BREI DIAMOND

# Wings of Light and Shadow

*For the girls who carry the weight of the world on their shoulders.*
*I hope you find the person who will take some of the burden.*

# 1

# Astriel

Flying. Wind roaring past my ears, muscles straining against the exertion of a steep climb. The sensations quieted my ever screaming mind. I straightened, high enough human eyes could not perceive my form beyond that of a bird, the stark white of my feathered wings stretching flat. I surveyed the forest beneath me, keeping a watchful eye for outsiders.

There had been more hunters in my land than ever before, searching for whatever manner of beautiful or terrible magical creature to add to their king's menagerie. Most met their fate at the hands of their own ignorance, underestimating the savagery of the inhabitants of this enchanted place. Even my own people did not venture into the tangled wood that surrounded our territory more than was necessary. We may have been blessed by the land itself, but the creatures who roamed held no such sentiment. But those who were more clever, venturing far too deep for comfort, too close to Phaedra, the official fae lands. They were mine.

I landed on a bare cliff, jutting out of a stony mountain, sucking breath, I peered over the treetops, towards the sprawling human kingdom, ever-encroaching. Closer and closer to the borders of my home. A number of them in the closest village had started building a stone wall, embedded with spiked iron on the forest side. A feeble attempt to keep my citizens out, or to discourage the other creatures of the wood. Humans, idiotic and childish humans, never understanding that attacks on their land were only ever retribution or warning, to stay out of ours.

I pricked my ears at a rustling to my east, long and pointed sharply at the tip, they were attuned to the sounds of the forest, an advantage over most opponents. A tree a few hundred feet from the initial sound exploded with hundreds of black birds pouring from its branches. It could have been a beast hunting which disturbed them, but the fine hairs standing on the back of my neck prickled in a familiar way. *Humans.*

With little thought I leapt from my post, diving low to cut between the lush canopy, landing silently as an owl in a massive gnarled oak. The leather slippers adorning my feet padding softly against the rough bark as I ventured closer. The forest was entirely silent. I crouched within a thicket of climbing vines, pulling my wings in tightly. Not daring to move once I found my spot, at risk of alerting the intruders before I could strike.

A twig snapped beneath me and I tipped my head in the direction. Two humans, young, not even yet teenagers, crept beneath me. *Sending your young into my lands, and yet we are the monsters.* I watched them move slowly through the bare dirt, breathing heavily as their heads swiveled. They could sense my presence, not knowing what predator watched them, or from where.

I watched for any indication that they traveled with a party. If they were part of some hunting group I couldn't see, when a sharp and ugly smell filled my nose. *Iron.* These young then surely did not travel alone. The poorest of their kind did not carry iron, that cold determination filled my blood as I surveyed them. I tried to glean their intentions, but with iron there was often only one option. They were sent here for a single purpose: To kill my people.

The pity I felt for them evaporated, replaced with a rage that burned beneath my skin, turned my vision red. I felt for the blade strapped between and wings and silently unsheathed it. A long silver sword that when it caught the light revealed delicate and intricate protection runes cascading down its center. I steadied my breath, listening closely to the forest for a moment longer, I heard nothing else, and leapt to the ground behind them.

I landed hard, intending for them to hear me, stretching my wings to their full imposing size. They both turned, eyes wide and wild with fear. The shorter of them tripped over himself, falling backward, mouth agape in a silent scream. The taller wielded a small iron dagger, gripping and re-gripping it in his sweaty palms. He held it ahead of him like a sword. I relaxed ever so slightly. *This youth is no assassin. T*he silence simmered between us as I studied them, the only sound in the quiet was their own ragged breathing.

"Why do you venture into these lands?" A question, asked like a command. I waited, but their fear stole their voice, and though the taller one opened his mouth to speak, no sound emerged.

"I will ask once more before I slay you where you stand. Why have you come?"

The shorter one, from his place on the ground, found his shaking voice. "We don't mean to offend," His eyes traveled to the simple silver circlet atop my head, and his eyes grew wider. "Agrona, we are no threat to your people, our family is starving."

*Agrona,* the name the human's had designated for me when I took over protecting these woods, I smiled as they said it, painting the perfect picture of a terrifying legend for them to leave with. I looked them over again. They were indeed quite frail. Their faces gaunt and their dirty, torn clothes hanging limply from their frames. A worn wooden bow in the hand of the fallen boy and tattered quiver slung over his back containing only two un-embellished wooden arrows supported his story. My fury winked out entirely, but they would not know that.

"And that?" My voice still hard and cold. I pointed my sword at the taller one, indicating the small blade in his hand, which shook violently as he started to speak.

"Stolen from a lord in our land. Protection, not malice." I considered him, tipping my head slightly. Allowing their fear to still their blood. Enough that hopefully, after this day, they would be wise enough to never return.

"Two admitted thieves enter my land, with an iron blade, and a quiver of arrows. I don't see how I can possibly let you live." I let it linger, watched the blood run out of their faces, not breaking their stare.

"Please, our family will starve without us, we won't ever return. This was a mistake. I'm sorry, I'm sorry." The taller one begged while the shorter one began to cry.

"Enough, enough." I gazed down at my blade, feigning consideration, "And stand up boy, I can't bear to watch you grovel for your life from the ground." He scrambled to his feet, eyes downcast, refusing to look up at me.

"And you," My blade once again pointed at the taller, "drop that pitiful excuse for a blade." He did without thinking, perhaps without meaning to. Then kicked it away, without my having to command it. I smiled internally, these are smart boys, they will not return.

I lowered my own blade, returning it to the leather sheath strapped to my back. Tangible relief filled both their eyes, and confusion. "You will leave here, immediately." I opened the satchel strapped to my belt, burying a hand within, "You may never return." I extracted a cloth wrapped bundle from inside, dried meat I had been carrying for my patrols. "If I so much as catch your scent on the wind again, I will kill you both before you can scream."

They nodded, their feet readying to run. I threw the bundle, it hit the taller boy in the chest and fell into his hands. I let a sneer color my face. Bright white teeth, too long canines glinting in the dappled light. "Now leave."

# 2

# Astriel

I did not return to my home in the heart of the city that evening. Instead, I found myself in a tavern. Weary from the day's patrol, weary from every day's patrol. The tavern was quiet, near empty. A green skinned fae behind the bar poured me a drink, her own wings glimmering iridescent rainbow in the soft candlelight like those of a dragonfly. She set it gently in front of me, her eyes, entirely black, searching my face as she did so.

"Long day?" She asked, as she grabbed a rag and began drying rinsed glasses from the wash tub.

I nodded slowly. My wings drooped behind me, the longest feathers brushing the hardwood floor. Throwing my elbows on the bar I covered my face with my hands. She did not push the matter.

Elia owned the tavern, my favorite in the city. Having hosted many meetings and gatherings here, it became a sanctuary of sorts. And while we were not necessarily close, Elia's understanding of my need for discretion and her ability to brew the best mead was critical. Thus, I held her in very high regard.

"Two more humans crossed the wall today carrying an iron blade." I offered as I grabbed for the overfilled glass.

She paused her drying for a single moment before continuing. "Fae hunters?"

I shook my head, and emptied the drink before pushing it across the bar for a refill. "Misguided children, they will not return." She nodded solemnly, perhaps the only person in Phaedra who knew, despite my reputation, I did not kill indiscriminately, or often, that I did not revel in it. She knew I let them go.

"It seems there are more and more everyday." She ventured, filling my cup from a pitcher. A honey flavored concoction, enchanted with something else, something for relaxation, I supposed. I watched it swirl with the magic as the muscles in my shoulders loosened. Without having to tell her, she new exactly what I needed.

I nodded again, "They are hungry, their king cares not if they live or die. But I cannot have them come here." I emptied the glass again. Unspoken between us was the fact that if humans with foul intentions entered here in high enough numbers, there is not much I could do to hold them off. I had been trained well enough, but it was only me.

"Where is everybody tonight?" I asked, scanning the near empty room. On a normal night I would not have been able to find this peace at Elia's, bustling with tradesmen and nobility who gathered here regularly, vying for my attention as well as hers.

"Equinox night, my lady. Everyone is at the fires." Her eyes did not meet mine as I looked at her.

Groaning, I buried my face in my hands once again. "I

completely forgot." She nodded solemnly. "I suppose I must show my face."

"It is your honor." She jested, smirking a little as she peeked at me in her periphery.

These holidays were created to celebrate the changing season as well as to give thanks to the warrior class. Another season without invasion. Dancing and drinking and revelry until sunrise. Today was the autumn equinox, the last equal day until the darkness of winter befell us.

I dreaded these holidays not only because at the end of the day my body ached from flying, but because I was the last of my class of warriors. The Seraphim. A people with feathered wings and legend of descending from the angels themselves. *A load of shit.* If there was anything angelic left in my blood it had been corrupted long ago.

I pushed myself from the bar, dropping a couple coins next to my empty cup. "Wait," Elia pushed another large glass towards me, "drink this before you go."

I glanced at it and looked at her with a raised eyebrow, "What is it?"

"For the nerves, so you can actually enjoy yourself." The corners of her thin lips quirked up.

I lifted the cup, peering over the rim, inside was a swirling crimson liquid tinged with gold. I sniffed it and it smelled like berries, and something sweeter I couldn't place. I drank without further question, warmth radiating through my body. My ears rang as it hit my bloodstream and my eyes widened as the taste coated my tongue. It only took a moment to realize what she had given me.

"Have a joyous equinox my lady." She grinned

8

# 3

# Astriel

I arrived at the party in full swing, having gone by my own home first to change. Trading out my worn working leathers for a more appropriate attire. My dress, a fine white silk low cut in the front and completely open in the back so my wings would be on full display. It's hem barely kissing the ground as I stood, concealing a fine pair of supple leather sandals, lacing up my legs to the knee. *An angel, an embodiment of good, always in white. If only they knew.*

My light hair had been tousled atop my head in delicate waves, a more formal diadem perched atop. Delicate silver jewelry decorating my ears, neck, and wrists. I had drawn a thick line of kohl around my eyes. The stark silver of my irises shone even more intensely against it.

Despite my reservations on being here, I felt divine. My chest warmed and eyes hooded. The intended effects of the concoction that tricky barmaid had slipped me. Though I smiled at the gesture. It had been a berry wine, spiked with maca powder and her own sort of magic. A drink to give me energy to get through the event, and an aphrodisiac. It seemed Elia thought I needed to unwind. *Perhaps not the worst idea.*

The fuzziness I felt intensified as I gazed skyward, towards the canopy of the massive and ancient tree that stood in the center of our small territory. *The tree of life.* It was revered as good as a god here. On this night, one could almost feel the power radiating from it, urging the celebration on.

My gaze fell back down, upon the party goers strewn about the grassy plain. Dancing, singing, and kissing in the long-cast light of the fires that dotted the open space. Fae of every variety, color, class, and power. They approached me periodically, offering drinks, food, thanks, and blessings. They thought of me much more than I was, but I had to let them. I had to become larger than life so they could live theirs peacefully. I bore the burden alone, but without remorse.

As I moved through the crowd, I took note of the children playing, fluttering on tiny wings if they had them, simply skipping or running if they didn't. I took a moment to admire their innocence, playing with their budding powers together. Young fae of every territory throw floating orbs of water at each other, capturing light between their palms, summoning little gusts of wind to take the winged children higher. Their laughter was like the tinkling of silver bells, their peace made my exhaustion worth it.

Seraphim carried no powers like that as far as I knew, or at least I didn't. Powerful wings and fighting prowess, that is what we had been gifted by The Mother. As a child I ached to play with magic like the rest of them, with no such luck. Perhaps the more powerful of my kind, maybe they had a certain magic I just couldn't remember, but I did not know.

I pulled myself out of my reverie. My eyes snagged on

a male I recognized. I smiled at the handsome enough woodland Dryad who stood on the other side of the fire. *He would do quite nicely for a night.* I slinked up to him, clinking our glasses together in greeting.

"Astriel, you look fantastic this evening." He greeted me with a wide smile.

"You as well, Silva." I took him in, long and lean in the way Dryads often were. A bit on the thin side for my usual taste but absolutely serviceable. He wore a green tunic and brown pants. Most likely the same clothes he had been gardening in all day if the dark smudges on his knees were any indication. I took a deep breath, he smelled like peat moss and citrus. Perfectly serviceable indeed.

His eyes flitted to my wings. They rustled softly as I tried to dampen my desire that was rapidly swelling. Not for the night, just long enough to pretend to be at least half as pious as most people wanted to believe. I watched a wandering waiter approach and drained my glass before setting it on his tray and replacing it with a fresh one.

I cleared my throat, "So, how is your equinox?"

"It is good! As you may well know we are putting in our root vegetables and..." Silva talked and talked and talked while I smiled and nodded, my ever emptying glass finding itself refreshed in my hand by passing waiters. The muscles in my back began to ache once again as the effects of Elia's potioned drink started to wear off. I knew that if I let it, then listening to all this droning would be for nothing, I would collapse asleep into my bed before I could even slip out of my shoes.

"Silva," I interjected when he stopped to take a breath, "It's getting late, would you like to walk me home?" I flashed him another smile as I said it.

It looked as if all of the words he had been ready to hurl fell out of his head as he nodded, holding an arm out for me to take. I silently thanked The Mother for it. I finished my drink before letting him lead me away from the fires and festivities, back to the city proper.

He found his voice again on the walk home, and only shut up long enough to climb on top of me. I liked Silva, he was kind and passionate and good. But he knew what these sporadic couplings meant. Which is to say they meant nothing. But for a swaggering male, even a sweet one, being able to boast you bedded the feathered fox was currency. It was a trade off I was willing to make for an hour or less of my evening where my thoughts wouldn't consume me.

And he was... fine. Enthusiastic, maybe a bit clumsy, but he tried. Which is more than I can say about some of his friends. But as he gathered up his clothes and headed for the door, those whispers of self loathing and unspoken regrets I had accumulated over the years would slink back into the room. There was no amount of work, or drinking, or casual sex that would drive it away completely. But at least for tonight I was sated.

\* \* \*

I was content to let exhaustion take me under into another night of fitful sleep when the sound of sharp knocks jolted me awake. It was still dark, sunrise well off. Far too early for visitors. I groaned as I threw on a ratty shirt and a pair of shorts and started for the door.

"Silva, if are back because you forgot something you could have gotten in the morning so help me-"

When I swung the door open, it was not Silva, but a meek looking Pixie with skin like storm clouds and eyes like rain that stood at my entry. "Clovis, what are you doing here?"

Her eyes widened like she hadn't expected me to know her name, but she spoke, "The council has gathered and they request your presence."

"At this hour? What happened?"

Her foot tapped anxiously on the stone stairs, "They request your presence." She repeated.

Her reluctance to tell me sent a nervous chill down my spine, "Give me five minutes."

* * *

The Pixie girl urged me to a meeting hall further down the street. She offered no more information and I knew better than to keep pestering her about it. It was clear that this was something that she was either sworn to secrecy by her lady, or she also didn't know. Either way, the council would be sure to enlighten me to whatever crisis they had cooked up this time. Every time they got together it seemed they were able to create crisis from nothing.

I groaned internally at the thought of it. I focused on just keeping pace with Clovis. She was near running down the cobblestone street, her delicate wings fluttering nervously. There was only one building with lights on, all others being closed for the equinox celebration.

I wasn't as put together as I would have liked to be, wearing a simple white dress that fell to my ankles, light stains of old mud coloring the hem. I had thrown my hair into a braid but strays fell around my face. Under normal circumstances, I never would have allowed them to see imperfections like these. It was a fracture in the very careful illusion of regal strength I had been forced to adopt in my role. But, when we finally reached the door to the meeting hall and I ripped it open to step inside, the somber faces of the nobility of every territory made my blood run cold.

Something was, in fact, very wrong.

# 4

# Astriel

The other ladies and only lord who had already taken their seats beckoned me to do the same. But my skin prickled, and their hesitation to disclose whatever had their faces so drawn kept me on edge. I couldn't quit pacing.

"Will someone please tell me what is going on here?" I near begged, my voice raising.

Morrelin, the eldest, a male with marbled golden skin, lord of the Nymphs, spoke first. "A girl has gone missing."

I gawked at him, frozen midstep.

"There is a human encampment in the western forest, we believe that is where she has gone to." Said Shyla, her inky black eyes settling on me. She was a Selkie, Lady of the Waters.

"A human encampment." I breathed, "In our forest? Why was I not informed?"

"It was only just discovered, a foraging group spotted their fires." Shyla said flatly.

I tried to find my breath, I had seen nothing of an encampment during the day, which means they were stealthy, and perhaps aware of my patrols. I bit my lip, and fell in the seat across from the rest of the council. The high, narrow back of the chair to accommodate wings dug into my spine. They all stared at me apprehensively, silence blanketing the room.

"I will go out tonight, find the girl." I finally said, hands balled into fists in my lap.

"It is not recommended." A small voice to my right, Jarrah, the redheaded Pixie with glowing delicate wings looked frightened. "They are wearing the king's uniform. They are fae hunters."

"All the more reason!" I nearly shouted into the silent room, slapping my palms on the table top. They just looked back at me, stunned silent. "We cannot have fae hunters this close to the city, if this problem is not tended to then all of our people are in danger." I steadied myself and took a long breath.

The Nymph lord spoke again. "We can rally some troops after the equinox, you will need numbers, we do not know how many there are."

I shook my head. "If they are royal fae hunters they very well may be gone by morning. This needs to be resolved *now*."

The rest just looked on solemnly. They knew it was true, but it was not ideal. It is a dangerous thing for a lone fae, even a Seraphim, to attack an encampment of unknown size in the night. But they had left us with no other option. I stood, nodded at the group, and without another word, strode out.

\* \* \*

I flew back up the street to my home as quickly as my wings would carry me. The terracotta tiled roofs blurred into orange smudges as I soared over top of them. My front door nearly came on the hinges as I barreled through it, my feet barely touching the ground. I stalked into my bedroom, kicking off my shoes as I went.

I needed to change quickly, there was no time for preening. I shrugged off the simple dress, leaving it in a pool of silk on the floor. I threw on my wrinkled base layers, and grabbed for my fighting gear. Leather chest plates, shoulder pads, arm and leg guards. My sword sheath next, strapped down my back, then one on my thigh for daggers. Strapping blades to wherever they would fit, I needed to be ready for anything.

I donned an enchanted circlet. An heirloom of my kind to help in battle. I hoped I would not need it. At last I yanked a pair of boots with a silent step enchantment, and launched myself out the front door, slamming it behind me.

I flew west, high above the treetops, and scanned the canopy below me. There was so much forest, even with a general direction to follow, I had a lot of ground to cover. I saw only darkness for several miles until, nearly imperceptible in a thick grove, a dot of yellow. A fire. I dove, silent as the night itself.

\* \* \*

Landing in a clearing on the forest floor, I listened intently. There was a raucous directly ahead, the sound of men drinking and celebrating. Celebrating their catch, or their

17

kill no doubt. The warmth that had radiated earlier was replaced by an icy cold. They would regret entering this forest. And they would die for touching one of my fae.

I stalked softly through the underbrush, my steps making not a sound, even as I traversed leaves and twigs. I peaked beyond the last stand of bushes between me and the sounds of men. In the clearing was a sprawling circle of wagons and tents. This indeed was an encampment, maybe thirty men strong. I didn't see them yet, but I heard them. I crept to my left, to catch a glimpse of what lay within the makeshift barrier.

These fools were in fact drinking, I spotted dark liquid in uncorked bottles. Some in hand and some discarded near the fire. They laughed and blabbered to each other, slurring their speech and warming their bare feet by the fire. Though they wore the king's colors, and the entire place stunk of iron, they certainly didn't act like fae hunters. Hunters would know better than to let their guard down in my forest.

Creeping another few feet to the left, looking between two more of the wagons, I spotted her. She was bound at the wrists to the spoke of a wheel. Tear stains marked her dirty face, wetting the strip of cloth that gagged her. I felt the rage again, like a blinding light behind my eyes. My circlet began to hum a warning. An owl sounded somewhere to my right. I would end them all and feel nothing.

One of the men stumbled over to the fae girl. A Pixie I realized, her wings looked crumpled behind her. Her beautiful delicate, paper like wings. *How dare they.* He kicked at her foot and leaned against the wagon, slurring vulgarity while she tried to put distance between herself and the man but couldn't. He leaned down to whisper something in her ear, but it was when one of his stubby, dirty, revolting human hands rested on her knee that I could stand it no longer.

I sprung from the bush two daggers already unsheathed and hurled them at the man by the girl. He looked shocked, genuine fear entered his glassy eyes as the blades pierced his chest. He fell a moment later, taking one final breath before he collapsed. I retrieved a new blade as I ran up on the Pixie, and cut through the binding ropes before turning my back on her. *Why would the king's men use ropes?* My own massive wings shielded her from the rest of the group as I turned on them.

"Run!" I shouted over my shoulder. She leapt from the ground and crashed into the brush.

The other men just stared at me, two more falling as I launched more blades at them. Though appalled, they did not charge, did not reach for any weapons of their own. The smell of iron grew stronger. *The king's men had used ropes.* My breath caught as realization dawned, my circlet thrummed loudly against my temples. That had not been an owl. These were not the king's men. *It was a trap.*

I poised to run when a blinding pain seized my leg. I looked down, an iron tipped whip wrapped around my ankle. Before I could think, its wielder yanked it back. I fell onto my front, the wind knocked from my chest. *One breath in.* Flipping onto my back I threw a dagger in the direction of the attacker. But the whip's handle lay on the ground, unmanned, and my dagger buried itself in a tree.

I kicked away at the whip and it fell loose, my mind clearing as the influence of that cursed metal abated. When a new pain struck me in the shoulder. I grasped for it, every breath burned and my thoughts scattered to the wind as I felt for it.

*Fuck.* My fingers found purchase on the foreign protrusion, it burned against the skin of my fingers as I steeled myself and pulled. Yanking it out stole the air from my lungs once again, the sound of metal grating against bone echoing in my ears. In my hand was an iron dart with a thick black residue on the tip. I discarded it, cursing. *The girl is safe, I've got to get out of here.*

I strained to stretch my wings, to take flight as the darkness tunneled my vision. My wings wouldn't work, I couldn't will them to move, to do anything. They had gone limp against my back, dragging in the dirt. Whatever that dart was coated with, it was doing its work. I watched through narrow vision as the true king's men approached, wearing iron, wielding it. I threw two more daggers, unable to see if they struck their target as gravity pulled me down. I blinked, over and over, trying to clear my ever narrowing vision as I felt myself slump against the ground. The cold bite of iron on my wrists hissed and burned as the world went dark. *The girl is safe.*

# 5

# Astriel

I awoke to more darkness. The ground beneath me seemed to sway. I couldn't tell if the movement was the cause of my nausea or the iron cuffs that tethered me. My wrists were welted from it. Even in the dimness I could see that blood had dried in thick rivulets to my fingertips.

The pain was so debilitating I could barely think. I steadied my breathing, closing my eyes as another wave of nausea overtook me. Swallowing, I pushed it down. I opened my stinging eyes, and looked around.

I was in what appeared to be a large cage, covered by a heavy cloth. The hard wooden floor groaned beneath me as I swayed. I strained to listen past the sound of my own blood pumping past my ears. Hoof beats, footsteps, wood creaking, whispered conversation. *I'm in one of the wagons.* My breath caught in my throat as the smell assaulted my senses. The bars around me were iron. Shackled in iron, surrounded by it. These men were certainly on a fae hunt, and I was their prey. I just hoped desperately that I was the only one.

One of the men must have heard chains rustling as I moved,

21

and lifted a corner of the cloth to peer in. Bright sunlight shone around him, I had to shield my eyes from it. With the sun so bright, it must have been midday. *How long had I been unconscious?*

When my eyes adjusted and I glared back at the man, I saw a moment of shock, maybe fear on his face. He quickly schooled it into the hard mask all fae hunters wear. They had been taught not to show fear to my kind, that we could smell it. It was a bullshit fantasy that humans had invented. But even if I couldn't smell it, I now knew he felt it. This generation of humans had never encountered a fae like me before, my eyes looked predatory in the dark, I knew that, and now he did too.

The cloth fell back closed, "It's awake." I heard the frightened man shout to someone, his voice still quivering though he had tried to steady it.

The wagon came to an abrupt halt that rocked me hard enough that the chain pulled taut, cutting into my skin. More footsteps, more hushed words shared between them. I braced myself. Looking down, all of my fighting leathers and blades were gone, even my circlet was missing. I cursed them.

I was wearing only my base layers, a black cotton tunic and pants. Even fully covered I felt exposed, off balance without the solid weight of my blades. They moved closer. I made myself bigger and my wings spread wider. I pulled myself to my knees, wincing as the metal once again opened a wound on my wrist as I straightened and the short chain pulled against the ring in the floor. *No weakness. They have no idea what beast they've cornered.*

Men on each side grabbed the cloth and pulled it back. The sun was blinding, I fought the urge to recoil against it.

Around me, I hear several men suck breath as my form is unveiled in full light. But my eyes are on the man astride a horse directly in front, who did not react.

He wore more finery than the rest of them; they all wore the uniform of the king's men, green tunics emblazoned with the lion crest across the chest. But his was more formal. The sword that hung at his hip was a shining silver to their dull iron. *Their leader,* I reasoned. His horse snorted and tried to back away at the sight of me. He steadied it before dismounting, handing off the reins to another man. I bared my teeth as he approached the heavy barred door that separated us.

He just laughed, and stepped closer. And I could see a long, jagged scar running down his jaw from his ear to his chin. But otherwise, he was strikingly handsome, for a human. Dark hair that fell in soft curls around his shoulders, piercing molasses eyes.

I could have found him quite attractive in fact, if it weren't for the circumstance of our meeting, or that he was made uglier by the sneer he wore, accompanied by a darkness, hollow behind those brown eyes. I could almost feel the number of my kind he had witnessed lay slain, I would revel in making him pay for it.

Blood dripped against the wooden floor and he stared down at it, casual, unconcerned. Every drop that spattered against the worn wood beneath me mirrored my own pounding heartbeat, thundering in my chest. The sound of war drums. His eyes again met mine.

He spoke. "If you can be a good little fae, we can get you out of those shackles." I said nothing, just hardened my stare. Such a typical human man, I wouldn't give him the

23

satisfaction.

I watched as he pulled a ring of keys from his belt. Choosing one, he thrust it into the lock. He turned it and the door swung open. I made as if I would lunge at him, the silent group of men now surrounding us recoiled. He did not.

"Oh come now, behave, I know that must hurt." His eyes fell to the blood on my hands, some already dried and flaky, some fresh, the coppery smell invading my nostrils. "We are going to be spending a lot of time together. We could be friends." He smirked, and I only just refrained from making a face of disgust.

As he stepped inside I raised my wings higher, spreading them until they filled the space. A threat. He tutted, and snapped his fingers, gesturing towards me. A man on each side of the bars wielded a long weapon, a crescent shaped blade on a long wooden handle and pushed them within the bars between us. As the highest blade found its place just below my chin, I cut eyes at its carrier, he did not react, one of the more seasoned hunters, I suspected.

My eyes fell back on their captain, who was stepping closer, key ring in hand. He knelt in front of me, reaching for my wrist. I hissed, but dared not move as the iron blades inched closer to my neck. He looked at me through his thick brows and just shook his head, still smirking.

His gloved hand closed around my wrist and cuff, and he turned it over to expose the keyhole. Blinding pain erupted again, and I tried not to yank away, to trigger his blade wielding guards. But he felt me stiffen, breathing hard through my nose. He stared intensely into my eyes, a warning of his own. Mere inches away, I could smell him, oak moss and cedar and sweat. He did not break our stare as the first

24

cuff fell away, but his hand remained.

I kept still as stone, breath trapped in my throat. Neither of us moved for a long moment. I couldn't look away from his deep brown eyes as they cut through me. Unwilling to break, smart enough not to attack, not yet.

He set the first hand down gently against my knee, and wrapped his leather clad fingers around the other. Turning this one over more gently, the key found its place and turned. The second shackle fell away. Again, his hand lingered.

I watched his lips as he wet them, "Now that's a good girl."

On reflex I yanked my hand back, eyes darkening at him. The guards tensed, blades grazing the soft skin of my neck, I felt a single stream of blood flowing where one kissed my flesh.

He smiled, a broad toothy grin that did not reach his eyes. It made my stomach churn, "Easy boys, she's behaving. Don't damage our catch."

He lifted a hand, removing the glove that encased it, and extended a finger beneath the blade. I tensed again, as his calloused finger brushing every so lightly against my throat. His face was closer to mine now, but no longer was he looking in my eyes, instead his gaze fell where blood was trailing past my collarbone and towards my breasts.

Under any other circumstance, I would have ripped his head off right there. His feather light touch flicked through the bright red, surveying it, before placing it between his lips.

His eyes locked on mine. "Interesting." When he blinked, his gaze seemed dreamy and far away, before clearing and connecting with intensity to mine once again. "Get some more rest, we will be there soon."

And just like that, the captain strode away. Leaving the

discarded cuffs anchored to the floor, the iron still humming. The door behind him closed and locked, the blades retreated, and the cloth once again shrouded my world in darkness. I released a breath I hadn't realized I was still holding.

# 6

# Astriel

I couldn't tell how much time passed as I lulled in the place between sleep and wake. The caravan did not stop, and they did not lift the cover again. All I knew is my mouth and throat were hoarse with thirst, and my stomach rumbled ever louder as the time passed. I curled in a tight ball in the center of the platform, my wings tucked in close, afraid for any part of me to touch the metal of the bars, or the shackles whose chains rattled with every bump. Just being this close to so much iron was slowing my healing to a crawl.

As the cart finally jerked to a halt, the cover was pulled away and I raised my head to a starlit night. The burns on my wrist still shone a shiny soft pink, but no longer the angry red welts they were. The men around me bustled and unloaded the other wagons. I moved to stand to get a better look, wobbling, my legs straining against the weight after so long laying down. The lightness in my head threatened to pull me back down to the hard floor. Without thinking, I grabbed the bars for support and recoiled as the sizzling iron once again burned my skin. I cursed, but managed to stay upright.

I was dizzy, tired, and hungry. *Focus, pay attention.* I blinked away the pain and the confusion and took in my surroundings. There were seven wagons, mine was the last in line, I looked ahead as the rest were uncovered, hoping desperately none of the others contained any more of my people. I breathed a sigh of relief when I only saw meats, exotic birds in small cages, and polished treasures strapped down. All looking to be human in origin. *Thank The Mother, everyone else is safe. The girl escaped.*

I turned my attention to the humans, carrying items inside of a massive building. My eyes followed the stone walls up and up. The sight drained the blood from my face. *A castle.* My breath hitched in my chest, and for the first time since seeking out the hunters, fear slithered up my spine. The human king, this was his castle, I was his prize. My blood turned ice water in my veins.

I heard a suppressed cough from behind me and whipped around, too fast, wisps of darkness threatened to coat my vision once again. I took a deep breath and pushed them away. By the door was the captain, that ever present smirk still plastered to his face.

"Look who survived the long journey without causing even a single stir, what a well behaved fae you are indeed. I wish they were all like you."

I snarled, and only a moment of exasperation crossed his features.

"Are you ready to meet your new master?" He asked, a fake and cruel question that had the fear not been tightening around my heart would have me boil with rage. But I remained stoic, silent and strong. I would not allow this man, this human, to take satisfaction in my fear. Even if I had to ball my hands into fists to hide the shaking in my fingers.

He opened the cage door. He and the two guards that flanked him coming in, hands on the hilts of their swords, but none against my throat this time. A fatal mistake, or it would have been, if I had any strength left at all. He closed the distance between us in a few short strides, and stopped close, too close, our chests nearly touching.

His scent once again filled my nostrils. *Oak moss and cedar.* I simply glared up at him, allowing no emotion to line my face outside of the contempt I knew swirled in my eyes. He was a good head taller than me and filled my vision with the bulk of him. *Touch me and I'll rip your throat out, bastard.* He chuckled as if I'd said it out loud, and held up a new pair of shackles.

I didn't move, trying to sort out how I would handle this, the best course of action for a situation I had never planned for, never trained for. He must have sensed my distraction and once again grasped my wrist in his own rough and now un-gloved hand. It was warm, and though the calluses earned through years of sword training scraped against my skin, his hold did not hurt. Instinct moved me to pull away but his grip tightened, another warning burned in those dark eyes.

In any other world I would have been strong enough to break him and his lackeys against these bars, but the dizziness of hunger, of thirst, of the proximity of so much iron had drained me into a feeble creature. I was no stronger than the desperate and starved human children I had chased out of the woods the day of the equinox. I hated myself for it.

I broke his gaze and looked down as a click, and the sensation of cool metal snagged my attention. He had locked the new shackle on without looking, it stung. Still, my blood screamed *danger* as he locked it in place, but it did not burn me like the iron cuffs had.

As if he had once again read my mind, "Steel, it will still subdue you, but it won't damage your pretty skin."

As the words left his mouth his thumb brushed against the back of my hand, and something snapped. I yanked away from him, successfully this time. I swung the shackled arm in a wide circle as I stepped back, the dangling cuff flying wildly on the chain. His eyes widened for just a moment as I brought my arm down, hard as I could manage, and the loose metal ring struck him on the temple. He stumbled back a step and his men charged me. I let them take me to the ground, turning a wicked, predatory smile at him.

I glared over my shoulder as his men locked the other shackle on, behind my back this time. He straightened, lightly touching the gash I had left in his eyebrow and the bruise already blooming on the outer corner of his eye. And he laughed, a self satisfied but genuine laugh.

"Good," He smiled as he dabbed at the cut with a handkerchief he fished from his back pocket, "I was afraid you would be no fun." And he laughed again, and my own smile faded, he had wanted a reaction. *I fell into his trap, for the second time.*

His men hauled me to my feet and drug me out the open door, tossing me to the ground at the bottom of the steps. I grimaced, small stones digging into my shoulders and face. My joints screamed with the impact. Strength threatened to fail me again, but panting, I used a wing to push myself over.

Facing him, I glared at the captain. He stood a few feet away from me, his face hard. With the wave of a hand, he silently commanded his men. They moved behind me, just out of my periphery. Their hands once again rested on the hilts of their swords.

"Stand up." He commanded me, his eyes burning into mine.

I looked away.

"I said, stand up, or these fine gentlemen will be forced to motivate you."

I did not move, did not react.

He snapped his fingers and his men approached, fully unsheathing their swords now. I felt the blades graze my wings, if either of them decided it, I would never fly again.

"Last chance," He drawled, "Stand. Up."

I felt the pressure of the blades increase and panic rose like bile in my throat. My feathers smoldered against the iron. I couldn't breathe, I couldn't think, I wouldn't win this, we both knew it. His eyes left mine as he started to nod to his men.

"I can't!" I blurted. The first time I'd spoken since the attack, my voice hoarse from thirst and lack of use. I stared down at my own lap, defeated. "I don't have the strength. I can't stand."

That self satisfied smile returned, and he waved off his men. They sheathed their swords and roughly grabbed beneath my arms, hauling me to my feet. I met his eyes again, "Then you are ready to meet the king."

* * *

The men half guided and half dragged me down a long and

wide gilded hall. I kept my eyes on my own feet, on my own reflection in the intricate tile laid beneath them. My hair had long since strayed from its styling, and fell into my face in tangled curls. My feathers were in disarray and dirty. The kohl had long smudged in ugly half moons beneath my shining eyes, or else it wasn't the kohl, and it was dark circles from the neglect of the journey. I couldn't tell, I couldn't bring myself to care.

I could see the boots of the wretched Captain ahead as he guided our way. He walked with purpose and confidence, his long strides nearly silent on the reflective stone. He stopped abruptly as the tile changed to plain shining black, Obsidian glass. A rare and expensive fae magic nullifier. I could hear people being addressed formally, but the blood was roaring in my ears again, dulling the sounds of everything around me. My eyes were starting to ease closed, accepting the spindly fingers of unconscious wrapping me in a warm cocoon, when my head was wrenched backward by my hair.

I stifled a yelp at the sudden pain and my eyes shot open, taking in the sight in front of me. My heart hammered, eyes widening when I saw him. There he was, the fae killer king.

# 7

# Astriel

He sat on a massive glistening obsidian throne, flanked on one side by a smaller seat, occupied by a cloaked figure, a woman, whose face I could not discern in the shadows. The king himself was a frail old thing, his fingers, which bulged at the knuckles from arthritis, tapped impatiently on the armrests. His gaunt face was near gray, speckled in age spots and covered in a sparse and patchy beard. His crown seemed almost too big. If he moved too much, I suspected it would slide right over his eyes.

I could have laughed at the absurdity of it all. That this was the human man, feared across the continent for his ruthlessness, but he was only a husk, an empty shell of what used to be a man. I would have laughed, if I had not seen his eyes flicker when he looked at me, a darkness residing beneath the deep blue of his irises. It was indeed the spirit of the killer king, even if his body was failing him.

I realized suddenly that the captain and the king had been speaking while I stared, and I focused as best I could on their conversation, but I was tired, so, so tired.

"She will look better when she is cleaned up and fed, I can assure you she was quite the beauty during the ambush." he spoke in a neutral tone.

"What is she?" The ugly king.

"Valkyrie I think, we've never caught one of her type, must be quite rare."

"Valkyrie? No demon then, truly only a fae." The corner of his mouth curled, an insidious smile as he appraised my dirty and weakened form before he turned back to the captain.

I snorted, I hadn't meant to, but these humans are so ignorant. I wouldn't have suspected truly how little they knew. But it was enough, both the captain and the king suddenly trained their piercing eyes on me.

"Is something funny?" The captain asked, tipping his head, feigning sincerity.

"The Valkyrie are a myth." Despite my exhaustion the venom had seeped back into my voice, and I found the strength to carry my own weight, and right myself. I shrugged off the guards, with my hands still bound behind me, they allowed it.

"They pray tell, fae, what are you?" The king asked, irritation coating every word. *I will slice you to pieces.*

With the last of my strength, I tensed my shoulders, muscles straining against the positioning of my wrists and hands. I raised and spread my massive wings to their full size, even bedraggled and dirty, they blazed an unnatural bright white in the well lit room. Both the men's eyes and their guards widened and traveled upward, taking in their sheer size and span.

"I am Astriel Calderon of the Seraphim, and you will regret the day you removed me from my people." I smiled a predator smile at that horrible, pitiful king. I reveled in watching the blood drain from his face. To my right, the captain's mouth gaped ever so slightly. As the darkness once again snaked into my vision, I let it. Before it overtook me, I could have sworn that from beneath the woman's dark hood, I saw a smile. Then the world slipped away.

# 8

# Keelan

The fae fell backwards to the ground, her crystalline eyes flickering and dimming as consciousness escaped her. My men stationed at her flank only barely avoided being taken down by the spread of her still outstretched wings. On instinct I lunged for her, ordering my men to lift her, to get her off her wings from where they crunched under the position she fell in.

"Get her to a room." I ordered the guards who fumbled and struggled to lift her.

"Stop." A voice came from behind me, the woman in the smaller throne stood and took a few steps forward. My men froze in place, looking between me and the cloaked figure. I nodded tightly that were to obey.

"Your Majesty, I will take things from here." Deliana, the king's sorceress and right hand.

She waited for the king to rise from his throne. He mumbled some thanks or otherwise, and ambled out of the room. She turned her attention back to me and pulled back the hood of her cloak. Her dark eyes that flickered with malice and barely restrained flame leveled themselves on me.

"She's… different from what we have previously seen here." Deliana started, squinted eyes trained on me.

"Perhaps so, a captured fae nonetheless." I raised an eyebrow at her.

"The king, when he got word of your capture, initially wanted her dead. He wanted to make an example of her." She ran an appraising gaze over the crumpled female at my side. I fought the urge to glance over.

"Is that so?"

"It is. But I imagined how you might object, this being such a valuable catch." She waved a hand to punctuate the point. "So I offered an alternative."

"And what is that?" I did not waver under the witch's piercing stare. A game she played that I was far too familiar with.

"As you are well aware, the king has had trouble finding a suitable match to produce an heir." An indirect accusation, I kept my face neutral. "He has decided that this beast would offer an… advantageous alliance, if they were to be wed."

My pulse quickened, but I steeled my expressions. "I'm not sure if this *beast* would take kindly to such a suggestion." I responded through gritted teeth, watching as a shadow of a smile curved at the witch's mouth.

"*The king* has considered that," Deliana strode down the steps, closing in, stopping less than a foot in front of me. "The king has also considered the fact that such a… spirited fae may react poorly to the circumstances. Which is why he suggested a binding."

"A binding?"

"Yes," My gaze followed as she stalked over to the unconscious fae, twisting a piece of silver-white hair around her finger, not looking at me as she continued, "just as a bit of motivation to keep her in line. I figured you would be up to the task."

"That would not be wise." I tried to hold onto the disinterest I so carefully plastered to my face, but I could feel it cracking with every word. It was an unfathomable, and needlessly cruel suggestion. Either the witch did not understand the weight of binding two people together, or she delighted in the pain it would cause.

"That is not your place to decide." she dropped the tendril and glared at me once more.

"It is both of our fates you are toying with. I can ensure the Seraphim will cause no trouble. But I will not partake in this."

"Of course it is your choice." Deliana drawled, "You can either submit to the order of the crown, as is your duty. Or we can dismiss you, but I think you know the consequences if that is your chosen route."

I stiffened, hands clasped tightly behind my back, "I would like to confer with the king. I do not think he understands the gravity of-."

"I am the voice of the king in such matters and thus what I say is good as law." Her voice pitched up ever so slightly, before she leashed it.

"Then it is you who does not understand, she will be more volatile if this is the route you take. And will be much less inclined to your other *proposition*."

"The *king's* proposition." She chided, "That is why she will be bound to *you*."

The witch approached me once again, gliding a single pointed nail down my chest as she spoke. It took everything inside of me not to slap her hand away, she could see it on my face, and loosed a cruel laugh, "You can charm her, convince her to be pliant to our needs. Unless, that is, you have some objection to the crown finally siring an heir."

Those all seeing ember eyes found me again, and I lost my words. It was precarious. If I refuse, I lose everything. If I agree, everything is lost. I could not find the words, so I just stared down at her, barely containing the scowl that pulled at my mouth.

"Good." She clapped her hands in front of her, "I'm glad you've come around, follow me. And bring the fae so we may work out the details."

# 9

# Astriel

I awoke in a large, lush bedroom, disoriented, dirty, even still wearing my shoes. I ran my hands across the soft fabric of the bedding, appreciating the weave, a haziness still dulling the edges of my senses. I surveyed the room, taking in the stone walls, the thick tapestries, and the bare surfaces of the many pieces of fine wooden furniture. The clouds in my mind began to dissipate.

In the castle, I was somewhere in the king's castle. I lunged from the bed, finding myself unshackled, seeking out anything I could use as a weapon. Still dizzy, still weak. *Mother above, when was the last time I ate?*

I didn't know where exactly I was, but I remembered the journey, remembered the king, the show I had put on for them. I smiled a bit at the thought despite myself. A heavy door carved with intricate patterns stood across the room, and I moved towards it, using the bedposts and furniture as crutches to get me there as my legs wobbled with the hunger that tore at my stomach. I yanked hard on the handle. Locked, from the outside. I pounded on it.

"Back away!" I heard a guard yell from the other side as the lock clicked, without thinking, I did. I stumbled over the edge of an intricately woven rug, but stayed upright as I created distance between me and whatever lay on the other side of that slab of wood. The door swung open, three guards entered, none I recognized, and a woman. My heart dropped as I saw her, not a human woman, an elf. Ears, long and pointed like mine, but without wings, she was beautiful, in the ethereal way only elves could be, but with sad eyes.

"Do not be afraid my lady, I'm here to help."

I rushed her, grasping her hands between my own, the guards gripped the hilt of their blades, readying to strike. But she shook her head softly, and turned her gaze back on me. She wore clothes in the human style, a long pale blue dress that covered her to the collarbone. Not finery by any means, but not the clothes of an ordinary servant. Her golden hair, traditionally long in the Elven territories with an otherworldly shine of spun gold, was cropped short at her chin, and looked dry and frizzy, like limp straw.

"What have they done to you? I will get you out of here. I promise. I just need a plan, and to regain my strength, I will get you home." I had forgotten the guards, I was frantic, panicked that she was here, that more of my people had been taken, but also bitterly relieved to see someone else like me.

"My lady, please, steady yourself, I am home. *We* are home." My heart splintered inside my chest, and my hands fell to my sides. I just stared at her, taking a mindless step back. I could think of nothing to say. *What have they done to you?*

"Let's get you in the bath my lady, once you are cleaned up, Sir Keelan will explain everything. Over breakfast." A soft smile.

"Sir Keelan?" I asked, as she led me, lightly gripping my still sore wrist, to the bathing room. I followed without thinking. I didn't even hear as the guards silently filed out of the room.

"The man who brought you here." That icy feeling filled my gut once again. *The wretched captain.*

The Elven woman undressed me while I mulled over the events of the past... Days? Weeks? Mother above I don't even know how long it's been, how long I have been absent from my people. The panic started to set in again, but a gentle pressure on my bare waist nudged me towards the now filled bath. I allowed it, sinking into the sweet smelling water that filled the copper tub.

I folded in on myself as she scrubbed my arms, rinsed and preened my wings, laid me back to wash my hair. It felt good, and I cursed myself for letting it feel good. This is a terrible thing, I need to get out of here. But I had to be smart about this if I wanted to get myself out. I needed to play a part, I realized, like I hoped the Elf was playing.

"What is your name?" I asked her, as sweetly as I could muster.

"Farryn." She responded softly, still cleaning my hair, lathering it with something that smelled like lavender.

"How long have you been here?" I tried to look up at her, past my lashes, but she kept her attention on my hair.

"Since before this king," She responded as if it weren't the most horrible thing she could have said, the most crushing thing I've ever heard. "It's hard to keep track of time with humans, they come and go so swiftly, like waves lapping against a lake shore." She smiled to herself then, like watching humans be born and die was something she enjoyed. I was horrified.

"You were taken."

"I was liberated." She pondered but never paused her task. "When I left, things were very tense in Allesyna, I was nothing. Here I reside in a palace, get to do and say what I wish, for the most part. It's better."

I sucked breath, Allesyna? She was not from my city then, she had been taken from somewhere so much further away. *How far do these humans travel to capture fae?* The thought broke when her gentle hand rested on my back, pushing me upright. She moved in front of me, standing me up slowly as water ran off my body and wings. My vision blurred with the threat of tears.

"It's an adjustment," She spoke softly, toweling off the drops of water that clung to my skin, "the first while is hard, you will learn to love it."

I wanted to scream. I wanted to grab her by her shoulders and shake her until whatever spell she was under broke and she remembered this was not her home. But I just stood there, mouth agape. My naked body erupted in goosebumps as my skin chilled.

"Let's get you dressed." Her pleasant smile, an ever present feature it seemed, did not reach her eyes. I followed her back into the bedroom, leaving a track of wet footprints as I went. My eyes followed her as she moved about the room, all of her movements automatic. Her gaze seemed constantly faraway, like she was daydreaming.

The clothes she has laid out seemed inspired by fae fashion, but with the forced modesty of the human world. A dark green velvet gown delicately embroidered in gold thread, with fitted sleeves to the wrist, and an open back to accommodate my wings. Farryn tugged at the heavy fabric

43

as I appraised myself in the long mirror embedded in the door of the hardwood wardrobe. It looked good on me, I realized, though I wouldn't admit it. I couldn't remember the last time I dressed formally in any color other than white.

Farryn buttoned the high neck in the back and my eyes ran across my reflection. I had lost weight on the journey. Sharp hip bones pressed against the flowing fabric where a fullness used to be. My face, which used to have a softness, now seemed too sharp. But my silver eyes still glowed in the dim light. At least I hadn't lost that in the darkness of the cage.

She left my still damp hair cascading down my shoulders, the lightness of it only serving to make me look even more pale, the purple smudges beneath my eyes, dark and ugly. She returned my circlet, which I thought had been lost, or stolen in the attack. She placed it gently on my head and I listened for it. It stayed silent, at least for the moment, there was no immediate danger.

She tried to pat a rouge onto my cheeks and I batted her away. These people had starved the color out of my face and I wanted them to see it, no facade of beauty would cover that. She only nodded at me with that smile which seemed to tighten almost imperceptibly. As if she understood, but did not agree.

Farryn linked arms with me as we left the room. The door had not been locked, I realized as we entered the hall. She nodded politely at the guards as we walked, whether it was a greeting or an assurance I wouldn't cause a fuss, I couldn't tell. I wouldn't though, not yet. I needed my strength, and information, before I made a move on these humans, at full strength they would be no match, and I would fly out of here with ease. At least that's what I told myself, what I needed to believe.

The dining hall was a spectacle, by human standards. Gaudy gold filigree decorated near every surface. Even the dark red wallpaper, with its intricate patterns of overlapping birds in flight, was detailed with it. The long and massive table that stood in the center was carved with images of serpents, men in battle, and many other such stories I couldn't absorb. I was too focused on the feast that lay upon it. Chicken, turkey, lamb, beef all in different manners of preparation, as well as complex vegetable dishes. Even knowing this food would not compare to that of my home, my mouth watered. *So, so hungry.*

Farryn guided me to a heavily carved wooden chair at the head of the table, still built to accommodate my wings, but not in the way of my people. Instead of a long slender back, it was short and wide, my wings were to go over, instead of around. Another clumsy recreation of what my people had perfected. I looked up at Farryn as she filled a glass with a dark red wine. It smelled sweet, but with a tinge of bitterness, no hint of the enchantments Elia would have provided. A twinge of pain bit at my chest.

"Sir Keelan has instructed you to begin, he will be joining you shortly." Farryn offered an encouraging smile, and squeezed my shoulder with one graceful hand, before turning on her heel and disappearing into the hall.

I hadn't realized how much peace of mind her presence offered me until she was gone. I sat alone, not even guards in the room. The vulnerability of my situation crept back in. But I pushed the fear away, the food on the table commanding my undivided attention, and I heaped piles of it upon my plate.

Shoveling spoonfuls of potato and chicken and pepper into my mouth without regard of if they may have been tainted, if this is what kept the Elf girl subdued. I would deal with the consequences later. I tore into the food, even as bland as it was, I couldn't bring myself to be disappointed. My starving body didn't care.

A man clearing his throat broke me from the assault on my plate. The captain- Sir Keelan, I remembered, stood to the left of the table, near its center, a respectable distance away, appraising me. He leaned against the back of a chair, attempting to appear casual, unruffled. But I could read the way his muscles tensed, the way his hand rested on the hilt of his sword. As if he knew, with my strength returning, I could tear him to bits if I pleased.

I swallowed, and set down my utensils, eyes cutting around the room. Five guards lined the walls now at equal distance from each other. *Good, you're smart to be afraid of me.*

I set my gaze back upon him, surveying his appearance. On this new day, he was dressed much more casually. Wearing a flowy white shirt, open at the collar, and tight fitted black pants filled out with what I now to could tell were well muscled legs. His sable hair, shoulder length and curly, looked windblown.

When our eyes met again, they seemed a shade lighter. I could not perceive the cruelty I knew were contained within them, only curiosity, maybe a touch of nervousness. The bruise I had given him colored the outer corner of his eye, though not as severely as I had expected it to be. Neither of us moved or spoke for what felt like an eternity.

"You look better today." A simple statement, no emotion.

"That tends to happen when one is given food, drink, and bathing." Bitterness tinged the edges of my voice.

"You gave us quite a fright last night, collapsing after your little show." He pulled the chair he was leaning on from under the table, angling it towards me. He lowered himself into it and leaned back, crossing an ankle over one knee.

"Will the king not be joining us?" I didn't care how they felt about the collapse, I saw what I needed to see. The memory of the shock filling their eyes bolstered my pride.

"He is busy. I have been tasked with keeping an eye on you." He absently picked at a pile of rolls on the table.

*You'll wish you hadn't been,* I thought, glaring at him. With considerable effort, I tamed my desire to lunge across the table and rip his throat out. At least for now. "So, *Sir* Keelan*,*" I let my distaste coat the words as I spoke them. "Are you a knight or a blade for hire?"

"I am anything I need to be, whenever I need to be it, at the pleasure of the king."

"So you are his lap dog."

"To you, I am merely a babysitter." He smiled, tossing a torn off piece of the roll into his mouth. *Wretched, wretched man.*

"Perhaps I will just kill you then, and walk out of here. If you are my only obstacle." My grip tightened around my fork where it sat on the place mat.

"Oh, I would not attempt such a thing." His face turned serious. He discarded the bread in his hand and leaned forward, rolling up the sleeve on his right arm. But his eyes did not leave mine as he revealed an intricately drawn knot inked into his skin, directly below the elbow.

I recognized it immediately, fae who had found their mate

would often have them inked together. The Serch Bythol, a symbol of everlasting love for most. A curse for me if genuine. Blood drained from my face as I stared at it, a gut wrenching dread pooling in my stomach. I ripped at my own sleeve, tearing at it until the threads burst and revealed what I had feared. On my own skin, in the same spot, drawn in glittering silver, was the twin knot.

My breath caught in my throat. It couldn't be true. It was impossible. *No, no, no.* I moved to stand, wine spilling against the table and carpet, the chair behind me tumbling several feet as I stumbled backwards in the panic. I clutched my chest, the tightness unbearable. There was no illusion of bravery or uncaring now, only pure, unadulterated terror.

"How- how could you?" My eyes widened at him, unbelieving. I couldn't even find the mind to scream at him, I couldn't see, couldn't hear, my lungs would not fill. My voice was failing me, throat constricting. It didn't make sense, humans shouldn't be able to carry fae runes, and yet he did, and yet he *bound us*. I felt sick.

My mind would not accept this, far worse than any cruelty I ever imagined humans could inflict, even as I hated them. Beyond merely physical, this was a spiritual violation, a death knell. The room around me was spinning. My organs- my very soul collapsed under the crushing weight. I blindly sank to the ground, trying to catch my breath. My lungs were paralyzed.

"The king's order, he suspected you may be too... unpredictable, that you may cause undue harm to his court." A tinge of something in his voice, a hint of emotion I couldn't read, something I couldn't focus on as the world collapsed inward. He was upon me now, trying to lift me from the ground, but I was separate from my body, my limbs not listening to the screaming in my mind to run, to fight, to do anything. Automatically, my wings tightened around me, a feathered shield against his touch. He knelt in front of me, lifting my chin from my knees, gentle but firm touch. He placed a flat hand on my chest, a pressure to slow my quickened breaths. I looked into his eyes, which bore into me with such intensity, and such genuine remorse.

"I'm sorry." Was all he said as he stared at me. Because somehow he knew, he understood why. He knew what he had done.

"I won't hurt anyone, I promise. Please, you have to get it removed, you have to unbind us." I was begging, crying at him pathetically, tears now wetting my face. I would suffer anything to avoid this fate he had forced on me. My eyes begged him even when my voice failed as he knelt mere inches from my face.

"You know I can't." He whispered.

And I broke.

I sobbed harder, my ribs near cracking beneath the crushing grip of my own arms as I pressed into myself. Everything around me blurred as fresh tears filled my eyes, as I retreated inside myself. His heavy hand was still firm against my chest. But it was useless, I could barely feel it, I didn't even have the mind to pull away. He had ruined me, marked me with one of the few permanent runes, a knot that whispered to the other from beneath my skin. *If you die, we die together.*

# 10

# Astriel

I was still sobbing when the captain gently scooped me up from the floor. I wanted to fight him off, to tell him to let me go, but I could only manage a few halfhearted beats on his chest with the side of my fist, he did not react. When my strength once again failed me, I just closed my eyes, silently praying to whatever gods or spirits or anything that would listen to save me, or kill me. I didn't care which. But none answered. He kept his eyes ahead and said nothing more.

I could have endured torture, pain, lashings. I would have gladly accepted any manner of pain these humans could have tried to use to break me, but not this. My soul was shattered into paper thin shards. And this man, this human would never truly understand what he had done to me. He had already killed me, binding me to his fleeting lifespan. I would never be able to find my mate, never marry, never even return to my home with this cursed binding. My people would have to continue on without my protection.

He deposited me gently in the bed I had awoken in. Already made up with new sheets and covers. I turned from him, wrapping myself in my own wings and shaking as each breath rattled through my body, until my entire core hollowed out, nothing left. I tried to curl into myself, to keep shrinking until I faded out of existence. I heard him slowly retreat from the room, pausing at the open door.

"For what it's worth, I really am terribly sorry." The door latched behind him, but did not lock. There was no reason, there was nowhere I could go.

* * *

For several days I did not leave the room. Farryn did her best to keep me alive, but she just as well could have left me to rot. It changed nothing. I did not fight her as she fed me, made me drink, bathed and dressed me like a doll. My mind was elsewhere, I couldn't bring it back to my body. The world around me was a haze of muffled, faraway voices and fleeting forms, in and out.

"Astriel. Enough of this." The first voice that cut through the mist around my mind, the first time I had heard my own name since being here. Keelan. But I ignored him. I didn't want to see him. My executioner. "You have to get up, you're wasting away in here, don't forget my side of this binding too, you're killing us both." He cursed under his breath.

*Good.* I rolled away from him. I couldn't bring myself to care, not about my own well being, and certainly not about his. Absently, I felt myself being lifted, but the heavy fog was rolling back in. I could still feel his warm hands on my skin, his breath on my ear. The sensations threatened to pull me out of my stupor but I wouldn't let them. I sunk further into the haze, as deep as I could go.

And then, pain. Freezing sharp shards burning my skin and wings. My eyes shot open to Farryn standing in the corner of the bathing room, looking apprehensive. Keelan standing above me, scowling. I tried thrashing against whatever assaulted me but I couldn't see it. Then the mist released me, and I realized where I was. The *bastard* captain had thrown me into a frigid bath, fully clothed. I laid my eyes on him, and suddenly the darkness that had filled my head for days lifted, and all I could see was red.

I lunged at him, feet slipping on the cold metal as I tried to vault out of the tub, I hit the ground, on my hands and knees, hard. The force rattling my bones. Keelan took a few steps back. That soft, self satisfied smile once again playing at his lips. "There's my girl, I thought you lost that fire."

"I will kill you." I snarled, lunging again, ready to pounce and tear at him until he was flayed open. He backed into the bedroom, casually, unafraid. Just as I closed in, arms outstretched and ready to claw that grin off of his face, his hand encircled my wrist, redirecting me, the other grabbed my waist and spun me face down on the bed. Feet still on the floor and hinged at the waist. I tried slapping at him with my wings but he stayed just out of reach.

I pawed at him with my free hand but he just grabbed it as well, wrenching it behind my back with the other. Holding both wrists in a single strong grip. He leaned over me, his chest pressing on the space where my wings erupted from my back, I shuddered at the sensation. I felt his breath caress the point of my ear. He was winded. At least I was able to accomplish that much.

ASTRIEL

His voice was a low growl in my ear, "If you need to be angry with me, we can take it to the sparring field. But you are not spending another moment in this bed."

"Get off of me." I spit through gritted teeth.

He pushed off and I righted myself, still huffing, rubbing my only partially healed wrists where they were pinched against each other. He backed away, raising his hands to placate me. His clothes were wet from where we had touched, and I could see the definition of his chest though the thin material now plastered to his skin.

"Not as much of a worthy opponent as legend would suggest. Disappointing." His eyes raked over my too thin form, on display with my wet clothes slicked to my body, "Have you always been this weak? Or are you just out of practice?"

I didn't bother to respond, only glaring as I studied him, trying to glean what exactly his goal was here. He did look terrible. Dark, heavy bags dragged beneath his eyes, his now wet clothes were rumpled, his hair frizzy and unbrushed. *Good.*

"Leave." I commanded simply, pointing to the door. Out of the corner of my eye, I saw Farryn grimace at my tone from the bathing room entryway.

"You will dress and meet me in the sparring ring. You need the movement, and some sun. You look like death." Not a flicker of humor in his tone.

"I'm not going anywhere with you." I growled at him, stalking to the other side of the bed, creating distance, dripping water as I went. Farryn looked fearfully between us, and quietly excused herself before disappearing entirely into the bathing room, not wanting to be in the middle of whatever was about to occur here.

"Well you can't stay in here for the rest of your life like a corpse. I won't allow it." His voice was strong, demanding. But he did not approach. Just stood there, stiff backed.

"I am not one of the savage men you command, what you do or do not allow is none of my concern. You and your wishes mean nothing to me." I held his stare, vibrating in my skin. "Not after what you did." The last sentence was low, venomous. I held out my arm to him, pointing to the silver mark inked into my skin.

"You have sentenced me to misery and death. You have taken *everything* from me." My eyes were burning, tears threatening to spill over once again. But I pushed them back and just stared at him.

"It was not my choice." His voice crackled, "It was commanded and I obeyed. I do not relish in this situation and don't wish to be tied to you any more than you wish to be tied to me. But you cannot kill us both because you don't understand the forces at work."

"There is no understanding. You made this choice, and I will kill you for it."

"Then you can kill us both in the sparring ring." The final word, a dismissal yet a command. He stormed out of the room, door slamming behind him.

I tried to catch my breath as Farryn crept back into the room on light feet. I leaned forward against the bed, hands tensing and un-tensing, my breathing ragged. Everything around me swirled in rage, and despair. As I regained my composure, Farryn carefully placed a stack of clothing near me on the bed, a white training tunic and pants.

"Go. Hear him out." She spoke softly, her voice like a

harpist's melody, soothing. "He is a hard man, and does not always say what he means. But he was correct, there are things at work here that you do not, cannot understand."

"Then tell me." I spit at her, more harshly than I had meant to.

She brushed off my ire, understanding that it was not meant for her. But she shook her head, "Not for me to say."

I exhaled slowly through my nose, governing my emotions, the shaking in my hands. But I nodded.

"Then let's get you dressed, my lady."

# 11

# Astriel

I was to meet him in the gardens behind the castle, an area provisioned off for these activities. Across the short cut grass lay a paved circle dedicated to sword training. Farryn had pulled my hair into a tight plait at the back of my head, I wore my circlet once again. A touch of familiarity in this foreign world.

Keelan was sitting on a stone bench, head in hands. And I stared at the sky before daring to approach him, feeling midday sun warm my skin. *How long had it been since I'd seen the sun?* The perfectly clear sky and light warm breeze made my wings twitch. I dared not take flight, but oh how I ached to.

"There is a ward around the entire estate." A voice cut through my reverie. I hadn't heard him approach, but he stood in front of me. Wearing training clothes similar to mine, but in black, with a dark brown leather plate strapped to his chest, he had a dagger strapped to his thigh.

"How high?" Even if I couldn't soar I might could lift off, just feel the wind beneath my wings once more.

"High enough. If you were careful." He watched me, tentatively, his eyes softer now than they had been since I'd met him. I considered it, briefly.

"Another time," I sighed, afraid that if I started I might not be able to land again. "Let's just do what we came here to do."

I had been able to dampen the emotions that raged under my skin for now, but they still lingered. He nodded solemnly, as if understanding. As if he possibly could. I stalked over to the stone circle, not looking at him.

I was eager to get in the ring. Yes, to work off some of the anger and hurt, and maybe to repay some of that hurt to Keelan. But also to try to discover how exactly this human man kept besting me. I was built for battle, it was in my blood, and yet, in the forest, and just earlier in the bedroom, he had rendered me defenseless.

I could blame drunkenness and surprise, and that poison tipped iron dart the night of the forest, and the neglect I had forced upon myself for the bedroom. But even then, I should be able to dispatch ten human men at a time without breaking a sweat. I didn't want to think of why I was suddenly so weak.

I reached for a blade and he caught my wrist, "Not yet," Keelan said softly, and placed a bundle in my hand, "First, eat." The cloth fell open and inside was a small meal of bread, cheese, and dried meat. My mouth watered.

I nodded at him and retreated to the bench. He followed, not sitting but watching me closely from a few feet away as I scarfed down the meal. I didn't dare acknowledge him as he appraised me, watching as the bundle emptied. I wasn't eating for his benefit, just to take the edge off the gnawing hunger pangs that I was becoming all too accustomed to.

When I finished, he handed me a canteen of water, I guzzled greedily, feeling cold rivulets running down my neck. Before it was snatched out of my hand.

I glared at him, "You're going to make yourself sick if you drink too much."

But he wasn't looking me in the eye, he was looking at the still angry pink welts that decorated both wrists from the shackles. I wiped my mouth and stood abruptly, pushing past him back into the circle. An anger, reignited, boiled in my blood. The marks would surely leave twin scars, even with my healing, iron *always* scarred. I entered the ring and turned on him, my face a forced mask of casual interest.

"How do you want to do this?"

"Hand to hand or weapons, lady's choice." He answered, stalking confidently into the ring, hands stuffed into his pockets.

The swords that I had initially reached for had left my mind. I wanted to feel it, personally, how this man was able to fight so effectively. "Hand to hand. Don't hold back." I took a wide stance, schooling my breathing, hands in front of my face and softly open. I was ready for this.

He raised an eyebrow, unbuckling his sword belt with one hand and tossing it to the side. He pulled his lone dagger out of the thigh scabbard and tossed it as well, far out of the ring. He shrugged, "As you wish."

He leapt before I had registered his movements, closing the distance between us in a single stride. I deflected his first reaching arm but lost my footing, a swift kick caught my heel and ripped me off my feet. I braced to hit the ground but felt strong hands on my back as he caught me and thrust me back to my feet. He retreated a few steps as I regained my composure.

"How did you-" But he was on me again, I ducked his grasp and punched at his midsection. He sidestepped and I tripped forward into empty air. A pull on the back of my tunic yanked me backwards, I collided with his hard chest and his thick arm wrapped around my throat, his other grasping at my waist, my wings pinned tightly between us. I wrenched at his arm, not pressed hard enough to restrict my air, but solid enough that I couldn't break his hold.

"Do you yield, El?" His breath warm against my neck.

"Don't call me that." I grunted, leaning back against him, before thrusting myself forward and launching him over my back, using my wings to push him off, into the air. His grip loosened and I slipped him. He landed hard on his back, the smug smile on his face finally gone as the air was knocked out of his lungs. He rolled back over, into a crouch and lunged again. But I had landed a blow, and my confidence had returned.

He kept low to the ground as I leapt over him, a single wing beat lifted me out of his reach. I landed behind him. Once again solid in my footing. I pushed toward him as he turned, my fist connecting with his scarred jaw, he stumbled backwards, but grabbed at my tunic, and I went tumbling after him.

He was now beneath me, on his back as I moved to straddle him, pinning his arms to his side with my thighs. My hand pressed hard against his torso, wings flared, shadowing him from the sun. I could feel his heart thundering beneath my palm. I reared my fist back once again and held it there.

"Do you yield?" My turn to ask.

His eyes flashed with something I didn't recognize, and

his smile returned. My heart dropped. An imperceptible movement, and a moment later it was my back pinned to the ground. One strong hand braced my arms to the ground over my head. His other was placed against my heaving chest, fingers splayed over my collarbones. The pressure was light but immovable.

I grunted as I struggled against him, somewhat surprised I was unable to break his grip. He rested the majority of his weight on my hips. It kept the pressure off my wings, but also served to lock me in place. He cocked an eyebrow from where he hovered over me as I tested his holds.

There was no amount of thrashing, or bucking my hips or trying to leverage his weight against him that I could use to dislodge him. My eyes narrowed in defiance. His, shadowed and dark, danced with amusement. We stayed like that, panting from the exertion, eyes locked, while I refused to accept defeat.

He decided for me, releasing my wrists and leaning back. The weight on my chest lightened, his fingertips running so softly downward I couldn't tell if I had imagined it or not. With all the grace of a jungle cat, he lifted himself from me, and extended a hand. I grasped it, scowling, letting him pull me to my feet.

We once again found ourselves chest to chest, breathing hard, hands still clasped between us. When, without warning, the mark on my arm *burned*. I recoiled, growling at it as it glowed, and then faded back into faint silver lines. I looked back up at Keelan, who still stared at me, into me. I could see his own tattoo fading back into its subtle color. I didn't know how to deal with the raw emotion on his face, so I turned away.

For a moment, I had almost forgotten about my circumstance, the high of sparring a familiar distraction from the reality that was now crashing back down around me. Farryn had urged me to hear him out. I had promised her that I would try. But the reminder of it, of the mark, brought those feelings bubbling back to the surface.

I hated the captain. I knew that, I knew intrinsically what he had done to me, the unforgivable ruin he had sowed. And yet, it wasn't hate that I was feeling when he pinned me to the ground. Wounded pride, maybe, but also something deeper, something *warmer*. I knew what it must be, some sort of self preservation in the magic. The mark was trying to eat away at my anger, trying to turn the tide of my feelings towards him.

But I couldn't allow it, he was still the enemy. An enemy that may just contain important information I would *need* if I wanted to get out of here. They were both right about one thing: there were forces at play here that I didn't understand, that my people didn't understand. But if I could figure out what those things are, I could make all of this worth it. I could play nice until I discovered what he knows, and then find a way out when I got what I needed. I just couldn't let myself forget the monster that he was.

I cleared my throat, "Let's just get a drink." I walked away from him, not daring to gaze down at the silver knot that had soured my mood. When I reached the stone bench, I positioned myself on the far end, giving Keelan a wide berth. He remained standing, eyes fixed on the canteen I had tossed to him, or his arm, I couldn't tell.

"So, how did you do that?" I asked tentatively, eager to break the tension that had formed like a wall between us.

61

"Do what?" His attention snapped back to me and he took a swig of water, then handed the canteen back over.

"Move like that, I didn't think- I guess I hadn't realized humans were capable of that." Birds were chirping overhead, I looked up at them.

"I've been training for a long time." He said simply, his mouth quirking up at one corner, "I think you're just not used to anyone challenging you. I mean, when was the last time you even trained with the Seraphim? You're rusty."

The look on my face must have given it away, because the playfulness fell from his. "It's been a long time." I admitted, not looking directly at him. Still watching the birds above coast in wide arcs against the cloudless sky. "The rest are gone. As far as I know I'm the last like me alive." My gaze dropped and my eyes locked on him then, and the pained expression on his face made me regret it.

"What happened to them?" his voice caught in his throat, pity. *I guess the mark is doing its work on him too.*

"I'm not exactly sure, I was young. My parents had sent me to a school in the city, to learn all the nobility skills I was sure I would never need." I laughed a little bitterly. "I was never supposed to be the lady of my territory. With three older sisters, I should have been the last in line for the responsibility. When I returned, everyone was gone, no one would tell me what had happened. The more time went on the harder it was to ask."

He watched me with such intensity it burned, not speaking, not moving an inch, so I continued, "That must have been somewhere around 200 years ago now. Immediately I was appointed the *Lady of the skies*, and protecting our lands and our borders fell to me."

62

I took another drink of water and loosed a sad breath. I hadn't spoken of these things to anyone, not in a very long time, I hadn't realized how badly I wanted to, "And now they have no one. I am here, tethered to you, trapped in this castle, with all the other sad eyed captives that claim to love it here, and my people are unprotected."

I scoffed and shook my head. The realization dawning, I was confessing the weaknesses of my city to a fae hunter. *Idiot.* My eyes fell to my feet. A maelstrom of emotion threatened to spill over but I refused to let it. I would make this worth it, I was still going to find a way home to them. I would make his pity worth it, and use it to my advantage. I finally looked back up at Keelan, who still said nothing, his jaw clenched.

"Anyways," I suddenly felt exposed and vulnerable. The way he was looking at me was too intense, too searching, like he could read my thoughts at a glance, "This was fun, I guess. I'll be in my room if you need me." And I walked away. He did not follow me, and did not look back as I retreated inside the castle and back into my room. I waved Farryn off when she tried to ask me how it went. I needed to be alone.

# 12

# Astriel

I awoke the next morning to breakfast on my side table, eggs and potatoes. I pulled the tray into my lap, eager for a hot meal. When I raised the glass of orange juice from the tray, a piece of paper fell from it. I picked it up, studying the pristine handwriting.

> *I'm sorry about yesterday, I didn't mean to upset you.*
> *When you rise, meet me back out in the sparring ring.*
> *We need to talk.*
> *- Ke*

I crumpled up the paper and tossed it across the room just as Farryn entered, she watched the paper fly and bounce off the far wall. It wasn't a cruel note, in fact, it was most likely exactly what I wanted. But rage, self loathing, something close to mourning ate at me. It made me dread the next inevitable run in with the man who despite his role carried a soft understanding in his eyes. I had failed to keep myself on a tight leash yesterday, and had gotten scrambled, started revealing vulnerabilities to that man. And he revealed nothing, I didn't care to risk that again. Whatever his story was, I decided I didn't need to hear it.

She looked at me sadly, placing a set of clothes on the bed. I did not meet her gaze. And instead stabbed a potato with my fork. *Leave me alone.* At our first meeting, I had been overjoyed to know I would not be captive alone in the world of humans. After my confessions yesterday, it just made me sad. I left my people open to become like her, leaving them vulnerable to more attacks. I wanted to cry and scream and break everything in this room. But I just sat there, staring at my breakfast, frozen. A single tear hit the tray.

Farryn must have seen and I felt her climb onto the bed next to me, moving the tray and pulling me into her arms. I grabbed onto her, craving that comfort I had never been offered before. I was overcome with the distinct feeling that if I let go I would float away, fade to mist. I was wracked with sobs as she held me, smoothing my hair with her hand.

"It's going to be okay," she whispered into my hair, "Everything is going to be okay."

I cried harder, "It's not me," I mumbled into the front of her dress, "My people, they needed me, I kept them safe. The humans, they are going to destroy my home because I am *not there.*" I would have given my life to my people if I knew it would keep them safe. And now it feels as if I've given my life only to see them destroyed.

"It is going to be okay my lady," Farryn spoke so softly I could hardly hear her, "But you need to speak with Sir Keelan."

I pulled away from her then, her touch suddenly feeling soured. I stared into her green eyes that shone like emeralds.

She still didn't get it, and still favored this human man over her own kind. She knew what the rune meant, the fate that it spelled out for me and she still defended him. I shrugged her off and refused to look at her, instead pulling myself off the bed, creating distance. I busied myself by fishing around in my wardrobe for clothes, not daring to look back at her. It was a harsh reminder. I had no allies within these walls.

"I left you more training clothes on the bed, my lady." I ignored her. Instead, I opted to pull out the clothes from the night I was taken, which apparently had been laundered. The tight black shirt and loose pants, fitted for me, made for me, by my people. I had no weapons and thus no need for the leathers. I didn't even put on shoes, just my circlet as I stormed out of the room. Loose hair whipped behind me when my pace quickened.

I didn't know where I was going but I knew I needed to be far away from Farryn, far away from Keelan, away from the guards and the illusive king. I needed to be alone. I snaked through long hallways that blurred into indiscernible smudges of color. I took countless turns, trekked up and down curving staircases until I was really and truly lost in the labyrinth of the sprawling castle. Whispers of my inadequacy, of this grand failure drowned out every thought.

I stomped further and further into the keep. Not caring where I ended up, not knowing if anyone saw or tried to stop me. There was nothing but the incessant roaring in my mind. When my breath burned in my throat, I took a moment, bracing a hand against a cool stone wall, unadorned with the priceless wallpaper that had been plastered to most every other hall I had found myself in.

This was an old wing of the castle, one that was not often

frequented if the cobwebs and faded dye of the rug beneath my bare feet was any indication. Ahead was a small plain door at the end of the dead end hallway. My head spun with fatigue as I swayed towards it, wishing I had gotten at least a little of that breakfast down before I had stormed off. When I reached it, I tried the knob, dull and tarnished. A soft humming filling my ears as I touched it, it turned. I pulled open the door, the hinges squealing, and beheld a set of stone steps descending into darkness.

I carefully stepped down, the circlet atop my head continuing to thrum quietly. Better judgment would have told me to turn around, find my room again. But I was so angry, so tired. Whatever was going to happen would happen. And that would be it.

I descended. The only light came from the hallway above, through the sliver of the door I'd left ajar. As I stepped lower, darkness blanketed the stairwell. I hugged the wall to my left, testing every crumbling step before trusting it with my weight. The climb down was slow and long. The only sounds I could hear were my own feet tapping against the cold stone and the constant thrumming of my circlet, which had grown stronger now. *Danger, danger.* It whispered in my ear, I disregarded it. My focus solely on finding where these stairs led.

If I had still had a family, maybe I would have been more cautious. But the fallout of those years after the rest of the Seraphim vanished had left its mark. Even as suitors threw themselves at me I shunned them, I knew better. Bedding me was a social currency, marrying me would have been a powerful alliance between territories. They had no interest in Astriel, only Astriel's wings. I had shut down the part of me that craved romance and companionship long ago. *No one to love, no one to lose.* Melodramatic maybe, but certainly an easier way to live.

I thrust myself mind, body, and soul into my people, patrolling the forest everyday, showing up to every social event. Going home meant only collapsing in my bed, weary muscles screaming at the end of each day. I allowed myself the touch of another at the seasonal events, fleeting and mostly unfulfilling, but it was something to do, a break from the monotony.

Two hundred years, I realized. I had been doing the same thing for *two hundred years.* And yet, the grief never fully subsided. I woke and flew and trained and drank and slept. Sometimes reading on the many nights that despite the all encompassing exhaustion that pulled at me, I wasn't able to sleep. That was all, never stopping long enough to really think or feel, not allowing the ever-present voices that screamed my failures at all hours to catch me idle. I shook the pain of it away before it could overtake me. Around another curve in the stairs, I spotted a dim light.

I followed it.

When I reached the bottom of the stairs I was overtaken by the room they opened into. A massive, sprawling underground library, lit with low burning candles on every shelf end and interspersed down the walls. I couldn't spot the far end from where I stood, just shelves overflowing with so many different kinds of books. I stepped slowly down the first aisle, running my fingers across the spines of the dust coated tomes. Some I thought I recognized, a few were in languages I had never encountered, and many so old I couldn't decipher what had once been embossed on their spines.

My bare feet padded against the ancient stone flooring beneath, smooth and worn from centuries of people walking between these shelves. The thought made my heart flutter. There was something so special about finding a place like this, with so much secret history. For what felt like hours I explored the cavernous library, touching the spines of hundreds of books but not unshelving any. Just appreciating the forgotten, albeit dusty charm of this place.

\* \* \*

As I perused, my stomach growled angrily, reminding me of the lack of breakfast. I had no clue of the time, no telling how long I had wandered these aisles. Looking, but selecting no books. I turned back at the vast amount of library I had not yet explored and sighed as I bid it a final silent farewell, preparing to summit the stairs I had come down. I had almost reached the entryway when I heard a *tap, tap, tap* on an aisle to my left. My circlet had been humming the entire time I was down here, so I paid it no mind as the sound pitched up as I followed the sound down an between the stacks.

My head swiveled as I followed the constant tapping, but every step I took, it sounded further away. Until, on the wall shelf, just at eye level, I spotted it. A book bound in rich violet, seemingly untouched by the heavy layer of dust that coated everything else. Its gilded spine, a striking shine in the candlelight. As I approached, I was able to make out the title. *The Winged War.* I had never heard of such a war in my lessons.

It was thick, and I could almost hear it beckoning me, begging me to peruse its contents. Curiosity took over as I reached out, a single finger perched on top of the spine, shifting it out just enough that I could get a better look. My circlet thrummed ever louder but I could barely discern it, as if the call of the book was louder, more convincing. I had braced to pull it out entirely when my binding rune sent a jolt of electricity through my fingertips, and I jumped backwards, a short yelp escaping my lips.

I stared down at the traitorous ink as it glowed, but it did not fade like it had last time. It seemed to glow brighter and brighter until—

"El!" A voice whispered-yelled from behind me, Keelan had appeared suddenly, somehow having tracked me down. I sneered at him.

"Don't call me that! And I don't want to talk to you." I whispered back, and turned my attention back to the shelf.

"Don't touch that!" He was closing in on me, no doubt about to wrench my hand away, for daring to do something without his explicit permission. His little project, lunging at the leash.

"Try to stop me." I whispered back, turning completely away from him and tipping the book the rest of the way out, feeling the weight of it fall into my hand. I turned to look at him, triumphant. His face paled.

"What have you done?" Was all he could say before ear shattering screams erupted from every direction around us. The very ground trembled beneath our feet.

He grabbed my arm roughly, "We need to leave. Now." No longer a whisper. I felt for weapons I was not wearing, panicking at the empty air where I should have had blades. He grabbed my hand iron tight and dragged me through the aisle as I stumbled behind him, trying desperately to keep balance. In his other hand he unsheathed the sword that hung at his waist, and it wielded it ahead of him.

Dark shadows flitted around us, encroaching ever closer, the walls seemed to scream in hoarse grating voices, *Thief, catch the thief.* I ran after Keelan, who brandished his sword at the shadowy beasts as they flitted closer, somewhere between being corporeal and not of this world. *How do you fight darkness personified?*

We had almost reached the staircase when one dipped between us, revealing a razor sharp talon that tore at my arm, breaking my grip as I fell face first into the stone. I heard myself cry out.

Keelan turned on his heel, eyes wide with panic. I picked myself up, dripping blood on the floor. I took off in another run towards his outstretched hand as another creature dove behind me, ripping into my calf, I fell again, pain screaming up my leg. I tried to shut it out, but there was more than just the gash, something that burned like fire as it infiltrated my veins, tightening the muscles, slowing every movement. My lungs ached. Keelan grabbed me beneath the arms, hoisting me as his blade shone in the candlelight, slashing in every direction, where it connected with the shadows was the sound of hissing, the smell of sickly sweet rotting flesh.

I limped as he near dragged me, throwing me onto the stairs, "Climb." He commanded. The pain coursing through my body and the fear in his voice urged me on.

On hands and knees I pulled myself up the slippery stone, and he walked backwards behind me, fending off the spirits that entered the corridor. I heard their strangled cries before they splattered against the hard stone. I kept climbing, chest burning and body aching, my strength trying to fail me. The silver light of the glowing rune was the only illumination as I crawled up and up and up. The soft silver shone harshly against the red that now covered my skin, dripping onto the steps, the warmth of it sticky against my skin as I climbed.

I could see the door, nearly reach the knob as the darkness that had been lingering so close in the past weeks coiled up my spine and wrapped around my vision. The last thing I heard was Keelan yelling. And then nothing.

# 13

# Keelan

I slammed the slatted wooden door behind us as I yanked a now unconscious Astriel into the hall. Beyond the barrier, intermittent thudding of the shadow creatures sounded, still desperate to finish the job. My shaking hands were running over her body, assessing the damage. She was pallid, her lips, normally a rich pink, were tinged in blue.

"We need help!" I screamed into the abandoned halls, hoping desperately someone was near enough to hear.

The gash in her arm was bleeding profusely, and the tattoo that adorned it flickered with its spectral light. In a panic, I ripped a strip of fabric off the bottom of my shirt, wrapping it around the wound and tying the knot as tightly as my trembling fingers would allow. I yelled again.

My gaze traveled further down, locking in on another pool of blood beneath her leg. As gently as I could, I turned her over. Another, longer and deeper gouge tore open her left calf. I blanched at the sight of it spilling too much blood on the worn carpet. I tore at my shirt again, and tied the makeshift bandage around the wound with as much pressure as I could get on it.

"Somebody help us!" I screamed again, and this time the distant sound of boots answered. I yelled again and again, urging them faster. When three of my men turned the corner, they all halted at the sight. A fallen, bleeding angel with my hands wrapped around her mangled leg.

"Don't just stand there! You two, come here and help me lift her. Edward, go fetch the doctor." The two I called over sprung back into action at the command, gripping at Astriel's limp form, and my lieutenant tore off back the way he came. "Be careful with her wings. Try to keep pressure on the wounds."

We ended up in my chambers, it was closer, I told myself. But in honesty, there was a compulsion to stay close, to keep an eye on her. I had seen battle, I knew the signs of death, Farryn would be useless in making sure she made it through this. Might allow her to fade away completely. The royal doctor cursed repeatedly as he inspected her wounds. Bloody gauze filled a tray as he tried to stanch the bleeding. I stayed by the door, watching the doctor work, but doing my best to stay out of the way.

So I paced, running my hands through my hair, down my jaw. Occasionally I forced myself to sit at my desk chair, only when the doctor cut too many annoyed looks in my direction. But staying stationary only increased my restlessness. I was at the point of madness when there was a knock at the door. I sprung up to answer it as the doctor finished stitching the wound on Astriel's leg.

Edward poked his head in, face hard, "Deliana wants to speak to you."

I groaned internally, but steeled myself, and stepped into

the hall, closing the door behind me. Edward moved himself back to his post on the other side of the door frame.

"What can I do for you Deliana?" I asked, crossing my arms.

She was wearing a dark violet cloak, it shadowed her face, but the glowing orange embers in her eyes tore through the darkness, piercing into me. "What happened?" She demanded.

"There was an accident, the fae is injured."

"Will she live?"

"Too soon to say."

"You were supposed to be watching her." The sorceress cursed, and then turned on me again, her eyes piercing. "I will see her." She moved towards the door, without thinking, I moved my body to block her.

"You will not. The doctor is working. I will be sure that he keeps you updated on her condition."

"How dare you deny me." She spit, closing in on me, "If she dies-."

"I am well aware, Deliana. But I am not killing her. She went off wandering because, if you dare believe it, she's having a hard time with accepting the binding and her purpose here." I sighed, running a hand through my hair. "I warned you of this. I'm working on her. But you need to let her rest and recover or your endless wrath will be for nothing."

She scoffed and shook her head. She opened her mouth as if to say more before turning on a heel and tearing off down the hall in the other direction, her thick cloak billowing behind her. I cut my eyes at Edward, who was already looking at me, almost imperceptibly shaking his head.

I huffed an irritated breath and stalked back into the room, leaning against the door as it snicked shut. The doctor looked up at me and offered a weak smile, having dealt with Deliana plenty himself. She was a terror in the castle, even when she wasn't using her magic to intimidate and control. She had been a pest since she was appointed nearly a century ago, when the previous sorcerer wound up mysteriously dead. I shook off the thought.

"How is she doing?"

The doctor set down his needle, snipping the thread and using forceps to tie the knot. "The wounds will heal, but there is nothing I can do for the venom. She will have to weather it, but she is strong." The elder doctor stooped to collect his supplies, his forehead, heavily lined with his years, was furrowed further in thought.

"What is it, doctor?"

He shook his head, "Not even most fae survive venom of the wraith, especially as much of it as she received. But she is unlike any fae I have worked on. What is she?"

"Seraphim." I bit out, eyeing the doctor, trying to glean what he was getting at.

"Hmm. Perhaps she is different then. For both of your sake, I hope that is true." The doctor's gaze fell to the mark on my arm, beneath the rolled up sleeve of my shirt. I clasped my hands behind my back, concealing it.

"Just make her well, doctor. The rest is none of your concern."

# 14

# Astriel

I awoke in an unfamiliar place, on a plush bed that was not mine, in a room that was much too dark. I tried to raise my head, but a blinding pain at the base of my skull stopped me, and a roaring headache set itself off between my temples. I heard, but could not see someone stirring. I knew who it was before I heard him speak, the scent of oak moss and cedar permeated the entire space.

"Don't move. You're okay, you're safe, we made it out." He had moved to the bedside near silently, and I appraised him through my eyelashes. I could hardly think, but I needed to speak to him, to apologize for nearly killing us both, to thank him, to ask the million other questions I knew I held. I made an attempt to speak, but no words escaped my too dry mouth.

"Don't try to talk, the poison from those wraiths nearly took you from us." So it was wraiths. I could have laughed if my body were in better condition. The human king had a library of wraiths, of course he did. Keelan rested his calloused fingers lightly against my shoulder, tentatively,

77

as if he were afraid that the touch may shatter me.

"And somehow," he forced a small laugh, "you made it out with this." He lifted something into my eye line, but I couldn't focus on it.

*The Winged War,* I've thumbed through it a bit now, not exactly easy reading. I don't know why you held onto it through all that, why you wouldn't just leave it behind." He seemed almost angry at me, or pleading, like he wanted answers I didn't have. I don't remember clutching the book as we escaped. I don't think I knew I still held it as I crawled up those steps.

Someone else entered the room, and Keelan's presence left me, my skin turned cold where his fingers had been. I heard them speaking softly to each other, unable to make out the words, or who the second person was. I turned my attention back to my own body. Everything *ached* so profoundly. Like every bone had been snapped, every muscle torn.

It took all my concentration to lift my right arm, the one with the rune, the one that had been mauled. From just beneath the mark all the way my wrist was heavily bandaged, a rosette of light pink blooming through the thick gauze. Below it, even without my vision clearing, I could see veins of black snaking across my hand, up my arm. Hideous and angry, radiating from the dressings. I let the arm fall, and winced, squeezing my eyes tightly against the throbbing.

The muffled conversation paused, and then continued. I strained to listen but could make out none of what they were saying. Consciousness was slipping again, the room falling further out of focus and the voices of those speaking falling quieter and quieter. I tried to fight it, tried to grab something that was real, that was tangible. But there was nothing within reach. And I was so, so cold. A soft voice from the far reaches of my mind whispered, *Let go, the pain will end.*

The darkness claimed me again

\* \* \*

I stood in a forest I recognized, though I couldn't place exactly from where. Morning light shone through the foliage, dappled light warming my skin. Birds chirped cheerily overhead, and I watched a hare race across my path. I walked along a deer cut trail, my white dress, my equinox dress I realized, whispered against the foliage as I passed. *Such a peaceful day for a walk.* I brushed my fingertips across the ferns which coiled in on themselves at the contact, a smile forming on my lips.

I heard the sounds of a celebration ahead, and followed them, as the thick woods opened into a glen, I saw my people, laughing and drinking together. They cheered as they turned and watched me emerge, raising their glasses in unison, "To the return of the lady of the skies! Astriel has come back to us!" I laughed with them, their smiles contagious. I took a gulp from a flute I hadn't realized I'd been holding, savoring the fizzy drink. *I made it out, I'm home.*

"It is so good to see again my dear." A familiar voice from behind me, my mother's voice. I turned. My mother, father, and sisters stood together, all smiling at me. Their great white wings gleaming in the early light. I ran to them, arms outstretched. We collided, tears welling in my eyes as they wrapped me in a hug.

"I never thought I'd see you again, I didn't know where you had all gone." I held my mother at arms length, pulling out of the familial embrace. Studying her serene face, silver eyes stared back at me, "I missed you so much." I again buried my face in her chest, savoring the warmth. Breathing deeply I inhaled cinnamon and cloves, the smell of her that I could never forget.

"You didn't look for us." A voice to my left, Amira, my eldest sister. I turned to her, breaking the embrace, retreating back a step. Her smile had faded, her eyes turning dark. I stumbled away from them, none of them were smiling now.

"You didn't even try." Two voices at once, the younger twins, Aziria and Aida, spoke in unison, accusing me.

"I wanted to, I was so young, you didn't even tell me you were leaving, the council forced me to stay. I wanted— I wanted to find you." Hurt gripped my chest as my burning eyes met those of my parents, no longer silver, now black.

"You failed us. We screamed for you, you didn't hear us. You didn't care. *You didn't come.*" My mother, the serenity had left her face, her fists clenched at her sides. Embers floated behind them, their wings on fire.

My breath caught in my throat as I stumbled back further. "You failed us. And now you have failed your people. You're a disgrace to our family and to the Seraphim line." My father, his empty eyes cutting into me, burning a hole through my chest.

Their wings had turned black as cinder, smoke thick in the air as fire licked up their bodies. A wind whipped around me as I sobbed, as I begged for their forgiveness. They just stood there, their inky eyes condemning me for my failures. I could hear their collective voices on the air. Though their mouths didn't move as the blaze consumed them: *You are the reason that we burn.*

They crumbled into ash on the wind and I turned, trying to run away, to retreat from the flame that now spread across the grass. My legs wouldn't move, turning leaden beneath me. I fell to my knees, sobs racking my chest. My fists pounded at the hard ground. *My fault.* The whole glen erupted in flames around me, my people, no longer drinking or laughing, screamed in terror.

"You didn't save me." I looked up, a little Pixie girl stood in front of me with crumpled and broken wings. The flames burned at her floral party dress. "They caught you and they came back for me, it wasn't enough. You failed." Her little voice morphed into something cruel, I shielded my eyes as she too screamed, and turned to ash.

I forced myself to look up, my face dirty and streaked with tears, the burning grass encroaching, the heat scorching my wings. Ahead of me, the only person standing, the only one not ablaze. I laid eyes on the cruel face of the killer king.

He remained silent, with a vicious grin bearing down on me. Behind him stood the tree. The tree of life, the lifeblood of my people, of the world at large. It burned too. Ancient branches crackling and groaning as they fell to cinders, crushing the houses that stood beneath, red embers climbing into the sky. The air itself seemed to scream around me. Again, I tried and failed to stand, thorny vines crawling across the dead earth wrapping themselves around me, digging into my skin, tearing my dress, tightening around my throat.

*Your fault.* The disembodied voices swirled. The vines tightened, cutting off my airway, threatening to snap my wings, scraping against my clenched eyelids. *You will burn with us.*

# 15

# Astriel

Screaming echoed off the walls, my screaming. My wings clamped in a tight shield around my body. I couldn't breathe, the smoke clogged my airways, the vines strangled my voice. There were hands on me, shaking me, pulling at me. I fought them off, confusion and pain dominating my senses.

"Astriel! Astriel wake up, it's a nightmare, it's not real!" A voice I recognized. *No, I can't watch anyone else die.*

Panic gripped me and I shot my wings backwards, colliding with the owner of the voice and the rough hands. A great clattering and loud groan sounded behind me as they connected. It was enough to spur my body into action. I jumped from the bed, not my bed.

My vision was still blurry, pain made my hands shake. I grappled blindly for anything I could find to use as a weapon, but the side table was cleared, the drawers empty. I was still fondling around in the dark when strong arms wrapped themselves around me, pinning mine to my chest. They held me like a vice, tightening while I struggled against them, pressing me against a hard body.

I thrashed and screamed again but the force did not yield. "Astriel, breathe. It's me, it's Ke, you're safe. It was just a dream, you're safe." A soft voice. A warm hand pressed against my bare chest.

"Deep breaths. Come back to me." That warmth softly tickled my ear and neck, my mind starting to clear, the panic subsiding, the heat of the flames dissipating into nothing. I blinked. *Keelan*. Keelan who was still alive. Keelan who was solid and strong and *here*.

I tried to steady my breathing, to follow the slow rise and fall of the chest I was held against. As the world came back into focus, I leaned into him, my trembling body weak as the panic ebbed away. I rested my head on the shoulder behind me, legs wobbling, and he nestled his face against my shoulder.

"I'm sorry," I croaked, tears running but for a different reason now, "I didn't mean to hurt you. I'm sorry I hurt you." The voices of others that I had hurt echoed in ears.

He made soft shushing noises as his grip began to loosen, moving to lay me back on the bed, "You didn't hurt me, I'm okay. You're okay, you're safe."

My vision focused as he moved in front of me, resetting the covers I had rumpled in my sleep. He combed back the hair that was stuck to my tear stained face with his thumb. Concern marred all of his features even in the dim light.

Satisfied with his work, he cleared his throat and turned away, wiping his hands on his sleep pants. I watched him as the pain reemerged, and the memories flitted back, images of murderous shadows and the feeling of their razor sharp claws. I remembered being attacked, I remembered the stairs. I did not remember getting here.

"How did you find me?" He stilled mid step, not turning to face me, and was silent for a long minute.

"I had a bad feeling, like a vibrating in my head," He said finally, his voice low, "So I went looking for you. Farryn said you had stormed off, the guards lost you somewhere in the south wing. But, it was almost like when I called for you I could hear you. Or I would catch a whiff of your scent or a feeling, a pull down certain hallways, something so intangible I thought I was imagining things. But when I came to that door, and found it open, and *knew* that you had somehow found your way to that cursed library—"

His voice caught in his throat, I didn't dare breathe. "I panicked, afraid you had already chosen a book, afraid you had already been torn to shreds."

"You got there just in time."

"No. If I had gotten there sooner I could have stopped you from taking that book, and you wouldn't have *nearly died*."

It was startling to hear him say it. I had imagined my own death hundreds of times, what would kill me, when, how it would happen. But never had I imagined someone watching it happen. Someone hoping that it didn't.

"Hey, Ke?" he finally turned to me, brown eyes burning with some emotion I couldn't place.

A war raged in my center. I knew what he was, the kind of man he was capable of being. I couldn't even begin to the imagine the atrocities he had committed in the name of his king. But there was another side, the side that came to find me, the side that soothed me from my nightmares. The way he looked at me now, those were not the eyes of a heartless murderer. Still, I cursed myself for the question I was about to ask.

"Could you stay with me?" My voice was barely more than a whisper.

"I'll be in that chair, just a few feet away."

"No, I mean here, in the bed, where I can sense you. So I know I'm not alone." I chewed on my lip, this was so incredibly stupid.

He seemed apprehensive, but I shifted, pushing myself closer to the center of the bed, wincing as my bones protested, making room. It was just to keep the nightmares at bay, and I was manipulating him into trusting me. Besides, he is acting this way because we are binded, confusing magic trying to save itself. That's all it was, I could almost believe it.

"Okay," He shuddered a deep breath, eyes piercing as they searched mine, "as long as you promise not to launch me into the desk again." He pulled himself under the covers, stiff, laying flat on his back, staring at the ceiling. Not looking at me.

But I lay on my side, facing him, not daring to cross the inches of air like a wall between us. I tucked the bandaged arm under my head, ignoring the ache. "I make no promises, but I'll do my best." I offered a weak laugh, but guilt gnawed at my gut, "I really am sorry, I was so confused, I didn't know who you were."

His breath halted for only a heartbeat and then resumed, "It's okay. Get some rest."

All at once, I stopped fighting the exhaustion and closed my eyes, I could almost hear his heartbeat in the darkened silence. *He is still the enemy, don't forget that.* I chided myself, even as the comfort of his warm body beneath the covers eased me back towards sleep. *Still the enemy.* And yet, I had no more nightmares. Just empty, dark sleep.

# 16

# Astriel

When I awoke, Keelan was gone, I groaned into the pillow. Propping myself onto an elbow, I relished in the sun glowing through the sheer curtains of the window. For the first time, I was able to properly survey what I assumed to be his bed chambers. Simple in design, with not much aside from the necessary furniture.

There was the bed in the center, a wardrobe in the corner, and a writing desk against the wall near the door, a large crack along its front surface. One of the drawers now sat crooked in its slot, the handle gone. From last night, I imagined. Or whatever night it had been.

I had no way of truly knowing how long I slept. But the damage to the desk was severe, and guilt lingered in my chest. *That had to have hurt.* As I moved, I grimaced at a pinch in one of my wings. I couldn't reach it without my other muscles screaming and the pounding in my head threatening to return.

I spotted a crystal glass on the nightstand, and lunged for it, too fast, pulling at my stitches. I couldn't bring myself to feel the pain. My mouth was too dry and lips too chapped. I chugged it greedily as I considered how long the wraith poison had kept me under. Days? Weeks? I wouldn't know until I could ask someone, ideally Keelan. I had a lot of questions for him.

Out of the corner of my eye I spotted another note, pinned beneath a small brown vial. Wiping rogue water from my chin and neck I replaced the empty glass, and plucked the note and vial from the surface.

*I have to take care of a few things, I will return soon.*
*Please try to rest, you are still healing.*
*If you leave the room I have ordered a guard to escort you.*
*Drink from the bottle, it will help.*
*Stay out of trouble.*
*-Ke*

I caught myself smiling at the note as I set it back on the side table. Short and to the point, so indicative of *him*. Despite the mild irritation of being ordered a chaperon, I could concede it probably wasn't the worst idea. Radiating pain that cut up my limbs when I so much as flexed my toes. I eyed the bottle in my hand once again, wincing as I popped the small cork. I sniffed it, and it smelled like nothing.

I squinted my eyes at the bottle, wondering what manner of human concoction lay within. But I sucked it down in a single gulp, waiting for bitterness to coat my tongue, stick in my throat. Instead, a warmth bloomed in my belly, a familiar warmth, I stared down at the unlabeled vial again. *Enchantment.* He had somehow procured a fae tonic, the lingering sweetness confirming my suspicions.

As the warmth spread I felt my muscles loosen and their ache subside. I flexed my wings for the first time in who knows how long, and relished in the satisfying stretch.

I swung my legs over the side of the bed, the cold wood creaking beneath my feet. Pleasantly surprised that when I stood and the pain was present, but manageable. I extended my good leg, just a bit to test it. I was sore, but mostly fine. The tonic was already doing its work.

I stood carefully, testing the weight on my bandaged leg, it ached, and I took a step further, I could nearly hear my joints groaning as I moved, hinges in desperate need of oiling. *Step, step, step.* I was not fast, and a blind man could have seen the limp, but I could walk. That had to be enough for now, I desperately needed to bathe.

Getting to the bathing room was mildly trickier, with fewer things to brace myself against, I hopped slowly on my good leg, letting the other hover off the ground until my balance tried to fail me. I flicked the water on straight away as I lurched into the edge of the tub, hot as it would go. I perched myself on the rounded lip, before I could soak, the bandages needed to go.

I started with the wrappings on my leg, not knowing how long it had been, and thus how healed the lacerations would be. Remembering the event made my stomach flip, everything about it was so vivid, the feeling, the smell, *the sound* of inconceivably sharp claws tearing me open. At last the gauze fell away, A long straight line cut across the calf at a diagonal, stitched closed but still red and swollen. It would be a horrible scar without access to a fae healer, I already knew.

With some idea to the extent of my healing, I tore off the

bandages on my arm more quickly. A similar sight greeted me. Though shorter than its cousin on my leg, It was still an ugly thing. Here, the shadows of black veins lingered under the surface, snaking up my arm, but appeared to avoid the rune near my elbow. Instead, creeping around it, not beneath it. I learned young that wraith poison was nearly always fatal, even with magic healing. I was not surprised it still intended to do its work even now.

I pushed the thought from my mind, the worst was over, I had survived it. I supposed I should have been grateful for that fact, though I couldn't discern how exactly I truly felt. I pushed the thought from my mind, throwing my legs over the lip of the tub and allowing myself to sink slowly into the scalding water. I bathed in silence within the tub I knew was his, soaking my sore muscles until the water ran cold.

# 17

# Astriel

I hobbled my way out of the bath, emerging feeling fresher than I had since my arrival. I still limped, steadying myself against the foot board of the bed as I pivoted, but something new caught my attention. On the bed lay a set of clothes, no doubt provided by Farryn. I looked them over, fingered the fabric, and gasped.

A fine linen camisole in a dark navy blue, with a deep cut neckline and a low, open back, embroidered white geometric motifs at the edges. Below it, a matching pair of flowing pants, so lightweight they seemed to flutter of their own accord even in the still air. I squealed and I clutched them to my chest, bouncing mostly on one foot. I recognized these garments, this cloth, those embroidery techniques. This clothing in the fae style, made by fae, sourced from the fae lands. They still smelled of home: florals and incense and casual magic. I breathed them in.

I carefully donned the pieces, savoring the sensation of familiar fabrics brushing over my skin, softer and lighter than human weaves. I turned, facing the long mirror held within the wardrobe door. They fit perfectly. The top, flowy but fitted, was cropped slightly above the waistband of the pants, exposing just a sliver of midriff. Thin fabric hugging my curves then flaring loosely, comfortably.

I twirled in them, ungracefully, relishing how it moved against my skin, a near sensual sensation. By the door I spotted a pair of leather slippers. Soft, expertly crafted, and once again, a perfect fit. I donned my circlet which had been placed on the writing desk. Looking and feeling like home.

\* \* \*

I opened the heavy wooden door, a task made much harder by only having full use of one arm and the opposite leg, but I managed. The guard who has been stationed just outside offered me a hand as he watched me wobble, I took it gratefully. I allowed him the burden of my weight as I righted my footing which had gotten tricky in the narrow gap I had only just been able to provide myself in the doorway. As I straightened and looked at him he offered only a subtle bow, an unexpected sign of respect.

"Apologies, my lady, but I've been given precise instruction to accompany you today, considering your condition."

"So I have been told," My hand still rested on his, "What is your name?"

"Edward, I am the lieutenant to the captain, here at his personal request." He looked uneasy, trying desperately not to gawk at my wings, or my clothes, quite scandalous by human standards.

"Well Edward, as you can probably tell, I have not quite regained my balance since the… accident." I wasn't sure how much he knew, how much he was supposed to. Especially considering the grave error that I had made was my own to bear. "Would you mind taking me to the gardens, I think some sunshine would do me some good."

He nodded, ever the gentleman, gently releasing my hand and instead offering the crook of his arm. I took it, trying to study the man out of the corner of my eye as he let me set the pace of our walk.

"So where is your captain anyways?" He tensed ever so slightly, but his face remained neutral.

"He had a meeting, pertaining to matters I am not at liberty to divulge." I fought the urge to roll my eyes. Then, remembering my mission, I realized I might not get this kind of time with a guard again, and sweetened my face the best I could, leaning into him a bit closer than strictly necessary.

"Why is it that I have never seen the king? Excluding that first night?" I looked up at him all doe-eyed and innocent, he only glanced down at me from the corner of his eye.

"The king does not often take audiences, and he is giving you time to adjust before you are acquainted. You did not arrive in the kind of mood to discuss diplomacy."

"Diplomacy?"

"Between our nations."

"There isn't any."

"I believe that is what the king seeks to remedy."

I halted my shuffling steps, pulling away so I could turn full faced towards the man, confusion creasing the space between my eyebrows, "Were you there that night?"

He swallowed, his throat bobbing, "I was there from the

first night." The night I was taken, referred to so casually, as if what he had witnessed or partaken in was just a trip to the market, not the upending of my existence. I started walking again, not taking his arm. The air had turned suddenly tense. I believe he felt it too.

"So then you know, that the experience certainly didn't *feel* very diplomatic." We both kept our eyes forward, no longer touching, both choosing our words very, very carefully.

"Perhaps I have spoken above my station." He had already said too much, but I needed to know more.

"What kind of relations is the king seeking if he is willing to take such measures?" Silence.

"Is that why he ordered I be binded to the captain?" More silence, and the hint of a scowl pulling at his face.

"That never should have happened." He spoke suddenly, harshly, an open opposition to his king.

"Why did it?" I did not have to try to sound meek, I could barely force the words out.

"He knows what you are, the strength you wield, he fears it. He only contends with power that he controls." His voice was so low I could barely hear it.

I took a deep breath, contemplating, "How did he do it?" My mind was racing, my own voice low as a whisper, "it shouldn't have been possible, not with a human."

He looked at me then, straight on, a hard and sad look, before cutting his eyes away, "His royal adviser is a sorceress, she performed the task when— after you collapsed."

The woman next to him, on the smaller throne, I realized, I assumed her to be a consort, but a sorceress...

He spoke again, hurriedly as we passed the open threshold and into the gardens. "When you revealed what you are, the nature of the power you yield… My captain tried to dissuade the king, convince him against it. But Deliana, the witch, she holds sway with the king, he trusts her above all else." That scowl again.

"Why Keelan?" The lieutenant poised to answer, but froze, I followed his gaze ahead. entering the gardens from the back gates was the captain himself, striding over, straight towards us.

"It was an honor to escort you, my lady," Edward stepped further away, and bowed deeply, "Please, enjoy the gardens." And he turned on his heel, and disappeared back into the castle, just as Keelan approached, his face unreadable.

"I told you to rest." He stopped two feet in front of me, his eyes scanning, noting where I strained and the unwrapped injury on my arm.

"I was only coming out to enjoy the gardens, your guard made sure I arrived safely." I shot back, mind still reeling.

He seemed to relax, and then his eyes skimmed over me once again, his time over my clothes, how they fit, where they lay open on my stomach and chest.

He took a deep breath, "Do you like them?" His face was taut, expectant. *Nervous?*

"They are from you?" I pulled at the hem, assessing them once more. He nodded once, only barely. "Where did you get them?" It hadn't occurred to me they might have been acquired by his band of hunters, stolen from other unlucky fae.

"There is a street market, in the next town. A suspiciously beautiful woman sells them." He winked at the subtext.

I broke into a grin. *He bought them for me.* I took a step towards him, stumbling a little on the loose rocks. He sprung forward to balance me, extending a hand.

But instead, I wrapped my arms around his neck, leaning into a tight hug, "They are lovely" I breathed into his shoulder. He froze in place, shoulders tight, arms open, shocked at the sudden intrusion. I felt him relax under my grip, and his arms wrapped around my waist. So gently, the touch of a man appraising a porcelain vase.

It was only because I needed him to trust me, so I could gather information. I reminded myself once again. That is the only reason I am embracing this man. *The enemy.* But something had softened in my chest.

"I'm glad." was all he said.

# 18

# Astriel

We wandered the garden silently for many minutes. Until I tired and took residence on a stone bench beneath a blooming wisteria tree. I breathed in their smell, sweet like summer. Keelan stood ahead of me, the entire walk his eyes cut back to the healing wound on my forearm, slicing down through the fading band of scarring from that first day in iron shackles. He scrutinized the dark veins that while waning, still snaked their way up my arm.

I tucked it against me, feeling the weight of his stare. But I finally had him alone, in a moment of peace. And I had so many questions. Even more since my illicit conversation with his lieutenant.

"I know that half a year has not passed since my… arrival, how are all of the flowers in constant bloom?" I did not deign to look away from the purple blossoms flitting above my head.

"The wards that were put in place, they provide security as well as certain luxuries. A blizzard could be blazing outside these walls and it would still feel like late spring. Keeps the gardeners employed." A wry chuckle.

"Who put in the wards? Surely not the king." I smiled when our eyes met, the dappled light through the blooming foliage dancing across his face.

"The kings have always had sorcerers close at hand, several centuries ago a particularly powerful one set up the wards, they have stood against weather, time, and attack ever since."

*Impenetrable shields.* I pondered on it a moment, until I noticed Keelan's gaze bearing down on me. No malice, no concern, he was just *looking at me*, a gentle glittering in his eyes. I cursed the warmth that climbed up my neck, reddening my cheeks. I did not want to like this man. I shouldn't.

"Either there is a monstrous bug on me or I sprouted another set of wings." I laughed nervously, "Why are you staring at me like that?"

He just shook his head, a soft smile playing at his lips, not the cocky smirk or the forced grin, just a gentle upturn of the corners of his mouth.

"I was just thinking about the library, how I'm glad things didn't go worse." His smile faltered, "How I'm glad you made it through that."

"I'm sure you are, considering our circumstance." I responded, running a fingertip absently over the mark, and then, "Wait- did they wound you? Were you poisoned too?" Sudden panic as I realized in the fallout, I hadn't known if he made it out unscathed. My eyes cut over him, scanning every taut muscle for a sign of those telling black veins. I was certain humans couldn't survive wraith venom.

He shook his head, "The wraiths didn't touch me because I wasn't the thief." He gave me a look and I made a face at him.

He smiled again, and bent away from me, lifting his shirt at the side, "The only injury I sustained from the whole ordeal was *this.*" He revealed a massive bruise coloring his ribs, dark indigo in the center with a yellow green tinge at its border. I stood and moved closer, outlining the discolored area with a light brush of my finger, he shivered at the touch.

"I did this." I said softly, following the bruise, higher, where it wound under his shirt. As I tried to lift it, following the bruise further across his back, Keelan gently grabbed my wrist, stopping me. His eyes burned into mine, but he just held my hand away and lowered his shirt.

"I'm so sorry." He loosened his grip as I lowered myself back onto the bench, "You lied. You said I didn't hurt you."

"You didn't," A mischievousness glinted in his eyes, "That damned desk did."

When I didn't return his grin he continued, settling next to me, "Astriel, you were confused, and having a venom induced nightmare, you were afraid. I don't hold that against you."

I stared down at my hands clasped in my lap, trying to shake off the memory, the foreboding of it. It had felt like more than a bad dream, it felt like an omen, a warning.

"What did you dream about?" Keelan asked softly, leaning forward to try to see my eyes through the silvery cascading hair that obscured my face. I turned ever so slightly away from him, so he could not see the tears threatening to spill. *He serves the crown. He will betray you, the mark means nothing.*

I contemplated not answering, not wanting to reveal another weakness. But he was so sincere. And besides, it was just the fever, the fever that nearly killed me. It probably meant nothing, I hoped it meant nothing. I took a shallow breath, forcing the words from my throat.

"I was home. I saw my family, and the girl— from that night. Everything, everyone was on fire. The tree was on fire." My throat tightened, the visions coming back in pieces, "They were all burning, and they told me I would burn with them. And the king was there, just watching, smiling down at me as my whole world burned and there was nothing I could do to stop it."

Keelan didn't speak, he just watched me, "When I heard your voice, when you tried to wake me, I thought you would be there too, that it would show you there, burning, with everything else that I— I couldn't bear to see it. I couldn't watch anyone else die"

He picked up my hand, holding it gently, interlacing our fingers. He apologized, voice barely above a whisper. I finally looked back at him. I could see it in his eyes then, red and rimmed with moisture. Guilt. The guilt for everything that had happened, yes the wraiths but also, *all of it.*

Like my being here. Like my being brought here was his sole responsibility. And maybe it was, but I could see it now, clearly, the pain that lived behind those brown irises that shone like honey in the sunlight.

I sniffled, wiping my eyes, shaking off his grip and the cascade of emotions. "Do you like it here?" I asked suddenly, surprising even myself that I had voiced it.

He took a deep breath, rubbing his hands down the thighs of his pants, "At this point, it's all I know. It feels like I've always been here. I wouldn't know how to be if I were anywhere else."

"You could leave." I offered.

"I'm afraid it's not that simple."

"It never is." I scoffed, shaking my head, "Can I ask you

100

something else?"

"Anything." He responded, and I could feel the sincerity in his tone.

It was a fact that had confused and irked me since our night of revelations. I needed to ask it before I lost my nerve, so I steadied my breath and trained my eyes on his. "Keelan, why was I bound to you and not the king?" His eyes darkened, but he did not break the stare.

"Astriel, there is something I need to show you."

# 19

# Astriel

He brought me to a trophy room, in a part of the castle I had not been to, through a door tucked behind a massive tapestry. Glittering jewels littered every wall and surface, artifacts and ancient weapons from even before my time filled glass cabinets and shelves. The collection was expansive, and ruefully beautiful. So many manners of treasure no doubt looted more than gifted. Breathtaking nonetheless. I ran a finger down the wooden edge of a display full of fine jewels, my breath hitching as I surveyed pieces of jewelry that no doubt amassed to the value of a small kingdom itself.

Keelan stood near the doorway, still as stone as I ventured further into the room. The aching in my body started to return from all the walking of the day, every step sending a jolting pain up my ruined leg. I did my best to ignore it, to truly absorb the types of valuables I would likely never again get the chance to appreciate.

I turned a corner, passing a large cabinet of ancient looking books. Even the carpet beneath my feet was so intricate and finely woven it stole my breath. I was about to call over my shoulder and ask Keelan why he brought me here, why it had been so important. But then I saw them. On the wall, above a large table littered with papers, trapped in a shadowbox of glass and iron grates, was an enormous pair of night black wings.

I couldn't tear my eyes from them, the dark feathers that seemed to absorb light shuddered, still alive, still aware. They nearly thrashed as Keelan strode next to me, not looking directly at them, hands shoved deep in his pockets. They would have dwarfed my own, even folded I could glean the size of them. Built for flying high, and fast, they would have been a sight to behold, under any other conditions. A chill ran up my spine as I took them in, my stomach turning as they writhed against their bindings. When I turned to Keelan, he stared at the floor, pushing at a stack of papers with his boot.

I could hardly breathe, "Why did you bring me here?"

"So you would understand." He finally looked at them, and they threatened to tear their decorative prison off the wall, feathers sizzling where they collided with the iron, "They're mine."

I just stared at him, trying to make myself understand what he was telling me. And all the pieces started to fall into place. I suddenly understood why he was so strong, so fast. Why he recoiled when I touched him, why even to sleep he wore a shirt, why he had been so careful with my own wings, afraid to touch them, afraid to look too long. He brushed back his hair, and for the first time I noticed the pointed tips of his ears. He was like me. Keelan was Seraphim.

"They stole your wings."

# 20

# Astriel

"One would think, after the cursed library fiasco you would be less inclined to wander into places you're not welcome." A voice cut from the darkness behind us and emerged from the shadows. From a door I couldn't see, entered the sorceress, Deliana.

"Hello witch." Keelan greeted the woman, contempt lacing the words. The hood of her coal gray cloak pulled back to reveal a face so striking I struggled not to look away. Her dark hair, tinged with flashes of crimson was pulled into a complex knot of braids at the top of her head, her eyes blazed like fire in the dim room, black and orange burning embers. Her full lips pursed in what I could only assume was an ever present grimace. When I looked at her, only one oppressive emotion held true: fear.

Keelan sauntered between us as he greeted her, taking long, slow strides. He stopped in the direct center, and faced her down, "We were just leaving."

A wicked smile crept across her lips as she glared past him, at me. The weight of her gaze was crushing. I could almost feel phantom hands groping my body as she looked me up and down, "How are you feeling, Astriel? Those wraiths nearly killed you, would have been a waste of so much hard work."

"Don't talk to her." He was breathing harder now, the casual posture gone. His eyes fixed on the witch, jaw flexing.

"Leash yourself, boy, we haven't even been properly introduced." She locked on me again, "Well I guess I know you quite well winged one, I took a trip through your mind on the long night of the binding. You are a sad, sad thing." I wasn't breathing. *She was in my mind. What did she see?* Keelan just glared at her, hands fisted at his side.

She cut her eyes back at him, "Oh no," a smirk was forming on her full lips. "I was afraid this would happen."

She tapped a long fingernail against her cheek, feigning concern, but her eyes glittered, "We had to bind you together for our protection and now our handsome knight is smitten." I stood still as stone, frozen under her suffocating stare.

She sighed and flitted over to a table on the other side of the room, leaning against it, that horrible smile growing wider. "You poor fool, it's going to finally break you when... oh, well you know."

"That's enough." Keelan barked.

"What is she talking about?" But he wouldn't look at me, the two of them stared at each other. Keelan fuming, Deliana amused.

"You haven't told her?" Fake surprise, and she leveled herself at me once again, "My dear, the reason you are here, why you get the nice room, why none of us get to play with you…"

"That's. Enough." He gritted his teeth, vibrating.

105

"She's going to find out sooner or later." She was loving this, dragging it out to toy with us, with Keelan.

"Once you are well, you will serve a very important role in this kingdom. So lithe and beautiful, young and fertile," She paused, inspecting her pristine fingernails, "You are to be wed. And you will bear the king's heir."

I went cold. She kept talking but I couldn't hear her, couldn't see her. I couldn't breathe, couldn't force air into my lungs. My mind shut down, turned to dust in my skull. I watched myself from outside my body.

Absently, I turned from them as Keelan and the witch traded loud insults, and he didn't see me leave. I walked out on shaking legs, through the tapestry and down the long hallway. This had to be another nightmare. I couldn't bear for it to be real. It couldn't be, it was too much, it didn't make sense, why a fae? Why me?

It struck me all at once. It was a ticket into the fae kingdom, not just Phaedra, even the continents. The last of my territory, any child of mine would be next in line. But I was no ruler, the warrior fae were never revered for more than their fighting ability. The king must not know that, not understand that in Phaedra our child would not be royalty.

But a merged bloodline *would* open up the borders, the Seraphim were the defenders of everything outside of the immediate territories. He could march his armies in unencumbered. I was shaking, that couldn't happen. I wouldn't.

\* \* \*

Lucidity returned and I found myself back in the gardens. I was deep in the hedge maze, sitting on the ground. Weak, tired, a pounding reverberated all over my exhausted body. Looking down I realized why: the wound on my arm, while the cut still healed, the black veins had thickened and darkened once more, now reaching up to my shoulder. The poison revived, surging in earnest towards my slow beating heart.

I had thought that surviving would be the only way to protect my people, to escape. But the walls were closing in now, there was no escaping this. I could only see one way out. Only one way to keep them safe from the world destroyer that disgusting king wanted to plant in my womb. Clarity at last.

I laid flat against the soft earth, watching the stars shine and rotate above me. A faraway voice whispered in my mind, like me but different. *Your martyrdom is a game of pretend. Admit you're tired, that you're done, and it will end.* And I was, I was so incredibly tired.

# 21

# Astriel

I was in Keelan's bed, turning over, not remembering coming here, or being moved here. He laid next to me, fast asleep. I took him in, breathing in his oak moss and cedar laden scent. He was naked, turned away. I watched him, the steady rise and fall of his chest with each breath. Smooth tanned skin contrasting harshly against the angry scars on his back, shining in the moonlight that filtered through the window.

I reached out to touch them, softly, not wanting to wake him. The place where wings should have been, should have erupted into beautiful dark feathers. I was angry. They stole the most precious thing to a winged fae, and kept it just alive enough to turn him into a monster. He shivered at my touch, but did not stir awake.

I pulled myself out of the bed, body no longer aching, no longer fighting the venom that had tried so hard to take me. I pulled on a silk robe, tying it around my midsection, taking one more look at him before turning the knob on the heavy wooden door. I slipped into the corridor, quiet as the night. Cold tile met my bare feet as I padded down the abandoned hall, no guards, no evil sorceress prowling for her next meal. I knew exactly where to go.

Hallway after hallway, twisting and turning until I laid eyes on the tapestry that hid the secret door. A woven picture of wolves attacking a deer. Blood spurting from the creature's neck, staining the edge of the image crimson. I felt the call, the gentle hum that spoke in hushed tones from behind the cloth. I slipped behind it, snicking the door behind me.

I followed the call, curving around the ancient books, treading over discarded parchment and weaving between stacks of boxes full of trinkets and weapons and jewels. I laid eyes once again on those magnificent wings. My blood boiled as they lay still, as if asleep in their cage. I would free them. All it took was a single silent wing beat and I was on the table, hands roaming over the glass case. The wings stirred, as if they sensed me. I hushed them, and they fell still once again.

I reached for the lock, before I even touched it I felt the heat. Iron, enchanted with some sort of protection, I needed the key. I could see it in my mind, worn around the neck of the killer king, strung on a length of rawhide. I could get it, easily, I would just have to make it into his chambers, my stomach lurched at the thought. The thought of what he wanted from me, what he expected me to give of myself, what he felt he was entitled to.

The wings flailed softly once again, and I tried to calm them, whispering promises of freedom, but they struggled harder, battering against the glass and iron, feathers falling to the bottom of the case as they were beaten or burned off by the metal grate. I could not soothe them. That laugh, the witch's laugh, echoed around the room, from every direction, there was no escape.

*Kill the king.* The wings commanded in a whisper. *Kill the king and steal the key.* I stared at them, mouth agape as their disembodied voice grew louder, from every direction. *kill the king. KILL THE KING.*

* * *

Dirt stuck to my cheek, in my mouth, in my hair. The sun had not yet risen, and the dark purple fading into soft pink was the only indication that day was coming. I looked down at my arm once again. The worsening of the wraith poison was no dream. Those killer veins still throbbed, dark and threatening, taking up so much of my arm. The healing gash on my leg had worsened too, the more severe injury, but further away from my vitals, the poison seemed not to try as hard to travel from there, but it still spread.

An exposed root dug into the muscle of my right wing, pain pulsing as I sat up, suddenly nauseous. Another wraith dream. *I would exterminate those creatures if I could.* I was tired of the vague prophecies, the subconscious warnings. But at least last night, it had been a direct order, from somewhere deep inside, something I somehow hadn't considered. It was the true solution, the only one that would work, that didn't include me throwing myself onto a spear. The one that would free the only other Seraphim I knew to be alive, Keelan.

I would kill the king.

# 22

# Astriel

The guards found me wandering the garden, confused and stumbling. I felt like death from my night in the maze, but still acted weaker, more ill, more disoriented. I needed to stay ill for a while longer to buy time. When they saw the dark veins, the hollowness of my eyes, the men were gentle, supporting me at the elbows while I stumbled through the castle halls.

Though no doubt they had been sent by Deliana to return me, expecting a fight. I had squashed their fear of me, I had to. I wasn't the mighty warrior defeated as I had been that first night. I was a tired, broken girl, still a fae, but no longer a threat.

When Keelan caught word that I had been found, he nearly tackled me in the hall, shoving away the other guards as he crushed me in a hug, before holding me at arms length, looking me over, cursing as he took in my appearance. Beyond the wounds themselves, I was in an appalling state. I had caught a glimpse of myself in a hall mirror.

I was gaunt, and pallid. My silver eyes turned gray, no

111

glimmer within them. My white hair slicked to my skull. My dirty wings felt too heavy to carry, so I let them drag on the ground. Such a terrible, pitiful sight.

I looked the worst I ever had. This was not like the first time, where the venom had tried to kill me in a hurry. No, it was taking its time now, savoring it, feeding off of my turmoil, growing stronger with it.

He swept me into his arms, so carefully. Through his chest I felt his erratic heartbeat as it battered against my shoulder. I could see it in his dark eyes, he hadn't slept. I tried to mutter an apology but came out jumbled and wrong. He just shushed me as he pounded down the hall.

My head started to spin as the last word I could manage left my tongue. "Healer."

He nodded, understanding. Not a doctor, a healer, a fae healer. I needed fae magic to stop the infection. Quickly.

He took me to his room once again. It was closer, I reasoned. Though I suspected it had more to do with keeping an eye on me, the binding magic doing its work on him, manufacturing feelings where there wouldn't be otherwise. Protecting me was as much about nobility as it was self preservation.

The swirling thoughts were pounding against the inside of my skull as I lay atop the covers. It would make sense, beyond the mark, for there to be an inherent protectiveness. Now that I knew he was Seraphim, I understood that fierce loyalty to our own is as natural as water, it was woven into our very being. And he felt responsible for my suffering. He knew the circumstances of my arrival, its *purpose*. It ate at him.

He would not leave my side for any reason, not until

the healer arrived. He made sure I ate, drank, and bathed. Scrubbing my skin when I couldn't force my limbs to move. Despite the intimacy of it, the magnitude of being laid bare in that way, he never faltered. He never made it seem to mean anything more than a task to be completed.

I had tried to bat him off the first night, insisting I could handle it myself. But as steam filled the room, making the air heavy in my lungs, the world started spinning around me, and I tripped while stepping out of my pants. I took a tray of soaps and oils down with me. The considerable clattering alarmed him, I was sprawled out on the floor when he burst through the door. I was not to leave his sight until I was healed.

Fair enough.

He had dismissed Farryn, but wouldn't reveal why, no matter how much I hounded him, no matter my pleas that he needed a break, needed to rest. I wasn't sure if he slept, slumped over in the ornate wooden chair at his desk, which still bore the marks from when I had thrown him into it. He refused to sleep in the bed, even when I left him space.

From time to time I would hear Deliana in the doorway, demanding entry, trying to send him on some fool's errand. But he would not budge. He would not let her cross the threshold, not her or anyone else. Only his lieutenant was allowed a post outside the door.

"I have been tasked with protecting her. Ordered to do it." He would gesture the mark that decorated his own arm, "I will not leave my post." And she would scowl, or pose some vague threat, but ultimately leave.

I worried for him immensely in those days, watching the

circles under his eyes grow darker and deeper, seeing his hand rest stiffly on the hilt of the sword he always wore as he glared out the window, flexing his jaw with the scar that cut across it, stark white in the sunlight.

On the evening of the third day, when the aching in my blood became too painful to sleep, I rolled over to look at him, eyes closed, laid back in that chair, head resting on his fist. His clothes were rumpled, his other hand still on the gilded hilt of that sword he wouldn't remove.

"Keelan, How did it happen?" His eyes shot open, momentarily alarmed at the sound, and then relaxed.

He knew what I was asking. He shifted in his chair, the wood groaning with the weight of him. He chewed his bottom lip, carefully considering how to answer. After loosing a shaky sigh, and he pulled himself up a bit straighter.

He reached an arm over the desk, his finger tapping the violet cover of the book I had stolen from the wraiths, *The Winged War*. His silver tattoo flickering in the light as it moved. He had been reading it the days I stayed with him, something to fill the time I guessed. He would sometimes scowl at the pages, his brow in constant furrow as he flipped through them.

"This war," he paused, considering, and I let the silence linger between us. "It was a brutal, dirty thing. Who actually started it was lost to time. But I remember it starting for *me* the day human forces began marching through our forest, two hundred and thirteen years ago."

He paused, his voice choked, "My friends and I were on the mountaintop, having a meal after training. Back then, I don't know if you remember, Seraphim life was a state of constant combat training."

I did remember, since I was old enough to walk or learn to fly I trained. All Seraphim did. It was almost a necessity in our territory, high in the mountain peaks of Phaedra, a place I had admittedly not spent much time in, and I had not returned to since my parent's disappearance. We were a warrior class, a protector class, we were made to defend. And it was the cornerstone of our culture. *Was.*

He continued, "The horn bellowed, and we were gathered in the great hall. We were to assemble that night to push back the human forces. As the sun set, we took flight. I was only just old enough to fly with the aerial legion. Hundreds of us, wingtip to wingtip. It was supposed to be a quick battle. We expected them to retreat.

"As we descended on them, their sheer numbers were overwhelming. They were heavily armed, and they just kept coming. Both sides sacrificed greatly in the battle." His eyes glazed as he went somewhere far away, overcome with the memory. "The battle raged for weeks, and we were making steady progress, pushing the human lines back. But we didn't know that while we were occupied in the forest, another troop had come from the other side of the mountain, they climbed, found our territory undefended, and slaughtered every injured, elder, and child that remained. All but one I suppose."

My heart stopped. I was away in the capital, at a school for nobility children. I wasn't in the mountains when the attack took place. I had never even been informed of a war, no one would speak of it. *Why wouldn't anyone just tell me?*

He looked at me sadly. It seems he had connected the dots of my history before I had. He had actually been there, he had seen it first hand. Keelan took a shuddering breath, and then continued, "We fell in great numbers as the war waged on, but so did the humans. I watched everyone I have ever loved fall at the hands of these mortal beasts.

"I was injured, and taken prisoner by the human forces. A fair few of us were at the end, as we were overcome. But as their numbers dwindled and the last Seraphim was either killed or captured, they retreated, and ended it there.

"Those of us who were captured were brought here, for the then reigning King Byron to decide our fates." Another shaky breath, "Most were executed, publicly. But the king brought me here, told me that I would work for him. I was young and terrified, but I refused him. I would not be a traitor to my people. I told him I would rather die.

"He would not let me. For months he kept me just on the precipice, experimenting with different torture methods, how to break a fae without killing them, without killing me." His voice wobbled, but he continued on, "Everyday, in that dark chamber, everyday I refused him, spit at him, cursed him, willed myself to die so it would be over. And then one day, instead of doing our usual dance, he brought a saw, and tore my wings from my body."

It gutted me, imagining the pain, the sounds, the smells, *the screaming*. I tried to blink away the image. Living with the anguish that having such a fundamental part of him so crudely ripped from his body. Seraphim are nothing without their wings, it is so wholly tied to who we are. I desperately wanted to go to him, to comfort him, to do something to ease the pain that cried out from behind his eyes. But I was frozen in place, stunned silent.

"I was sure it would kill me, I prayed that it would, but even apart from me, they *lived,* like a creature all on their

116

own. They tried to return to me, beating down Byron's men, my wings *fought* more than I did, more than I could. He had them taken away. And left me for days, just hanging in that cell.

"When he returned, he offered me a choice: work for the crown until his bloodline ended, at which time they would be returned, or he would burn my wings. Either way, he told me, I would live, with or without them."

"So you took his offer." I barely whispered. He looked at me, a tear running down his face as he did. And he nodded.

"I did his bidding, betrayed my own people, sacrificed so much of myself for the hope of one day being free. For *two hundred years.*" He shook his head, the hatred for himself, for his actions reddening his eyes. "When this king was born, an only child, a single heir, I crafted a plan to finally end this curse: I would prevent him from ever marrying, from ever siring an heir of his own, however I could. I would finally be free."

I remembered the king then, so old, so withered, with only his horrid sorceress at his side. But no queen, no children. "How?" It was all I could choke out.

"I killed potential consorts, sullied relations with neighboring nations who had daughters, if they were inclined, I bedded them myself to taint them in the eyes of the king. I did whatever I had to do. If he found out and killed me, that would've been fine too, but he never did. Either way, I knew my curse would end with this king."

"And yet you brought me here, knowing the king's plan."

"No," his voice was weak and low, "The king collects fae as servants, as exotic creatures for his menagerie, or presents for his allies. He had different plans for you but it shouldn't—

he never would have…" His voice broke, trailing off. He stared at the ceiling, avoiding my gaze.

"I suspected what you were, but wouldn't bring myself to believe it, convinced myself you were anything else. I thought- I knew that there were no more Seraphim. When you revealed yourself as what you are, and then collapsed…"

His eyes fell, and he tapped the book once more, staring at it bitterly, "The thing about books from the cursed library, is that they are not written by man or fae, there is no bias, no agenda in their contents, it is simply an account of what occurred. The full ugly truth scrawled out on these pages. Which is why they are guarded by those malicious spirits, truth like this comes at a cost."

The venom in my veins seemed to purr at the words.

"What it says is that our kind was the only target for that attack. That it was not the goal to invade the city at large, only to slaughter the Seraphim. They took us out, so that when they launched their next invasion, it would be easy, met with minimal resistance. Every king after Byron has planned to invade the fae again, conquer our lands, but the fae woods were so savage. When I sent men into those woods they either perished or came back scared shitless, refusing to return.

"They would rave about a beautiful demon with enormous feathered wings and blades made of light itself. A spirit of the forest who would appear out of nothing and disappear on the wind if she let them live. They claimed she was a specter with eyes made of quartz that could see directly into a man's soul."

He almost smiled as his eyes became dreamy, still faced up at the ceiling. "That demon became legend, and I was able to deter the king because of it. I convinced him that we would not be able to rally forces when so many feared what lay within the forest."

He looked at me now, an unyielding stare that told so much, even if he couldn't say it, "He commanded me to go personally, with a small army to kill or capture the demon. I planned to fail, to slay some of my own men, and spin a tale of unending power that decimates armies." He grimaced.

"And then that drunken savage captured the Pixie girl. Claimed she would be good bait, I could have throttled him for it, I was going to. But then I sensed you, you were already coming." Neither of us breathed as he paused, but his eyes didn't waver. "And suddenly, I had successfully captured *Agrona*, The Demon of the Woods. And all of my men saw it, there was no way to spin the story unless I killed them all, perhaps I should have.

"I tried to break you down, scare you just enough before our arrival that the king would not see the legend I knew you to be. I needed him to dismiss you as a threat, and I would find a way to get you out, or... something. But unfortunately, you are indeed Seraphim, and wholly unafraid." He loosed a wry laugh, and a tight smile, "And when you fell, I'm told the king was delighted that I had succeeded in capturing the spirit so many feared. He wanted to have you killed. Displayed for his people to see that even a legendary demon can fall at his command.

"Deliana, the witch, offered a different route. Claimed that if he bore an heir with fae blood, especially of such infamous lineage, he could simply walk into Phaedra, claim them as his own, a powerful alliance, a silent takeover."

He rose from his chair as he finished the thought, cutting

his eyes away from me, striding over to the window and peering out. I followed him with my eyes, and he kept his back turned to me. His hands were shaking, and I realized I was too. I was horrified, for him, and for me, for what this meant for my— for our people.

"Deliana suggested the Serch Bythol as added assurance, to keep both of us in line, as she has been suspicious of me since she arrived. I wanted to beg her not to, beg her to convince the king not to allow it. I wish I had pleaded harder that they did not understand the depths of its meaning, the consequences of being marked in such a way. But Deliana would have relished in my groveling.

"I had to keep up a front that I didn't care for you, that she couldn't use you against me. I couldn't risk it. She had already persuaded the king to agree to the mark, and he did, then commanded that I be your personal guard. She knew how protective I would be of you because of what we share, and she could already sense our connection. She knew it would destroy me when the king claimed you. Just as a personal touch for me refusing to bed her, I suspect."

He was no longer glaring out the window and into the night, his gaze instead fell to his own forearm, to the fine lines of his half of the mark. "I still don't know what to do."

I looked down at my own mark, the black venom still skirting around it, despite my worsening state. We sat in tense silence as he let me consider everything he had told me. But I had no words, so I let silence reign in the darkened room.

# 23

## Astriel

The healer arrived at dawn. Keelan nor I had slept that night, both still reeling from his stories. Him, having to relive the horrors, me, having to grapple with them for the first time. But we also hadn't spoken. Neither of us willing to cross the ocean between us.

Keelan just took a post near the door when the Nymph came sweeping in. Her name was Charterea, sent at Keelan's request from a neighboring kingdom. *Another captive fae.*

The healer bore no wings, and could have easily been mistaken for human if she didn't move as if floating just above the ground when she walked, or else it felt that the ground moved with her, urging her forward on a phantom wave. She carried a heavy looking woven bag, no doubt filled to brim with all manner of enchanted concoctions.

She tutted as she looked me over, running her glowing hands over every inch of my body, feeling for the infection, how far it had spread, chattering the whole time.

"Human castles all look the same, they are so drab."

"It is everywhere, you should have called for me sooner."

"Your wings are so beautiful. Would you be willing to donate a feather as a tip for this service? I've never worked on a Seraphim before."

I tuned her out, letting her do her work as my eyes kept falling back to Keelan, who watched her like a hawk, hand still stationed on the hilt of that sword. He was haggard after several days of not sleeping, his tangled hair tied back haphazardly. But those piercing eyes were clear, his stance every bit the warrior I now knew him to be. Every move she made, he assessed her, tracking her movements like she were a vicious beast, poised to attack. There was no easing his paranoia, I knew. So I tuned him out too, and turned back to examine the elder fae.

She wore a plain, unflattering dress in slate gray, the fabric was bulky, and worn well past its best years. Her hair, with streaks of silver poking out in every direction was pulled into a bun she probably wore for the whole journey. It occurred to me that I had never seen a fae with signs of aging, never above middle age. I wondered how old she must be. I wondered how long she had lived among st the humans, how long she had been held at the mercy of the crown in her kingdom.

"I see congratulations are in order." My attention snapped to her, as did Keelan's. But she just kept fussing, digging around in her bag.

"What are you talking about?" I asked, my throat full of thorns.

"Your mark, my dear! It's not everyday someone finds their mate, especially not a mate they are so smitten with they would bind themselves." She ran a sharp nail over my tattoo. "Might have been the only thing keeping you alive, dear."

122

"Oh it's not—" Keelan spoke for the first time since the healer arrived. I cut him off.

"Can you step out for a moment?" I addressed him.

"I don't think—"

"Ke, please, just for a few minutes." My eyes pleading.

He studied me for a moment, then cut his eyes at the Nymph. He cleared his throat, "Two minutes, and I'll be right outside."

I watched him and he exited, shutting the door harder than he needed to, making a point to the healer, reminding her of his strength.

Charterea halted her distracted digging when we were alone, and focused her attention, eyes bright and sharp, directly on me, "What is the matter, sweetheart? I mean besides the obvious." She asked, with maternal concern.

I searched for the words, "A spell like the Serch Bythol, does it manifest emotions between those binded?"

She studied me for a moment, and then the inked symbol, it seemed to create its own light as she watched it, "You did not choose to be marked." It wasn't a question, but I shook my head, and she sighed.

"The Serch Bythol is its own breed of rune magic, more ancient than any of us. But no, I don't think it can *force* two people to fall in love, if that's what you mean." She started rummaging again as my face reddened.

"I don't mean love I mean—"

"Sweet girl, whatever you are feeling is from you entirely, not a silly rune."

"But, one day," I swallowed, the words tumbling out before I could stop them, "will this mark prevent me from actually achieving a mating bond? Like being binded, will it prevent

123

me from being *bonded*?"

Her focus swung to me again, hard and serious, "My girl, you already are bonded."

And Keelen stalked back into the room.

# 24

# Astriel

Charterea gathered all of her things up in a hurry, and left a handful of bottles on the nightstand, muttering instructions of when to take what, and then thrust a list of ingredients into Keelan's hand before floating out the door. I heard her snap to her escort that is was time to leave. Ke surveyed the list.

"Healers are always an odd type, what did she have to say?"

"What are you talking about?" I asked, perhaps a bit too loudly, I cleared my throat, and grabbed for one of the tincture bottles, studying the label. I popped the cork and took a swig, grimacing at the flavor. *Not one for taste enchantments I see.*

Keelan stared down at me, eyebrows furrowed, "Everything okay?"

"I will be when I actually get this poison out of my blood." I laughed nervously. He didn't seem convinced but didn't press, at least for now.

Did he know? About the bond? I mean he must. And when did it even happen? Wouldn't I have felt it? Did he feel it?

I decided that at least for now I would say nothing. If he already knew, then he probably assumed that *I* already knew. And if he doesn't know, then it is certainly not the time to tell him, with everything regarding the king and… me, looming around the corner. *Well, at least the tension from last night is broken now.*

I decided not to think about it, the tincture was already doing its work, despite the bitter taste of it still coating my mouth, I felt warm, and my energy was returning again. I savored the sensation, my muscles loosening, the tightness in my chest starting to abate. Even the drab colors Keelan had adorned his room in appeared a touch more vibrant.

I threw my legs off the side of the bed and Keelan lurched towards me. He took my hand and rested his other on my shoulder, "you need to rest, let the medicine do its work before you strain yourself again."

"If I lay in this bed any longer I'm going to burst into flames. I'm just going to take a bath."

He helped me stand and nodded, "Alright, I'll help you."

I pulled away, trying to ignore the hurt in his face. I suddenly felt… bashful. I hadn't before, but now, knowing, it felt different.

"I can handle it." I said, averting his gaze.

"The last time you said that you tried to crack your skull open on the tile."

I pondered, "You may sit outside the bathing room, with the door open, but I will bathe myself."

He narrowed his eyes at me, "What did she say to you?"

"Nothing!" I quipped back defensively, "Is there something wrong with a lady wanting a little privacy?"

"There is when she should be conserving her energy to heal

from something that tried to kill her. Not once, I'll remind you, but twice."

Then his mouth curled up at the corners mischievously for the first time in what felt like forever, "Astriel," He said my name slowly, drawing out every syllable, "I've already seen you in all of your naked glory, several times." I slapped at him as his grin widened. I stalked towards the attached room, trying not to limp too visibly.

"Pull your chair over, you'll sit here, *outside* the bathing room." He just raised his hands in defeat, that smile still pulling at his lips.

"As you wish."

To his credit, he did not peek around the door frame even once. Even while I undressed with some difficulty, grunting and groaning quietly as I could when the movements sent spears of pain up and down my limbs. But with the medicine I already felt less stiff, and I was able to finally step out of my clothes without incident. But I winced when I dipped myself into the water, still sensitive to the heat of it.

"Everything okay? I'm not looking." I heard him smiling.

"I'm fine. *Smug prick.*"

"I heard that."

"I would hope so." He chuckled to himself, and I found my own lips quirking up at the corners.

I soaked in the bath for well over an hour, trying to sort out everything that had happened here, with me, with Keelan, what he revealed to me last night. What the healer had revealed. The nightmares, the warnings, what I intended to do.

"Hey, Ke?"

"Yes, El?"

127

I rolled my eyes at the nickname and leaned my head on my hands on the side of the large tub, water sloshing quietly at my movement. I saw only his boots, kicked out and relaxed through the open doorway. The medicine the healer had given me was doing its work in my body but it also left my head feeling clearer than it had been in weeks. The ever present tightness in my chest that screamed louder than my thoughts loosened.

"You told me last night how you've prevented the king from siring an heir thus far."

"That I did."

"Well I'm thrilled you didn't decide to kill me."

"Our matching beauty marks did a good job of taking that off the table." I heard him chuckle.

"What if you bed me instead?"

His boots disappeared, I lifted my head as I heard a clattering on the other side of the wall, and coughing.

He poked his head through the door, a wild look on his face, "I beg your pardon?"

"I mean you could beg." I smiled but his face turned deathly serious, and it faded.

"Astriel, this isn't a funny thing. Even if you're serious I don't know that it would work." He stepped fully into the doorway, forgetting our agreement, I didn't mention it.

"Why not?"

"Well for one you're not human, so the rules are different. For two, he would just as soon kill us for it. And for three, I can't imagine that— I mean surely you have…" He made a vague gesture with his hands and let himself trail off.

"If you're asking me if I've gone to bed before the answer is yes."

"Then it's pointless anyways, you're already tainted."

"Excuse me?" I shot him a vicious glare.

"No I mean— I would never— what you do and with who is obviously your own business I just mean—" He took a deep breath to steady himself, "I would see you as a partner, he would see you as a possession, that is the difference."

"So you see me as a partner?" I was toying with him again, enjoying watching him squirm, especially after his comment about all my 'naked glory'.

"Well I imagine—"

"You've imagined it." I was beaming at him now, hands gripped on the edge of the copper tub as he struggled to find his words.

"I think that healer slipped you something a little more than medicine." He sighed, but he was smiling softly now too.

It felt so good to see him smile after I'd been the cause of so much pain for him. I studied his face, the faded scar on his square jaw, which I had wanted to rip back open when I'd first met him, now seemed a fitting addition to his face. Those brown eyes glittered in the flickering candlelight. Further down, for the first time I really let myself take in the shape of him, tall and lean, but strong, with wide shoulders and toned legs.

"Why are you undressing me with your eyes, Astriel?" His voice was playful, but soft.

"I just don't know how I never saw it before, that you're a Seraphim. It seems so obvious now."

He smiled at me, a tinge of sadness in his eyes, "You know why."

I nodded, and then asked, "How much time do you think

we have before…"

"I don't know," He released a long breath, and then sauntered over, sliding down the edge of the tub to sit on the
floor, both of us forgetting my bid for privacy, "Once you
are healed enough, Deliana is going to demand for it. You've
already squandered her timeline so thoroughly. So, a week,
maybe two."

I rested the side of my face on the tub's edge, my wings
drooping back into the water.

"I bet Deliana is regretting tethering you to me by now."
I laughed wryly. "Especially since you keep bringing me to
your chambers, I can't even remember what mine look like
anymore."

He didn't say anything, but I could feel him looking at me,
"You'd think she would have been more concerned about us
spending so much time together," I raised my head to look
at him, inches apart, "I mean, anyone else—"

Before I could finish my thought, his lips were on mine,
softly, cautiously exploring. Without thinking, I leaned
further forward, bringing myself closer to him, returning the
pressure. His hand cupped my cheek, warm and gentle. The
callouses that hardened the tips of his fingers grazing my jaw.
But he broke the touch, his eyes wide, panicked, searching
mine. My mark, the binding, was glimmering in the dim
light, and his was too.

"El, I'm sorry, I shouldn't have—" He started, and before I
could process my own movements, I grabbed his face with
both hands, pulling him back to me, crushing our lips back
together.

This time it was not soft or careful. He returned my
ferocity, my hunger for this. His hands were on my neck,

my shoulders, my back, exploring me. My hands slid down his neck and chest. I gripped at his shirt, undoing the buttons as quickly as my fingers would allow. We moved to stand, together, in harmony, his hands sliding to my bare waist. Feeling me, but also lifting me, even in this moment conscious of my weak points. Water ran off of my wings as I rose. I smiled into his mouth. Rubbing my hands over his bare chest, over his shoulders, under the open collar.

He tensed as I crossed to his back and I froze, pulling my face from his, "If you don't want me to… Tell me what will make you comfortable, what will make this good."

He grinned, and brought his face back down to mine, our lips only grazing, and he breathed, "You. You will make it good." And his mouth crashed back into mine.

His hands only left my rapidly heating skin to pull them out of the sleeves of his shirt, and they were back, traveling lower, cupping my ass, kneading it I undid his belt. "Hold on to me." He growled into my mouth as both hands clamped the backs of my thighs and lifted me. I wrapped my arms around his neck, clinging to him, our mouths still exploring as he carried me, dripping water, to the bed.

He set me down delicately, despite the urgency I could feel coursing between us. I spread my wings behind me, flattening them against the bed. He took a step back, panting. He fixed his gaze on me, his eyes studying every exposed part. He had seen it before, but not like this, not when it was *for* him. "Are you sure that this is what you want?"

He was asking about the act, but also about the rest of it. He was asking if I wanted him, and everything it entailed. He was asking if I accepted the bond, entwining not just our bodies, as the mark did, but our souls.

Fearful anticipation filled his eyes, and my heart cracked at the sight of it. He had given so much of himself to things outside of his control, unwillingly and painfully. And yet he saw me, and all the darkness that hovered around my sharp edges, all the pain I could cause him, all the pain I most likely would cause him, and yielded to *me*. He offered himself, laid bare in more ways than physical.

I nodded, slowly, still breathing hard, "Yes Keelan, you are what I want." And I meant it, with every fiber of myself. Beyond the lust that clouded my vision and boiled in my blood. Beyond knowing that he was *like me*. Even knowing that it could tear me apart, the things we would have to do to find peace outside these walls. He smiled for just a moment, relief flooding his features. And then his face turned animal, he kicked off his boots and pounced.

The weight of him, the sensation of our bare chests colliding stole my breath. Our mouths connected again, opening to each other, tongues dancing. My legs wrapped around him as my hands traveled across his chest, down his back, entangled in his hair. His mouth left mine, trailing kisses across my jaw. His tongue trailing down my throat, lower, his teeth scraped my collarbone, biting down. I arched into him, moaning softly.

I could feel him against me, through his half buttoned pants as I pulled him closer with my ankles that locked together behind him. I reached between us, trying to release him. I wanted to touch him, feel the solid length of him. But he grabbed my wrists, pinning them together above my head with one one rough hand.

"Not yet." He snarled against my skin.

His mouth found the peak of my breast, tongue swirling,

and I cried out, grinding against him. I needed more, my body screamed for it. The heat that radiated from my center overtaking me, erasing everything but him, the feeling of him against me.

His free hand traveled lower, grazing my skin, burning like fire as it ventured ever closer to part of me that ached for him. He grazed my inner thighs with his knuckles, venturing closer, his thumb drawing soft circles around the place I silently begged for him to touch.

"Keelan please." I was breathing hard, and he lifted his eyes to me, dragging his grinning mouth to my other breast, nipping at my skin as he went. I groaned, raising myself up to him again, tightening my legs around him, doing anything to increase the contact, to urge him to give me what I desperately needed.

"Such a greedy little forest demon," He whispered, his mouth traveling again, running down my stomach, "You know those men would call you *Death on Angel's Wings* when you ran them out of those woods." I could feel his smile against my skin traveling lower. I could barely breathe, barely think.

"Looking at you now, I get it, your intoxicating danger." He paused, his mouth hovering at the hinge of my hips, the feeling of his hot breath alone threatening to send me careening over the edge, "If only they knew, that I could make the death angel beg."

He released his grip on my hands and fell to his knees at the side of the bed, yanking me roughly to the edge as he threw my already trembling legs over his shoulders. Pain and injury forgotten, his mouth was on me, hands gripping my thighs, holding me tightly to him. My free hands wound themselves into his hair as the force of his tongue ripped the air from my lungs.

In long sweeping strokes he set my body on fire, my world dissolved until I could feel only him, only the places where he touched me. Finally, his tongue flicked at my aching core and I shattered beneath him, my back arching off the bed, the universe collapsing around us. I bit my lip to stifle the scream that tore at the back of my throat. Stars exploded behind my closed eyelids.

When I opened them, he was above me again, hooking an arm around my back and lifting me to the center of the bed. His eyes were dark and hooded, still consumed by lust as he removed his pants and I saw the rest of him. The full, straining length of him. Before he could position himself, I pressed a hand to his chest and flipped him onto his back, hovering above him.

*My turn.* My lips raked down the column of his throat, painfully slowly. While his hands traveled hungrily down my waist, across my hips as I teased at him. I clamped my mouth on the join of his neck and shoulder and sucked. His hips bucked beneath me and a low groan that was almost my name set goosebumps erupting on my skin. I released him for only a moment, just long enough to whisper into his skin, "It seems I am the one making you beg."

I heard him growl, yanking at my hips once again, pulling them until my entrance only just made contact with his rigidity, and he held me there. "You really are a demon." He breathed, smirking up at me. Our noses nearly touching as we both panted, chests heaving.

I didn't blink as I lowered myself onto him. Inch by inch. I watched his face as I did, reveling in the way his eyes rolled back, his breath hitched. I savored his low growl as I reached the base. And then I halted, and just held there, accepting the fullness of him, adjusting to it. His eyes connected with me again, burning into me, still hungry. I lifted myself again, watching his eyes shutter with the sensation.

I raised an eyebrow at him and asked, "Well? Are you going to beg for it?" He laughed and snarled in the same breath, using my hips to pull me down, join us, as he raised up to meet me. My whole body quaked as he did it again, and again. My pleasure building for the second time. I raked my nails down his chest as he took me. No more teasing, just ravenous desire coursing between us.

As we both approached that precipice, edging closer to climax, our words turning to incoherent babble, I felt it. Like a bowstring, notched and being pulled tight, the bond seemed to materialize into something solid. No longer a silent plea to be near him, but a tether, stretched between us. I could tell Keelan felt it too, and the thrust of his hips intensified. That *snap* of it being locked into place was the final piece to go crashing over the pinnacle.

My wings spread to their full length as lightning exploded inside me, the force of it extinguishing every candle in the room. I fell into him, my hands on his chest keeping me upright. We both gasped for air, smiling at each other. The only light in the room, the glowing lines of our marks.

"You are so beautiful." Was all Keelan said as those brown eyes drank me in, all of me.

# 25

# Astriel

"I've been wanting to do that since the day in the sparring ring." Keelan whispered, grinning, his voice still husky as we lay side by side. Still naked, hands held between us and our legs tangled together.

"I'm just that irresistible, huh?" Smiling as I said it, our faces close, our breath mingling.

He smiled back, "Clearly."

"Is that when you knew?" I asked quietly.

"That is when I suspected, when the mark first reacted to you. I *knew* when you were in trouble in the library and your mark called to me, helped me find you."

"I'm sorry. That was... bad." I winced at the memory.

His other hand trailed the valley of my waist, fingers drawing lazy circles against my skin while he considered, "When did you know?"

"The healer told me," I responded meekly, "I had convinced myself that whatever I felt for you was a consequence of being binded, that it was some sort of protection in the magic. I hadn't even considered that it could be... I didn't know what it would feel like. And I haven't been exactly thinking straight since I've been here."

His eyes searched mine, and he took a shaking breath, "We could leave," I could hear it in his voice, the fear, the desperation, "I could get us out of here, we could go back to Phaedra, finally be free of this."

"But your wings- if you leave they will burn them." My heart ached, remembering the sight of them, trapped in that box, for two hundred years they called to him, and he couldn't reach them.

"If you give the king…" His voice was hard, eyes darkening, "If his heir is half fae, I'll never be free. I'll be subjected to at least another several centuries of *this*. And what it will do to you, I won't be able to stand it."

He tried to smile but his eyes were glazed, no longer looking at me, "It would be enough to see you soar, to be there with you." He was willing to sacrifice so much, for me, for my happiness. I felt his fingers slide, running down the length of my wing, feather light touch that made me shiver and sent goosebumps erupting over my skin.

"Deliana told me, while you were ill that— That when you are… expecting," his face turned hard and solemn, "they intend to clip your wings."

My heart stopped, the earth cracking open, threatening to swallow me, "They can't do that." I croaked, throat tightening. I could feel the thorny vines from my nightmare, tightening like a noose around my windpipe, tearing at me.

Keelan untangled us and turned over, looking at the ceiling. But I still stared at him, unable to look away, unable to find the words. Tears burned at my eyes again but would not fall. "They would let you keep them, as a symbol. To prove that you are in fact what they claim." His voice faltered, "Astriel, if you stay, you'll never fly again."

Something inside of me cracked, my chest cleaved open at the thought. I had met fae with clipped wings from the human realm. I had seen the faint scars that ran over that critical tendon. They were husks, ghosts of themselves. As if severing that connection also sliced at their souls. I couldn't bear the thought.

I choked, but forced myself to speak, "In all this time, why did you never kill the king?"

His voice, void of emotion, "Oh I want to, I would have. But a little spell his sorcerer thought up prevents me. If I kill him, my wings burn. My hands have been tied."

That resolve, the clarity I felt the night in the maze revisited me. *Kill the king.* If I end him, we will both be free. I could get us out. Keelan could finally end this lifetime of sacrifice and be happy. We both could, I could make it happen. It wouldn't be hard.

I decided then, in the dim light that there was no alternative, this would be the only way out, for both of us. I knew what I had to do. Keelan wouldn't like it, but he wouldn't have to know, not until it was over. He would find out what I had done when he was reunited with his wings.

"Let's get some sleep." Was all I said, and we did.

# 26

# Astriel

I rose before Keelan that morning. The days of sleep deprivation finally catching up to him. But I felt so rested, so satisfied, even the aching in my bones seemed lessened. I looked back at him as I stood, I had never seen him so at peace, his strong back relaxed, light cascading over the defined muscles. Muscles that used to carry his wings.

He had faded scars peppering near every inch of skin, the marks of centuries of fighting and torture still evident, all over. The marks that emerged where his wings would have been were worse than I could have imagined, even after all these years they still looked fresh. Not like the light white scar that ran the length of his jaw, these were barely scabbed over wounds, refusing to give up hope that his wings would return. I would get them back, I would set him free from this living hell.

Digging through Keelan's wardrobe, I tossed aside piles of leather sheaths and discarded garments in the bottom until I found a set of my clothes, extra from my prolonged stay here. I picked them up, a sniff indicated that they were, in fact, clean. They were simple, comfortable, selected so I could rest and heal.

Heal.

I looked down, the gash in my arm was still raw and red, but the dark veins had retreated, nearly imperceptible. I looked at the injury on my leg and observed the same. Not all the way gone, but nearly. Something inside me knew it was not the medicine that had done it.

*'Might have been the only thing keeping you alive'* Charterea had said about the binding, about the bond. I had survived even when I didn't want to, even when the voice in my head offered peace and I accepted it. Ke willed me to live, had *needed* me to survive. And taking on the bond, solidifying it, had allowed my healing to accelerate. It was just another reason I needed to do this. Another reason I needed to set us free.

I dressed, quickly and quietly. Tiptoeing to the side table, throwing back another dose of the healers concoction. I set down the empty vial, wincing at the sound, fearing it would wake him, but he did not stir. I took one more look at Ke, watching his chest rise and fall with each even breath and padded out of the bedroom, softly snicking the door behind me. Once in the hall, I locked eyes with the lieutenant, so seemed startled to see me. "Edward, I would like to request an audience with the king."

The lieutenant had initially tried to dissuade me, tried to get past me to open the door. To ask Keelan if it was the wise choice. I wouldn't let him. I tried to tell him that it was Keelan's idea that I finally meet the king. That he wasn't to be disturbed, that he needed to rest. But even as he quit arguing and just looked me up and down to check the state

140

of my healing, I could see the reservation in his eyes. *So he knows more than he's letting on.*

I denied the suggestion to change clothes before our meeting. I was not trying to impress him, I didn't want to. I needed to speak with him. That was all. I am still healing, I reminded the well meaning lieutenant. My relief was palpable when Edward finally gestured for me to walk with him, and I did, not taking his arm this time, strong enough to carry myself.

The silver dagger I had swiped from Keelan's wardrobe and tucked in the waistband of my pants pressed cold against my back.

* * *

I was once again ushered into the dining room where my world was shattered months ago. Months. So much time had passed, and I barely noticed. I sat at the center of the table, the only other chair at the head, where I had sat, the remnants of wine staining the wood beneath the new runner.

For several minutes I sat alone, picking at my fingernails as I waited for someone to fetch the king. Reservation and fear gnawed at my gut. *This is the easy part.* I reminded myself. While I never particularly enjoyed killing, it isn't difficult. The body reacts when it knows it is in danger, the mind only passively involved. Of course, this was a different kind of danger, but anticipatory adrenaline still rendered my palms clammy against my lap.

After what felt like an eternity, the king arrived. He entered slowly, stooped forward and suppressing a cough as he ambled in. He wore only a lush robe and slippers, not even a crown. Not the killer king I had imagined at all. He looked so old and so... frail. He fell into the chair, and it groaned beneath his weight. "So we finally are properly introduced, *Agrona.*"

I suppressed a grimace at the name, the false moniker a sign of how little he knew about me, how little he truly cared. I was nothing but a thing to him, a potential alliance, an incubator. I felt the rage boiling up again before I leashed it. With effort, I softened my face into an easy smile, a disarming smile.

"It has been too long, Your Majesty." I managed, tipping my head forward as a subtle bow.

He waved a hand, and a servant, human it seemed, appeared with a decanter and filled his glass with a deep red wine. "Where is my captain? He is supposed to stay by your side until—" He caught himself, "For the time being."

I played ignorant, "I have not seen him yet this morning. I requested your audience as soon as I rose."

"So you are feeling better then." He took a long drink of his wine, some of it spilling out of the corners of his mouth and dripping down his bearded chin. He wiped it away with a sleeve.

"The healer did her work well." Was all I said in kind.

"Glad to hear it," He waved again and a platter of food was placed before him, another servant placed one in front of me, "Please, eat." He gestured a knife at me and the platter, eggs and bacon. But the sound of smacking as he chewed discouraged my appetite.

He looked up at me, mouth full, "So, I hear Deliana

informed you of our proposition." I nearly scoffed, but I let it die in my throat.

"Indeed she did, I wanted to meet with you to discuss the particulars." My stomach churned at the facade, the lies I would have to swallow to get my chance, "An alliance between our lands would be unprecedented."

He nodded, wiping his mouth but leaving little flecks of bread decorating his beard. "I am a gentleman," he started, bringing a hand to his heart as he suppressed a belch, "Now that you are well, I will set the date and we will be wed within a week. And then when we announce the coming of a new heir we will travel together to Phaedra and inform your people that it is a joint territory."

*A week*. He turned his attention back to his plate. It was so nonchalant, just a business dealing, not even to be negotiated, as if it was already done. I started to reach for the dagger. Two steps and I would be on him, and this horrible dealing would be ended before it could begin.

I watched him, wholly unafraid of me, not even deigning to gaze up as he tore into his breakfast. Only servants stood stiff backed against the walls, staring into nothing. No guards. For whatever reason, he didn't think me to be a threat.

I steeled myself, this worked in my favor, unarmed and unprotected. It would take a heartbeat, maybe two, to free us of this fate. I gripped the handle of the blade, leaning forward. A door slammed open to my left, commanding my attention.

Deliana and Keelan stormed into the room. The hand that gripped the dagger's handle swiftly fell back into my lap as they entered. I schooled my features and smiled sweetly at both of them. Keelan, still bearing harsh purple smudges beneath his eyes, cut me a sharp look before softening his face back into that impenetrable mask of indifference.

Then he turned his attention to the king. My eyes, against my will, traveled over him. He wore his more formal working uniform. I couldn't help but picture the events of the night before, biting my lip as I remembered his touch, his taste. But my eyes traveled lower and along with his sword, he also wore his dagger sheath, which hung empty.

"My apologies that she bothered you so early in the day, your majesty. She has a tendency to wander if I don't keep an eye on her." Keelan sauntered over to me, taking post behind my chair before ordering a servant to fetch another for him and the witch.

Deliana regarded me suspiciously, and floated over to the shoulder of the king.

"Your Majesty, you should have alerted me of this meeting. She is still a fae."

The king roared with laughter, slapping his hand on the table, spewing crumbs, "Deliana look at her, I hardly think I am in any danger here." I did indeed look like the picture of compliance. Sitting with my hands in my lap and my wings drooped ever so slightly, still a touch too thin and pale from the many ordeals of being here. I forced a smile.

"Besides, when discussing the matters at hand, a lady's desire for privacy is best to be respected." He nodded at me, and I returned the gesture. Feigning an appreciative smile.

The servants set the other chairs, Deliana at the right hand of the king, and Keelan on the other side of me, mostly at my back. Deliana was whispering in the king's ear as he continued the attack on his plate when I felt a hand on the small of my back, softly brushing through the feathers of my lowered wings. I stiffened, the soft touch making my skin scream, and then felt the whisper of the blade in my waistband being plucked out.

I turned to him, alarmed, but he was already leaning back in his chair, having taken the wine glass that sat next to my plate. I spotted the dagger I had stolen back in its sheath at his hip. How he knew where it was, I wasn't sure. He just watched the king and Deliana lazily as he sipped, not regarding me at all. I suppressed a snarl at him, but just turned back to the king and his sorceress, waiting to be addressed again.

"How did you end up in the cursed library anyways, Agrona?" He looked up at me for a moment but his focus was still on his plate, the witch now sat back in her chair, seething with irritation about something I didn't hear.

"My adjustment here was... hard," I chose my words carefully, "I was seeking some sort of refuge, a touch of familiarity. I got lost and when I came across the door it... called to me, so I entered. I didn't mean for it to become such an ordeal."

He looked at me now, tearing off a piece of bacon, leaning forward with his arms on the table, "You were attacked by those dark beasts, so you took something. What book?" Genuine curiosity, no hint of anything else.

"It's called *The Winged War,* I haven't had a chance to read it but I believe that it is about my people-"

"Oh! You could have just asked ole Captain Ke, over there! He remembers it." he turned his attention to the male behind me, "You were there, weren't you?"

Keelan nodded tightly, but didn't speak.

"I suppose I'll have to ask him about it." I tried not to let my gaze linger on Keelan, despite knowing what he must be

145

feeling, almost being able to sense it. *The bond* I suspected.

When I looked back to the king he was running a finger through the egg yolk pooled on his plate. He locked eyes on me again, and there was a fogginess I hadn't noticed before. He sucked the yolk off his finger and started to stand, taking a heavy step towards me.

"May I touch your wings? I've never seen a fae with feathered wings before."

Everyone else at the table stood simultaneously, including me. I took a step back, trying not to visibly recoil. Keelan directly behind me, stiff backed, with his hand hovering over the hilt of his sword, but not touching it.

"Your Majesty," I tried to steady my voice that threatened to shake with panic, "It is considered untoward to touch a fae's wings outside of… intimacy. They are very sensitive."

He stopped in place and let his hand drop, color erupting on his sagging cheeks, "I see," He cleared his throat, looking to Deliana and Keelan before nodding at me, "My apologies, I didn't mean to offend, but they are beautiful."

I offered a tight smile, but my attention was on the male who stood behind me. I felt him tense when the king approached, and could feel him trembling. I suppressed the urge to turn to him, to soothe him and assure him that everything is okay.

Deliana came upon the king now, "Your majesty, since you've finished breakfast, perhaps we may discuss a few things," she cut those eyes of hellfire at me, *"privately."*

# 27

# Astriel

Keelan and I exited the dining call, walking silently in step until the balmy spring air of the gardens brushed my skin. I turned my face to the sky, letting the rising sun warm me.

"Are you out of your *mind?*" Keelan suddenly hissed, turning fully towards me, darting his gaze all around to ensure we were alone.

"I don't know what you're talking about." I responded coolly, not halting my pace, not daring to look him in the eyes. My heart pounded in my chest, at what I would have done. If even another minute had passed before Ke and the witch barged in, the king would have been dead.

He grabbed me by the elbow, spinning me to face him, "Astriel," He kept his grip firm, but not hard enough to hurt, "I woke and you were gone, Edward had to tell where you had run off to. When I found the dagger missing—" His voice caught for just a moment, and his mouth set in a hard line.

"I don't even take audience with the king. What were you thinking? If I hadn't come, if you had—"

"I had it handled." I snapped at him, pulling my arm from

147

his grip. I felt my wings flare behind me, punctuating my frustration. "You forget that I am not some fragile thing, he is only a man."

"And when Deliana found out what you had done— if she even knew what you intended to do, and I wasn't there-" his voice trembled in his throat but his eyes still burned with anger, with fear, "She would have killed you without a second thought."

"She would try. I am built and bred for this Keelan, you forget." I meant it, but my voice faltered.

"You are no assassin." Keelan said softly.

My blood stilled, the gravity of it all came crashing down, my legs buckled beneath me. I had been so sure, so ready. My desire to break his curse, the need to set us both free, the clarity I thought I felt, it had been wrong. *I had been wrong.* I could have compromised everything, endangered the both of us. My knees hit the ground as I buried my face in my hands.

"Keelan, I can't live like this—" It was all I could choke out before the tears I had been holding back finally escaped me.

And I knelt on the ground, shameless and broken. And I wept. I wept for my people, and the life I left behind. I wept for Keelan and the bond that would undoubtedly kill us both.

"Then we will leave." he whispered as he knelt down next to me, pulling me into his arms.

"We can't, your wings—"

He shushed me, holding me tighter, his chin resting on the top of my head, "I would rather they be turned to cinder than watch you hurt like this."

And I heard the pained sincerity in his voice, "You mean more to me than anything else, I would sacrifice everything

I have, everything I am, if it meant you would be safe, if you would be happy."

And he would be sacrificing everything if we were to leave. He would be giving up the very thing he had turned into a monster to save. Two hundred years he served the crown and was forced to turn away from everything he believed in. All for the glimmer of hope that he would one day be reunited with his wings. And he was willing to give up that hope, *for me.*

I wanted to fight him on it, wanted to insist that we would find a way. But I couldn't see any way out, the walls were closing in and I didn't know what to do, so I just nodded. Even as it crushed my soul to force him to make this choice. I was so tired of fighting, of plotting and scheming and dreaming in riddles I couldn't solve. I just wanted it to be over. I needed this all to be over.

# 28

# Astriel

We decided to occupy our own chambers that night, to prevent suspicion and pack. He had given me an old rucksack from deep in the depths of his wardrobe, but as I surveyed the items occupying my own, I realized there wasn't much that I would care to take.

I donned the set of clothes Keelan had given me and my circlet. Stuffing a set of training clothes and my layers from that first night into the bag. Then drained one of the healers concoctions and pocketed the last two. *I will need my strength.* The flavor was still revolting, but it was effective.

We agreed to meet at midnight in the gardens, Keelan's guards having been dispatched elsewhere for the night. Evidently, the lieutenant ensured they would be occupied. I wondered absently if he was some manner of fae I didn't recognize, or if he was just blindly loyal to his captain. It didn't matter in the grand scheme of things, I appreciated him nonetheless.

I ducked out of my room as the moon rose higher into the sky, sack slung over my shoulder, eager to get to Keelan, desperate to get away from this place. I had pulled on my boots from that first night, enchanted with the silent step. I thanked the Mother that they were still here.

The only sound as I snuck into the hall was the soft click of the door. I locked it from the inside, to buy time in the morning if anyone came sniffing around. *No going back now.* I stepped lightly, despite the already imperceptible sound of my footfalls, ears straining for evidence of anyone else wandering the halls at this late hour. But I was only met with more silence.

Down the hall, around a corner, past the dining room. I hugged the edge of the corridor, the curve of my wing brushing against the ornate wallpaper, eyes flicking from side to side. The only sound I could discern was the pounding of my own heart. My circlet remained dormant. Two more turns, one more long hall and I would be out in the open air. My breath caught in my throat. I turned a corner, too fast, and locked eyes with the king.

I spun on a heel, flashing out of his eye line. I pressed myself against the wall, praying he didn't see me, willing myself to disappear against the wallpaper. I could hear his shuffling steps, his labored breath.

"Who's there?" He called out weakly, "I saw you, who's there?"

I forced my breathing to steady as I cursed in a whisper. So close, I was so close and with one misstep I would ruin everything. I ran my hands along my body and cursed again. No blades, I forgot for a moment that here I didn't have the luxury of weapons. I would have to make due, worst case, I could outpace him, easily. So long as we were quicker than the guards he would surely summon, or Deliana. This would not be the end of the line.

One, two, three deep breaths and I stepped out into the open hall.

As I did, his eyes fell to me again, "Oh, Agrona, what are you doing up at this hour?"

That name again, that false moniker that marked me as a slayer of men. And yet, no fear showed in his features.

I steadied myself to face him, "Your Majesty, why are you—" but the gleam in his eyes stole my voice.

He looked so weak. Not in the way all humans looked weak, but like a snared rabbit, clinging to life. His sparse hair was disheveled, his beard sticking out in every direction as if he had been running his hands up through it. He was stooped and his thick robe threatened to come undone, it appeared he didn't wear anything underneath. The key I had seen in my vision swung violently with every wobbling step against his chest. I looked down and noticed he was only wearing one slipper. Without thinking I stepped towards him, reaching out.

His attention caught something on my shoulder, my bag I realized, "You're leaving." A sadness seemed to fill his hazy eyes as he said it.

"I have to." my voice soft, careful.

"Why? We have barely gotten to speak, surely you don't find me so detestable."

I scanned his face, looking for anything other than the wild and tired confusion that seemed to mark him all over, "I can't marry you. I can't be a pawn in this game of power."

"A pawn? But you came here, you wanted—" His hand pressed against his sweat slicked forehead as if he was fighting against a mighty headache.

"I was brought here." I stepped towards him again, hands outstretched as if I were settling a spooked horse, "Remember? The night Keelan brought me, in shackles, in the throne room."

He shook his head, stumbling and I reached forward to steady him, my hand on his elbow. "You sent him into the fae woods to catch the demon, and then kept me here to produce an heir."

There was no recollection in his eyes as I held him, up close I realized I was at least a hand taller than him, and that feeling I felt when the two boys stalked through my woods came rushing back. Pity, and a misplaced protectiveness. My eyes traveled further down the hall, two more turns and a long hallway and I would have been at the threshold to the garden, to freedom.

I looked back at the shriveled king, "Which way is your room? Let's get you back to bed."

He pointed in the other direction and started ambling, I matched his slow steps, hand still on his elbow. I could feel my limited time ticking by, but I couldn't just leave him like this.

"Your wings are so beautiful," He mused, and I lowered my eyes to him, "I didn't know there were fae with wings such as yours."

As he said it, a memory emerged from our breakfast together, when I intended to drive that dagger into his chest. *'I've never seen a fae with feathered wings before'.* I remembered that Keelan and I had shot to our feet, both protective over my wings. But Deliana had stood too, all too eager to wrangle the king from the room, from what he might say next.

"Your Majesty," I started slowly, "Keelan had wings like

153

mine."

He twisted his head to gape at me, "No, no, no. Keelan has no wings, he is an elf of some sort. He pledged his allegiance to the crown before I was born."

"That's not true," I rested my hand on his forearm, keeping my voice barely above a murmur, "Your ancestor, King Byron, stole his wings after the war, to keep him here. They are pinned up in the trophy room. You wear the key to their cage around your neck."

"What trophy room? This key is for... Well, I can't quite remember. But I wouldn't do something like that, at least I don't think I would." And suddenly I could see it, the soft shimmering that sometimes glinted around his head. A misted blindfold someone had placed over his eyes, into his mind.

*Deliana.*

There was no telling when the last time the king made a decision for himself. He certainly wasn't in the condition to. Perhaps this morning, in the dining hall, was a glimpse behind the glamour, still confused, still infected with her influence. But away from her, he had been kind, not the killer of legend. Certainly not the kind of man I had expected him to be, nothing like the cruel king I had met on the night of my arrival.

We had come up on the massive doors that led into his bedchambers, and he mumbled some thanks for the escort. "Your Majesty," He turned to look at me once more, the recognition seeming to slip from his mind even as I stood in front of him. "May I take that key? As something to remember you by, a parting gift?"

He blinked, and then smiled at me, the smile of an old man

154

who enjoyed having company, and I felt a pang of sympathy for him. With shaking hands he pulled the rawhide over his head and held it out, "My dear, if you can find a use for it on your journey you are free to take it. It's doing me no good if I can't remember what the blasted thing even belongs to."

I took it by the cord, the iron of the key singing a violent song in proximity to my skin. And I smiled back at him. There was a momentary flash of lucidity, of pain and sadness and helplessness, but no malice, none of the dreaded killer king. In a blink it was gone, and he turned from me on unstable legs into his chambers, and shut the door.

# 29

# Astriel

I turned back into the hall, leaning against the closed door. My heart raced, a thundering pulse roaring in my ears. I looked at the mark on my forearm, its light seemed to pulse in an unwavering order. *Go.*

So I ran.

At some point I shucked off the rucksack that pounded against my back. Sprinting in silent step down the abandoned halls. I slid around corners, tripped over carpets. I whispered to the rune that glowed brighter on my arm with every step, "Tell him where I am, where I am going." I had no clue if the message would convey. If that's even how the bond worked, if he would hear me. I didn't have time to linger on the thought. I pressed on.

When I reached that giant terrible tapestry I ripped it away from the door, yanking the smooth wood open with enough force to take it off the hinges. Before I even entered the room I could hear the beating of the wings, their voiceless cry to be set free, and I was going to answer them.

Like in my dream, a single wing beat lifted me to the top of the table before the glorious wings. Like in my dream I shushed them, willed them to quiet, and they did. As I clasped the wrought iron lock it burned into my skin violently. It branded my flesh with hideous power, but I could barely feel it. My circlet thrummed loudly at my temples. Palming the key, it burned sharp and icy, I couldn't bring myself to care as I sent it home. I twisted, and relented, the mechanism clicked and the lock fell open.

Stars erupted in my vision.

One moment I was on the table and the next I was flying, not by force of my wings, but something worse. And then I was crashing through the glass display of books, colliding with tables of treasures as I careened through the air. Wood and glass splintered beneath my body as I shattered the tables on the far wall. Pain radiated from my center back as I pulled myself forward onto my elbows.

Before me, Deliana stood, cloak whipping around her on an unseen wind, those embers in her eyes turned to a roaring blaze. Her face crooked into a hideous sneer.

"You just have to ruin *everything.*"

# 30

# Astriel

"You stupid, insolent girl." Her voice burned with whatever blazed beneath her skin as she stalked up to me. I tried to right myself, to climb back into a fighting stance before she could approach. But that phantom wind forced me to the ground again.

"Do you have any idea what you have done? The centuries of work you are laying to waste? And for what? For a crippled fae male? Because he stuck his dick in you and now you think you're in love?"

She saw my eyes widen and smirked, "You think I don't know what goes on inside my castle? You think I don't have ears in every corner of this wretched place? You are not the first doe eyed girl he's taken to bed to get what he wants, and you certainly won't be the last."

"What are you even trying to accomplish here?" I needed to buy time, I needed to find a weapon, I needed to release those wings that were beating so ferociously at their cage. The open lock shook with every movement, but did not fall from where it hung,

"Girl, you have no idea what forces are at play here. I worked for *years* to break down the mind of that idiot king to do my bidding. I was *this* close," I palmed the floor around me, shoving aside scattered jewels and smooth precious stones, looking for anything to grab onto as she closed in on me, "and you just can't leave well enough alone."

She grabbed me by my collar, wrenching me off the ground as she spit in my face, "If you won't submit, then you will just have to die."

The door behind us flung open and a wild eyed Keelan burst into the room. She snarled up at him just as my hand found purchase on a large shard of glass that had been shattered with the force of my body. I swung it blindly, the sharp edges tearing my palm, and it sliced open her bicep. She released me as she stumbled back, gripping her arm that spewed blood on me and the carpet. I choked on it as I hit the ground and that white hot pain threatened to take me under.

"The wings!" I shouted to Keelan as he rushed to me. I pointed with a bloodied hand and he followed my gaze, they thundered against the glass and iron, shaking the walls with their force. Books and stacks of boxes tumbled with the great power that boomed around the room. A candle had tipped, lighting a stack of papers on fire. Deliana looked at them and grinned.

Keelan took off running towards them, vaulting over fragmented remains of furniture. I tried again to lift myself, shuddering against the pain that wracked the entirety of my body. In just a glance I looked over my shoulder, my right wing hung limply. One movement and I could feel the shattered bones grinding against each other. I stifled a cry before trying and failing to haul myself to my feet.

He had almost reached them when I heard Keelan cry out. I snapped my attention to where he was pinned to the wall, three glistening black blades erupting from his arms and stomach. Obsidian daggers, fae magic nullifiers. Not only would he not have access to his Seraphim strength, but they would slow his healing to nothing. The truth was a pounding behind my eyes. If I didn't get to him, he would only have a matter of minutes before he bled out.

My eyes found Deliana, who stood across from him, more of those roughly hewn blades floating around her, as if she had summoned them out of thin air. She cut her eyes at me but did not turn away from Keelan.

"I should have tried harder to shatter your mind the moment you entered these walls." Deliana spoke with low precision, "You would have married that demented old fool, bore his bastard halfling spawn. And we would have been united without a fuss."

"Why?" Was all I could choke out, my face was wet, with blood or tears I couldn't tell. Fire spread all around us.

"Because of the tree!" She shouted, the force of her own spelled wind threatening to drown her out, "Because when I control the tree I own everything. Kingdoms will bow and fall to my mercy."

And I saw it again, the nightmares, everything burning. My people burning, the tree burning. She would destroy everything in her path. I fell forward, hands fisted on the carpet as the truth in that vision sapped at my strength. But I kept my eyes on her, knees tearing against broken glass.

"I spent the better part of a millennia influencing royals and their armies to do my bidding. The other fae were more than happy to bend to my demands. Your feathered friends were the only ones immune to my influence."

Her smile turned molten, "That is why they all had to die that day." My vision blurred as she spoke, "I led the troop up the mountain. *I* ordered that not even the crying babes be spared. I even remember your mother."

And suddenly the world went silent. Only the faraway thudding of Keelan's trapped wings broke through, his distant yelling. Beyond that, my world narrowed to Deliana.

She spoke again, "She stayed behind you know? Sent her family out to fly on the front lines so she could *tend the children*. A coward's excuse to avoid battle." She looked at me directly then, "I remember the fear in her eyes when she begged me to spare her people. I remember how she screamed your name when I plunged that obsidian shard into her heart."

I screamed, but there was no sound, the last thing I saw were Deliana's eyes widen. My vision filled with pure, blinding light. And then inky darkness.

# 31

# Keelan

I had been waiting for her in the gardens, worry tightening in my chest as the minutes ticked by. We agreed to meet at midnight, and the large clock built into the castle wall was ticking closer and close to one. I fought the urge to check on her, to find her. *She's coming.* But a tightness gripped at my chest.

I was just about to reenter the castle when the mark that decorated my arm flickered. I studied the fine lined ink as it began to shine brighter, a light tingling radiated through my whole body. *Hurry.* A voice seemed to carry on the wind. *Find her. You know where she is.* Without thinking, I broke out into a run. I knew where to go, like I had when she wandered into the library. A sixth sense to find her.

My boots pounded against the stone floors as I stormed down the halls. I passed her bag where it had been discarded, falling open on a rug. Panic thundering in my chest. I knew where she had gone, I knew what she intended to do. I had told her, urged her to stop, and she just couldn't help herself.

162

*Stubborn, strong willed female with a death wish.*

I only just spotted the open door pushing aside the massive tapestry when I heard the scream, and a reverberating sound of breaking. I closed the distance, dread pulling at me as my mind emptied. As I crossed the threshold, the sight before me drained the color from my face. Deliana had Astriel in a steel grip, her head falling backwards. Her eyes were full of shock and panic and they fell to me. But her hand moved on its own and I watched as she gripped a broken piece of glass and slashed it though the witch's arm.

The sorceress released her and stumbled backwards, Astriel hitting the ground hard as I started towards her, but her shining moonstone glare stopped me in my tracks. She raised one shredded and burned hand, pointing to the other side of the room. In a command that I couldn't force my body to disobey, she shouted, "The wings!"

I turned towards them, their lock hung open, shaking with the force of their struggle. Their call pulled at me, and mindlessly, I sprung towards them, closing in as the witch fully turned her attention to me. Only a few feet away, a few more steps, and I would be upon them. A hand reaching to grab at the lock, if I could get them, I could save us, I'd have enough power to end Deliana. I could save Astriel.

A mind shattering force stopped me in my tracks.

The obsidian burned like ice, freezing my blood and obscuring the thoughts from my brain in a glacier, it drowned out the sounds around me. All I could hear was the ringing in my ears, the rush of my own adrenaline. I looked down at myself, blood running in rivers where the blades had struck, dug so deep into the wall I couldn't move without them tearing

163

deeper, flaying me open.

I had to do something, either reach the wings or reach Astriel. I couldn't stay pinned to this gods forsaken wall. I groaned, out of the corner of my eye I could see those massive and dark feathered wings thrashing against the case. They called to me, begged me to release them, but I couldn't hold my focus on them. I couldn't will myself to want them, not when the bond that threatened to strangle my heart pulled my focus.

I forced my failing vision to clear, craning my head to Astriel, who was addressing the witch from her place, crumpled on the ground. One of her wings was broken, I could tell that much, and based on the angle of her foot, so was her ankle. She was covered in blood, I couldn't tell how much of it was hers.

I couldn't hear them, not over the pounding in my own head, the beating of those wings, the crackling of the fire around us as it spread rapidly across the room, threatening to swallow us all if I didn't act. I pulled against the shards, they wouldn't budge. But I kept pulling, using all of my strength to separate my arm from the wall. With a sickening tear, one arm was free.

The shard that punctured it still dug into the wall. Pain was a distant feeling, I couldn't let myself feel it, not when I had to get to Astriel, when I had to shield her from the witch's wrath. But I could feel the warmth of my own blood, the weakness setting in. I was losing too much of it, too fast.

I brought the free arm down, grasping the blade that dug into my stomach. I yanked on it, nothing. *Free the other arm.* I stifled a cry as my fingers wrapped around the blade plunged into my other bicep and yanked. palms tearing against the razor sharp edge. I felt it give, just a little. I wrenched on it again, gritting my teeth, and it came free from the wall.

I slumped a little, breathing as hard as I dared, every breath moving against the blade that still tore through my middle. I cut my eyes to the witch, her focus was no longer on me, she was glaring at Astriel, a wicked grin curling at her lips. Her floating blades pivoted in air, turning their points to her. My hands, together, wrapped around the glass in my stomach. I had to free it, I had to get to her.

My fingers tore deeper against the razor sharp edge of the obsidian as I pulled. But my attention stayed locked on Astriel, who was crying. Her hands planted against the tattered carpets beneath her. I pulled again and it gave way. I dropped it as I lunged forward, running to her. Pain returning, I stumbled.

Her silver eyes glowed, brighter than before, glinting against the ever growing flames threatening to consume the room and everything inside of it. I reached out, still too far away. The air around her seemed to tremble. Absently, I heard a clatter of metal on wood behind me but I couldn't tear my gaze away. A crackling light surged from where she crouched. Time slowed, as the world exploded around us.

A blinding luminescence forced me to shield my eyes, and when I made myself look back out into the blaze. Astriel's wings were fully extended, but they were no longer feathered. They were made of that brilliant light itself. Bright as a sun.

I looked around, the witch was shielding herself with her torn arm. The daggers fell around her in slow motion. I watched the flying debris float in midair as the light overtook them. The fire around us extinguished with the force.

I looked back at Astriel, her face blank, her features

165

obscured. A power that swirled around her, and shot outwards. I advanced on hands and knees towards her, unwilling to feel the shredding of my skin as I crawled through the wreckage. Fighting the all consuming oppressive weight that emanated from somewhere within her but also all around. I screamed her name but the force absorbed it, there was no sound in the room at all.

And then a burning at my back. An earth shattering boom that threatened to fracture my very bones. And a wind, powerful enough to lighten the air around me. I looked up, and saw, for the first time in two hundred years, my own wings, on my back. They seared my skin, bonding themselves to the flesh they had been torn away from. And I felt a wholeness return. Despite the forcefulness of the light that filled the room, familiar shadows once again snaked around my hands and shoulders.

The obsidian wounds slowed their bleeding and I found myself rising to my feet. I leveled my glare at the witch, who turned her attention to the shadow my wings cast as they swallowed the light that blanketed the room. Terror colored her face as I took a single step towards her. Her skin turned red and blotchy, withering beneath the light and darkness. The light grew to a blinding beam. I blinked, and she was gone.

Astriel's cosmic light winked out, and she collapsed.

# 32

# Keelan

I ran to her, readjusting to the weight at my back. That heavy, incredible weight I never thought I would feel again. I slid up her, not only did she no longer shine but she was ashen. Even the subtle sheen that usually glittered across her skin like a fine gossamer was gone.

When my shaking hands found her and skittered across her bare skin where her clothing had torn she was cold. With trembling fingers I gripped her shoulders, shaking her. I knew I was crying, I knew I was yelling her name but she didn't respond. The only sign of life was the shallow and uneven rise and fall of her chest.

I scooped her into my arms, mindful of the wing that hung limp behind her. I had to get her out. I had to get her somewhere safe. She needed a healer.

I winced as I lifted her, cradled against me, her head lolling over my arm. My wounds screaming at the strain. I couldn't force myself to care, it didn't matter. Only she mattered, I had to save her. I tripped over fallen and scorched debris as I carried her, but stayed upright. As soon as we made it out the doorway, into the clear hall, I took off into a run, stretching my wings behind me, testing them, trying to remember the way they feel. The hall was only just wide enough to accommodate the spread of my wings as I beat them, urging myself faster, urging myself to fly.

I only prayed I remembered how.

As soon as my boots crunched on garden gravel I beat my wings in earnest. Screaming muscles in my back from centuries of disuse would have kept me earthbound were I not in the throes of wild panic. I failed everyone, my fellow soldiers, the people of Phaedra, myself. I would not fail Astriel now, not when she had given so much for me. Not when she was willing to sacrifice everything even when I begged her against it.

With a few more beats, I was airborne. A rocky start, but I held tight to Astriel, crushing her into my battered chest. She looked so small, so frail in my arms, not the steadfast warrior I knew she was. As we approached the wall I could feel the ward pushing against me, not wanting to let me pass. I screamed into the night, "I am the Captain of the Kings guard! I will pass!" and the pressure relented. I soared over it, and into the open sky.

As the world spread before me, a curious feeling tightened my throat. *Real, genuine freedom.* I would have laughed or cried at the feeling if it were not the limp weight in my arms. It would be an hour flight to Phaedra, I only hoped I had enough time. The mark on her dirty and damaged arm flickered. A candle on the verge of being blown out.

From the air I watched sprawling towns turn to fields of cattle and sheep, and then forest. A few townspeople spotted us in the cloudless sky, some yelling a warning to their families, but it was unavoidable. I didn't have the strength to fly high enough to keep from sight.

Her limp silver hair whipped around her face, mingling with the shadows that slinked down my arms. Reaching for her, and then retreating, as if afraid her light would return and dissolve them to nothing. They seemed to ask a question with each gentle caress. The same question that burned in my throat but would not dare cross my lips as her broken wing fluttered freely in the wind. *Did she forfeit her flight so that I may once again have mine?*

I steeled myself. Focusing only on the whisper of wind through my feathers and the destination ahead. I did not allow myself to feel the aching muscles in my back or focus too closely on the ever quieter sound of Astriel's heart against my chest. As long as I flew she had a chance. "Please El, stay with me. Come back to me." I whispered against her cold neck.

The forest beneath us was deadly silent, a quiet passage over what I knew were dangerous lands, even for the fae. Not a rustling of leaves or evidence of beasts graced my ears. The forest itself quieted in our procession. A threat of mourning. I pushed away the thought. Ahead of us I could only just make out the streetlights of the city capital on the horizon, pushing through my growing exhaustion, I flew faster.

As we broke past the edge of the woods, I started yelling. I ducked lower, closer to the tiled rooftops that clustered as we entered the center of the capital. I flew lower still, barely above the cobblestones. My voice, hoarse and foreign to me, echoed off the decorated structures around us. Lights flickered on in surrounding buildings as I tumbled down into the street.

"Somebody help us!" The scream tore from my throat as I crouched, cradling Astriel. "We need a healer!" Doors opened around as all manner of fae peaked out, and I heard footfall descend on us. Someone was lifting her out of my arms, someone pulling me away at the shoulder.

"No, no, I must go with her. Please, let me go with her."

# 33

# Astriel

The darkness was unfathomable. An impenetrable void, full of disembodied whispers and swirling wind. Alone, I stood, or floated, I couldn't tell, my body was so far away. *You've earned your rest.* A voice that was not a voice echoed against oblivion. A cold embrace.

*You can be at peace. The worst is over. Come home.* My thoughts were foggy, but an expectant calm settled in my mind. I knew, absently, and without fear, that somewhere far away from me my body was dying. But the void spoke kindly, it was an offer, not a command.

"Keelan?" I found myself asking, or thinking. The endless space around me seemed to still, to quiet, the distant voices seeming to consider, to contemplate.

*The binding will be broken, he will be left behind.* A compromise, I realized. A bid to un-tether us, allow him to live if I decided to release my hold on the physical world. I wasn't afraid, there was only an unrelenting sense of calm, the promise of rest. But I could still think, still reason. I knew what I felt for him, in a logical, faraway place in my mind.

"What if I want to stay?" I found myself asking. The absence considered again, ebbing, seeming surprised, if a void can experience surprise.

*You will return. Pain will return. The consequences will be yours to bear.* Something tickled at the back of my neck, like a soft embrace, a probing. *The choice is yours.*

# 34

# Keelan

The night and following day passed in a tense flurry. Firm hands guided me to a chair in the living room of the quaint home as healers and helpers scurried about. After my own wounds had been tended, they told me I could stay, as long as I kept out of the way, at least until the worst was over.

I spent the following hours taking in my surroundings. My first time back in Phaedra in two centuries, the same but different. I had never spent much time in the city center in my youth, staying mostly atop the mountains in Seraphim territories. No reason to do that now though, if those towns are otherwise abandoned. The thought made me hurt for Astriel, who had weathered a loneliness which, while not the same, mirrored mine.

I was surprised to learn however, that *this* was the dwelling Astriel had chosen for herself. As I knew her, she was so refined, so casually regal in her countenance. But here she resides in a small, squatty bungalow partitioned off of a quiet street. While away from the hustle and bustle of the inner city, it still sat on the edge of the city proper.

Floor to ceiling windows took up more space than true walls, in every direction facing a fenced in yard that only contained the ghosts of landscaping. Flowerbeds overgrown with dead weeds, a stone path obscured by wild, untrimmed grass. The wooden fence, while maintained to offer privacy, had clearly been in need of a paint job for longer than she had been gone. But inside, thick, dark curtains obscured the solemn view. They were not often pulled open, it seemed, if the dust collected in thick layers on the rods were any indication.

The walls were mostly bare, and furniture was sparse around the common areas. The chair I sat in was the only one that showed signs of any use. It was nestled in a corner, near an overflowing bookshelf, surrounded by stacks of novels with cracked and worn spines. The plush floral upholstery was worn where I could imagine she tucked her feet up against herself to read, leaning into the gleam of the stained glass floor lamp encasing an enchanted, ever glowing ball of light to the side. Across the wide area rug sat a matching couch, that before the other guests invading the space had cleared it, was covered in discarded clothes; jackets, scarves, and leathers. As if she shed her outer skin as soon the front door locked behind her.

\* \* \*

I rose from the spot I had occupied near exclusively since arriving, and wandered into the kitchen for a glass of water. In this room, I was met with more of the same. The white cabinets were mostly empty, save for a few spices and unopened jars of preserves. On the wooden counter top sat only a towel, resting on it were a single mug, plate and bowl. I checked the drawers for cutlery, and it was the same, a single spoon, fork, and knife haphazardly thrown within the one nearest to the sink. *Not much for entertaining I guess.*

But I understood why, even as my heart threatened to shatter. She had been left alone, grown alone, and lived her life alone. She would probably see all of these prying eyes in her home as an invasion, even if it was a necessary one. I sighed, gazing out the window above the sink where I'm sure some well meaning nurse healer had pulled them open.

The sun was setting again, painting the sky orange, I tore my eyes away from it, trying not to think of how long I prayed I would get to see that sunset from this side of the forest again. I blinked away the threat of some painful emotion and ran some water from the old and sputtering tap into the mug.

"Oh umm, excuse me?" A meek voice sounded from behind me. I turned, nearly knocking a basket of baked goods someone had brought off the kitchen island. Cursing, I righted it, still not re-accustomed to the added sprawl of my wings.

I cleared my throat, "Sorry," The Pixie girl I had been introduced to as Clovis stood on the other side of the island, shifting her weight from one foot to the other, a perpetually anxious creature it seemed. "What can I do for you?"

"She's asking for you—" She didn't get the chance to finish as I slammed the mug on the island and barreled past her, only half aware of the nervous fluttering of her wings as she flitted out of my way. I could hear her now, panicked, my name on her lips in a weak and scared cry, and the shushing of the healer I knew hadn't left her side. My heart tightened as I wrenched open the door to her bedroom.

She was being held down by a nurse healer on each side, thrashing against them, confusion lining her face. Her wild eyes leveled on me, and she stilled, her resistance against the females who held her softening. I tried not to let my tangible joy show at the thought that my mere presence calmed her.

"Keelan," her voice still hoarse, but quieter now, "I thought I lost you."

# 35

# Astriel

Even with blurred vision I could make out Keelan's familiar form in the doorway. It must have been night, I figured, as the hall behind him was completely dark. He crossed the distance between us in no more than two steps, batting away the unknown hands that had been braced against my shoulders. I reached out to him, desperate to hold him, to feel him against me.

An unexpected pain ripped a cry from my throat as I leaned forward, and I felt his strong arm wrap around me, easing my aching body back down to the bed.

"Don't try to move, you're hurt."

"What's new?" I tried to smile as my head hit the pillow and an odd sensation came to the surface, it was my pillow, in my bed. The realization hit me, an internal stampede. I was home, Keelan was in my room. *Oh Mother, Keelan is in my house.* I groaned, the place was a disaster when I left. He probably thinks I live like a pig.

"What's wrong? What hurts?" Keelan leaned over me, worry etching his brow.

I stifled a pained laugh, but a grin crept onto my face at the absurdity of my concerns, "Excuse my mess, I left in a hurry."

He grinned down at me, shaking his head, "Glad to see you made it out with your priorities intact."

"We made it out." I was suddenly choked, tears threatening to spill over, "You got us out."

"*You* got us out." He softly chided, and the light in the room seemed to shift. I blinked, my focus drifting over his shoulders.

"Your wings—" the choke turned to a silent cry as I reached out, my fingers grazing the soft feathers that were once again a part of him. "You got them back."

He nodded, flexing them. They dominated the space, absorbing the light in the room. I observed a dark mist that wrapped around his shoulders and arms like a tamed snake. He caught my stare, "Shadow Wielding," He held out a hand and the wisp wrapped around his arm, coiling in his palm, "An affinity I've had since I was young. I didn't realize they would come back when my wings were returned."

I stared at the swirling cloud, trying to understand. Even in all my studies, I had never encountered mention of such a thing. I stuck out a finger, not quite touching his palm, and the wisp reached out a tendril and circled my finger, dancing across my skin. It was cold, a drafty breeze, but comforting.

"I think my shadows were more concerned about your well being than mine," Keelan chuckled, "I didn't realize they had favorite people outside of me. They were barely even afraid of your light."

I rested my hand on my lap as the shadows retreated. And looked up at Keelan, "My light?"

His expression shifted, "What do you remember?"

* * *

He ran me through the events of that night, not shying away from the bitter details, not failing to chastise me for my recklessness either. I was almost as pleased to know my message down the bond translated as I was appalled to learn of this *light* that I didn't know I contained. A light that may or may not have almost killed me.

I took a deep shuddering breath as all of the information settled, trying to make sense of it all.

"So she's just… gone? Like escaped?"

"I honestly don't know," Keelan buried his face in his hands, his elbows resting on the edge of the mattress where he kneeled on the floor. "Maybe? I would hate to assume she's dead if she's not, but I've never seen a power like yours. I don't know how it works."

I stared at the ceiling, "So most likely, we will have to deal with her again."

"Most likely."

"But for now we are good."

"As far as I know."

I loosed a heavy breath, turning back to look at the male at my side, who I so desperately wanted to wrap myself into despite the pain that throbbed at a deafening beat all over. I let my mind wander to the thing I hadn't wanted to consider since waking. I tried to push it down, but it was bubbling to the surface now, with every aching movement.

"Do you think I'll regain use of my wing?"

Keelan's eyes closed for a moment as he picked up my hand, holding it between his against his lips. "I'm told these healers are the best in the city. If anyone could fix you, it would be them."

I nodded, trying to push down the emotions that roiled in my gut. I turned my eyes back to the ceiling. Keelan's locked on me, there was no hiding anything between us now. He could probably feel what I was feeling even if it wasn't written all over my face. But he said nothing, just held my hand to him, his breath a calming warmth.

# 36

# Astriel

The next few weeks passed in a haze. Elia came to visit the first week, bringing with her a large growler of some brew she had cooked up just for me. I could have kissed her for it, even a single glass doing more than the healers' concoctions to dull my pain and quiet my mind. Which I appreciated, mostly because they kept the nightmares at bay. Though to my dismay, I was under strict order to not leave the house. Even the walk to the shops was too far, according to one of the healers. And flying was out of the question.

When the sorceress tossed me like a rag doll across the room, she broke my ankle, a simple enough fix. But she also succeeded in turning the bones in one of my wings to splinters. The hard eyed healer told that she was able to set them back into position, but warned that if I 'trashed' her hard work, then I was on my own. So bed rest it was, fair enough.

There was also the nasty business of the wraith venom. Which thankfully, had become so diluted that the gifted healer had no issue. When she cut my stitches however, she had no qualms complaining about the work the human doctor had done. She tried to sketch a few healing runes to fade the appearance of the scars, but they just sizzled and faded.

It was a shame, but I could live with it. Even the burn scars on my hands, the shadow of a lock and key, would not fade with the runes. And the already set scars from the iron shackles were more of the same. It seemed whatever damage I had done to myself at the castle was content to leave its mark. A permanent reminder of what we had been through.

The first two weeks, I was barely allowed to even leave the bed. Ke stayed by my side the entire time. He didn't seem to mind that he had to cook all my meals and guide me to the bath, thankfully. We went on like this, a routine of weakness that while I had grown used to it, still made my skin itch. I was stir crazy and tired of being endlessly doted on. And when Ke finally succeeded in driving me crazy with his fussing, I urged him to get out and explore.

The consequence of his exploring though, is that he started shopping. For his first trip to the markets for more food, I gave him signing rights to my account. Evidently, I hadn't done much spending of the ample salary allotted to me by the council. The number startled me as much as it did Ke, and he just looked around, noting all of the things that needed changing. I waved him off and told him to use his best judgment. I downed another glass of Elia's brew and ambled off back to bed.

* * *

I tore through new paperbacks Ke bought for me as he turned his attention to the house. He brought back dishes and new bedding and all the things I had been too busy or too disinterested to buy for myself. I just let him, if he needed to keep busy to stay sane then at least we had that in common. The real change happened when he replaced my curtains with pale blue gauzy strips that let the light in. I didn't dare say it, but I liked the change. For so long this place had served as no more than a box to eat, sleep, and read in that I forgot it could actually be... homey.

Besides his home making, Ke went about reacquainting himself with Phaedra, running errands and meeting with the people who summoned him. And despite the calm domesticity we had fallen into, he still kept a distance between us. He slept on the couch, for fear of hurting me. And as far as I can tell did not even think of intimacy outside of caring for me. And *that* nearly hurt more than my slow healing.

We didn't talk about our previous coupling, or the bond that hovered over our heads, or where those things played into our new dynamic. I was fairly confident he was just trying to be mindful of my limitations. But I couldn't help the voice from somewhere in the back of my mind that kept chanting that he regretted our one night together. I didn't have the heart to bring it up.

At the end of that second week, the hard eyed nurse returned. She pinched and pulled at my wing so hard it felt like she wanted to make me squeal. But she deemed me fit to return to my daily activities, still barring flying. But I was excited to be cleared to get the hell out of this bed.

* * *

I glanced around the room, it had been tidied by the many people who had been in and out during my initial healing. I would have appreciated it, had the shame of how it looked before not made me grimace. Hardly anyone came into my home under normal circumstances. And I was too busy or tired or uncaring to do more than pick up enough of my laundry to have it washed. I dug around in the closet until I found something suitable, an old shirt and pants set I hadn't worn in years. Nothing beautiful, but comfortable, and that was fine.

Slowly padding into the kitchen, I opened one of the cabinets. One that normally sat mostly empty was now full of dishes, a matching set of four for each. I pulled down a new and colorful hand blown glass. Admiring it before I half filled it with Elia's brew, the last in the vessel. *I'll have to go visit her, see if I can persuade her to make me some more.* The relief was near instantaneous, and I closed my eyes as muscles loosened and the aching ebbed. *That female really is a miracle worker.*

I took in the other changes Ke had made. There were fresh cut flowers in an ornate vase on the island, wisteria blossoms. The kitchen faucet had been replaced with one that did not sputter when I rinsed the glass. A new plush rug ran in front of the sink, patterned in a way to imitate thick moss. Everything was *clean*. I never considered myself a particularly dirty person, but now that everything has been scrubbed down, it shone in a way I hadn't known it could.

On the counter was a trio of wooden bowls in varying

184

sizes, full of produce. I grabbed a peach from the smallest one, appraising it before I sunk my teeth into the soft flesh. An involuntary groan vibrated in my throat as the sweetness of the juice coated my tongue. I had been fed all manner of hearty soups and stews during my bed rest but nothing compared to the simple joy of our local fruits.

"Do I need to leave you two alone?" An amused voice from behind me. I whipped around, startled at the sound.

Keelan was leaning against the kitchen doorway, smirking, hands stuffed in his pockets.

"You're here," I mumbled around the bite, and swallowed, "I thought you'd be out for the day."

"Your council members decided to postpone their meeting, so I thought I'd check on you. It's good to see you up and about." He crossed the kitchen in a few short steps, stopping so close to me the shadows at his shoulders tickled my cheek. Then grabbed a pear for himself from the bowl and retreated, leaning against the island.

"What have those busybodies got you doing these days?" I asked, trying to ignore the pounding in my chest at his proximity.

He assessed the pear in his hand, not yet taking a bite, "Mostly just inquiring about your condition, and bugging me to work out my wings so I can take over your patrols." He took a bite and tucked into his cheek before he continued, gesturing to me with the fruit, "You made yourself such an asset to their peace of mind here that they are desperate to get someone back into the skies."

I scoffed, taking another bite and chewing it while I considered, "They want you to take over my patrols?"

"They want *you* to start doing patrols again but I keep

telling them you're still healing. I mean Mother above, they saw your condition when you got back but they are so frantic." He released a heavy sigh, "I don't know how you dealt with these people on your own. Especially the Nymph, he's always acting like there's a crisis and he's the only one in the world who knows how to fix it."

I smiled at him while he shook his head, frustration lining his forehead. "They've always been that way, but they also basically raised me after my parents disappeared. I guess I'm used to it."

Ke looked me over, "They also want to know if you'll be fit to attend the Spring equinox tomorrow."

*Another equinox? Had I truly been gone that long?*

"Yes," I groaned. "I'll be there. Mother above I can't believe it's already nearly spring."

"Not a fan?" He was smirking now.

"Even when I'm not proving to everyone that I'm still alive, it's just a big show. Dress pretty, act demure, strong and detached, yet soft and caring. It's an exhausting ordeal. But I need to be there."

"I don't think when I was young we even came down from the mountains for Equinox, we celebrated in our own city."

I watched for any sign of emotion as he spoke, but he gave nothing away, "I don't remember any of that." I admitted softly, eyes trained on the half eaten peach, "What was it like?"

"Mostly stealing liquor from our parents," He laughed. "But there were always fires and a big relay race around the mountains. The females would build this giant flowered effigy of the Mother in the center of town and the musicians would play all night while we danced." His eyes glazed, lost in the memory.

"It sounds beautiful." I whispered, that ever present ache of what I lost tightening in my chest as I said it.

He shook his head and looked at me again, taking another bite of the pear, "So what? You've just been doing this forever?"

"You saw the state of my house," I half laughed as I gestured around, "My life for the last two hundred years has been flying over the forests by day and charming the locals by night. I don't even know what I would do with my time if it were any different."

"Well," Ke started, tossing the core of his pear into the trash, "I look forward to seeing you in action."

"I'll warn you, we are going to get some looks when I start walking around with a tall, dark, and handsome piece of eye candy on my arm." I winked at him playfully, taking another bite of my own fruit.

He placed a hand over his heart, bowing dramatically, "That is a sacrifice that I am willing to make." And his grin was wide and genuine.

# 37

# Astriel

The next morning, when I stumbled out of the bedroom wearing only another giant shirt, Ke was already in the kitchen making breakfast. Even though he must have heard me yawning and flat-footing it on the hardwood, he did not turn.

His attention was fixed on whatever he was heating in the pan. But my gaze fell to his bare back. It was the first time I had the opportunity to really see him, wings and all. His back, which had been strong and muscled since I'd met him, now appeared nearly Olympian in its definition. The urge to reach across the room and run my fingers over every bulging inch and feather nearly overtook me.

"Astriel, you're awake. Breakfast is almost ready." Ke chirped, turning towards me and grinning. I let my eyes linger a little longer in the place where his naked torso disappeared into the waistline of his pants before clearing my throat and heaving myself into one of the bar stools. Keelan's evident amusement made it clear that he did not fail to notice my staring.

I pushed away the urge to cross that boundary we hadn't even discussed, "It smells good, what are you making?"

He slid a plate across the island towards me, a veggie omelet with a smiley face made of tomatoes gracing the surface, "Oh wow, and here I was thinking you only knew how to make stew... Fancy." I smirked at him, raising an eyebrow.

He turned fully towards me, leaning against the counter and dramatically resting the spatula across his shoulder like a mighty sword, "Astriel, you will come to learn that I am a male of many talents."

I had hated that cocky smile when I met him, and found it revolting when he wore it. Now, it made butterflies dance in my chest. Everything about him radiated a cool confidence. And now that we were back in Phaedra, he released the ever present tension he wore like armor. His movements were loose and fluid and he wore some level of a smile almost constantly.

"You're undressing me with your eyes again." His amused voice cut through my thoughts, "And your omelet is getting cold." My face warmed and I cut my eyes back to my plate, picking up the fork.

"What are you thinking about?" He asked, head tipping to the side.

"You just seem happy, and relaxed. I don't know if I've ever seen you actually happy." I speared a piece of egg, resting my cheek on my propped up fist as I chewed.

"It's easy to be happy here. Even when I have to deal with your bossy council." He laughed, "The people here are full of life and so at peace, they just *live*. I hadn't seen that in... ages."

\* \* \*

As morning passed and the sun started its descent to the horizon, I hauled myself out of my reading chair. Bookmarking the page and resting it on the pile of other books I had read too many times to count. Ke had gone to the garment district in search of an outfit for himself that he would deem appropriate for the celebration tonight. I had been dreading getting ready, busying myself with anything I could to take my mind off the impending obligation.

The mood did not lighten as I dug through my closet, inspecting all the many gowns I had acquired, and yet finding nothing that felt right. My months of wearing casual color left the sea of white fabric bland and uninteresting. I had just covered my bed in all manner of white silk, organza, and chiffon and Ke walked in. Eyes wide as he surveyed the leaning stacks of dresses.

"What happened in here?"

I just looked over at him, shoulders slumped and face distraught. "I have no idea what I am going to wear tonight."

He stepped over to the bed, running his fingers over the piles of fine fabrics, appraising them. "They are all white."

"I know." I had forgotten, he's never seen this part of me. "It's part of my public image the council groomed me for when I was young. You said the humans called me 'Death on Angel's Wings' but here, I just have to play the part of angel." I clarified, smiling weakly, forehead still creased while I glared down at the pile.

"Do you like it?"

"It's tradition. I don't mind, I just don't know which one

of these is good for tonight. Jarrah is sending her girl over with a flower crown so it's got to match."

"What kind of flowers?"

"Ivory gardenias, what else?" I rolled my eyes.

"Do I need to wear a particular color?" Ke looked momentarily concerned.

"If you let them start picking your clothes they'll never stop." I looked him up and down. "Whatever you're having made will be suitable. Remember, for everyone else it's just a party." I gave him an encouraging smile, and then turned my attention back to the stack.

Keelan grunted some sort of confirmation and walked out of the room. So, I continued my search for *anything* that would be deemed appropriate for my 'grand return' in the council's eyes. Down the hall I heard the front door open and close. Keelan striking off on another errand.

\* \* \*

I settled on a strapless gown that was more lace than fabric. Patterned with a sheer mass of lace roses, it was woven tighter to be made more opaque around my chest and at the pinnacle of my thighs. It did not fit as it would have before losing so much weight and muscle. Though it fell looser than it was designed to, my assets were still displayed beautifully beneath the flowy wrappings. It was the perfect combination of ethereal and sensual. And despite the fact that it was yet another white dress, it was still beautiful.

I donned all my usual silver jewelry after I dressed. Studs

and dangles and connecting chains decorating every spot in my pierced ears. Around my neck, I hung a delicate chain with a large drop pendant, the center bezel containing a feathery green stone.

*Seraphinite*, a gift from my mother on my 10th birthday. The stone of our people. I fought the painful memory and the heavy emotions that clouded my thoughts. *Mother above I wish I had more of that elixir.*

Once my hair was tamed into a braid down my back, I finally settled a viney diadem that the flower crown would be secured upon and slipped on a pair of delicate leather sandals. *The same sandals from the last equinox.*

I tried not to let the realization further sour my mood. But my chest still beat an uneven rhythm, my breathing coming in short pants. I took a deep breath, willing the unease to pass, and appraised myself in the mirror. Though a nagging feeling of dread settled in my gut. I did my best to ignore it as I swiped on a rosy lip tint. These events had always been a nerve wracking burden, but now, being back after so much time away, knowing the kind of reception would be waiting for me, my chest fluttered with nerves.

Just as I was entering the main room, fixing a silver cuff in the shape of a snake around my bicep, Keelan strode through the threshold.

He stopped short as our eyes met, hand grasping the knob of the still open door. He wore an entirely onyx black ensemble, the collar of his shirt open. He had pulled his hair back into a bun, curly strays framing his face. It was a far cry from anything I had seen the past few weeks. The lines of his body accentuated in the perfectly tailored garments. In his free hand he held a white box with gold engraving.

"You look incredible." He said, breath hitching.

"So do you." I responded in like, my heart thundering beneath my ribs as I took him in.

"Oh uhh, Clovis caught me on my way up the walk, this is for you." He cleared his throat and held out the white box, finally closing the door behind him.

I took it, but couldn't force myself to look away from him. In the dim light his eyes were dark. Not in the sinister way they had been when I first met him in the forest, but shadowed and heady. My wing feathers rustled under his penetrating stare. A warmth bloomed in my chest as I found the strength to finally turn away. Crossing the living room, I set the box on a chest of drawers in front of a mirror and opened it.

Inside was a beautiful crown of fresh cut gardenias, the smell intoxicating as it wafted out of the box. Keelan stayed unmoving in the threshold as I pulled it out and delicately positioned it on my head. My eyes kept flicking to his reflection as I struggled to adjust it so that the hidden hooks of the diadem would secure it atop my head.

"Here, let me." He said, striding over.

I turned to him, looking through my white lashes as he gingerly arranged the woven stems into place. This close, I could feel his warmth, and that familiar scent of oak moss and cedar wrapped around my senses. Intoxicating in its own right, I breathed deeply and felt that nugget of dread loosen its grip. He backed away a step, assessing his work, and then dropped his eyes back to mine.

I said nothing as his hand raised again, tucking a loose strand of hair behind my ear, his thumb lightly brushing over my cheek. I leaned into his touch, eyes closing for just a moment. When I opened them again he was still staring.

"Perfect." He breathed, and reluctantly dropped his hand.

I straightened, and smiled up at him, mind still foggy. "Are you ready for this?" I asked, though something in my core screamed against it. A warm urge to tackle him right there on the rug and forgo this night entirely. I had a suspicion that if I suggested it he would not object.

He nodded and presented his elbow for me to take, "It would be my honor to escort you."

# 38

# Astriel

We meandered down the street, arm in arm, and in uneasy silence. I kept my eyes on the cobbles ahead of us, trying desperately to keep my shoulders loose despite the pain and swirling anxieties that crept in now that I was out of Elia's elixir. I did not want Ke to worry.

We had gone several blocks before he broke the silence, "Is something bothering you?" He asked, not looking down at me, just keeping his gaze ahead.

"I'm fine, just taking in the peace before we get into the frenzy." It wasn't a complete lie.

"Aren't you excited to see your friends?"

"Friends?" I huffed a laugh, "Elia will be working at the tavern, and... yeah no that's not..." I blushed at the realization that I couldn't finish that sentence, that I never had true friends that would have been at these events.

He stayed silent for a long moment, our footfalls, the only discernible sound on the abandoned street. I tried not to squirm, tried not to let him sense my trepidation. I had done this hundreds of times, gone to these events, rubbed elbows and smiled until my cheeks hurt. But I couldn't shake the unease that sent my heart racing. This should be easy, this should be familiar, but I could barely breathe.

"Is your loneliness by design or circumstance?" Ke suddenly asked and I gawked at him, stopping in place.

"I am not lonely." I broke his hold and took a step back.

"I'm not trying to be a dick, I just-" He sighed, "El, from what you've told me and what I've gathered, you spent two centuries not engaging with this city at all outside of necessity."

"Because I don't *need* anyone. Like you said, *necessity*." I sneered at him, and started walking again, picking up the pace. I could hear his footsteps gaining on me as I turned into a side street.

"El. El, stop it." I ignored him until his hand wrapped around my elbow and turned me, "Astriel stop."

"Why does it matter to you so much? Who I keep company with? Worried about who I'll be meeting?"

He scoffed, "Astriel, I'm just trying to understand you. I mean we've spent enough time together, we are bonded for fuck's sake and you still hold me at arm's length."

"We are *binded*." I spit at him, yanking my arm out of his grip. Deliana's voice weaseling its way into my mind, not for the first time. *'You are not the first doe eyed girl he's taken to bed to get what he wants, and you certainly won't be the last.'* "I don't know what misguided sense of duty you've placed on me but it is wasted. We are out of that castle, you are free of me."

"I don't want to be free of you." He reached out a hand, his face softening. I took a step back. My breath came in short pants, panic I couldn't control overtaking my senses.

196

"Then what do you want from me?" My voice pitched up.

"I just want you, Astriel." I rolled my eyes, deflecting from the pained sincerity in his voice. "I'm trying to figure out why, even though we— even after everything we've been through, you won't let me in. The last few weeks have been nothing more than small talk, I don't understand why all of a sudden you won't let me get close to you. I want to know why you don't let *anyone* close to you."

"Oh I let plenty of people close to me," I turned my face hard. "As a matter of fact, there are some people who *will* be excited to see me. I actually have an equinox tradition with a few of the males that will be there. So it might serve you to make yourself scarce tonight."

As the venomous words left my lips, a flash of hurt crossed Keelan's face. And in the same instant, a heavy stone of regret settled in my gut. But I had already gone too far, the words struck with deadly intent.

"You don't mean that." He shook his head, "But, if that is what you want then consider it done." He plunged his hands in his pockets before crossing in front of me and taking off into the dark sky.

I fought the prickling of tears that burned my eyes. I deserved this. He felt obligated to me by circumstance and I enabled it with my passive flirting and undeniable ache for him. I should have squashed it before anything started. Even though it's going to hurt him now, it's for the best.

I leaned against the wall behind me, not caring if it marred the pristine white of my gown. This whole persona was a lie. I was not perfect or angelic or anything to aspire to. I was a black hole that good things fall into. Better that Keelan knows it now.

# 39

# Keelan

I shouldn't have pushed her, but I didn't know how to get her to open up. *Wrong method apparently.* Whether it was just the stress of this holiday or something else I couldn't see didn't really matter, something was wrong, even before I set her off. In the castle she told me I was what she wanted, I knew I wasn't imagining those lingering looks or the heat in her face when we teased each other. She could act like I meant nothing to her but I wouldn't let it run me off. I had plans for tonight that I had to finish preparing for, and I needed to see them through.

I would give her some space to cool down, and then I would go to her again. But I didn't know when that would be, and the idea of her going to bed with another male made my blood boil. If it's what she wants, then fine, I'll go to a tavern and rack up a tab until I forget about it. But it's not. When we had been together it was beyond anything else I had ever felt before, I felt the bond that night, I know she did too. I know that I couldn't imagine bedding another female, surely she felt the same way.

I caught an updraft and coasted on it while the thoughts roiled through me. There's no telling if she would even come to the celebration now. She might just turn around and go home. I would go to her if she did. I would show her exactly what our bond means and how she can't just cast me out because closeness is a foreign concept.

*Misguided sense of duty.* Mother above surely she is not that blind. The thought made my skin bristle. I could see the trees and fires growing as I flew closer, and I resolved myself to calm down as I descended upon them. No matter what happened tonight, I would show her that she cannot scare me away with cruel words, no matter how they stung.

* * *

When I landed, the party was already in full swing. As I stalked towards a refreshments table I noted the many looks I got. Some venturing towards near fright at the other fae took in the scope of my dark wings and the shadows that accompanied them. I imagine that I looked quite frightening compared to what these folk were used to. Even in my youth it was uncommon for Seraphim to venture to the capital. I'm sure many of the residents have never seen a dark winged fae. Their standard is Astriel, a blinding light compared to my darkness.

I reached a table, grabbing a flute of champagne, swirling it while I unconsciously searched for Astriel in the crowds. I couldn't see her. *I shouldn't have left her alone on the street.* Anything could happen without my being there to escort her, what if she fell and was hurt, or what if she tried to fly and her wings gave out— no. I just beat her here, that is all. I'd be telling myself that until I was laid eyes on her.

I edged closer to one of the large fires, facing away from it as I spread my wings, enjoying the warmth that contrasted the unseasonably crisp evening. I sipped from the glass, the sweetness warming my chest as I swallowed. I looked down at it, wondering what secret effect it would have. It was certainly enchanted.

I kept my head on a swivel, most of the people here wore muted earth tones, her white would stand out like a beacon. *By design of that horrid Nymph lord no doubt.* How she continued to bend to the will of that council was beyond me. Maybe they planted the seed that she needed to be alone. Maybe they insinuated that a lone pillar of hope is all she could be. If so, it was bullshit. Given the chance, I would tell them that much.

Most likely she just never knew any different. In the mountains I knew what it was like to be othered. Shadow wielders were uncommon, and often seen as a bad omen among st the elders. Even though Seraphim wings came in a variety of colors, black was nearly as rare as white, and had been unheard of for generations. It's hard to create a circle when you are so unlike all of your peers.

I looked around at all the different types of fae that wandered the space, some with insect-like wings, a few, bat-like and leathery, but most of them were without wings entirely. Of course she must have felt like an outsider, there is no one here that is anything like her. *There is no one else in the world that is anything like her,* I mused.

Maybe that's the real reason why she doesn't want to be

seen with me now that we are back. I would shadow her glow. She is heaven incarnate. So what did that make me? A devil? She would be right to think that. She knows what I was forced to do during my time at the castle, things I chose to do. She wouldn't be remiss to run from my darkness.

But she let me stay with her, let me hold her in moments of weakness. I could almost smell her piney and floral scent. From the moment I saw her it wrapped around me like a noose, even when I couldn't act on it.

\* \* \*

The party goers gave me a wide berth when they passed me, not braving the refreshment table I lounged by. I realized it was likely because a grimace had been contorting my face as I stood there brooding. *Not a great first impression, Ke.*

I was just about to drain my drink and grab another before stalking off into the shadows when someone approached me.

"You're new." She said matter of factly, her azure eyes glowing in the firelight as she looked up at me.

"I am." Was all I grunted in response, looking her over. She was a water sprite by the looks of it, soft features and a petite frame. Her dark hair cascaded over her shoulders like a wave, crashing at her hips. Her dark blue shimmery dress cut clear down to her navel.

"Well that explains why you're over here all by yourself. I'm Marina."

"Keelan." I did not have the energy for this, I needed to

find El.

"I've never seen anyone carry darkness the way you do," her eyes glinted as they ran over my shoulders, following the wisps that curled thicker around my chest and wings in response to her scrutinizing stare. "All the males here are such do-gooders, it's nice to meet someone who has a little grit to them."

I cut my eyes over her. Her chest and cheeks were flushed, and her breathing heavy. I fought the urge to roll my eyes. "What makes you think that I'm that?"

"I mean look at you, literally shrouded in darkness. Standing alone and looking pissed. Are you trying to tell me you aren't that?"

I just shrugged and looked back over the crowd. My heart jumped when I spotted Astriel in the distance. Her wings were tucked tightly to her back as different people approached her, talking emphatically and taking her hand before wandering off. I could tell even from a distance her dress was dirty, and her face was red.

"Are you like our Lady of the Skies?" Marina asked, not deterred.

"Something like that." I responded, eyes still focused on her, she had drained three drinks already. And I could see the tight grin plastered to her face as she addressed everyone who spoke to her. A well built male held her hand for longer than necessary and my jaw tensed. She did not look at me.

"Everyone thinks she hung the moon. But really she's just a drunk bitch." Marina spat, following my gaze.

I finished my champagne and set the glass on the table to my left crossing my arms. "Is that how you speak of the one who protects your very way of life?" My voice was tight as I turned to the sprite, eyes hard.

Her breathing quickened, "She disappeared for six months after our last equinox, and who's to say if she actually does anything. She comes to these events, smiles and drinks and tells everyone what they want to hear. But she doesn't actually want to be like us. She thinks she's better because she's got some crazy bloodline. Like that makes a difference."

She rolled her eyes, "A lot of males want to take her home just because she's different. She does it too, keeps them drooling after her just for the satisfaction of it."

I sneered at her, "You would be wise to watch the way you talk about her around me, you have no idea what she has sacrificed for this place."

Marina bristled, a viciousness edging her voice, "I've heard she's not even a good fuck," her hand found and rested on my folded forearm as her voice lowered, "I could get her off your mind, save you the trouble."

I took a step back from her, anger heating my blood. I locked eyes on her, speaking low and even. "That's my *mate* you're bitching about. So I'll say it again. Watch the way you talk about her around me."

Her face paled and her mouth hung open like she considered saying something else and thought better of it. She turned on a heel and scurried off to the other side of the fire. I shook off the feeling of her touch. I shouldn't have said it, El and I hadn't discussed... anything about us. She would be upset if she caught wind of it, that I was making bold declarations on her behalf.

Looking for Astriel across the field once again. Her eyes locked on mine for just a moment before finishing yet another drink and turning back to her people. Not a glimpse of emotion in the brief look. But it wouldn't deter me. Let her simmer, there are things I need to take care of anyways.

I would be back for her.

# 40

# Astriel

Keelan was across the field, camped out at a drink table and chatting up a girl I had met a few times. She was beautiful, it was no wonder he would like her. My chest tightened, and I drained another flute. I had driven him away. I made that choice. I had no right to be upset about it.

I felt his stare the moment I arrived, after walking several more blocks in the dark. The back of my dress was lightly stained from where I tried to keep myself from collapsing against a wall. And I could feel my face was still puffy from crying. I hoped to everyone else it looked like a consequence of drinking, and it soon would be.

I tried to keep myself from looking at him, the mere sight of him triggering a pang of remorse that clenched in my chest. I said such awful things that I didn't even mean, and to what end? *He doesn't deserve that.* I instead turned my focus on the many people approaching to offer their well wishes and inquire about where I had been. I would just tell them I had been in the human realm, not caring to share the gruesome details. But when their eyes ran over the fresh scars, I could see the horror in their faces. Thankfully, none of them asked.

I don't know how many drinks I had tossed back before Silva approached, a wide grin taking over his face.

"Welcome home Astriel. I trust you are doing well."

"Silva, it's so good to see you again. I'm doing much better now. Still sore of course." I flexed my wings to demonstrate their tightness and reluctance to spread.

"Does that mean you'll be resting after the festivities? Or would you like some company?" His half smile was hopeful, and I knew what he was asking. But despite my quick words with Ke, the thought of actually acting on that habit with Silva made my stomach flip.

"I'm sorry Silva, I'll be exhausted by the time this night is over."

He nodded, disappointment coloring his features before he schooled it back into that easy, lopsided grin, "I understand. You know where to find me if you change your mind."

I smiled weakly at him, "That I do."

He nodded a shallow bow and disappeared back through the crowd. My shoulders were aching already. Even though I had a brief respite from the onslaught of well-wishers, I knew it would be temporary. They would be coming and going all night, eager for me to ease their minds.

*I could always just leave.* I showed my face, surely people would understand if I didn't have the energy to be here all night. I needed to talk to the council, see what they thought. I surveyed the field, but I didn't see any of them. They were probably huddled up in some building discussing one of the many things I wasn't to be privy to.

Okay, so then I would give it another few minutes and then disappear, I could handle that. I grabbed at another drink off the table, which was now littered with empty glasses. I couldn't bring myself to count them or care. I looked around again, Keelan and the sprite girl were gone. *Probably off together.* I drained my drink, and started walking.

I didn't necessarily have a destination in mind, but I figured it would be a better look if I as least appeared to be mingling. I camped out too close to one of the central fires, savoring the passive burn that made my skin tingle. The people milling about would smile if we locked eyes, but most seemed to be content wrapped up in their own lives. I watched as couples paired off and spoke closely, their faces inching closer together, tentative hands finding solace in each other.

"You're going to catch yourself on fire standing this close." A gravelly voice from behind me cut though my contemplation, oak moss and cedar invading my nostrils.

"I thought you would be off with your new friend." I responded, not turning, trying and failing to sound unbothered.

"El, can we please talk?"

"So you can accuse me of being cold and distant and lonely again? I don't particularly have an interest in that." I responded, turning my head to look at Keelan over my shoulder.

He wore a tight smile. "I won't say a thing about it. I just want to show you something."

"Show me what?" I asked, eyebrow raised.

"It's a surprise, but we will have to fly."

"Keelan I can't fly." I scoffed, turning back to the fire.

"I'll carry you. Please, let me show you this." His voice was tinged with hopeful desperation, I softened at the sound.

I studied him over my shoulder for a long moment,

knowing this would be a bad idea. "Fine, but we have to get away from everyone first."

He was smiling, "Of course, my lady. Follow me."

\* \* \*

We took off from a clearing hidden from the general party goers, far enough away that hopefully any prying eyes wouldn't be able to tell exactly what they were seeing. Being cradled in a male's arms wouldn't exactly project strength. Despite my frustration and bid for distance from him, the feeling of his body pressed against mine melted my resolve.

We flew away from the tree, and past the city proper, and over Keelan's shoulder I watched the lights of the still lit buildings fade into a cluster of glittering dots. The air as we climbed higher turned frigid, biting into my exposed skin. I shivered, and Keelan's grip tightened on my waist and legs, his warmth leaching into me.

"Where are we going?" I finally asked, looking up at his face, a mask of concentration.

"Into the mountains." He responded, eyes trained on the terrain ahead of us.

I waited for him to continue, but he didn't, so I settled my head against his chest, breathing in his heat. "I wish I had at least brought at drink."

His laughter rumbled through his chest. I couldn't help but smile. "We are almost there." He whispered into my ear, tickling my neck.

He climbed again as we approached the nearest mountain,

soaring over the foliage as we shot into the sky. I leaned my head back, savoring the brisk air tearing past my face, a sensation I hadn't felt in months.

Keelan suddenly dove hard, sending my stomach into my throat. I squeaked involuntarily and wrapped my arms around his neck, my eyes shut tight. An entirely different sensation than diving when I'm the one flying. The lack of control set my nerves on edge.

"It's okay, we are about to land." He whispered, amusement evident in his voice.

# 41

# Astriel

Ke was smiling wide when my shaking legs were once again planted in solid ground. He had dropped us on a stone outcropping on the side of Mount Rynn, the tallest of the three peaks at the northernmost edge of Phaedra. The only illumination of the cliff was a large half moon and the glittering stars, casting a soft glow over the mountainside forest. I knew that this mountain would have been the one the Seraphim township resided on, but we were not near it, as far as I could tell.

"What are we doing here?" I asked, wandering to the cliff's edge, gazing over the darkened forest rapidly descending below.

"I wanted you to have a taste of a Seraphim Equinox." He said softly, gesturing behind him with one arm. In the center of the bare space lay a large blanket. On top of which lay two unopened bottles of champagne.

"I thought you said you kids stole liquor?" I joked, still appraising the spread, a smile pulling at my lips.

But he was beaming, "The people of the capital are squares,

only sparkling wine apparently." His eyes glittered in the starlight.

"When did you do this?" I asked, striding over to the blanket.

Ke followed a step behind, "When you were sulking at the bonfires."

"I wasn't sulking." I mumbled, and then more strongly, "What if I didn't let you bring me here? Quite a gamble, captain." I nudged him playfully with a shoulder.

"If you refused to join me, I would have come up here alone, drank both bottles, and enjoyed myself immensely. Though I would have probably had to spend the night up here." He chuckled, throwing himself on the blanket, leaning back on his hands. "The last time I tried to fly after drinking too much I woke up in a phoenix nest wearing nothing but my underwear."

"How in the world did you pull that off?" I couldn't stop the wild laugh that escaped my lips.

"Wish I could tell you." he grinned, his eyes following me as I lowered myself onto the blanket, "But I don't remember, probably just some run of the mill young male theatrics. I think I remember there being a dare involved."

I shook my head, picturing a youthful Keelan causing trouble for no reason other than being young. Even as the thought quirked up the corners of my mouth, I couldn't help the pang in my chest that he had been pulled from it. Or selfishly, that I never got to experience it.

"So what is this place?" I asked, shaking off the feeling and once again gazing out at the barren space, "Some sort of lovers' lookout?"

He feigned hurt, "You think me so cliché? Surely you know

I'm more creative than that."

I laughed despite myself, "Then where exactly are we, Ke?"

He shifted, looking past the cliff edge, "I used to come here when I was young and needed to be alone. My dad was a hard male, and when I disappointed him, which I often did, this is where I would go to get away from him." His tone changed, less playful, but not exactly somber. Like the facts carried an emotional weight with them.

"Did he die in the war?" I asked before I could stop myself.

"No. He was cut down in a petty duel with a male he accused of cheating him on meat prices." Keelan responded, a bitterness edging his tone.

"I'm sorry." Was all I could think to say.

"Don't be," He smiled again, "tonight is about enjoying the beautiful things of the Seraphim. Now relax, the show is about to begin."

I tucked my knees to my chest, watching Ke as he smirked and grabbed one of the bottles, popping the cork with the thumb of one hand before handing it over to me. I took it and pulled a long swig, savoring the renewed warmth that blossomed in my chest.

When my arm dropped, I noticed Keelan staring at me, "What?" I asked, suddenly self conscious.

"I'm just appreciating you." He said, voice thick.

"For drinking?"

"For being."

My cheeks heated, and I forced myself to look away, back into the sky. Unsure how to respond, I simply said, "The stars are beautiful from up here."

"Do you ever come here? To the mountain, I mean." I heard him pop the cork of his own bottle, and take a long drink.

I shook my head, "This mountain always felt haunted. And because I didn't know what happened to the people that were here, I didn't know what kinds of ghosts would remain. I was always too scared of what I would find." As I said it, wind whispered through the trees, as if confirming those fears.

I took a shaking breath, shuddering against the chill and brought my chin down, turning to face Ke. He leaned back on an elbow, the champagne bottle in his other hand propped up on his hip. His always intense stare was painfully piercing. It took all of my willpower to not shy away from the fierce gaze.

He shook his head and took another pull from the bottle, swallowing, his eyes again found mine. "I cannot imagine how hard it must have been growing up without—" he made a sound of disgust, "You lost so much."

"You were ripped from it," I sighed, "*that* is pain. I never knew what was lost. This is the only life I've known. Before I met you I didn't even know that outside of vague memories of my family, that there were other Seraphim."

"They shouldn't have kept it from you."

"What would that have done? It fucked me up enough to think I was miraculously the only survivor of my immediate family. Telling a kid they survived their entire people only because they were hidden away at some boarding school would have been worse."

I bit my lip, fiddling with the hem of my dress before taking a long drink from my bottle. "There would have been no way for me to make it out without some weird damage," I bit out a tight laugh and threw myself backwards, laying flat on the blanket, wings sprawling. "It was an impossible situation, I don't blame anyone for how they handled it."

"I wish I could have been here, so you would at least know you weren't completely alone." He looked down at me.

"You were in the castle, living your own nightmares. You were more alone than I was. You really and truly thought you were *alone*, the last of your kind."

He finally heaved himself over and lay on his back next to me, interlocking his fingers over his stomach. I felt the tips of our wings lightly brush together at the proximity, and suppressed a shiver.

"That's not wholly true. When reports started coming in, years after I had lost hope, about a demon in the woods," I heard him smile, "something in me knew that somehow, someone had made it out. And when they described you..." he trailed off.

"I fought beside your father. And all of us loved your mother fiercely." He looked at me, silently inquiring whether he should continue. I nodded, even though I was unsure if I wanted to hear what he intended to share. He nodded back and faced the sky.

"They were as close as we had to royalty. We revered your family as community leaders. I don't know what you remember, but your father was the general of our army. A great male who was absolutely fatal on the battlefield, but not bloodthirsty. He always tried to mediate before he permitted duels or battles or any level of violence.

"Your mother was a teacher, a healer, and a confidante for anyone who needed her. And she was so loved for her boundless care. Your sisters were much the same. Your family line was the lifeblood of our way of life."

When he turned his head to me, I was staring at him, silently begging him to continue. No one ever talked about

214

my family, my memory of them fleeting I didn't even know what to ask. Keelan had known them, had respected them. A foreign emotion boiled beneath my skin.

He continued, "Seraphim carried wings of every color, often corresponding with their affinities. Your father's were a rich ochre, indicative of his abilities on the battlefield. Your mothers were a sage green so light they almost looked gray, the color of healers. All of your sisters carried wings of canary yellow. I can't remember what that affinity was, but we just saw them as joy personified."

My breath was quickening as he spoke. I thought back to my nightmares, and the memories I thought I had of them. I only ever saw them with white wings and eyes like mine. I wondered if any memories I had of them were genuine, or if I had invented them all.

His voice changed went he went on, "I remember when word spread of their youngest. A little girl with eyes like clusters of stars, hair like spun moonlight, and wings of unfathomable white. It was unheard of, the last white winged Seraphim was rumored to have been the immediate descendants of the angels themselves.

"You were sent off to that school at five years old if I recall. None of us knew why, and especially no one was explaining to me, just another rowdy kid. Looking back though, part of me thinks they knew that something horrible would happen and wanted to keep you from it.

"All of this is to say, when I heard stories of Agrona, of *Death on Angel's Wings,* I knew it had to be you. And when I was ordered to go and *retrieve* you, I considered every possibility to fail, or to stop it, or simply to leave. But I was such a coward. And when I saw you, strong and beautiful and so fiercely protective, it was like something that had broken all those years ago snapped back into place."

His chest shuddered a heavy breath, "Astriel, knowing you were out there somewhere was the only thing that kept me breathing some nights."

He kept his eyes trained on the endless space above us, but I could see the moisture welling in his eyes. He blinked it away.

I opened my mouth to speak, not knowing what I was going to say but wanting to comfort him, when his eyes cleared and he raised a finger to the sky.

"Look, it's happening. This is why I brought you here."

When my eyes turned skyward, I audibly gasped. The darkness above us had erupted into ribbons of multicolored light. They moved and wriggled like fish swimming upstream, and the colors shifted before my eyes. They looked fluid, suspended rivers that could drip those colors upon the land.

"What are they?" I whispered, incredulous, and I stood, unable to tear my eyes away from them. I felt I could reach up and run my fingers through them, and wear the cosmic colors upon my skin.

"Auroras. They only appear on Solstices and equinoxes. On the mountaintop, when the celebrations started winding down, we would extinguish all of our fires and sit in darkness, *this* is the soul of a Seraphim equinox."

"I've never seen them before."

"You can't see them from the capital. Our oral history tells us that this was a gift from the heavens for us alone. A beacon that we are the chosen people of The Mother. I doubt anyone in the capital even knows they exist.

Something that ached in my chest for my entire life seemed

216

to ease as I watched the sky dance. I felt that if I listened close enough I could hear the song they moved to. I wanted to be a part of them, to move with them, to hear what they were trying to tell me that was just out of earshot.

Keelan was suddenly next to me, his chest rising and falling rapidly with his heavy breathing. His rough grip pushed down at my shoulder, "Careful, El. Come back to me."

The spell broke just enough that I could turn my attention to him. My wings had spread as if I were about to take flight, the tension in my shoulders suggesting that if he hadn't stopped me, I would have leapt off the cliff without even thinking. I relaxed them, taking a deep breath. I felt high, the blood in my veins vibrating like a swarm of bees had found their way beneath my skin. It was *euphoric.*

# 42

# Keelan

I was nervous that the turn in conversation would ruin our evening, but as soon as the sky flared with the aurora, I knew I'd made the right choice in bringing her here. She was spellbound by the flow of colors, and any other night I would have been too. But I couldn't tear my eyes from her.

I mirrored her movements as she stood, and followed her to the edge of the overhang. The kaleidoscope of hues glinted off her moonstone eyes. Even her hair seemed to absorb the colors, like they belonged to her alone.

I watched as her body tensed, like given the chance she would take flight and disappear into them. When I clapped a hand on her shoulder, and she turned to me, the aurora above looked like it responded to her. The bands appearing to dip closer, almost as if they wanted to touch her as much as she wanted to touch them.

When her wild eyes met mine, they were clear but distant. She was looking at me, but she was still seeing the aurora. The feathers of her wings reflected a pastel hue of the many colors overhead, the urge to touch them threatened to overtake me. But I would not steal this moment from her. True joy sparkled in her eyes, and I wanted to watch the feeling bathe her features for as long as she would let me.

And then, in the tight breath of a single moment, the lights in the sky winked away.

"Where did they go?" Astriel pulled away from me, frantically searching the skies.

"They only last for a short time." I choked out, but my eyes ran over her tensed form, the air squeezed from my lungs. "In the sky at least."

She turned to me quizzically, before she noticed herself. Her very skin swam with residual glowing colors. I couldn't help but feel like she had absorbed some of the heavens themselves, like she was made of the same stuff as they were. She produced her own light, a faint rippling of liquid rainbows.

"What is happening?" She asked, more in awe than fear.

"I— I don't know. I've never seen—" All I could do was shake my head, mouth agape and hands outstretched.

The phantom glow slowly faded, and we were once again only illuminated by the moon and stars.

"I could hear them." She said suddenly, her eyes, once again swirling in shimmering silver, tore into me.

"Hear what?" I asked but I still scanned her, searching for remnants of what we had both seen in her skin.

"The lights. The auroras, they sang. I couldn't understand them but if I was able to get closer I would have been able to, I know it."

I felt the blood drain from my face as my eyes found hers again, "They... sang to you?"

She nodded, "You couldn't hear them?"

219

I shook my head slowly, trying to piece together what she was telling me. "I think we need to go back."

# 43

# Keelan

I dropped El off at the house, forgetting about the festivities in the center of the city. I was only able to urge her to keep the singing auroras to herself, not to tell anyone. My mind was a flurry of information I only half remembered and needed to confirm.

She did not fight me as I ushered her inside and made for a quick escape. During the flight home she had slipped in and out of lucidity, alternating rapidly between whispering to herself and studying me. I wanted to believe it was just the vast amount of drink she consumed that night, but I knew better. Perhaps it *had* been a mistake to take her to the mountain.

When I shut the front door, I could still hear her mumbling something about a song of the heavens. I needed to be quick, so I could get back and keep an eye on her. I didn't understand this mental fever, even though I had my suspicions. I needed to get to the library.

I flew across town, the streets were deserted with everyone at the tree side celebration. I only hoped someone there would be working. As I closed in on the massive stone structure, domed at the top in intricate stained glass, I breathed a sigh of relief. There were lights on, someone would be inside.

My feet had barely connected with the pavement when I pushed through the stained glass door. A mousy female behind the main desk started at my intrusion. I stalked up to her as she sat upright, closing the novel she had been absorbed in.

"Sir, is everything alright?" The librarian asked, holding her body tense.

"I'm sorry if I scared you," I offered, running a hand through my windblown hair, "I'm in a hurry. Do you know of any books about Seraphim history? Stories of origin or cosmic legend? Powers of the originals?"

She maintained eye contact but I could see her gaze was not focused on me. She had retreated inside her mind, no doubt flipping through her mental files of what this building contained. I watched her, resisting the urge to impatiently tap my fingers on the wooden surface of the desk.

Her eyebrows suddenly jumped and she shot up from her seat, "Follow me." She beckoned with one hand. She led me to a set of stairs behind a plain wooden door at the back of the main room.

"The capital collected many books that survived the attack on the Seraphim all those years ago; they never got shelved on the main floors." She said as her wooden soles clacked against the stone staircase.

"Why not?" I asked absently, eager to just get down here and find what I'm looking for.

"I was supposed to, but some of these texts... it felt like

looting to just *claim* them as ours." She shivered as she said it, and I nodded.

The further we spiraled down, the darker and dustier it got. Whatever lay at the base of these stairs hadn't been visited in a very long time. The stairwell began to open up as we reached the bottom, revealing a squatty room piled with crates and crooked shelves. Ancient looking books stacked in every corner.

"This was all they could save, I'm told. Hopefully it'll contain what you're looking for."

"Would you mind helping me look?" I tore my eyes from the forgotten collection. Looking directly at the librarian, who had relaxed and now carried herself with an easy confidence.

"Of course." She said, and started digging in one of the nearest crates.

"I never caught your name." I mused as I fingered through the spines on a shelf by the stairs.

"Moira."

"Keelan." I responded in like.

She paused her rummaging. "You're the male who brought Astriel home."

"Mhmm." I pulled down a book that looked promising.

"Are these for her?" She asked, and I could feel her stare on my back.

I carefully considered how much to share, "Yes. She has been so desperate to reconnect with our culture." Not a complete lie, but certainly not the truth.

"Is she okay? Moira asked, turning back to her search.

"As okay as she can be." I breathed, not looking at her.

It was silent for a long moment, both of us unsure how

to proceed, only the sound of shuffling books between us. "She's always been different." Moira stated simply, and I paused my search, a defensiveness budding in my gut. But she continued, "She's perceptive. More so than she will admit, even to herself."

I calmed, and focused on the books in front of me again, "That she is." I wasn't sure what she was getting at, and I was tentative to offer too much.

"Well," Moira cleared her throat, perhaps sensing my unease, "I found a few to get you started. I know you're in a hurry, and I can keep looking for next time you come by." When I looked back at her, she wore a soft smile, and held four thick leather bound books in her arms.

I collected the two that I had found, and smiled tightly back at her. We climbed the stairs again, Moira leading the way. I shut the door to the basement and followed the librarian to her desk. She took the dusty books out of my arms, her fingers brushing my hand as she did.

Something flicked across her eyes and her easy smile faltered for just a moment. I studied her as she wrapped the stack together in brown paper and then secured them with twine, but she had returned to the easygoing and bubbly librarian, the hint of whatever troubled her gone.

"It'll be easier to fly with them like this." She said, handing me the bundle.

I watched her, searching for any indication of that curious feeling in her features. But it was long gone, she just looked at me, no emotion beyond polite professionalism on her face. She was small, thin boned and lacking any substantial musculature. Just a librarian, certainly not a threat, I reasoned with myself. Even as that familiar wariness tickled at the back of mind. I shoved it away.

"Thank you, I'll come by again when I'm done. I appreciate the help, truly."

She nodded and her eyes sparkled, "Hey, tell Astriel to come by when she feels up to it. I've been saving recommendations for her while she's been gone."

I couldn't help myself, I smiled back, "I'll be sure to let her know." And as my hand rested on the doorknob and started to turn, I looked back at her one more time. She glanced at me over her book, a mischievous grin on her face. She winked, and a stirring in my chest hinted to the fact that she knew more about Astriel, and more about what I was doing here than she let on.

\* \* \*

The sight that I beheld upon reentering El's home was beyond words. Her dress was draped over the back of the couch, one shoe by the door and the other kicked down the hall. She wore one of my shirts, hiking up around her thighs as she sat cross legged on the floor in front of the coffee table.

She had pulled off her diadem and flower crown, which were both now haphazardly being worn by the glass shade of her reading lamp. Her white hair stuck out in all directions. On the table in front of her was a scattering of papers she frantically sketched on. More papers had been pinned to the wall, charcoal illustrations of constellations and the auroras.

I hadn't been gone long, she must have started as soon as I left. She did not look up as I entered, so absorbed in her work she didn't hear me.

"El, what is all this?" I asked carefully, setting the bundle of books on the floor next to the door, slipping off my shoes and undoing another button of my shirt.

She looked up, her charcoal pausing in mid air. "Ke, you're home." She smiled, but her silver eyes were clouded and distant. Something flashed across them.

I crossed the room and settled on the couch, picking up one of the papers. "What are you drawing?" I asked softly. Smudged geometric diagrams littered the page, utterly indecipherable.

She ran her charcoal darkened hands down her front and through her hair, leaving black streaks in their wake. "The stars." She said simply, "The Aurora showed me. Math of the heavens."

She gestured to the wall behind me, standing. "Look. You can see the music in them." She strode over, pointing at a page of dots connected with straight lines. She stabbed at it with a finger. "They are connected, like the strings of a harp, we could play their song. We used to know the way they sing."

I gaped at her, "Astriel, I think you need to get some sleep. I don't—" I lost my voice as her eyes locked on mine, glittering in the dim light.

She crossed the room, putting her hands on my shoulders as she stopped in front of me, pushing me back onto the couch. She lowered herself, knees resting on either side of my lap. Her head tipped to the side as she settled. Her loose hair cascaded over her shoulders in messy curls. She ran her hands down my chest, but her eyes were locked on mine.

"Astriel," I breathed, my heart was thundering, "You're

drunk." I kept my hands planted firmly on the cushions.

She shook her head, "No." Her voice was thick, "I am awakened. You showed me something I couldn't even imagine tonight. You fill gaps in my mind and soul I hadn't known existed. And you keep doing it no matter how much grief I cause you."

I moved my hands to her hips, to lift her off of me. "El, let's go lay down and get some rest." That crazed look still whirled in her eyes, but they were clearer now. Her hands clapped over mine, leaving charcoal fingerprints where they rested, holding us together, the shirt riding higher so that I touched her bare skin. Her hips shifted, pressing against me. A groan rumbled in my throat against my will, and a smile pulled at her lips.

"I can hear your song too, Ke. The space between stars call to you."

I cocked an eyebrow, trying to stay focused with her this close to me, her scent invading my senses, our breath mingling. "What are you talking about?"

Her hands left mine where they rested and reached past my face, her soft fingertips grazing the arch of my wings. I shivered, and her smile widened. "I don't know anything about shadow wielders, and I don't know much about your life at all. But when the sky sings for you it is soft, and mournful."

Her eyes were unfocused again, and I watched as my shadows reached towards her, wrapping around her arms. I felt her breath catch and her body tense as they brushed past her face, weaving into her hair. They thickened the air around her. She tipped her head further into them as her smile faltered, like the mist was whispering in her ear. "They

227

came to you as a child, you were alone."

"Astriel, please." I didn't know what I was begging her for, but my voice cracked. Pain bloomed in my chest as her eyes glazed, welling up at the waterline, unfocused. I searched her face, but as the wisps continued to thicken, she seemed to retreat further and further away. I grabbed her face, dispersing the shadows.

"Come back to me." I whispered.

Her eyes locked on mine again, a tear breaking away and running down her cheek and wetting my palm. "Keelan, I—" she shook her head but didn't break the contact, her own hands falling into her lap.

I shushed her, and wrapped my arms around her waist, pulling her into me. "I'm okay." I whispered as a sob racked her body. I didn't know what the shadows told her, what they shared without my permission. But it was bad, I knew that much.

"You won't ever be alone again." She mumbled into my chest. And I pulled her in tighter, pressing my lips against her forehead. I closed my eyes, breathing in her windblown scent. There were no words, nothing I could say to ease her pain.

So I just held her, praying that it was enough.

# 44

# Astriel

I was in my bed, alone. My head throbbing painfully to an uneven beat. I knew Ke stayed with me last night, that he let me curl into his chest and held me as the cosmic grip sent shock waves through my mind. I couldn't hear the heavens today, the aurora's spell having broken while I slept. I was grateful, it felt like a mania, a fever that boiled my blood and that I couldn't escape from. Even though at the time, it felt like freedom, like true clarity, I knew it couldn't be.

I groaned as I pulled myself to the edge of the bed, everything ached. But there was some satisfaction in the knowledge that it was an ache from hunching over the coffee table, or tensing in Ke's arms while he flew, or sleeping wrong, and not the ache of yet another devastating injury. It was a normal ache, I could have smiled about that fact.

I padded down the hall, still wearing on of Ke's shirts, not sure where exactly I had gotten it. I averted my gaze from the collections of drawings still pinned to the walls as I walked, doing my best to avoid the reminders of what I had become last night. But I knew they were there, the mental images of them burning behind my eyes. A silent call that they would not be ignored.

I turned into the kitchen, taking a deep breath as the crude sketches finally disappeared from my periphery. Why Ke hadn't taken them down, I couldn't say. He must have been as alarmed by my frenzy as I was, though he did not voice it. I groaned internally at the thought of how it all looked.

He sat at the island, bent over a book, with several others laid open, taking over the entirety of the surface. His wings drooped, grazing the wood floor. I crept quietly up behind him. Though he didn't immediately notice me, his shadows stirred at my presence.

"What are you doing?" I asked, my voice hoarse for some reason I didn't know. He turned to me, purple smudges coloring the space beneath his tired eyes. He hadn't slept.

"You're awake." He said, trying to sound cheerful, "Do you still… hear anything?"

"All quiet." I responded, rubbing my temples.

"There's coffee on the stove, it should still be hot." He gestured, but his eyes scanned over me. Searching for something. I pretended not to notice. Instead, I crossed the kitchen, pouring myself a mug of still steaming coffee from the percolator.

"You never answered me, what are you doing?" I asked again, savoring the scent of the spiced drink as I leaned on the counter.

"I went to the library last night. Moira says 'hi' by the way. She said she's been collecting recommendations for you."

"Moira!" My eyebrows shot to my hairline, kicking off another jolt of pounding in my head. I winced, but excitement overtook the pain, "Oh Mother above I need to go see her." I was giddy thinking about it, we had spent many late evenings together discussing books. The library being the only other place in Phaedra I visited with any regularity, by choice at least.

"See Keelan, I do have at least one friend in this city outside of Elia." I smiled into my coffee, savoring the chocolate and cinnamon he had brewed into it.

A tired grin graced his features in response, seeming pleased by the information. He pushed his mug to me, "You're making that look too good. Would you mind pouring me another cup?"

I nodded, setting down my own mug and snatching his up and filling it, setting the now empty percolator in the sink. I walked around the island and handed it to him. Leaning over his shoulder, I surveyed the open pages of the book he had been so enraptured by. I skimmed the passages, stories of ancient heroes and the battles they won. I rested one hand on the counter, swatting away his shadows that snaked across the air towards me, not ready for any more revelations they cared to share, if I could still hear them.

If Ke noticed, he didn't say anything, and instead took a long swig of his coffee and rubbed his eyes. "I'd heard stories from the elders about ancient Seraphim with the ability to commune with the celestials," he started, his voice tired and heavy, "I was hoping to find more information after what happened to you last night."

I winced, and averted his gaze, planting my eyes entirely on the book. I only had a vague recollection of what I had said last night, and in the morning light it made almost no sense to me. I probably looked mad to him, a drunk fae who had lost her mind after a night in the mountains. His careful tone told me everything that I needed to know, that he thought I might still be fragile from it, on the precipice of another episode.

"Find anything good?" I managed to ask, trying to keep my voice level.

I didn't want to betray how terrifying it had been, how past the beautiful songs, screaming and crying had penetrated that veil of terrific joy. I didn't want him to see in my eyes the darkness that swirled from the secrets his shadows spilled, the horrors of his childhood by the hands of his father, the all encompassing *grief* that gripped at him. I had heard it, seen it, and felt it all. I shook away the memory.

"Nothing yet, mostly just creation stories, some prophecies passed down from the originals that don't pertain to what I'm searching for." He rubbed his eyes again.

"Maybe you should get some sleep." I ventured, resting a hand on his shoulder, ignoring the swirling shadows that begged me to lend them my ear again.

"Maybe so," he said, slumping further, his forearms pressed into the counter top. "But you— are you okay?"

I offered him a weak smile, "I'm perfectly fine, just worried about you."

It wasn't quite true, I was reeling, but he didn't need to know that. His eyes ran over me again, brows furrowed. "If you want to talk about it—"

"Do *you* want to talk about it?" I cut him off a bit harshly. "It's not just the aurora we would be getting into." I pulled away, shaking off the almost tangible grip of his misty companions.

His eyes darkened, grim understanding lining his face. But

he said nothing, just pulling his mouth into a tight line. When he looked back down at the book, a tinge of regret pulled at my chest.

"Ke, I'm sorry. I didn't mean— that came out wrong."

"No, you're right," He slammed the book shut, "maybe I'll get more information out of you the next time it happens. Maybe the next time you start talking to the stars they will actually have something to say that's worth hearing."

I recoiled against the verbal jab, taking a steadying breath before responding. "There won't be a next time."

I didn't believe it. But I refused to accept the person I would become if this kept happening, if I couldn't control it. How would I be able to take to the skies again, watch the forests, if I crumble into a babbling lunatic without warning? I would suppress it, push it down and down until whatever channel I had opened snapped shut. And I would *never* return to the mountains for a solstice. I was right to avoid that place for all these years.

Ke looked at me, his anger waning and sadness replacing it in his eyes. "There will be." He hauled himself out of the chair, disappearing down the hall. I heard the front door open and shut.

I fell into his spot, burying my face in my hands, unable to stop the tears that spilled over. On some level I knew I would never escape this, I would never be able to just *be*. I would always have some curse or obligation I didn't understand following me. There would always be a heaviness that dragged me and everyone I dared care about down.

I had suppressed every feeling I had about the voices for years, for centuries. But the floodgates were opening now. Those thick barriers I had spent my entire life building were crumbling after the aurora. I knew the core of that truth, there was no escape. There never would be.

In my youth I thought the whispering I would sometimes hear in the far reaches of my mind were just that, just my own mind, my own grief, trying to sink me. They were still there, even now as I tried to lock them up, deep into my subconscious. But I had dealt with it. Alone. I could deal with it alone.

But I also knew that no matter how far I ran from myself, they would always be there.

# 45

# Astriel

Without thinking I found myself at Elia's tavern, and though it was bustling, she stilled when she laid eyes on me, concern lacing her features. At some point I had dressed, instinct taking over, I had mindlessly thrown on my working clothes. As I slid into a vacant seat at the bar, Elia strode over. Instead of the usual overfilled glass of wine, she pushed a short glass of clear liquid to me.

I didn't meet her eyes as I drained the glass. Even with all her skill, her enchantments couldn't conceal the sharp burn of the liquor. I only absently noted an earthy bitterness in the taste. But the warmth that filled my chest immediately quieted my mind.

"What's wrong?" She asked quietly, filling a mug with a frothy mead for another patron. It was only midday. Before, this would have been early for even me to be slumped over this bar.

I shrugged, "Same as always." She understood enough without having to pry, and replaced my glass with another, filled with the same biting drink.

I drained it again, resisting the urge to hide my face in my hands. I could feel the other patrons watching me. I straightened, even now I couldn't bring myself to show my weakness to them. Though I'm sure they sensed it.

I glanced around, this place was the same as I remembered it, dimly lit and loud with chatter. I narrowed my eyes at the many people who glanced my way. Most found something more interesting to stare at as our eyes met. Their nosiness was overpowered by their respect, or fear, or the grim emotion I was sure was written all over my face. I tried to ignore them, gesturing to Elia for another drink.

"How is your healing, Astriel?" Elia asked as she brought another drink, giving me a sidelong glance as I sucked it down without waiting, grimacing at the taste.

"I still hurt, and I'm not allowed to fly. Your brew helped immensely I must say." She wandered off, tending to other patrons, and then returned. "Could you make me some more?" I asked tentatively, trying not to seem too desperate. Her drink didn't only keep away pain and nightmares, but they also silenced the incessant noise inside my mind.

She shook her head, and lowered herself so only I could hear her quiet voice. "I'm afraid I cannot, my lady. It is not a daily drink like I serve here, I don't make it unless it is truly needed. It can be quite addictive."

I nodded, trying not to let the disappointment color my face, "I understand." *I'll try again later.*

Her eyes lingered on me, seeing more than I'd like her too. Years in the tavern gave her an almost uncanny ability to read between the lines, to hear the unspoken in her patrons. It was a skill that I appreciated almost as much as I resented.

"Where is your shadow wielder?" She asked suddenly, eyes

236

still trained on me.

I gaped at her, of course she had heard of him, or maybe he came here. "Running around." I said simply, not breaking her gaze.

I didn't know where he had gone, where he even would go. She made a noise I couldn't decipher the meaning of before walking off. I studied my empty glass, watching the warped reflection of me widen and lengthen, until she returned with a fresh one, and a tall glass of what I assumed was water. I cut her a look, and she just smiled knowingly before continuing with her work.

* * *

I didn't know how long I had been there, or how much I drank. But Elia, to her credit, asked no more questions, just replenished my glasses when they were empty and ushered off other guests if they tried to impose on my solitude. I would have to do something for her, some indication of my appreciation. The water glass still sat untouched on the bar.

I was just about to crumble into sweet oblivion when a guest found the seat next to me. Elia was at the other end of the bar, facing off with a Dryad who had become too rowdy, too busy to have noticed this one sneaking into my space. I couldn't will myself to look up from the bar to face whoever was disturbing my peace.

"Not in the mood." I slurred. I didn't have the mind to care how I looked or sounded anymore.

A glass slid across the bar, I reached for it, but another

hand snatched it up first. "Oh, I'm just here to enjoy a hard earned drink."

I looked up, the world spinning at the sudden movement. "Keelan, what are you doing here?" I was confused, and irritated. This was supposed to be *mine*, the one place I could go without having to be something for someone. His swirling mist branched out over the bar top.

"Elia sent her courier to find me, she figured you would need help getting home." He took a sip of the drink that was meant for me, "She was right, of course. You look like shit."

"Fuck off." I said, pushing myself off from the bar. He had no right to hunt me down here. Elia had no right to summon him. I had almost made it to the door when the ground seemed to jump up at me. A strong pair of hands grabbed my shoulders before I collided with the dirty floor.

"Alright El, come on. It's time to go home." I couldn't focus on his face, I couldn't focus on anything. Everything blurred and swirled together, and I couldn't make my arms work to push him off. So I just accepted his guiding hands as he pushed us out into the street.

"No flying." I blurted as the chill early morning spring air cut through my clothes. I was already feeling sick, I couldn't fathom being airborne right now.

"Obviously." Keelan quipped and I could almost hear him rolling his eyes.

# 46

# Keelan

She was nearly too drunk to stand, her boots dragging against the cobblestones as I half carried her down the abandoned streets. Her eyes were unfocused, clouded. I had seen her drink, and drink a lot, but I couldn't have imagined the sight when I entered that bar. Her wings so slumped they rested on the dirty floor of the tavern, the tips tinged brown with dirt. Her whole demeanor was different, an Astriel I had never seen before, a shell of herself.

When I returned to the house after taking a walk to cool my temper, she was gone. No note, no indication of where she was off to. I had waited on the couch for hours, running over what I would say to her, how I would apologize for snapping at her like that. I was beginning to doze off against my will when a knock sounded at the door long after nightfall, I lunged for it.

When I beheld a boy with a note, my heart fell. I read it, written in the fine script of the tavern owner I had met once before. My anxiety spiked. I should have known she would have run off. I could see it in her, that she was more rocked by the visions than she let on. I should have pushed her on it. I should have made her quit running.

I looked down at her, feet scraping and swaying. She was breathing heavily and kept shaking her head, eyes glued to the ground in front of her. "So, why all the drinking?" I asked.

"Doesn't matter." she hiccuped, stumbling. I scooped her into my arms, it would be easier to carry her than drag her all the way home. "Quit doing that. Someone will see."

I looked down at her, loose-limbed and petulant, staring at her own hand. Mother above she must have drank the whole bar. "Do you always drink like that?" She rested her head on my shoulder, eyes shut tightly.

"Used to." She groaned.

I kept walking, letting her adjust to the sway of my gait, silently praying she wouldn't ruin my shoes. When we turned down another street, further away from the few others making their own inebriated treks home, I finally asked, "Why?"

She opened her eyes to me, red rimmed and glassy. She waved off my shadows that started to slither around her arms. "Easier to make mind quiet, gets too loud."

"The heavens? You can still hear them?"

She shook her head and squinted her eyes closed again, "Mostly not the sky. Even as a child the whispers followed."

I sucked breath, and turned another corner. "Why didn't you say anything?" My chest tightened, I had known she wasn't being completely honest, but I couldn't have known she had been struggling with this for so long.

"I can deal," She groaned, tipping her head back over my

arm, "Agrona is not weak. Forest Demon is not weak. Astriel: Phaedra's beacon of hope cannot be weak." Her arm swung back and forth with every statement.

"The Forest Demon is currently slung over my arm like a potato sack." I tried to joke, despite the gravity of her words threatening to rip me off my feet.

I felt her body jolt as she huffed a laugh, "Not the most compromising position you've put me in, if you'll recall."

I felt my cheeks flush, and I squeezed my fingers into her ribs, making her squeal. When I looked down, she was staring up at me, a sadness swimming in her eyes even as she tried to force a smile. "Reach into my back pocket." I said forcing myself to turn my gaze forward, and not get lost in her glimmering eyes.

"So direct these days, Ke."

I shook my head, a grin pulling at my lips, "Dirty mind." I leaned down to whisper in her ear, her shiver elicited from my breath being more satisfying than I'd like to admit. "Elia gave me something to help sober you up. It's in the right pocket."

She reached back, her fingers grazing the skin where my shirt had ridden up, and brushing against my feathers as she found the pocket. I raised my arm as she pulled hers back through, surveying the murky liquid swirling in the vial. "What is it?"

"Do you ever actually know what she makes for you? Just drink it."

She popped the cork and threw it back, "Oh that's terrible." She winced, tucking the empty bottle into my breast pocket.

"Hair of the dog." I chuckled at her.

She rested her head against my shoulder again. We were

on her street, almost home.

"Why do you sleep on the couch?" She asked, her voice already clearer.

"I don't want to make any assumptions." I said softly. Admittedly, the couch was terrible, and I woke up every day with a new pinched muscle because of it. But we had never discussed it so, save for the night of the aurora, that's where I went.

"You don't have to. You can sleep with me... If you want. My bed is more comfortable at least."

I kicked open the garden gate and strode up the walkway without responding. When we were at her doorstep, I set her down. She was still wobbly but not necessarily at risk of falling over herself anymore. I looked down at her, she was wringing her hands. I couldn't tell if it was because she had offered something she didn't want to give or if she was nervous about my response.

"El, you don't owe me anything." I said carefully, staring at her down turned face.

"Do you wish it were different?" She blurted, looking away, kicking at the door frame with her boot.

"Wish what was different?"

"This. Us. I know I'm not the easiest person to... care about." She paused, a shuddering breath rocking her chest. "If we had met under different circumstances, if we weren't thrust together the way we were, do you think you would still have wanted me?"

Something cracked in my chest as I grabbed her face between my hands, "Astriel." She looked up at me, her eyes swimming, "I would have loved to court you traditionally.

I would have followed you around like a lovesick puppy." I smiled softly.

"Ke, you don't have to-"

"No. I mean it. I am sorry that we were pushed together like we were. I hate that a lot of choice was taken away from both of us. But I would have found you in any version of this life." I was shaking, I hoped she couldn't feel it.

I needed her to understand that she *wasn't* an obligation, that even when she drove me crazy I still craved her. "El, I have loved you fiercely from the moment you pinned me in that sparring ring. Binding or no binding, bond or no, I would still love you if you carved my heart out with a knife."

I searched Astriel's face, holding my breath. I might have said too much. I might have scared her. She didn't want something like this.

I wanted to tell her how I felt for months, but it was never the right time. I wanted to tell her when we made it back to Phaedra. I wanted to tell her on that mountain. I almost told her every morning when I first laid eyes on her. I was tired of *almost*, and *wanting*.

But there would never be the right time. We would forever be in crisis. Whatever happened I would deal with it. If she ran I would wait for her. I would wait a lifetime for her.

I opened my mouth to speak again, but then her lips were on mine.

# 47

# Astriel

I couldn't resist it anymore, all the fighting and running and pretending I didn't care was useless. Every time I tried to run him off he leaned in harder. No one had ever pushed me like he does, even though it made me want to throttle him most of the time. He was reliable, and sturdy. Someone I could actually lean on, who let me lean on them.

He had saved me more times than I could count. Not just from the dangers we found ourselves thrust into. He saved me from myself. He had been willing to sacrifice his wings for me. Not for some sense of duty or atonement, but for *me*.

I threw my arms around his neck, pressing my chest into him. We were still on the stoop but I didn't care if anyone saw. I couldn't focus on anything other than him. He froze, not moving for a long moment as I fell into him.

And then he wrapped an arm around my waist, the other grappling with the door handle. He didn't break our kiss as we stumbled inside. The door had barely shut when Ke slammed me into it. His hand cradled the back of my head as he collided into me.

I tore at his clothes as his free hand snaked beneath my shirt, his rough hand sliding over my breast. I moaned into his mouth, fire erupting in my core as he growled. His hands left me and gripped the back of my thighs, hoisting me up. My legs wrapped around his waist, careful of his wings.

He carried me down the hall, our mouths locked together in a feverish embrace. My hands roamed his body. Unlike last time, now, he had wings. Wings that would heighten every sensation. I intended to use them.

I rested an arm on his shoulder and gently stoked the curve of his wing, running my fingers through his feathers. He made a deep, guttural sound and I felt him stagger. He pinned me to the wall just short of the bedroom when he broke our kiss. I looked up at him as innocently as I could with the lust I knew was written all over my face.

"You are playing a very dangerous game." He panted, eyes dark. He ground his hips into me so that I could feel exactly the effect I had on him.

"I have no idea what you're talking about." I whispered, scraping my nail down his shoulder and up the muscle where his wing erupted from his back.

He threw his head back, groaning, his hardness pressing against me with more force. I gasped at the friction. "You are evil." He snarled, bringing his face down to my throat. His teeth clamped on the connection of my neck and shoulder. I cried out, my fingers digging into his back. By the time I regained my senses, I was being tossed on the bed.

Keelan stood to the side of me, pulling off his shirt. "Are you still drunk?" He asked, voice thick.

I shook my head, breathing hard, "Not even a little bit."

Even if I was, I wouldn't be able to tell, my heading was spinning and my muscles weak for a different reason now.

He smiled wickedly and climbed on top of me, his bare chest rippling with the movement. My mouth was dry. I reached up to touch him, and he pushed my hand away. I looked up at him, incredulous.

"If you want to play games, then I can play games." He whispered, and then sat back on his heels. His arms wrapped around me and I felt the low back of my shirt tear open. I gasped as he pulled it off of me, exposing my bare torso.

He lowered his mouth, his hot breath dancing across my flushed chest, "I'll buy you a new one."

He dropped further, wrapping his lips around the peak of my breast. His tongue flicked my nipple and I arched into him, a moan ripping from my throat. I felt his smile against my skin. My hands wound into his hair.

Rough fingers worked on getting me out of my pants. His soft lips dragged back up to my neck and I raked my nails down his back. As I felt the buttons release, I lifted my hips, and he pulled them off in one swift movement. In a flash he had ripped off my underwear.

"I'll replace those too." He leaned back in his position between my knees, his eyes raking over me. "Mother above I've missed this." He whispered mostly to himself.

I reached towards him, I needed to feel him, his weight on me. He leaned forward, but before my hands connected with his strong chest, one hand wrapped around both of my wrists and pinned them above my head. I whimpered, arching my chest towards him, but he raised up.

"I've had enough of you driving me wild without any consequences." His voice rumbled, and it set my heart thundering.

His other hand came up, brushing the arch of my wing. Goosebumps covered my body and I arched again, he dodged me. He rotated between palming my breast and grazing through my feathers. His barely there touch sent shock waves through my core. I clenched my eyes shut as he went back and forth, kissing and nipping all over. I was panting, opening my eyes to the ceiling as I tried to steady myself against the sensations.

"Let me touch you." I begged, and he just grinned in response.

Then without warning, he plunged a finger into me, and his mouth covered mine as I cried out, swallowing my scream. His wings spread around me, casting us both in shadow. He pulled away, watching my face as he pumped, driving me closer and closer to the edge.

"Keelan please. I need to feel you." He picked up the pace and the corners of my vision turned hazy. I was mumbling incoherently, trying desperately to contort my body into him but his grip held tight. Just as I approached the edge, my eyes closing as the pleasure became too much, his hand left me.

I snarled at him, my back falling into the mattress. "Son of a bitch." I choked out, blinking the haze away.

His laughter rumbled, and he finally released my wrists. Hoisting himself off the bed. I sat up on my knees, my legs shaking from the release I had been deprived from. He stood in front of me, unbuttoning his pants.

He still wore that cocky grin, "Something the matter, El?" He chuckled, breathing hard, and slipped the pants down his legs, stepping out of them, exposing his full length.

I climbed off the bed, standing in front of him. My bare

chest grazed his and my hand gripped him. A groan rumbled through his chest. I planted wet kisses across his torso, and tiptoed to nibble his neck and ear. I relished his shivering against my touch, the effect I had on him.

Planting a hand on his chest I rotated around him until he was facing away from the bed. My hand was still wrapped around him, pumping gently. His eyes that never left me were glazed with lust. If he really wanted to play a game of wills I would give him a run for his money.

I shoved him and he fell backwards onto the bed. I sank to my knees, and I watched his eyes widen. I gripped him again, running my thumb over his tip. He threw his head back, cursing. I lowered my face to him, running my tongue across the underside of his length. His hands fisted the covers. And I smiled. Painfully slowly I pulled him into my mouth, deeper and deeper until my nose tapped his lower stomach. I moaned around him, the vibrations resonating through his length. He made another rumbling sound and I pulled back up, swirling my tongue.

"You are a beautiful nightmare." I heard him breathe, his husky voice making the hair on the back of my neck stand up. I sunk his substantial length into my mouth again and stayed there, flicking my tongue around him.

I came back up, sucking my cheeks in around his tip as I felt his hands on my shoulders, "Enough." He growled, and pulled me on top of him, before twisting and pressing me into the bed. "You win, El. I can't stand it anymore."

His mouth was on mine again and his hands wrapped into my hair as he plunged into me. I wrapped my arms around his neck, tangling my fingers in his hair as my head shot back. I was already so close that just the feeling of him inside of me sent ripples of pleasure up my spine. He pounded into me with a ferocity that strangled any sound that tried to escape me. I could feel him tense as he mumbled sweet and dirty words into my throat.

"You are everything, Astriel. I love you. I love you. *I love you.*" The declaration punctuated every movement and I was dangerously close to shattering beneath him.

As the pleasure sent us both over the edge, together, the words escaped me before my own fear could stop them. It came out as no more than a whisper, my lungs still deprived of oxygen, "I love you, Keelan."

And we were both consumed by oblivion.

# 48

# Keelan

It took everything in me to untangle myself from Astriel. She looked so beautiful in the mornings, a baroque painting, wings sprawled and naked form only half covered. Her soft skin nearly glittering in the early morning light. I needed to quit thinking about it or I'd fly home and wrap her around me again.

Not only had much of the tension I had been carrying been relieved by our activities, but she loved me. *She actually loved me.* Even the fact that I had a meeting with the council couldn't bring down my mood. Their tedious tasks and fears would be water off my back. Even that insipid Nymph lord couldn't dampen my refreshed state of mind. Though I knew he would try.

\* \* \*

When I swept into the meeting room, the grin that I thought

would be a new permanent addition to my face faltered. In a chair at the head of the table, surrounded by the ladies of the council, dirty, slumped, and tightly gripping a mug of tea, was Farryn. When her eyes settled on me, they were filled with fear, and something else, something I couldn't identify.

"What is going on here?" I demanded, the rest of the room turned, a collection of emotions coloring all of their faces.

"She wandered into town this evening." Jarrah chirped from her seat.

"*This* is why we need patrols in the skies." Morrelin spit, he cut a vicious look at me. I ignored him.

"Farryn, what are you doing here?" I asked, crossing my arms, my voice was hard.

The gathering of fae turned to me, "You know her." Morrelin accused, not a question, mouth agape. I nodded.

Farryn lips wobbled as she looked up at me, her hands trembling around the mug. "Deliana took control of the kingdom. I ran."

It felt like I had been punched in the jaw. *Deliana is alive.* The fact threatened to send me reeling backwards. "How?" I growled.

Farryn's gaze fell to the floor, "She bewitched him, and had them married. As soon as she was appointed queen, she slaughtered him. She is rallying forces now to invade Phaedra."

I sucked my teeth, and turned my attention from the Elf, "Astriel needs to be here. Clovis, will you fetch her?" The nervous Pixie looked to her lady, who nodded curtly. She rushed out of the room, leaving us in tense silence.

I sunk into the high backed chair, Astriel's chair, that I had occupied for every meeting, running my hands through my hair.

"She needs to be contained," Morrelin boomed across the room, making Farryn jump, her tea sloshing over the edge of the mug. "We don't know her true intentions here. Anyone from the human realm cannot be trusted."

"She is fae." Shyla spit, her webbed fingers still running down Farryn's arm. The Selkie stayed crouched next to her, clearly a comforting presence despite her uncanny appearance.

"And yet she served the crown. For all we know she could still be serving the crown." The Nymph retorted, sour face contorted into a sneer.

"Farryn," I cut in, "How did you get past the wards?" All eyes turned to me, as if suddenly remembering that I too was forced to serve the crown.

"I was sent on a task to retrieve… supplies for Deliana, in preparation for a ball she is throwing. As soon as I was able to slip the guards I ran into the forest. I didn't know where else to go." She started to cry, and Shyla turned back to her, wiping her tears with scaled fingers and whispering words of comfort.

"I don't believe her." Morrelin stated, his arms crossed. I cut him a look but said nothing.

"What were you getting for her?" I asked.

Farryn set her mug on the table, hands trembling, "Deliana is old, and has to spell herself to stay youthful, and keep her magic strong." She rolled her left sleeve, pulling it up to the shoulder, "That is why she sent you out on so many fae retrievals." She addressed me directly. She twisted her body, revealing a cross hatching of angry scars on her upper arm. Wounds that had been opened, and then barely allowed to heal, and then opened again.

"What is that?" Jarrah asked, her voice pitching up and her wings vibrating behind her, tousling her scarlet hair where it fell over her shoulders.

"The key to her power is fae blood. She needs a constant supply to maintain control." Her eyes never left mine, "She keeps the fae you caught and bleeds them until they can no longer serve her. That is one of the reasons she needed Astriel. The more powerful the fae the more potent the blood."

My face paled. I felt sick, the fate I had sent so many fae to. I had no idea. "Mother above." Was all I could bring myself to say.

"You captured fae?" Morrelin turned to me, mouth agape.

I nodded, "I told you that I was under control of the crown. I was forced to." I hadn't shared details of my time at the castle with the council. I might have if I knew that *this* is how it would come out.

"We let you in on our meetings, and you are more of a traitor to our people than anyone." The Nymph roared, the other nobility turned to gawk at me.

"I am not on trial here." My temper was flaring, "You have no idea what I sacrificed to get back here."

"Apparently, we have different definitions of sacrifice." He was seething, baring his teeth. The ladies just watched. Farryn shrunk into herself at the intensity of the exchange.

"Oh you spoiled bitter lord, if you ever left these meeting rooms you might understand the complexities of the world at large." I shot out of the chair, my wings flaring and hands planted on the table. Out of the corner of my eye I saw Shyla flinch and Jarrah was fluttering in place, like she would shoot through the ceiling if given the chance.

"How dare you speak to me like that. I have been winning wars and protecting Phaedra longer than you have been alive you traitorous, lowborn, mongrel bastar—"

"Leash yourself, Morrelin." A stern voice from behind, I spun. Astriel stood in the open doorway, her eyes narrowed.

Morrelin froze in place. An accusing finger still pointed at my heart, flickering with some sort of Nymph magic, as Astriel strode in. The sound of her heels clicking against the hardwood was the only sound in the now silent room.

When I set eyes on her, my breath caught in my throat. She was resplendent, wearing a high necked and starkly white structured gown with a narrow cape that fell between her wings. The long sleeves hid the scars of her trials, no doubt an intentional choice. It was the most modest I had ever seen her dressed.

A pillar of nobility. she had braided her hair, strands winding around her circlet. Otherwise she wore no jewelry. The understated simplicity was effective. This was not the Astriel who dressed to entice and captivate her people. This was something else entirely.

I lowered myself back in the chair, resisting the urge to bow. She was every bit a queen. *My queen.* Astriel halted next to me, the piney floral scent of her easing the tightness in my chest. Her hands clasped softly in front of her.

"It is nice to see you again, Farryn." She said simply, face unreadable, nodding at the awestruck Elf across the table.

She turned her attention to the Nymph, a vein pulsing angrily in his neck, the magic he had been ready to unleash fading as he lowered his hand. "I have weathered your tantrums and accepted your temper for far too long,

254

Morrelin. But you will be very mindful of how you speak to my *mate*."

Her voice was low and cold. I watched Morrelin's face pale, his mouth hanging open. I would have beamed if I had not been frozen in place. Her authority was palpable, holding everyone in the room in an iron grip. "

Please, sit." She spread her arms, and the lord and ladies obeyed. Even Farryn straightened under her piercing silver gaze.

It occurred to me that the council hadn't seen Astriel since the night she returned. Based on their reaction to her, they did not expect her to come back with such encompassing force. I stared up at her, enchanted by the way she glowed. But her attention was elsewhere, she surveyed the room.

Jarrah had settled back into her seat, to our right, looking more relaxed than I had ever seen her, and almost… smug. Shyla moved from her position crouched near Farryn, but still sat in the seat nearest to her, hand resting on her forearm. Morrelin was stiff backed in the chair to my left, his hands fisted at his sides, barely contained rage written all over his face. I grinned, clasping my hands in my lap.

He cut his eyes to me, "Can't fight your own battles?" his voice low. I was just about to spit something back at him when I felt Astriel lean over, planting her hands on the tabletop.

She leveled her eyes at the lord, who straightened in his chair. She let him squirm beneath her stare for a long moment before saying, in a voice like ice, "Keelan is my proxy in this council when I am indisposed. I understand that you have been the only male in this room for the last several centuries and you feel threatened." He opened his mouth to speak but she just lifted a finger to silence him, "I am back now, and you will not run this council on the basis of intimidation, even though I know you would love to. But if you take issue with Keelan, then that means you have an issue with me. So tell me Morrelin, do we have a problem?"

The Nymph stared her down, venom in his eyes, but she did not falter. His eyes blazed, but he yielded, looking down, softly shaking his head. "Good." She stated simply, and straightened. "So please, someone fill me in on what is going on here."

Shyla took over the conversation, explaining to Astriel the events of the morning. She only nodded periodically, otherwise standing still as a statue next to me. As the Selkie finished her account, and turned back to the Elf, I felt Astriel tense. "So where will Farryn stay?"

"She shouldn't be allowed to wander." Morrelin grunted. Astriel appraised him, her eyebrow raised, the closest thing to a show of emotion since she had arrived.

"We have a vacant house in our territory for traveling dignitaries in our court." Jarrah offered softly.

"Then she will stay there." Astriel said with finality, nodding appreciatively to the lady of the Pixies. "If that is all, then we will take our leave and reconvene tomorrow." The ladies nodded, and the Nymph lord opened his mouth to speak, cutting his eyes to me before thinking better of it.

She nodded and strode out the door without another word. I sprung out of my seat to follow her out, not caring how it looked to the others.

# 49

# Astriel

I felt sick. When Clovis showed up at my door and told me an Elf from the human kingdom had showed up I did not need to guess who it was. I was in a panic, and wary. I knew Morrelin would cause a scene about it.

I was quite frankly surprised he didn't demand she be immediately executed. His leadership style still held influence from the infancy of Phaedra, when the territories were still being drawn and betrayal was more common than loyalty. I suspected that the Nymph acted more savagely during those times than most. I didn't want to think about it.

Deliana was alive. We would spend the day absorbing the details of Farryn's arrival. I would have to go see her and get more details, privately, this evening. And tomorrow I would face off with Morrelin again. We would have to figure out how to proceed with preparing defenses for whatever Deliana had planned, a tricky task when lacking any class of warrior.

I'd have to find a way to get information out of the castle. My head was throbbing. There was so much to do. I needed to eat and collect myself before I decided anything.

I walked at a brisk pace away from the meeting hall, and I could feel Ke closing in on me. We were almost to the end of the street when I cut off into an alley, the tightness in my chest becoming unbearable, nausea roiling. I had to get out of sight. When I reached the end of the closed off alley I folded over, bracing a hand on the wall, my breathing coming too fast and my lungs too tight.

"What's wrong?" Keelan bent in front of me, his hands on my shoulders.

I just shook my head, I couldn't form words. I used my other hand to brace against his shoulder, worried I was going to collapse into him. My vision was clouding, tunneling into a pinprick. The world was disappearing around me. Every sound was distant and far away. I was going to pass out.

The thundering of my own heart was the only sound as I felt myself being straightened against a strong body behind me. My breath was coming in short gasps, tears pricking at my eyes. A warmth pressed hard into my chest, forcing the ragged rise and fall to slow. I would have clawed it away if my arms weren't pinned at my side. A vice squeezing me tightly. But the pressure was working, my breaths coming deeper and slower. I leaned my head back into the shoulder I knew was Keelan's, pressing my eyes tightly shut to will the tears to quit falling.

The roaring blood in my ears dimmed and my trembling limbs began to relax. I could hear a voice, but I could barely make out the words. The hand on my chest pressed harder, I had to work to fill my lungs, but it helped. "Deep breaths El, come back to me."

That familiar voice, those words that worked like a spell

when Ke spoke them. I opened my eyes and the dingy alley came back into focus. I exhaled hard though my mouth, and I felt Ke's grip loosen.

"Better?" He asked, and I nodded, my head still against his shoulder. He released me, and spun me around to him. I took in his face, his dark eyes searching me, the white scar on his face, jumping as he clenched and unclenched his jaw.

"Sorry." I coughed, still dizzy.

"Does that happen every time?" He asked, hands still gripping my shoulders tightly.

I shook my head, "Only when I have to go against Morrelin like that. Normally I can get home first, but with Deliana—" My throat tightened again and Ke pulled me into him.

"It's okay, she can't get to you now. We will figure it out. She won't touch you." I nodded into his chest, trying desperately to keep my breathing even.

"There is one thing I wanted to ask you though, about the meeting." His face was serious. He held me in outstretched arms, eyes searching mine.

"What?" I asked, breath hitching again.

"Mate, huh?" He was grinning now, an eyebrow raised. I slapped at him, a smile twitching at my lips, fear melting away. He laughed. His eyes danced and I could almost see what they were saying. *There's my girl.*

* * *

Keelan flew off to fetch a meal from a nearby cafe after dropping me off at the house. We ate as he stood across

259

from where I sat at the island. I could feel his eyes on me, and I dropped my spoon and glared at him. "What is it?" I asked folding my hands.

"I've never seen you like you were in that meeting." He studied me, swirling his spoon in his own stew, "You were so powerful, it was incredible."

I felt my cheeks heat, and I turned my attention back to my meal. "I hate being that person." I confessed.

"Why?"

"I fell into it as I came of age and that ridiculous male treated me more like a wayward child than the equal they demanded I be. Morrelin was in charge of my physical training. For a long time our relationship was more that of family than adversary. I mean, for my twentieth birthday he had a blade custom made for me, to celebrate my ascension." I shook my head, looking back up at Ke. "I don't know when that turned sour."

"And the panic attacks?"

I shrugged, "I've had them since I was a kid. I can keep them mostly under control but after the castle— well everything changed after the castle." I saw a pain in his eyes, "Don't look at me like that." I said, my voice cracking.

He set down his spoon and rounded the island, spinning my chair to face him. I opened my mouth but he just pulled me into him, resting his chin on top of my head. I wrapped my arms around him, breathing in his scent. He said nothing for a long while, just holding me.

"I have to go see Farryn today." I mumbled into his chest. "I need more information than what she was willing to share with the council."

"Are you going to be okay?" He asked, not releasing me.

"She was kind to me. And she's terrified, a familiar face might be what she needs."

"There's something off about her story." Keelan breathed, loosening his grip and stepping back, his hands still on me.

I gave him a quizzical look and he sighed, "She said she slipped the guards and that just... doesn't feel right. I'm worried about what that would mean, if she lied."

"You think she's working for Deliana?" I didn't want to believe that, but with the witch it would be wrong to dismiss any possibility.

"I never trusted Farryn, if I'm being honest."

"Is that why you ran her off at the castle?" I asked.

He nodded. "I knew she reported to Deliana, I just didn't know if it was willingly."

A thought struck me, "Did she bleed you?" I asked, not recalling any scars like Farryn's on his body.

"No." He said grimly, shaking his head. "If I had known *that* is what they were doing, I would have taken my own life before continuing to serve the crown."

Even though the confession shattered my heart, I knew it to be true.

# 50

# Astriel

I sat in a high backed chair in the house Jarrah had allocated for Farryn, positioned on the southern tip of the city. It was cute, bedecked in flowers on every surface. A Pixie's favorite way to decorate. Farryn was sitting stiffly on a plush couch, her hands folded in her lap. She had changed into Pixie clothing, a ruffled purple dress that ended at her knees, lilacs embroidered on the bodice. It didn't quite suit her long Elven limbs but she didn't seem to care.

I wore a casual linen set and my circlet. Not wanting to be perceived as aggressive with either fighting garments or my council attire. Though, Keelan wouldn't let me leave the house without a small armory of daggers strapped to every concealed place they would fit. *Overprotective busybody.*

I shifted in my seat, the shape of the chair contorting my wings uncomfortably. The hilt of daggers at my hip dug into my stomach. The Elf had suggested tea. We sat across from each other in tense silence as we drank.

She kept looking me over, like she didn't quite recognize me, which I supposed she wouldn't. I looked much better than I had in the castle. I had started filling back out with good food. And now that I could leave the house and keep myself busy, I was starting to rebuild the muscle I had lost. Even the simple exercises and stretches I had been doing in private contributed to the subtle strength that was slowly returning. A testament to how much I had lost during the ordeals.

"I'm sorry about the meeting," I started, "I would be lying if I said it wasn't always like that." I offered her a smile that she did not return.

I cleared my throat, "How are you Farryn?"

"Fine." She said flatly, a tone I had never heard from her. "Phaedra is much smaller than I thought it would be."

"It is beautiful, and rich in culture." I said slowly, gauging her odd mood. "You will enjoy your stay here."

I looked her over, her hair was still the same dry yellow it had been in the castle, but her eyes were brighter. Her sharp angles had softened, like she had been well fed. But there was something in her face I didn't recognize. I fought a shiver.

She nodded, "So the forest is the only thing separating the fae from the humans?"

I raised an eyebrow, "The forests are protected by many against the humans." Lie.

"No one found me until I stumbled into the square."

"Fae are permitted to cross." Another lie, Morrelin was right, I thought bitterly. I needed to get back into the skies.

"How is Sir Keelan?" She asked, changing the subject and reaching for her teacup on the table. She averted my gaze.

I narrowed my eyes, "Better now. Still adjusting to life outside the walls."

She nodded, taking a long drink. "And you?"

"Healed." I said simply.

"I heard you still can't fly."

I suppressed a grimace, I don't know how she would have heard that. "I can fly just fine." It was probably true, but I still hadn't attempted.

"It must be hard, Keelan regained his flight, and you lost yours."

"I can fly." I repeated.

She just stared me down for a long moment, and then said, "Tomorrow I'm going to see the tree." She took another sip of tea.

"You are to stay here for a few days, until we can assess the situation."

"So I'm a prisoner."

"No, you're just… unexpected. The council is very protective over Phaedra for obvious reasons." This conversation was not going how I planned, this isn't the Farryn I remembered.

"I'm surprised you bend to their will." She said, appraising me, "They seem more occupied with trivial concerns than the reality of what goes outside of these borders."

"Our priorities are the same. Safeguarding the way of life for the people of Phaedra remains paramount."

"And yet they do not care about you, not truly." She countered. I bristled at the unfortunate truth, "Tell me Astriel, do they have any idea the thoughts that threaten to drown you?"

"You said you slipped the guard, how did you pull that off?" I asked, pointedly ignoring her question, desperate to take back control of the conversation.

She set her cup down, eyes bearing down on me again,

"You know, you two were selfish, taking off in the middle of the night like that." My circlet awoke, humming quietly.

"Excuse me?" I gawked at her. Setting my cup on the low table between us.

"Deliana was especially cruel in the weeks after you left. She took out her anger on every fae Keelan ever brought in. They are all dead now." Her voice was flat and void of emotion.

"Keelan is not responsible for that." I snapped at her. Hands balling into fists in my lap.

"No." She agreed, standing, "It's your fault. You were their source of hope, and you failed them." A smile curled at her lips.

The words struck, hard as a physical blow. "What the fuck is wrong with you?" I barked, rising from the chair. I searched her face for the signs of Deliana's influence but I found none. Her eyes were clear, and full of anger.

"Astriel: The protector of fae." She mocked, throwing her hands in the air, "Agrona: Demon of the forest." A wicked sneer contorted her otherwise pretty face.

"If you have an issue with me, please, don't hold back." I crossed my arms.

"The only thing you do with any consistency is protect your own interest and kill the people you claim to protect. You are a disgrace." I kept my face neutral. I wouldn't let her know those words that I had told myself for so many years stung coming from another's lips. It wasn't true. It felt true, but I knew it wasn't.

"We would have died in that castle."

Farryn stalked towards me, a grin spreading across her face, "There is still time."

My circlet threatened to vibrate off my head and a flash of silver glinted in my vision.

# 51

## Keelan

I wasn't proud of it, but I followed Astriel to her meeting with Farryn. Nothing would happen, I reminded myself. And even if it did she would be fine. I had personally strapped more knives to her than perhaps strictly necessary. I hoped none of them would be necessary.

But if there was any lesson to be learned from my time at the castle, it was that acting in caution is vital. I wish she would have let me come with her. She claimed Farryn wouldn't open up if I was there. It may have been true, but I didn't have to like it.

I camped out at an outdoor table in front of a cafe across the street, sipping on a spiced coffee. Spring was fully underway, so I had shed my jacket and sunned my arms and wings in the fresh warmth. The Pixie territory was beautiful in spring, even the buildings seemed to be in bloom. Climbing roses vined across the green terracotta roof tiles. I couldn't bring myself to truly appreciate it, to tear my attention away from the house my mate had ventured into. She had been in there for over a half hour, but it was quiet.

The streets bustled around me. Pixies carrying bouquets and potted plants down the street. I watched a young Nymph haggle for a deal on produce. It may have been Pixie territory, but it seemed all manner of fae with affinities for the natural world found their home here. Now that spring was fully underway, they kept busy. Some stared, or outright sneered at my darkened presence in their color filled oasis. I did not heed them, or else I couldn't, my attention solely on the building Astriel currently resided.

I suspected that when she once again emerged, Astriel would be less than pleased to see me here. *Overprotective busybody* she had taken to calling me in the weeks since the castle. I smiled at the thought, perhaps it was true. But it was simply a call I could not ignore, to be near her, to protect her.

She could handle herself, I knew that, with no small amount of pride. But something gnawed at me. There had been a bad feeling in my gut ever since the morning's meeting. There was something off about Farryn. Even when Deliana and the king lashed out, I had never seen her become emotional about it. Her tears seemed… performative.

I scanned through my memories of her. Farryn had come to the castle with Deliana when she was appointed, her personal ladies maid. And I had my suspicions that she served the witch in more ways than she let on, but I could never be certain. And until El came to the castle, she avoided me like the plague.

When El did arrive though, Farryn found reason to cross my path near constantly. She inquired about her state, our binding, if she was as powerful as the rumors suggested. I either ignored her or lied. Even then, not willing to feed any information to the witch.

I was very near dozing off, the warmth of the sun and the smell of honeysuckle mingling with tangible relaxation when a shot of fear jolted my body upright. I looked around, nothing in the street was amiss. But I saw a curtain flutter in the window of the house Astriel and Farryn were meeting in. I watched, it fell back into place, once again concealing the home's interior.

Maybe she had seen me, and was getting ready to come out here and grab me by the balls for not trusting her. But the minutes ticked by, and the curtain did not move again. My pounding heart beat against my rib cage, but I stayed seated. Just watching, waiting for any indication that I should act.

And I watched. Even as patrons on the street dispersed, even as the sun began its descent to the horizon. I kept my attention locked on the door, on the windows, on the alley to the side. My arm where the mark lay tingled, but I would not act, not yet. *She's fine.* I chided mentally, even as anxiety pooled in my gut. If she were in trouble I would know.

# 52

# Astriel

I grabbed her arm as she swung the hidden dagger at me, her teeth were bared as she clamped her other hand on the hilt, pushing harder. I shoved her off and she stumbled backwards. Instinct taking over, I found myself launching over the couch, creating as much distance between us as I could. She positioned herself between me and the door. Her eyes turned dark, a vicious grin spreading across her face.

"What are you doing?" I panted at her.

"My queen isn't done with you yet." She growled and her features turned feral.

She lunged again and I ducked the slice of her knife, reaching for the one I had strapped to my ankle. I had just gripped the handle, yanking it free when her hand came down again. I managed to knock it away but a sharp pain erupted at my shoulder. The cut was shallow, but burned like acid where the blade had connected.

I tried to ignore it and wielded my blade at her. "Let me leave, Farryn, I don't want to kill you." I threatened, my arm already aching.

"I can't." She stated simply, twirling the blade in her hand, "I would be more afraid of you, but that heaviness you're already starting to feel is from Leru. I only needed to land one blow. You'll be on the ground in a few minutes and I'll be able to drag you out of here."

I paled. Leru: A fast acting paralytic that would leave me awake but helpless. The realization settled like a stone in my gut. I had to get out of here, and fast. I'm a warrior, even in my weakened state. It's in my blood, I can do this. *Shit.* My dominant arm was already slackening at my side.

I launched myself at the Elf. We collided with the wall near the door, knocking picture frames from where they hung. Glass shattered as we struggled, and I heard her knife clatter to the ground. She grunted as the wind was torn from her lungs and I blindly swung my dagger at her.

I heard her scream, and I stumbled away, my vision starting to spin. A long and deep wound was leaking across her chest, darkening the fabric at the front of her dress. But that crazed look still glinted in her expression. "Last chance Farryn." I choked out.

My legs were wobbling, threatening to pull me down. She shook her head and lunged again, not bothering to retrieve her blade. Eyes wide and wild as she charged. Not the haze of Deliana's influence then, but something else, a frenzy that made the Elf savage, not seeming to care if she, herself got hurt. Only focused on the brutal attack.

She closed in on me before I could move, muscles weakening, growing increasingly more sluggish. Cold fingers wrapped around my throat, squeezing with an unnatural strength. The couch behind me prevented any retreat, I was pinned, dark spots erupting in my failing vision. My hands shot forward, tightly gripping my blade. Her body collided with mine, trying to force me over the couch back as I felt the crunch of bone and hot liquid coating my arm.

Her grip on me waned and she slumped at my feet. My lungs were filling too slowly, I stared down at her. She crumpled against the carpet, a red pool spreading beneath her. I couldn't let myself stop to think, to feel anything. She still stared up at me, unseeing.

I dropped the dagger, stepping over her, my foot tangling in the ruffles of her dress. I tripped, falling to my knees, the darkness swallowing up so much of my vision. I righted myself on shaking legs and lurched forward, hands outstretched, feeling blindly for anything that could support me. I knocked a vase of flowers off an entryway table as I fell into it, I felt them crash in front of my feet as I tumbled into the wall.

My body was failing, the toxin burning its way through my blood. I just had to get out the door, someone would see me, someone would know to get help. I slid against the wall, breathing, I had to focus on my breathing. I slumped as I reached the door, extending a trembling arm. My hand slipped off the knob, the hot blood that coated my fingers, slickening my grip.

I swung the other up, using all of my remaining strength to squeeze the handle and turn. The door popped open just a crack and I shoved off the wall, colliding with the door frame and pushing it open further. I tumbled through the gap and collided with the stone steps. There was no pain, my muscles seized fully. This was as far as I could get, my body no longer responding to my commands. I stared up at the blue sky.

The light around me darkened, the spots in my vision finally spreading until everything was cast in shadow. I was about to close my eyes and accept it as a face crossed my vision. Even with the mental haze I knew who it was. *How did he get here so fast?* But my mind was muddied, thoughts crashing into each other and breaking apart.

The world tilted and I knew I was being lifted but I couldn't feel it. My eyes shot to him, he was saying something, talking to me, but it sounded far away and distorted. I wanted to speak but my throat was constricted.

"Is she dead?" I tried to ask, but I had no idea if any sound had left my throat.

He looked away from me, into the house. His lips formed a curse I couldn't hear, but when he looked back down at me, he nodded. *Thank the Mother.* My throat tightened further, "Leru. Home." I forced the air out of my lungs, praying I had made any sound at all. I watched him curse again, and then I was folded into his arms.

It was such an odd sensation, being detached from my body and still completely aware. As Keelan took to the skies, I knew the wind would have been strong and cold. I couldn't feel it, even when I cut my eyes to my limp arms folded in front of me. But it was foreign. My body wasn't mine. It was just a dead weight I was trapped in.

It would only last a couple of hours, I knew that. Keelan knew that. But when I looked up and saw his face, saw the fear, and anger that lined his features. The ringing in my ears was a deafening roar. But we were crossing the city quickly, the fading daylight casting long shadows over the city. I kept my eyes on Keelan, trying and failing to clear my throat. I would have leaned into him if I could have moved my head from where it fell into the crook of his arm.

# 53

# Astriel

As soon my body connected the bed, Keelan ripped my top open, the ringing of my ears was fading, and I heard the fabric tear. "Not hurt!" I tried to yell but it only came out as a strangled whisper.

"You are covered in blood and you can't feel your body." Keelan growled as he ran his eyes over me. "You don't even know if you're hurt. I have to check."

I rolled my eyes, "Then bath." The muscles in my throat were frozen, but he still seemed to understand the garbled sounds.

"You'll drown." He said sternly, pulling my bloodied pants off and eyeing my legs. "I told you I didn't want you going in there alone. I knew we couldn't trust Farryn." He made quick work of undoing the straps of the leather holsters he had secured to me earlier.

He walked back up the side of the bed, discarding the leathers on the floor. He scanned my face, my neck and chest. I watched as he brought his finger up and tapped the clear stone in the center of my circlet. "I don't know why you bother to wear this thing if you never listen to it." I would have clenched my fist, or batted him away if I could. His eyes dropped. "Your fingers moved, that's a good sign."

I managed to successfully swallow, "Ruining my sheets." My voice was clearer, but not quite words yet, "Bath."

Keelan sighed, and scooped me back up, hauling me into the bathing room. He set me gently against the side of the tub as he got the water running and started undressing. Even as he did, a scowl overtook his face. I lolled my head to the side and tried to raise an eyebrow at him.

He still sounded irritated. "I have to get in with you if you want to keep your head above water." A groan rumbled in my throat but kept my eyes on him. He felt the water with his fingers and shook off the drops. Then stooped before me, and my eyes followed him, even now trying not to linger on his naked form.

He untangled my circlet from my hair and set it gently on the counter, sensation was slowly returning, and I could feel the heat of his breath on my face. "We are going to start training in earnest after your wings are cleared. I'm summoning the healer tomorrow, to see if you're ready."

I groaned again as he lifted me, and settled us both in the bath, planting me in his lap, between his long and muscled thighs. "You are stronger than a crazy Elf, and you should be stronger than me," He stated, a hardness in his voice as he gently rubbed a washcloth down my torso, rinsing away the now dry, flaky blood. "You shouldn't be this easy to incapacitate."

"You should see the other guy." I choked out, but I felt Keelan snarl against my hair.

"This isn't funny Astriel. If she was using a paralytic she

wasn't trying to kill you. If she had gotten you out of the city, I don't know that I could get you back."

I started to try to speak again but he wasn't done. "If Farryn wasn't lying about Deliana raising an army, then a knife in your boot isn't going to be enough. You are Seraphim, a gifted Seraphim, and you could barely hold your own in a one on one fight."

I moved to rub away a smear of blood off my leg but only succeeded in slapping my thigh before my hand sunk back beneath the water. "Sorry." I mumbled, my head falling to my chest.

Keelan gently lifted my chin, leaning me against him, He brushed my hair back with his fingers, running the washcloth over my collarbone. I felt him tense. "Did she try to strangle you?

"A little." Actual words, the muscles of my throat starting to release.

"Your neck is bruised. Mother above, Astriel that looks terrible. Does it hurt?" His voice was soft.

"Not yet." I tried to raise my knees and sit up but my feet slid, splashing water over the side of the tub. I breathed a curse.

We sat in silence while he rubbed the washcloth over my body. I could see small bruises blooming on my arms and legs, and a particularly dark one on my ribs. They were most likely more from stumbling and falling out of the house than the actual fight.

We stayed like that for a while. I slumped against him while he scrubbed away the blood, assessing scratches and bruises, searching for anything more severe. The cut on my shoulder had already clotted, not as deep as I thought it must have been. I cursed myself silently for allowing this to happen, for being so stupid. I should have known what she meant to do well before she acted. I was smarter than this.

I felt Ke take a deep breath, and I braced myself for the inevitable. He had been right, I should have listened to him. I already knew that. I didn't need him to tell me.

But he surprised me, breaking the silence in a sad whisper. "We are binded together, El. If one of us dies we both do. You need to learn to be okay with sticking together."

I mulled over his words, and swallowed hard. "That's not true." I turned my head, my nose brushing Ke's jaw as our eyes met. My voice was hoarse, but I could speak. I needed to before I lost my nerve. "I died before, after the fight with Deliana, or almost died. I was given the choice to sever the binding. You would have lived."

The washcloth froze in place on my arm, I felt his heart rate increase. "What are you talking about?"

I sighed, trying again to sit up, Ke's hand gently pressed against my back, helping me upright. He spun me, hands on my waist until I was facing him. I leaned back against the edge of the bath, my head too heavy to support. His face was tight.

"I knew I was dying, and I was in a completely dark place. But not bad dark, just empty. There was a voice, but it wasn't really a voice." I brought a weak hand to my forehead, "I'm not explaining this right."

Ke just stared at me, holding his breath. I continued, "It told me that I wouldn't hurt, and that you would stay. It gave me a choice. I could stay, and maybe never fly again, or I could go, and I would be free. Of all of it."

"You chose to stay." Keelan said, so low I almost didn't hear it. "Why?"

I shrugged, "I had something worth staying for."

Keelan reached for me, pulling me back into him, his arms wrapped around me in a strong but gentle embrace. Instinctively, I curled into him. "You know that's still no excuse." He muttered into my hair, "I can't lose you."

I ran an unsteady finger down his jaw, tracing the shimmering white scar, looking up at him, "I can't lose you either."

He leaned down and kissed me, his lips a soft brush against mine. He only barely pulled away when he said, "Then quit almost dying."

# 54

# Astriel

"The bones are fused. Try not to crash too hard into anything but you should be able to start re-learning flight." The hard eyed healer did not smile as she delivered the news. The muscles all over my wings were tender and sore from her pinching and prodding. She eyed the fingerprint bruises on my neck, but if she was curious as to their origin, she said nothing.

I rubbed my shoulder, "So, I can start training again?" I asked her.

She looked past where I sat at the island, towards Keelan, who was leaning against the counter top by the sink with his hands in his pockets. "Only sparring. No swords. No grappling. And in two weeks I'll check back in. *Take it easy on her.*"

I suppressed a chuckle as Ke's easy smile faltered like a child being scolded. He just nodded, and straightened as the healer stood. He cut his eyes over to me, shoulders tight. I'd never seen him be intimidated by anything, and yet here he was, withering in front of one of the few people in the world who vowed to never do harm. It was poetic.

The healer nodded to me, gathered her bag and strode out of the kitchen. But not before giving Ke another stern look. She let herself out the front door and I heard Ke release a breath he must have been holding. I couldn't resist anymore, I burst into laughter. He looked down at me, face still taut, but a grin tugged at his lips.

"Big, tough Keelan, scared of a nurse fae." I bit my lip trying to stifle another laugh.

"I don't think she likes me," he chuckled as he ran his fingers through his hair, "Apparently I should have stabilized your wing before *very heroically* flying us out of the castle."

I just looked at him, shaking my head, wearing a wide smile.

\* \* \*

Sweat was beading at my brow as I balanced on one leg atop a boulder on the outcropping we had come to for the Equinox. The sun was edging closer to the horizon, and I squinted against the harsh light. My thigh burning from the exertion, slipping from where I had been instructed to keep it aloft. Keelan whacked my ankle with a long stick every time the suspended leg fell. He claimed it was a necessary drill on re-learning to balance with my wings. It was terrible.

After the healer cleared me for training, Ke took off to meet the council, filling them in on the events of the day before. Better than letting some poor Pixie housemaid run across the scene we had left in the house. He informed me that

Morrelin was, in fact, as smug as I expected him to be. He had lamented that she couldn't be trusted, and my skin crawled at the thought of admitting that to him. So Keelan took the meeting without me, a fact I would be forever grateful for.

A sharp pain erupted on my shin and I breathed a curse, glaring down at the dark fae. He had ripped the long, narrow, and sadistically flexible stick off of a nearby tree to *motivate* proper form. He held it out, still suspended, poised to deliver another strike if he decided my stance faltered. "Focus, El."

I glowered at him, and he just grinned at me. *You want to learn how to fight like a true Seraphim? This is how we train.* He had said at my first major objection. But I agreed to this small torture, ignoring his smug grin when I conceded.

Despite the fact that he was not doing any considerable training of his own, he still dressed in what he explained were traditional Seraphim fighting leathers. The connected panels stretched over his broad form, and with every move, the thick straps that buckled the ensemble together cut into the muscles on his arms and legs. They were beautiful, and artfully crafted.

"I am focused," I lied, "This is just terrible."

"You want to fly?" He asked, raising an eyebrow and brandishing that infernal stick on his shoulder, "This is how we build your strength."

I stomped the foot that I had been holding up and put my hands on my hips, tucking my aching wings back in from where they had been painfully outstretched for who knows how long. "Just throw me off the cliff and I'll figure it out." I mumbled, hopping off the rock. I was frustrated, and not just because of the tedious exercises, but because I really was *weak*.

And with him I was realizing that none of the training I had done mostly with Morrelin in my youth, and then alone as I aged was nearly as effective as it needed to be. The harsh realization sunk in that all these years I was just lucky that I only confronted humans, who were weak and often scared. If I had to fight other fae I would have been, I *was* out of my depth.

"Shouldn't we be doing some real training? You know, for when we have to deal with Deliana and her hoard again?" What I wouldn't admit is that the prospect was terrifying. She had nearly killed us both at the castle, and the more I learned where my weaknesses lay, the more petrified I became that we would fail against her. I couldn't bear the thought that we might find ourselves once again in her grips.

"We will." He responded, eyes scanning. "Baby steps, I'm supposed to be taking it easy on you, remember?" I just rolled my eyes in response.

He appraised me as I stalked up to him, pulling at my own leathers, trying to force a cool breeze beneath them. Keelan had commissioned both sets from an artisan in the capital. Both were intricately tooled, and where his were swirling patterns that overlapped, depictions of wind and water. Mine were decorated with geometric constellations. Evidently, Keelan had taken some of my frenzied drawings from the night of the Aurora to the tradesman.

He presented them to me the night before, nervously shifting from foot to foot when I tore into the brown paper they had been wrapped in. I had been wearing the same leathers for decades, not that it mattered, they had been lost in the castle. But they had been plain, made for me by the council when I took to the skies as a teenager. These, by comparison, were incredible. I sat on the bed just turning them over and running my fingers over the fine details for hours, an unbreakable smile creasing my face as I thanked Ke over and over.

And I still appreciated them, loved them even, but they were thicker than what I was used to, and still desperately needed to be broken in. The way they stuck to my sweat slicked body was suffocating. The still air around us offering nothing in the way of relief.

"Are they chafing?" Ke asked, his demeanor changing back from hard ass trainer to concerned mate.

"No," I said, dropping my hand, "they are *hot.*"

He smirked, "We can agree on that at least."

I chuckled at him, an idea blooming in my mind, a way to make the journey up here worth it. "You're not tired are you?" A suggestive question, I lowered my lashes at him.

"Not even a little bit." His breath hitched, and he tossed his stick to the side.

"Feeling strong? Feeling fast?" I asked, looking at him out of the corners of my eyes.

"Oh, absolutely." He took a step towards me, reaching out.

"Then let's cool off." I said, winking. And I took off running.

His eyes widened, "Astriel what are you— *fuck.*"

I could hear his footfalls behind me as I took off for the cliff's edge. His strength building training was exhausting, and my legs trembled as I tore across the uneven stone. What he didn't know is that I had been privately, and lightly working out my own wings. It has been over seven months since I had last taken to the skies, and I was itching for it. He would have me doing drills for another month before he felt comfortable with my trying again. Mother above, he had carried me up the mountain today to train.

Granted, I knew I wouldn't be able to climb very effectively, but I could descend, I could coast. *He's going to be pissed about this.* I thought, smiling. I steeled myself as I tore across the cliff. I wouldn't have done this if Ke wasn't here. Even if I was confident in the fact that I could catch air, being supervised was safer in the instance that I overestimated my abilities. Which was a possibility, though I hated to admit it.

I was approaching the ledge and I felt Ke gaining ground on me. I urged my tired legs faster, and spread my wings. They were fatigued, but didn't hurt anymore. I heard him yelling from behind me. My heart fluttered with anticipation, my wings trembling in excitement. My boots connected with rolling gravel and I took one last pounding step, and then I was airborne.

# 55

# Astriel

Falling. The ground fell away as wind roared past my ears. My heart beat wildly as my feet kicked against empty air. I stretched my wings further, flattening them against the wind. They caught, and my straining muscles screamed against the sudden pressure. A wide grin split my face as I leveled. I was coasting high above the descending forest below, I was flying. I heard myself release a triumphant laugh. I didn't know if I would ever get to see the world like this again. It was beautiful.

A sudden presence caught my attention. I was shrouded in shadow, and wobbled in the air as I looked up. Keelan's enormous wingspan blotted out the sky. The first time I had truly seen his wings like this, airborne, fully extended. His sprawl dwarfed my own, a breathtaking sight to behold. He looked down at me, his face unreadable in the darkness he cast. The beat of his massive wings pressed the wind down on me, and I had to beat my own in earnest to compensate.

I urged myself on, faster, savoring the burn of exertion. The cutting wind cooled my overheated skin. But a different burn was boiling in my center. I looked back up at Ke, who had dropped several feet, close enough that our wingtips grazed with each beat. I had never flown like this with anyone, other fae couldn't go this high, or this fast.

"You are insane." Keelan yelled over the wind, but he was smiling too.

"You would have caught me." I yelled back, my eyes burning with emotion and the force of the winds we flew against.

I dropped again, ducking beneath him and then rising on his other side, as close as I dared soar next to him. His eyes stayed on me, and I could see emotion swirling in them. I wanted to bank or dive or climb into the clouds, but I leashed my desire. Better to take it slow, not push my luck. Baby steps.

So we just coasted together, over the receding forest and crossing the city. The Tree of Life swelled as we grew closer, it seemed to glimmer in the dying light. Even at this height I could see the fae on the ground with their heads upturned, some pointing. I loved this. I loved Keelan for being the reason I could do this again, and for being here with me. The emotion tightened in my chest, almost to the point of pain. For the first time, maybe ever, I felt whole.

"You are magnificent." I heard him say, his voice low, almost lost in the wind.

Emotion roiled within me, my skin was on fire. I could have stayed up here all day, but already my muscles were starting to protest, and a hot need was building in my core. I looked over at Keelan, his eyes were still on me, and I watched his features darken, an animal grin spreading across his face.

Without exchanging another word, we both turned to fly home.

\* \* \*

We lay naked in bed, exhausted and sated from our events after the flight. Soreness settled into my bones from training, but the afterglow of sweeping contentment eased the discomfort. Ke was on his back, hands woven together behind his head, eyes softly closed. I curled into him, breathing in his scent, the oak moss and cedar complimented with an atmospheric smell. The scent of the sky still clinging to him.

I breathed deeply and wriggled in closer, savoring his warmth. I dozed against him, hovering in the space between sleep and wake. The steady rise and fall of his chest lulling me into a relaxation that rivaled any other. Stolen when his chest rumbled, clearing his throat, my eyes shot open.

"El, as much as I would love to lay in this bed with you for the rest of our lives, we need to figure out what to do about... everything."

I sighed, turning my eyes up to him before rolling onto my back, "What first?" I asked, staring at the ceiling.

"You need to meet with the council to discuss patrols and the events with Farryn."

"Pass. What else?" I covered my face with my hands, but I felt Keelan's eyes on me.

"We need to find a way to get information about what is going on in the castle."

"How the hell are we going to do that?" I asked, nudging him with a wing, "We aren't exactly inconspicuous." I turned to him, he was wearing a grim smile.

"I'm working on that." He said, "There is something else."

I pulled my hands away from my face, and narrowed my

eyes, "And what is that?"

He hesitated, chewing on his lip. "We need to understand what happened to you during the aurora."

I groaned and sat up, throwing my legs over the side of the bed, "Why are we still on that? I told you, it won't happen again." I reached for a shirt, but paused when I felt Ke shift on the bed, wrapping an arm around my waist.

I felt his forehead rest in the center of my back, his hair tickling the base of my wings, "You don't know that." I kept my eyes on the floor in front of me. "El, you exploded into a ball of light and then *died* at the castle. You said that you've always been followed by whispers. You witnessed one cosmic event and were turned into a babbling maniac covered in charcoal."

I turned to him, eyes hard, "Okay," He conceded, "Not a maniac. But Astriel, if something like that happened during a battle? Or in flight, or even in a council meeting, it could be catastrophic."

"What is there even to do about it?" My eyes searched his.

"I don't know." He fell back into the bed, his hands raking down his face, "Start at the library I guess."

# 56

# Astriel

The morning sun warmed my wings and shoulders as I stood in front of the heavy oak door of the domed library. Keelan relieved me of my obligation to the council, leaving early to meet with them. I knew Morrelin was going to be insufferable, as per usual. I just hoped Ke would be able to keep his temper in check.

The trade off was that I had to come here and try to find information on my *affliction.* The stack of books Ke had sent me to return were shifting awkwardly in my clammy hands. I dreaded the dusty tomes that I knew were awaiting me. But I was actually excited to see Moira again.

The door squealed on ancient hinges as I entered the library, it was still bright, the massive stained glass skylight casting colorful rays across the shelves and sitting areas. I scanned the space as the solid door loudly swung closed behind me. I didn't see anyone, and my chin tipped upward, scanning the balconies of the two higher floors. There was no movement.

"Moira?" I called quietly, padding over to the large desk

I knew was hers. She wasn't there. I sighed, dropping the books in my arms onto the wooden top. The dull clunk echoed through the space, I winced at the disruption in the otherwise silent building.

I rubbed my clammy palms on my training pants, and leaned against the desk. I was meant to do more training upon my leaving here, from the house this time. More balance drills no doubt. Keelan wouldn't spar with me yet, the healer spooked him against anything too intensive. I could always just start sparring at him, he would have to defend. *There's a good chance I would get knocked on my ass though.*

I was lost in the thought when I heard the whine of hinges as a door I couldn't see opened and closed. "Astriel?" A voice from behind me. And then a loud squeal.

I had only just turned when I was crushed in a tight hug from the mousy haired librarian. "Moira!" I choked against her iron grip.

She released the embrace, and held me at arms length, her surprisingly strong hands still squeezing my shoulders. "You look great! I missed you! It's been too long." She hugged me again.

I cleared my throat and she took a step back. Her gold eyes scanned me. "I've been wanting to come see you, there's just been a lot going on." I offered meekly. "And the last library I was in tried to kill me." I tried to smile but the memory surged. *Why did I say that?*

"You found a wraith library." Not quite a question, but shock colored her face.

"Unfortunately," I groaned, leaning back against the desk, "No book is worth that hassle."

She just looked at me, questions swirling in her eyes, but she shook them off. And a smile broke out across her face, "So are you here for fun reads or did you new beau send you for more history lessons?"

I smiled back at her. "The boring stuff unfortunately." And I followed her as she turned, heading for a door at the back of the building.

"I like him." She said, flicking a playful look over her shoulder, "Hard to read though."

"He certainly is." I smirked, "I swear he's not as much of an ass when you get to know him." He never told me how their meeting went, but I could imagine he had been less than warm with her.

"Oh he wasn't too bad, just worried about you." I stared at the back of your head, "The equinox really freaked him out."

"What did he say to you?" My breath caught in my throat.

"Nothing." She responded simply. She halted, and turned to me, tapping a short nail against her temple.

"Oh right." I huffed a laugh. *Seer.* "You've got to quit roaming into people's minds, Moira."

"I didn't mean to, I swear." She held her hands up defensively but wore that roguish smile. And maybe it was true, all it took was a touch for her to see the hidden truths. "It's helpful though, I've been able to collect some books that might be closer to what you need. He's looking in all the wrong places."

"What do you mean?" I fell in step with her as she started walking again.

"He's looking for origin stories, but you're not an original Seraphim. Though I do believe you have some connection to them." She glanced over my white wings and I instinctively tucked them tighter. "And I got a glimpse of your drawings, which reminded me of sacred astronomy. You should bring them in so I can get a better look."

As she spoke I remembered why I liked her much. Anyone else who knew about what happened that night would have been frightened, or revered those ramblings and drawings as some prophecy. But she never saw me as anything more than I was, never saw me like the other fae. Our relationship was casual, no expectations or carefully crafted personas. I was always just Astriel with her, not anything more. And when she could just pop in and see whatever turmoil existed in my mind, there was no need for hard questions. It was a reprieve.

"I'll bring them tomorrow." I smiled to myself.

She yanked open the ancient door and we began our descent. "In my research, I found some divination methods that I wanted to try with you. If you can access that ability at will, it might not be triggered by events like the aurora."

"I'm not a diviner." My brows furrowed, but I kept her pace.

"You weren't." She corrected, "But something must have happened that opened up pathways that were previously closed."

She stopped at the base of the stairs and turned to me, "Astriel, this may feel new and scary, but these powers have always been within you, just dormant. You've run from the spirits trying to commune with you forever, it seems they won't be ignored any longer."

She turned and stepped further into the room, but I was frozen in place. "Quit snooping in my head." I tried to say it playfully, but anxiety turned my blood to ice. The voices had been getting louder, and harder to control. I hadn't even told Keelan, not wanting to worry him.

"It's my curse, I can't help it." She kept her voice light but her smile faltered. She settled into a chair at a long table in the middle of the room that looked too new to match the sagging shelves surrounding it. Unfamiliar items and open books littered the surface. "Don't be mad, I'm only trying to help."

I sighed, lowering myself to a chair across from her, "Just tell me what I need to do."

# 57

# Keelan

El was right to not want to attend the meeting. Morrelin was still absolutely insufferable about what happened with Farryn. The Nymph was painfully smug the entire time, steering the conversation back towards the subject even as the conversation shifted. I had given them the bare bone facts the morning after it happened, but he was still determined to demand more.

I was also learning that the ladies in the room were less inclined to participate in discussions when Astriel wasn't present. They just shared looks of nervousness or irritation when Morrelin and I argued. It seemed today would be no different.

"I have an informant inside the castle that I am trying to get in touch with. That is the best way to discover Deliana's plans." I raked a hand down my face, already exhausted.

"Anything you learn could be tainted, especially if she is capable of bewitching people to do her bidding." His face was already reddening, spoiling for a fight.

"Are we even confident that she is actually building an

army?" Jarrah spoke for the first time since the meeting, her voice low.

"We need to act as if she is until we know otherwise." I said softly, offering her an apologetic look.

"That's not enough!" Morrelin boomed, slamming his fists on the table, and I gritted my teeth, "We need to be proactive, waiting for her to strike is a mistake."

"How do you suggest we do that, Morrelin?" I seethed, "Phaedra has no warrior class, and I will not condone sending the people of this land to their deaths. We need to move mindfully."

"Then get your female back in the skies." That ugly vein was bulging in his neck again.

"Careful." I grated, "Astriel has only just been cleared to fly by *your* healer. I have been surveying the forest and all has been quiet."

"And how is she?" Shyla asked, her entirely black eyes trained on me, unblinking.

"She is well." I softened my tone again, "We are training extensively to rebuild her strength."

"And after the altercation with Farryn?" Jarrah spoke again.

I wouldn't have shared the knowledge of her injury with the council had it not been for the fact she had somehow acquired or hidden a poisoned dagger. If the humans were coating their weapons in Leru, then everyone needed to be aware. And I knew Jarrah carried guilt from the ordeal, having housed her, and trusted her.

"She recovered faster from the toxin than I have ever seen anyone. And the cut itself is very minor." Jarrah nodded and quieted again.

We went back and forth for hours, until a headache throbbed between my temples. When Morrelin went off on another tirade, my thoughts fell back to El. I wondered if she had found anything that provided any insight to her abilities. I had grown up hearing stories of blessed Seraphim who could commune with the originals. But they were just stories, and this felt different somehow, especially the way she seemed to be able to communicate with my shadows. They thickened and swirled with the thought. *Traitorous mist.*

I knew, based on her reaction, that they had shown her something of my childhood. I didn't want to revisit those memories. And I certainly would not have shared those horrors with her willingly, not unprovoked at least. But she hadn't brought it up again, and for that I was thankful.

But it gnawed at me, I had never considered my dark companion to be anything other than an extension of myself. Just a manifestation that accompanied the darkness of my wings. They had revealed themselves to be at least some level of sentient. I wondered what else they could do, or who else they had spoken to.

And then there was Moira, someone Astriel clearly held very dear, but she was a curiosity in of herself. When our skin connected, I felt *something.* And it had affected her, even though she was quick to hide it. I wondered about her affinities. I hadn't been able to glean even what manner of fae she was when we met.

She carried no wings, but she didn't necessarily look like an Elf. She was pretty, but not with the same devastating elegance. She almost seemed human. But she couldn't be, she acted like fae, hinted at a long life. It troubled me. There was a glint of understanding in her eyes when she looked at me, like she could see past my skin and straight into my soul. A shiver rattled through me, I would have to ask El about it.

I turned my attention back to Morrelin, who droned on and on and on.

# 58

# Astriel

I was going cross eyed staring into a black mirror. All I could see was a darker and distorted image of myself. The hand to my right, holding a pencil against the blank page of the notebook remained unmoving.

"Anything?" Moira whispered next to me.

I groaned and dropped the pencil, pushing the mirror away, "Nothing."

"Okay, well this isn't the only method we can try. There's runes and tarot cards and tea leaves-"

"This is hopeless." I breathed, leaning back and throwing my head over the top of the chair.

"Just as dramatic as ever I see." Moira shut the book she had open and shook her head.

I cut my eyes over to her and chuckled, "Maybe we should wait until the solstice, surely something will happen then."

She glared at me, "You're impossible." But a smile tugged at her lips.

We had been in the library basement for hours, scouring books and trying to access a line to the voices. Nothing was working. And even they seemed to be growing frustrated, the whispering that tickled the back of my brain would sometimes grow louder, but still unintelligible.

"I'm *tired*." I shot back. We had tried crystal balls, black mirrors, casting stones, and *nothing*. "I'm not sure cheap parlor tricks are going to help."

"They are not parlor tricks." Moira leveled her stare on me, a hand beneath her chin. I watched as she lost herself in contemplation. When her eyes cleared, they locked on my neck. "Before we give up for the day, let's try one more thing."

I groaned, "What?"

She reached out, gently brushing the seraphinite pendant around my neck, "Pendulum reading."

When her hand retreated, I grabbed the necklace, feeling the cold stone in my palm, "With a necklace?"

"It has a personal attachment, it's quite literally the stone of your people, let's just try it."

I gave her a wary look, but reached back to undo the clasp. She reached over me to grab the notebook that was still laid empty, and tore out a page. On it she drew two perpendicular lines intersecting. At both ends of one of the lines, she scrawled *yes,* and at both ends of the other, *no.* She slid the paper in front of me.

"What do I do?" I asked, staring at the parchment and tightly gripping the necklace.

"Hold it by the chain, dangle it over the intersection of the lines, and start asking simple questions."

I gave her a wary look, but positioned the necklace, the stone glinted in the light as it swayed an inch above the paper, and then stilled. "What do I ask?"

"Start with a question you already know the answer to."

I took a deep breath, rolling my eyes. "Are we in a library?"

The pendant hung still for a long moment, and then started slowly swinging along the 'yes' line. I heard Moira suck in a breath, but I didn't look at her, not wanting to influence the swing of the pendulum with any movement. It stilled again.

"Ask something else." She whispered. "Ask about the aurora."

I considered for a moment, what question to ask, "Was the aurora trying to tell me something?"

The pendant moved again, stronger this time, once again across the affirmative line. We both waited with baited breath as it continued its swing. It suddenly halted in the middle of the page, as if an invisible hand snatched it out of the air and held it still. I wanted to pull away, the uncanny feeling of being watched filling the room, but I couldn't will myself to move.

"I don't know what else to ask." I hissed at Moira, who was transfixed by the necklace. She reached out and rested a hand on my arm, but said nothing.

I sighed, "Is communing like this dangerous?" Strongly this time, the pendant swung almost angrily in the negative. A fierce no.

My hand was tingling, and there was a ringing in my ears. Moira was still locked onto the now motionless pendant, and I swallowed hard. I had something to ask, even if I was afraid to know the answer. "Is Phaedra in danger?"

The pendulum swung hard across the affirming line. I sucked breath, and I heard Moira gasp beside me. The chain seemed to be heating in my hand, and instead of easing into silence again, the pendant changed course, rotating in wide circles, no longer indicating a single answer at all.

"What does that mean?" I heard Moira ask, but her voice was faraway. The ringing in my ears grew louder, and my heart was thumping to an uneven rhythm. "Astriel?"

That blinding light overtook my vision again, and the world disappeared.

\* \* \*

I was standing in the clearing in front of the great tree. The midday sun bathed the field, bleaching the details of the world around me. There was no city, no Phaedra, as far as I could see. I was surrounded only by the grassy field sprawling beyond the tree, and then endless dense forest. I squinted, using a hand to shield my eyes. When I looked around, I was alone, and an uneasy quiet settled around me. Not even the usually present chirping of birds cut through the blanketed silence.

A voice, lilting and ethereal, cut through the soundless glen, "My daughter, you have finally answered my call."

A woman, tall and beautiful, white hair cascading well past her rounded hips. She wore a deep blue velvet gown that pooled at her feet. Her edges were blurred, like she was made of the air itself, but her features were distinct, strong eyes with color that seemed to shift in metallics boring into me. Atop her head was a crown of stars, not quite touching her, like they floated and swirled just around her, a galaxy in themselves.

"Mother." I breathed, and fell to a knee, lowering my head

in a deep bow, my hands planted in the soft grass. I had never seen her. There were no depictions. But in a distant place, an instinct, an ancestral knowledge, I knew who she was.

I felt her kneel before me, lifting me back into standing. I averted her gaze, "Look at me." I did, and for a moment, her eyes were quartz like mine, and then glimmering gold, and then an endless night sky. "I have called to you for centuries, why did you revoke me?"

Her soft gaze was piercing, as if she already knew the answer to any question she would ask, but wanted to hear it regardless. "I didn't know," I breathed, "I was afraid."

"Attempting to outrun your fate is an often painful and fruitless endeavor." She spoke, releasing my chin and clasping her hands together in front of her.

"I was a child." My voice was no louder than a whisper.

"I am sorry that you were burdened so young. It wasn't supposed to be this way. I hoped so much better for you, my daughter." Her tone softened further, understanding. "Unfortunately, even I do not rule the hands of fate, we all must bow to it."

"I don't even know what I am meant to do." Emotion caught in my throat, a sob I would not let escape me. "I had no teachers, no guidance for this... illness."

"I will admit, you have suffered far more than could be anticipated. This was not supposed to be your journey here. But my daughter, you are only ill in the ways in which you avoid the call. You know by now that taking vices does not quiet the sound."

I nodded, but said nothing. The goddess appraised me. "There is an imbalance. I can feel it in the tree, in the ground and on the wind."

"What do you mean?" I found myself asking, and she gave me a knowing grin.

"The sorceress you contend with, she has tapped into something powerful, something ancient and dangerous. It is not only Phaedra that will feel her wrath, she will rewrite creation with this tool." I moved to speak but she held a hand up, halting me, "I tell you this not to hurt you, Phaedra will fall. But unless it is dealt with, those you intended to save will burn."

"We cannot fight her, Phaedra has no army."

"Armies across the continents will fall, they will turn to dust when they meet this power."

"Then we have already lost." I murmured, my gaze turning to the cloudless sky.

The Mother's gaze did not waver, though her head tipped almost imperceptibly to the side. "The thing about this world," She started, pulling my attention back to her, "is that everything exists in a very delicate balance. Fire burns, water extinguishes. The bird eats the worm and then upon death is fed to it. Light and dark battle in the sky every day, neither winning or losing."

I listened to her, transfixed, trying to understand her message. She continued, "The wind carries you as gravity pulls you down. Your body heals, but it scars. Every force is a push and a pull, a give and a take. When something is taken, but not given, the power becomes misaligned."

"What does that mean?" I asked, my head spinning.

"Something has been taken." The goddess said simply, and then her soft and ever present smile faded, "I must leave you now, I have been here too long. But you must know, I am not the only one who wishes to speak with you. You will not find peace until you answer their calls."

She thrust out a hand, grabbing mine and bringing it to her. Her edges flickered, "Take this, and remember what you fight for." She did not release my hand when she said, "Stay in balance, my child. The angels bless you."

\* \* \*

"Astriel! Oh thank the Mother." Moira was shaking me. And when I opened my eyes, groaning, I was staring at her too close face, and then the ceiling behind her. "Holy shit, Astriel."

"What happened?" I asked, my throat dry.

"Your wings turned to light, for one." She was frantic, her voice laced with concern and excitement.

"Did you see it?"

"Whatever you saw? No. It's like you blocked me out. When I touched you it *burned*."

I loosed a shuttering laugh and hoisted myself into a sitting position. The chair I had been planted in was knocked over next to me. My whole body was sore, as if whatever I had experienced was as physically taxing as it was mentally. I was exhausted.

"What is that?" Moira pointed at my clenched fist.

I lifted the hand, and opened it, in my palm lay a heavy charm, like a silver coin strung onto a chain. One side depicted a collection of overlapping circles, like a blooming flower. I flipped it over. On the other was a six sided star with uneven points. Neither symbol meant anything to me, but it was real. The Mother had thrust it into my hands herself.

"Did you have that when you came here?" Moira asked, her voice tight.

I shook my head, "She gave it to me."

"Who did?" She asked, eyes wide.

"The Mother."

Moira paled, and pulled away from me, "Astriel…" But she didn't finish her sentence. There was nothing to say, there were no words.

# 59

# Keelan

She stumbled through the door like the weight of the world was pressing on her shoulders. My hand dropped from where it was buckling a bracer onto my arm, it fell to the floor as I ran to her. Her eyes were red rimmed and tired, and when I clamped my hands on her shoulders, searching her face, she slumped into me.

"What happened?" I asked, frantic.

She shouldered past me, collapsing onto the couch. I sat across from her, body tense, unable to read anything in her half-lidded eyes. She sat unmoving and silent for a long while, her chest rising and falling evenly. I almost thought she had fallen asleep when she started talking.

Her voice was laced with exhaustion, but it was steady. She did not falter as she told me of her research, and the vision. She weathered my questions about Moira's abilities, about the scrying, about the Mother's warning. She answered them all unflinchingly.

Finally, she paused and held out one trembling hand. When she unclenched her fingers a silver necklace fell and dangled.

She said nothing as I watched the charm softly glow in the afternoon light. I plucked it out of her hand and studied the delicate and intricate designs decorating both sides.

"She gave this to you? In the vision?" I asked, watching her slump further into the cushions.

She nodded, "It was in my hand when I came to."

I leaned backward into the couch, my leathers groaning as I loosed a heavy breath. I recognized these symbols, "This one," I started, flipping the side of interlocked circles towards her, "Is the seed of life. It represents inter-connectivity, and universal existence, a symbol of rebirth."

I watched her, her face betraying no emotions, but she listened, enraptured. I flipped the coin to the uneven star, "This is a unicursal hexagram. I've seen it displayed in priestess temples. It's an elemental symbol, used to invoke planetary forces and cosmic energies."

"So what does it mean?" She asked, reaching out.

I placed the pendant back in her hand, "Together? On the charm? I have no clue. But if She gave it to you, it must be important." I paused, considering, "Are you going to try divining again?"

She sighed, "Maybe tomorrow, Moira wants me to meet her at the library again."

I reached over, placing a hand on her knee and squeezed, "No training today, get some sleep."

But her eyes had already closed, her breathing slow and even.

\* \* \*

I stood in a glen at the human's edge of the barrier forest, a long sword strapped to my back. I resisted the urge to pace. When Astriel fell into a deep slumber, I just pulled her legs onto the couch and laid a blanket over her. When I picked up my dropped bracer from the floor, and quietly grabbed my sword from the umbrella stand, slipping out the front door, she did not stir.

I had told no one about this meeting, not even El. I would have, but she was so worn down from her vision, and I knew that I would just make her worry, or she would demand to come. I didn't want her anywhere near this. In the distance, I heard the mighty roar of a beast on the hunt. I ignored it, training my ears for a more subtle sound.

It was almost indistinguishable from the other sounds of the forest, just the crack of a twig, and then the call of an owl. I called back, waiting. I could just barely make out the rough hewn stone wall past the treeline, iron spikes jutting crudely from the mortar. But I could see no movement.

My finger tapped nervously against my thigh. I had snuck a letter out of Phaedra and into the kingdom. A dove with an encoded message that I hoped to The Mother could only be decoded by the intended recipient. I received a similarly encoded letter back when I left the meeting hall. *Where is he?*

As if answering my silent plea, Edward stepped silently from the underbrush, searching the area with a trained eye as he strode into the clearing. He stopped several feet in front of me. He looked me up and down, taking in my fae leathers, and the weapon on my back, my wings. He wore the uniform of the royal guard, the crest of a roaring lion emblazoned over the entire chest panel.

"I see you've been promoted." I said dryly, gesturing to the finery he was adorned in, the same I had worn.

"Someone had to take your place." he responded, a smile pulled at his lips.

We crossed the glade to each other, both grinning now, and clasped forearms. "Thank you for meeting me, Edward." I said as we broke the contact.

"You understand this is very dangerous for me." He responded, throwing a wary look over his shoulder.

I nodded, "I need to know what Deliana is planning."

"She has been wreaking havoc on the kingdom since you and Astriel left." He spoke low and sadly, "But she has halted fae hunts, at least to my knowledge, and has dispatched every fae servant in the castle."

"Not you though." I raised an eyebrow. His face turned grim. Edward was only half Elf, with no discernible fae features, save for an unnatural fighting ability. And, I hoped, more allegiance to Phaedra than the human lands.

"If she knew I would likely be executed."

"My sources say she has come into possession of an item of great power." I told him, not wanting to put yet another target on El's back by revealing her newfound abilities.

"I do not know of any items. But undoubtedly, her power has grown. It's like she can suck the life out of any living thing. The gardens are nothing more than kindling anymore." He kicked at a pebble with his boot.

I sucked my teeth, "What is she doing with this new power?"

"She slayed an entire town of people who refused to join her ranks. Her ascension to the throne has not been well received." He winced.

"So she is building an army?" The man nodded, and I cursed under my breath.

"She is doing something to the warriors, they have changed with her influence. It's as if they do not feel, do not think. They fight and they fall, that is it."

"Does she have plans to attack?"

"Not that I know of, yet. But she is clearly preparing for something. I will keep an ear open, and send word of anything important." I nodded, and Edward pivoted to retreat back out through the forest.

"Edward," He turned his head, looking at me over his shoulder, "Keep your head down. You are my friend, it would be a great tragedy to have to kill you because of something as trivial as betrayal."

An amused smile glinted in his eyes, "It would be a great tragedy to have to be killed by you, Sir Keelan." And then he was gone.

# 60

# Astriel

Moira was already in the basement when I turned up at the library the next morning, an envelope of aurora drawings tucked under my arm. I wore both my seraphinite necklace and the gifted charm, unsure which would be better for the pendulum work. When I descended into our unofficial workspace, Moira had moved the large table against a wall, and in the middle of the room lay a pile of blankets and pillows. I tossed the envelope onto the table, and gave the female a spirited look.

"Moira, I know we've grown close but I'm afraid you got the wrong idea."

She looked up from her work, momentary confusion coloring her features. She reddened as she glanced between me and the bedding, a wide smile creasing her face.

"It's so you don't hurt yourself, you tart." Her smile widened further, "But, if I wanted to bed you, you'd better believe that I could."

I batted my eyelashes and flicked a hand at her, "If only you could be so lucky."

Moira rolled her eyes and kicked another crate of old books out of the way, "Are you going to flirt with me all day or would you like to focus?"

I laughed, savoring the loose ease of the exchange. With the chaos of everything piling around us, the soft banter was heaven sent. Her playful presence was a welcome respite from the somber nature I had to take regarding nearly every other part of my life. I plopped myself into the middle of the pile, hands resting on the knees of my crossed legs. I schooled my features, "I'm not confident with how well it's going to go today. It's been pretty quiet since the last one."

Moira knelt in front of me, reaching out her hands. I took them. "If nothing happens, then nothing happens." she said softly, her all seeing eyes boring into me. "Progress is progress."

I nodded, releasing her grip and unclasping both necklaces, holding one in each hand. "I don't think I need the answer paper today. I want to try something different." Moira nodded back to me, and scooted back on the pallet, giving me space. I extended both arms, a pendant dangling from each hand. I took a deep breath in, and then my eyes closed.

I fell into a sort of meditation, trying to quiet my thoughts and open it to messages. I listened to my own mind. Since I had fallen into that deep and dreamless sleep, there had been no voices, no whispers, as if they were sated. But the Mother said there would be more.

If that were the case, I needed to access them now, in a controlled environment. The memories of the aurora haunted me, that couldn't happen again. Especially if there was an unknown threat brewing over the horizon. Especially if I had to face whatever Deliana had come to possess.

313

I shushed those thoughts. *Focus.* I tried to center on my breathing, feel the insignificant weight in my hands, passively listen to the steady beating heart of the female across from me. Every sound was heightened in the subterranean room.

In the back of my mind, a sensation, like a gentle shock. Something soft, tickling the base of my skull. I focused my attention on it, allowing the feelings to grow in intensity. It traveled down my neck, into my chest, across my arms. Goosebumps erupted in its wake.

Moira said something, but once again her voice was faraway and muffled. I listened, but there was no voice, only the physical sensations. I allowed myself to be bathed in it, and when icy phantom fingers skittered across my body, chilling my skin and breath, I let it. In an absent sort of way, I could feel both necklaces moving, the chain scraping circles into the bottom of my fist. And I felt it when the chains stilled, and the cold enveloped my entire body.

\* \* \*

A freezing cavern, no— the interior of a glacier. The walls were blue ice, the illusion of light shining from deep within them. I stood in the middle of a frozen river. Above, the ice walls collided, blocking out any view of the sky above. I was deep below the surface, how far, I couldn't tell.

Below my feet, I could see movement, a migration of fish perhaps. But they were just shadows, flitting out of sight. I puffed out a breath, forming a cool cloud in front of my face. Ahead was a narrow path carved into the ice, disappearing around a bend.

I started walking, deceptively stable on the smooth frozen surface of the river. The icy cave was long, with nothing distinctive to reference if I got lost. But there was no spirit, no creature that called for my attention. I was able to access… something.

But what was it? I kept walking, running a hand down the edge of the frigid pathway. The sound of dripping water was a hollow, echoing sound around me.

I followed the bend and the hall opened into a massive chamber, long and wide icicles bearing down from the high ceiling with menacing intent. Ahead was a break in the thick ice floor against the far wall. I strode over to it, listening to ice crackle and groan beneath my feet. The only sounds came from the shifting ice and my own breathing. When I gazed into the jagged hole, a broken window into the dark waters beneath, my breath caught.

Looking up from the cold abyss writhed a giant serpent.

I watched it stare, still as death, but did not recoil from it. Its skin was the white of a watery death and its eyes, glistening red marbles. All across its horrible head were jagged scars, if I looked deeper, I could make out the silhouettes of broken spears, swords, and arrows, still embedded in its impossibly long distorted body.

*You have finally answered my call, little dove. I have been patiently waiting for you.* Its silent voice echoed in my head, a snake coiling around my senses, tightening.

"What are you?" I choked out, fighting its oppressive presence.

*I am Andolir.* The creature's voice, a whisper on the still air.

315

*I have been trapped beneath this ice for a millennia, but there are rumors in the currents. I will be free soon.*

"Why have you called to me?" My voice cracked, and a low rumble in the water conveyed that my fear satisfied the beast.

*The tales of a world-bound angel travel far, little dove. Though you are not what I expected.* He raised then, his scaled snout poking out of the water, sniffing, huffing a frigid mist into the air. *You are not fallen. What are you?*

"Fae. I am Seraphim." The attempt to steady my voice was unsuccessful.

*Seraphim.* The creature chewed on the name, and took another deep breath, blowing the foul scent of death from its slitted nostrils. I fought the urge to gag at the smell. *But you are not like your brethren. You are not an angel, but your blood is like theirs. It would be delicious.*

I was trembling, "Why did you call to me?" I asked again.

The serpent was silent for a moment, considering. *Will it be you who sets me free? I hunger for a world outside of these frozen walls. I haven't eaten in so long.*

"I cannot release you. I wouldn't if I could."

*The water speaks to me. Even if it is not you, I will be set free. We don't have to be enemies, dove.*

"Quit calling me that." Despite my frozen body, anger roiled beneath my skin. "What do you want? I won't ask again."

*Your kind are so impatient. I haven't had company in a very long time, and yet you are so eager to leave me.* He sunk back into the water, but his ruby eyes never left me. *The World-breaker is awakened. It will set me free, but if it is not contained, my freedom will be short lived. I do not wish to be slain before I have even had the chance to hunt the shorelines once again.*

"What is the World-Breaker?" I asked, that familiar dread pooling in my stomach.

*It is an ancient weapon, older than even me.* It seemed to chuckle, deep in its body, a rumble that shook beneath the ice. *I have not seen it. I do not know what manner of weapon it is. But I can feel its power pulsing. It grows stronger everyday.*

"I don't know how I am meant to stop a power like that." This thing was toying with me, it enjoyed watching me squirm.

*Its wielder is sloppy. It knows this. The power will consume any human or fae who bears it. But not before untold damage is done to the lands you cherish.* He paused again, watching for my reaction. I knew it could see the fear in my eyes, its disfigured maw almost cracked in a smile. *There is a weapon I can offer you. It is not near as ancient, nor as powerful. But you may find it beneficial in your journey.*

"Where can I find it?" The beast watched me for a long while, assessing. I flared my wings. "I grow tired of this conversation, Andolir."

*So sweet to hear my name on the tongue of another.* That invisible presence wrapped itself around me again, squeezing, pulling the air from my lungs. *I will offer you the blade, for a bargain.*

I knew better than to bargain with any fae. But to strike a bargain with an ancient water snake, it could not end well. Despite the knowledge, I found myself asking, "What do you want?"

There was no question now, the creature was smiling.

# 61

# Astriel

I was wrapped in thick blankets, and I still woke violently shivering, my teeth clattering so hard I was convinced they would shatter. When my eyes opened, Moira was staring down at me, that panicked expression draining the color from her face again. I blinked, if I didn't know better, I would have thought there was snow on my lashes. I flexed a hand beneath the pile of blankets, my fingers were stiff, nearly numb. I could hardly bend them.

"What the fuck was that?" Moira, breathlessly whispered, rubbing my arms, trying to urge warmth back into my frozen body.

I couldn't move, and my voice cracked like ice when I tried to speak. I forced the words, "Lift the blanket."

Moira eyed me, but complied, and gasped at what she beheld. Clutched, frozen in my right hand, was an incredible, ornate sword. The other hand bore a long and deep gash across the palm, blood flowing and staining the blankets around it. I groaned as she lifted the hand, despite the fact my body was warming, my bones still threatened to snap.

Absently, I noted her scurrying off, and then returning with bandages, "Did you see it?" I managed to choke. While she wrapped my hand.

"No. It was like last time, you blocked me out." She looked up from her work to me, "Do you yield ice now?"

I shook my head, wincing at the cracking in my neck, "Thank The Mother though, cold like this is miserable."

Moira shook her head but offered a tight smile, "We need to get you home."

\* \* \*

By the time I sank into the bed, and Keelan paced in front of the foot board, Moira was slinking back out the front door. I had filled her in enough that she knew to be nowhere near the house when Ke discovered what I had done. She dropped both necklaces on the dresser, placed the sword on the couch, and offered not even a clipped farewell before sneaking out. *Smart of her.*

My body had warmed considerably, and now only the tiredness of the ordeal pulled me downwards. The soft bed I sat on beckoning me to sleep. I didn't want to discuss this now, but I knew we would have to. Keelan's shadows were a swirling warning.

"Are you out of your mind?" He bellowed when he was confident Moira was out of earshot.

"I did what needed to be done." I said, sitting up against the pillows. I leaned over then, sucking down the glass of water Moira had made me before her abrupt departure.

"You made a blood oath with *Andolir.*" He gripped the foot board hard enough that I heard a crack.

"Not a blood oath," I rolled my eyes, and wiped the water from my mouth, "It was just an exchange."

"You offered your *blood* to an ancient sea demon for a *sword.*" He spit back. The look in his dark eyes was pure fire, and his shadows danced.

"He just wanted a taste, he's been trapped for a thousand years. It was an easy choice."

"And what would have happened if he wanted more than just a taste? You can obviously be harmed on a spirit journey." He glared down at my bandaged hand, "Can you be killed? Or worse, what if he was marking your scent and as soon as he's free he's going to hunt you? Did you think this through *at all?*" He was yelling.

"Watch how you talk to me, Keelan." I pulled myself off the bed, squaring my chest at him. The exhaustion pulling at my bones was still there, but irritation urged my body on. "You wanted me to get the voices under control, and now they are. You wanted to find solutions to the Deliana threat, *I found one.* You don't get to be pissed at me for the way I solve problems."

He crossed the room until he was within reach, "Astriel, what you did was reckless and dangerous and I don't know why you can't admit that."

"It was no more dangerous than anything else we have done, Keelan. The life we have to live, the things we are going to have to do are *dangerous.* You know that." My wings stretched out as my anger grew.

"My source says that Deliana is building an army, with a power we haven't seen and don't understand, excuse me for being nervous for you." His wings stretched to match mine.

"Your source?" I asked, narrowing my eyes, "What source is that?"

His face paled and his feathers rustled, "It's not—"

"What source, Keelan?"

And red filled my vision.

\* \* \*

I was already halfway down the hall when he finished his sentence. I screamed in frustration, whipping around to him. All the heat was extinguished from his eyes. "You hypocritical, pig-headed male!" I yelled. "You didn't bother to tell me? After all the shit you've given me? After *Farryn*?"

"I was going to," he pleaded, his palms out to me, I took a step back, "but you were so tired. It was only a two minute meeting."

"With a man who serves the castle, Keelan. He had loyalty when you were captain, but what if that had gone away when you left?" My wings flung out so hard they knocked over the umbrella stand, swords scattered across the floor, I hardly heard it. "Or what if he did want to be loyal to you but Deliana had him in her grips? There was a very good chance that could have been a trap."

"I trust Edward." He puffed his chest but I could see in his eyes he couldn't justify himself further than that.

"So then what is this? Do you not trust *me*? Or is it some backwards Seraphim thinking about females that I had the pleasure to miss out on? Do you think I'm too weak to handle myself? Because if the issue was us keeping each other safe then you would have never gone out into those woods by yourself."

Tears were streaming down my face, but I didn't bother to wipe them away. He was just staring at me, dejected, and I knew my words had hit home. "Astriel, I-"

"You run around Phaedra like a rogue king, barking orders and trying to make a martyr of yourself. But, don't be mistaken, Keelan, as far as the politics of the territories are concerned, you serve *me,* not the other way around."

Before he could even open his mouth, the front door was slamming shut behind me.

# 62

# Astriel

I was furious. I took flight from my front stoop, not caring about how my untrained muscles strained. Unable to register that this was my first takeoff from the ground since the fall equinox. I just needed to get away from the house. I needed to get away from Keelan.

I flew to the library and checked the door. It was locked. The sun was well past the horizon now, which means Moira must have gone home. Exasperated and irritated with myself, it occurred to me that I had no idea where she lived. Until recently, I only saw her at the library. *I am a terrible friend.*

I considered heading across town to Elia's tavern. Knowing myself, I would just drink myself silly and kick off the fight again when I saw Keelan. Probably not the best idea. Even if the numbness of drink would have been a welcome respite. Better to let old habits die.

So I just flew. wide circles around the capital, towards the mountains, over the forest. I wasn't in fighting gear, but at least if I did some half-assed patrolling I would be doing something useful. There was no sign of Ke in the skies. If he was smart he would give me a wide berth.

On some level, I understood his actions. We had both been alone for so long. It's an adjustment to live with, to live *for* someone else. But that didn't make it hurt any less. We were supposed to be a team. *I guess that makes me a hypocrite, too.*

I flew higher, the burn in my wings quieting my too loud mind. Not voices, not right now, just my own roiling thoughts. The night wind roared past my ears, I breathed deeply, the sharp chill burning my lungs. The forest was dark, and the sounds of beasts on the prowl and chattering of nocturnal birds broke through the otherwise silent night. This was familiar. Alone in the skies, I was who I have always been.

When a cramp developed in my shoulders, I accepted that at some point I would have to land. On instinct I dove towards a mountain outcropping, a cliff I had used to rest, eat and survey the land all those months ago. I stumbled on the rocks, panting as I skidded to a stop too near the edge. Another harsh reminder of just how out of practice I truly was.

I collapsed against the wiry trunk of a scrub tree, groaning as I tried to massage my knotted shoulders. It was undeniably a beautiful night, clear and still. Only a light breeze rustling the sparse grasses and needle-like leaves of the tree. The bark scraped against my bare back, rough and grounding. I leaned back into it, dropping my hands to my side.

I looked out into the starlit sky, surveying the constellations above. They twinkled, a flickering candle flame, and despite myself, I found my frustration ebbing. This familiar, this was as close to contentment and peace as I had ever known. So much chaos had overtaken my life, but the mountain quiet wrapped me in a warm embrace.

I closed my eyes, savoring the moment. The breeze traveling up the open leg of my pants, over my arms, tickling my cheeks. My eyelids fell closed, only absently aware of the dull ache in my muscles. I breathed in the balmy air, warm even at this altitude. I would have been content to doze up here for hours if it wasn't for a gnawing at the back of my mind. An abstract pull I couldn't shake.

*Look. Listen.*

My eyes shot open, and I strained my ears against the soft rustling of the tree I leaned against. I could hear nothing, sense nothing amiss. But that feeling kept gnawing, pulling my attention towards the treeline. I leaned forward, eyes scanning the darkness.

Then I heard it, the rhythmic thumping of boots through the undergrowth, and the clinking of metal on metal. I scrambled to my feet, hurrying to the cliff edge. I gazed towards the sounds, and deep in the forest, a gentle glinting of firelight caught my attention.

Without thinking, I launched off the outcropping, diving towards the canopy. Instinct overtaking any sense of self preservation. As I descended, the sounds of the encroaching troops grew louder. They were still at the far edge of the forest, I noted. Diving further, I landed, too hard, in the high branches of a gnarled oak. A few of the men surveyed the surrounding area at the noise, but none looked up.

I scanned the group. A dozen men, wearing the royal uniform and heavily armed. Though the sun had long set, they did not make camp. Only torches held by a few of the men lit their continuing procession. I watched as they marched below me, a slow but steady pace. With horror I realized they intended to march through the night, directly into Phaedra.

I glanced behind me, towards where they would emerge from the wood. They came from the south, and would march straight though the farmlands, and then directly into the Nymph village. I reached backwards for a blade, my hand striking air where a sword should have hung. *Stupid.* I had not left looking for a fight, and I carried no weapons.

I couldn't take on all of these men unarmed. I calculated how much time I would have before they would break the treeline and unleash mayhem on my people. It wouldn't be long. But I would have enough time, only barely, to change and arm myself. If Keelan wasn't home then I would handle it alone. I would not have enough time to hunt for him.

I launched myself from the tree, silently as my wings would allow, back into the night air.

.

# 63

# Astriel

When I burst through the front door, Keelan started, pushing himself from the couch. If I had not been overcome with urgency, I would have slumped in relief. His hair was disheveled, as if he had been running his hands through it. He strode towards me, opening his mouth to speak. I silenced him with a hand in the air as I stormed past him.

"Not now." I said roughly, hearing his bare feet slap against the hardwood as he followed me down the hall. "Get dressed. Quickly."

He gawked at me, but pulled on a shirt as I shed my casual attire in favor of a tight shirt and pants, "What's wrong?" He asked, handing over my socks and boots.

"A dozen of the king's men—" I shook my head, "Deliana's men, marching towards the lowlands. Heavily armed, not making camp for the night."

I tossed him his breastplate from where our leathers were laid atop the dresser. "Now?" He asked. But he did not falter, strapping himself in and grabbing for his wrist bracers and thigh panels.

I did not look at him, buckling my own leathers on, my fingers fumbling with the straps. "Right now." I reached for my waist belt, but he was one step ahead, kneeling in front of me as he tightened it.

"Are you ready to fight?" He looked up at me, but his fingers did not stop their movement.

"No choice in the matter, now." I responded, pulling him up with my bandaged hand and thrusting his own leather sheaths against his chest. I took a deep breath, "They are only men, they must already be exhausted. We can handle them."

I opened the top drawer, digging through the pile for sharpened daggers. I set two on the dresser top for Keelan, taking two for myself, muscle memory had me sheathing them without looking. Ke grabbed my shoulders, turning me to him, "It's been months Astriel, you're still healing."

I pulled out of his grip, placing the daggers into his sheaths, and then cut my eyes back to his, "Then you had better have my back."

I shouldered past him, out of the bedroom and back down the hall, tucking a small blade into my boot. My heart beat to a wild rhythm in my chest. I opened and closed my fist over and over to conceal the shake in my fingers. There was no room for fear or panic now. As I reached the threshold, and reached for the sword laden umbrella stand, I paused, hand hovering over the many hilts. A tugging at the back of my mind halted my step.

I turned, Keelan was hopping down the hall, pulling on his boots. My attention pulled to the right, the sword I had bargained for with Andolir had been moved to the coffee table. The intricate etchings of complex knots glinted in the lamp light. It shone as if freshly polished.

I strode over, picking it up, feeling its weight. The hilt, a dragon with an impossibly open mouth, felt comfortable in my hand. The green stone in the place of an eye flashed as I turned it over. When I looked up, Keelan was watching, nervousness etched on his face.

"Let's go. We need to hurry." I said simply, sliding the sword into my scabbard. He nodded, eyes wary, and we took off, back towards the barrier forest.

# 64

# Keelan

I let Astriel set our pace, silent as we soared in the darkness. A new moon left us flying nearly blind. But she did not slow, did not falter as we approached the forest. Even in the minimal starlight I could see the hilt of her newly acquired sword gleam against her back. Why she had chosen it, I couldn't say, wouldn't ask, not until this task was complete.

Farmland turned to thick forest canopy. I kept my eyes on the trees below us, searching. My ears pricked to Astriel's anxious mumbling. Her eyes shooting back and forth across the thick foliage. Her braid whipped in the wind, the silver turned ashy in the dim starlight.

"Where are they?" I heard her grumble, forehead creasing as her moonstone eyes squinted, searching for them.

"Are you sure they came from this way?" I asked, bringing myself closer, only allowing myself to look at her for a moment before my eyes fell back to the dark woods.

"They were here." She whispered, desperation lacing her voice, so low the sound was nearly lost in the wind.

She opened her mouth to speak again when I heard it. The

snap of a bowstring, the whistling of arrows. Her name, a warning that had barely left my lips when I barreled into her. Wrapping myself around as we plummeted from the sky.

I gripped her tightly, my wings swallowing her form as we collided. She pulled against me as we rotated wildly towards the rapidly approaching canopy. The blinding burn of an arrow finding its mark in my shoulder weakened my grip, but I did not release her. Another in the wide muscle at the arc of my wing tore a scream from my throat. The iron burned in my blood immediately.

From the corner of my eye I could see individual leaves now. We were falling too fast, I wouldn't be able to brace us from the impact. At least not without breaking my own body in the process. So I tore us apart, and threw Astriel. I prayed that it was away from the origin of those arrows. My own wings spread, but did not catch wind, not fast enough.

Branches snapped and lashed at my body as I tumbled. I grabbed blindly, desperate to find purchase on anything that would slow my descent. Rough bark slipped through my fingers. It was only as the ground jumped up at me, that my hand wrapped around a branch. The sudden weight speared an agonizing pain up my arm and down my back, radiating from the now broken off arrow in my shoulder. The wood snapped.

I hit the ground with enough force to knock the wind out of my chest, but nothing broke. I lay on the uneven ground, sucking air into my protesting lungs. *Astriel. I need to find her.* I pulled myself up, too fast, battered body screaming against the movement. A groan escaped my lips, shredding pain in my wing as I fell against the trunk of a tree.

I reached back, fingers trembling, and wrapped my hand around the shaft of the arrow that had survived the fall. One deep breath, and I yanked it out, swallowing the pained sound that ripped at my throat. I took just a moment to assess it. The arrowhead still intact.

My blood sizzled on the iron, emitting a putrid smoke. I discarded it, the fogginess in my mind abating only slightly with the other still buried deep in my shoulder. A problem I would have to address later.

I unsheathed my blade, brandishing it in front as I tore, swiftly as I could, towards where I knew Astriel would be. That feeling was back, the tug of a thread, pulling me towards her. I knew to follow it, even in the oppressive darkness. I could track her even with the iron in my back dulling my senses. I would always be able to find my way to her.

A distinctly masculine shout, and cry of pain narrowed my search. If these men had been walking by any light, they had long extinguished it. Not even the smell of smoke lingered in the air. So I followed the sound, and the pull towards my mate. The clash of metal on metal pushing my feet faster, my pain forgotten, urgency overtaking all else.

\* \* \*

I broke from the underbrush into a clearing, frozen mid step at what I beheld. Two men had already fallen, limp, against the dirt. Astriel was addressing three more, surrounding her, swords drawn. She hadn't pulled her own sword yet, and instead parried their attacks with only twin daggers. She was faster than them, dodging their brutish attacks and swiping for their middles, their legs, stabbing for their ribs when they left their sides exposed.

I had hardly taken a breath as the three of them slumped in a morbid circle around her. The remaining soldiers did not hesitate, did not feel the fear any mortal man should have as they beheld her. *This* was Agrona. *This* was the Angel of Death. I saw it now, the force of nature, the legend she was known to be. Every movement was nothing more than a flash of white wings and silver. Only the rustling of a quiver tore my attention away.

I launched into the fray, cutting down the two archers who notched their arrows, leveling their bows at Astriel. Arrows struck at her feet as I collided with them, ruining their aim before my blade silenced them. I turned, two men sprinted in my direction, two more closing in on Astriel. *That only makes eleven. Someone is missing.*

I engaged the men, the iron in my shoulder rendering me weak enough that it was a near equal fight. My eyes kept cutting to Astriel. She was dirty, small cuts torn into her clothes, whether they were from blade or her own undoubtedly rough landing I couldn't tell. But she moved smoothly, not hindered by any major injury by all appearances.

A flash of silver and she only wielded one blade, and I heard a thump at my back. A glance over my shoulder revealed the crumpled corpse of a man, her missing blade struck deeply in his neck. *And that makes twelve.* I turned my attention back to the men who swung their blades wildly, no refinement in their technique.

I yielded a step as the men continued their assault, blood spilling as I cut into them. But they did not react, their attacks only halting with a mortal strike. I ran my blade through one of their chests, the crunch of bone sickening as one man fell. I only narrowly dodged the other's strike as he swung for my neck.

A quick glance to the side revealed Astriel had also dropped the second man, her final dagger jutting grotesquely from his eye. I watched as she dropped and rolled out of the way, finally unsheathing her sword. It sang against the scabbard, and she wielded it in front of her, still retreating. She was hesitating. *Why would she hesitate?*

I turned my attention fully back to my last remaining assailant, feinting as he launched himself towards me. I swung backwards as he stumbled past. Blade severed spine, and he collapsed. Still breathing, crawling on his elbows towards me, his legs limp behind him. I dug my sword into his back, a wet squelch the final sound as he stilled.

Panting, body vibrating, I turned to Astriel just as her sword met her attackers. The sound of clashing blades echoed across the clearing. My eyes widened as I watched hers glaze over. A scream tore from my throat as she fell to her knees, the emerald eye of the dragon flashing as her arm fell limply at her side. *No. Not now.*

I ran to her, too slowly. I watched the man raise his sword, preparing to deliver that fatal blow. Time slowed as my own sword fell from my hand and I gripped the daggers at my hips. Without thinking, I threw them both, one after the other. The first found its home in his rib, the other in the side of his skull. The light left his eyes as his body slackened,

334

falling to the side.

Astriel did not react, she only stared at the sky, wide eyes unseeing.

# 65

# Astriel

One moment I was in that forest, fighting side by side with Keelan, and the next there was the song of metal on metal. In a blink I was gone from the woods, standing in a white void. Not the same as the death void. That had been an unrelenting darkness. This was like the inside of a massive cloud. A mist covered space of light.

I could not leave the spot I stood in, but my head pivoted, searching for something, anything that might indicate where I was, what had happened. I vaguely remembered the sword, the sword I had chosen, but then balked at using. *But I had used it.* The memory was faint, but it was real. The sound of it when it collided with the dead-eyed soldier's own blade. It rang out like a death knell. Even now the silver peal of it echoed in my mind.

"You wield my family sword." A voice cut through the mist, I searched for its owner. A male appeared in front of me. Not fully corporeal, but solid enough that I could make out his features. Solid enough that I could see the ashy brown wings on his back. Wings I had seen once before, in a memory that was not mine.

"What do you want?" I spit at the male, Bastion. Keelan's father.

"So you know who I am. Interesting." He ran a hand through the image of his graying hair, "I haven't seen that sword in a very long time, where did you find it?"

"I pulled it from the hide of Andolir." I said as strongly as I could muster, when I looked down, the sword was in my hand, or at least a spectral depiction of it. Here, it had no weight, and yet I could feel its hilt in my hand. As solid as in the real world.

"So that is where that old fool ran off to." Bastion laughed wryly, his eyes still on the blade. "My father was its last wielder. They both disappeared when I was young."

"What do you want?" I repeated myself, even bristling, I tucked the information away for later.

"That sword is not for you to carry." He said, turning his hard eyes on me, "It belongs to my son." Something like pain flashed across his dark eyes. Keelan's eyes.

"Then I will return it to him." I responded, softer. "Though I hope you did not call me here just to discuss the blade."

"I have nothing to contribute to your journey, if that's what you mean." His voice was rough, gravelly. His face hard, with a violence in his eyes that made it almost hard to believe that he was related to Keelan at all.

"Tell him I'm sorry." Bastion spoke again, almost a whisper, "He didn't deserve— I was so lost after his mother passed. I couldn't be what he needed."

"That does not absolve you. Not for the beatings, for the cruelty." My voice hardened again. Those memories of his shadows had shown me, real as if I had been there, flitted through my mind.

"I know," his voice crackled, "but tell him anyway."

I nodded tightly, "Is that all?"

"You love him." Not a question.

"I do."

"Then tell him to go home. There is a loose stone in the hearth. He will find it there."

I opened my mouth to ask what he meant, but he had already dissolved back into the mist.


I stood there, waiting for the vision to end, waiting to return to my body. But it didn't fade. I was in the mist, alone, stuck. Panic rose like bile in my throat when I glimpsed a flash to my left. I turned to it. Breath catching as I beheld him.

"It seems you did make good use of that key after all." An old, tired voice. The dead king. But he looked stronger here, not the shell I had met. A soft smile graced his wrinkled face.

"I'm surprised you remember." I said, a grin playing at my own lips. "Thank you."

"Thank *you*," he looked different here, clear eyed, standing tall. "You leaving finally snapped Deliana's restraint. Her killing me was my first taste of freedom in decades."

"I should have done more," I choked out, genuine remorse pulling at my chest, "If I had known, I wouldn't have left you there."

"It was too late for me. You did all you could." His voice softened, "My last memory that was truly mine in that life was your kindness. That is enough."

"Why did you seek me out?" I asked, unable to stop myself.

A soft laugh, a warm laugh, "You are everything I hoped you would be, Astriel. I know you need to be getting back soon, so I will make this as swift as possible."

My name, not Agrona. He knew my name. "What are you talking about?"

"I saw the weapon she wields. She wore it when she cut me down." he paused, pulling at his neck, eyes faraway. I suppressed a wince at what she must have done to him.

"It is a crown. It is making her more powerful, but it fights her. She has had to change course in her ambitions, her plans have changed." He paused, as if he was decided what more he would say, "Her powers of suggestion are much stronger now. Those men you fought, they were not themselves. They did not feel fear or pain. That is what you will be up against."

"How do we win against an army like that?" I asked, a stone settling in my gut.

"It will go against everything you know, and everything you stand for. You cannot waste time battling with them. The source will find you. You already know that there is much which will be lost. There will be sacrifice, I am sorry to say."

"What kind of sacrifice?" I asked, breath hitching.

"I have said all I can." His eyes were sad. He rested a hand on his heart. "We all must pay the price for salvation."

And in a blink he vanished into nothing. And then I was gone, the light once again fading to dark.

# 66

# Astriel

I blinked. Vision clearing, back in the midnight forest. Keelan was shaking me, his frantic voice pitched up as his fingers dug into my shoulders. Rocks and twigs dug into my knees, a sticky moisture soaking my pants. I dared look around, men's bodies littered the forest floor. The one closest to me, only inches away, with twin daggers erupting from his head and chest, pooled blood beneath me.

I lurched backwards, stumbling as I pulled myself to my feet. Keelan yanked me into him, crushing me against his chest. I shook against him, wrapping my arms around his wide torso, breathing him in. Swallowing, my ears popped, and his voice came back into focus.

"Where did you go?" He released me, hands running over my hair, across my face, down my neck, "Thank the Mother, you came back to me."

I was dazed, Keelan's touch the only thing tethering me, his shadows snaking up my arms, appearing to take their own assessment of my state. "We were fighting, and then I was just... gone."

He nodded, eyes swimming, "As soon as your sword made contact you just fell. Astriel you—" His voice broke, "I almost couldn't save you."

I shook my head, looking directly into his still wide eyes, "It's not my sword." His traveling hands halted on both sides of my neck, I brought my own up, gently gripping his wrists. "Keelan, I met your father."

\* \* \*

We sat in the clearing, surrounded by the bodies of fallen men as I described what I had seen, who I had spoken to. Keelan listened in rapt silence, his face betraying every emotion. When I finished, he just stared at me, his mouth a hard line. I rested a hand on his knee, giving him the space to sort through his feelings.

"My grandfather's sword." He finally spoke after a long while, awestruck eyes traveling to where the silver blade gleamed, still laying in the dirt where I had dropped it.

"It seemed very important to your father that you be the only one to wield it." I offered carefully.

"He apologized," Keelan scoffed and shook his head, but his lips were tipped up at the corners, "that alone would make me think you were making the whole thing up if I didn't know any better."

I chewed my lip, pulling myself to my feet, holding a hand out for Keelan to take. When I pulled him up, his face contorted, a sound like a whimper only barely escaping his lips. Without so much as a warning, I grabbed his bicep and spun him. A broken arrow jutted out of his shoulder, a trickle of blood staining the back plate of his leathers.

"You self-sacrificing ass." I mumbled, smacking him against the leather of his chest plate when he turned back to me, "When were you going to tell me you'd been shot?" I spun him again, probing around the wound.

He winced, "Forgive me, I've had other things on my mind." I just glared at him where he peeked at me over his shoulder. "You're welcome by the way." His smirk faltered as my fingers prodded the tender flesh.

"I beg your pardon?" I raised an eyebrow at him, pulling the tiny blade out of my boot, wiping it on the closest thing to a clean section of my shirt.

"Oh you know, when a handsome male takes an arrow for a fair maiden, she usually says thank you." *Smug bastard.* But I couldn't keep the amusement off my face.

"What should a maiden say when her handsome savior chucks her into a tree just to fall directly into an enemy troop?" I asked, batting my eyelashes. I gave him no warning before I eased the blade around the arrowhead, dislodging it from where it struck bone.

He sucked his teeth, growling through the pain, "I believe she just starts digging around in his back with a knife."

I pulled out the arrowhead, still intact, and tossed into the treeline, "Then we are even." I grinned, clapping him on the sore shoulder.

# 67

# Keelan

Astriel rejected my bid for us to fly home, instead opting for a walk that felt near endless. I told her several times that I would be able to fly. But she would just look at me, and then run her eyes down my back, declining every time. After the first several attempts to convince her, she just poked the wound on my shoulder, gauging my reaction. Each time I groaned or recoiled, she would just give me a knowing look and keep her pace.

So we walked in companionable, if weary, silence. Through the low set farmlands, up the river walk, and finally into the capital. She strode like a woman made anew, unbothered by the exhaustion I knew must be plaguing her body. She hadn't slept, which, admittedly, was my fault for running her off after the fight about Andolir. I reached back, grazing the pommel of the sword at my back. I suppose I can't be too upset about it now, knowing the sword and its true origin. Even if I had a fair few questions about it that would undoubtedly remain unanswered.

I could have wept when I finally laid eyes on her squatty

bungalow. The sky tinged purple with the impending sunrise as we finally crossed the threshold. It was all I could do to kick off my boots as I entered, leaving my leather and weapons strapped on. Their stiffness may very well have been the only thing keeping me upright. I couldn't help the thought that it would have been so much swifter to just fly.

But now, slumping into a bar stool at the island, leaning over the counter top as she disappeared to find her medic kit, I had to appreciate the foresight. The ache in my wing was unbearable, and the opposite shoulder throbbed in beat with my heart. Flying would likely worsened the wounds, and if they hurt this bad *now*— A chill ran up my spine at the thought.

I watched Astriel stride back into the room, medic kit in hand. Her hair was windblown and messy, her feathers blood-spattered. Even so, her movements were sure and steady. She bore the marks of battle. Shallow cuts that had long since clotted in the places her leathers didn't cover, and a bruise that had begun to bloom on her cheek. But they did not seem to bother her.

We did not speak as she appraised me, and then began the methodical task of removing my gear. She piled my leathers on the counter, tossed our daggers into the sink to be cleaned and oiled. I just watched her through lidded eyes as she worked, adjusting my position when she nudged me, but otherwise not moving. I had almost dozed in my seat when she finally spoke.

"How much do you care about this shirt?" She asked, fingers trailing down the torn and stained shoulder.

"I don't." I grunted, the most response I could muster.

Her lips tightened into a thin line, and she turned towards

the kitchen, digging around in a drawer and pulling out a pair of shears, "Then I'm not going to bother asking you to raise your arms." She moved behind me, cutting and snipping in calculated lines until the fabric fell away.

"You need to bathe." I felt, more than I heard her say. Her breath on the back of my ear. "It will do no good to disinfect these if you're just going to dirty them again as you sleep."

I just nodded and let her guide me to the bathing room. I sat on the edge of the tub as she ran the water, and then knelt to undo the buttons of my pants. There was nothing sensual, nothing expectant in her actions. Even as she pulled my body into standing and stripped me bare before pointing to the steaming bath.

My thoughts wandered as I climbed in. I was absently aware as she, still in her own fighting clothes, sans the leathers, scrubbed at my bruised and battered body. But it was the message she had conveyed from my father that demanded my attention. I wondered if she would join me when I flew up to the ruins of my home. I wondered if she would even be able to bear it.

He left something for me there, something that he wanted me to find. A parting gift from beyond the grave. I suspected what it may be, though I did not dare hope. It was an odd thing to reckon with, having spent so much time hating him. And I didn't forgive him, not in the ways that mattered. But the sheer fact that he found a way to send a message through the veil did something to ease the anger I had been holding so close all these years.

Without my realizing, Astriel had guided me to the bed, positioned face down so she could dress the wounds. The bandage on her own hand was dirty and threatening to come unraveled, red penetrating the layers. I should have been tending to her. I didn't even ask if she was okay.

I steeled myself to rise, to offer her the same that she had given me. An act of care that I had never before been granted. I closed my eyes, taking a deep breath, shifting to brace myself. But before I could push myself up, she shushed me, and I felt her fingers comb through my wet hair.

The sensation was like a spell, I could not fight against the beckoning sleep.

# 68

# Astriel

Eyes still closed, I reached across the bed, feeling for my mate. Instead of the solid warmth of him, my fingers only met with empty sheets. I groaned, rolling to the edge, squinting against the bright light that illuminated the space through sheer curtains. Our leathers were still piled in the corner where I had left them after my own much needed bath. They were still in need of a good scrubbing, the stains of our battle darkening wide splotches. I pulled myself to my feet, trying and failing to rub the sleep out of my eyes.

Shuffling, I grabbed for a shirt, eyes unfocused. It was Keelan's, I realized, his scent of oak moss and cedar wrapping around me as I pulled it on. Looking around the room, I noted the rumpled covers, the red stained rags I could make out through the bathing room door, and the freshly oiled daggers that lay upon a towel atop the dresser. I must have slept like the dead for him to have put them there without waking me.

From the kitchen I could hear the soft clinking of dishes, I padded down the hall, following the sound. When I passed the few remaining drawings from the aurora, I did not shy from them. They were still indecipherable, but they no longer scared me. They may have opened the door to something I still did not quite understand, but the fear of it had lost its hold on me. I was at peace with this strange power.

That peace was solidified as I entered the kitchen. Ke's back was to me, preparing some variety of food that I could not see past his wings. He hummed a melody to himself as he worked. He did not hear me enter, so I just leaned against the wall, watching him. The places on his back and wing where he had been wounded were already considerably more healed than yesterday. His muscles seemed looser, though his entire torso was littered with angry bruises.

Shoving off the wall, I crossed the kitchen, he was so lost in the song he was humming he did not hear my approach. "What are you making?" I whispered into his back, wrapping my arms around his middle.

He started at the sound and touch, then relaxed into the gentle embrace, "Sandwiches." He said cheerfully, resting his hands on the counter as I pressed a soft kiss between his wings.

"How are you feeling today?" I asked, pulling away just enough that he could spin to face me, leaning his hips on the counter. I scanned his toned chest, equally as covered in bruises and shallow cuts as his back.

"Much better." He responded, pulling me into him. "What about yourself?"

"Still tired," I admitted, breathing him in, "What time is it?"

"Just after noon," He responded, planting a kiss on top of my head, and then reaching behind his back to grab a plate in each hand, "You should eat."

Reluctantly I pulled away, taking the plate he offered. As if in response, my stomach growled loudly. The sight of the simple meal made my mouth water. He slipped around me, striding to the other side of the island, setting his plate down before easing onto the stool.

"Those look like they hurt." I gestured to his chest with one half of the sandwich before taking a large bite.

"They do." He chuckled, "But I will survive. How'd you make out?" He tore into his own.

"Nicks and scrapes." I mumbled around the bite and then swallowed. "The tiredness is more from the impromptu vision quest than the fight itself."

"Speaking of that," Ke set his sandwich down, eyes boring into me, "would you join me on a trip up the mountain today?"

"Sure. What for though?" I took another bite.

"I'd like to go to my childhood home. In the Seraphim township."

I halted my assault on the sandwich, unease coiling in my stomach, "To find what your father hid?"

He nodded, not breaking eye contact, "I know you haven't been up there, and if you don't want to go it's fine I just thought—"

"I'll go with you." I interrupted him, trying to smile. "Besides, it's time I quit running from that part of my past."

A grin spread across his face in a wide arc, "Finish eating and we will get dressed."

* * *

The ruins were worse than I could have imagined. The scars of raging fires blackened the stone of every building, the roofs long burned away. Walls crumbled into piles of rubble from centuries of disrepair, shards of glass still crunched underfoot. I took in the heartbreaking sight, clutching Keelan's hand as the grief I had pushed aside for so long bubbled to the surface. Any signs of life had been long since washed away. Together, we strode through a necropolis.

"I didn't know it would be like this." Keelan spoke softly, as if afraid to wake the dead.

"It's horrible." I whispered, the sound choked and ragged.

We walked in step, no longer speaking. Wind rustling through the trees was the only sound that broke the oppressive quiet. We passed abandoned fire pits, the ravaged remains of masonry that looked to have at once been a small amphitheater, a headless statue of a woman with broken wings. The men who had come here left nothing intact. Only an entire culture burned to ash. They destroyed *everything*.

"Do you want to see your parents' home?" Keelan asked, squeezing my hand tighter.

I just nodded. I knew I would never willingly return to this place. This would be my only chance. So I followed him as we wound through the ruins, careful not to disturb anything from where it lay.

He stopped in front of a building, what was left of it. No larger or grander than any other we passed. It was so… ordinary. But I felt the pull, a recognition I couldn't place. I had few memories of anything before I became a ward of the capital, and yet, somehow I knew this was my first home.

I broke Keelan's grip, walking slowly towards the deteriorated building. Stepping over a scattering of stone at the threshold, I took in the space. The base of a hearth still stood on one wall, but there was nothing else. Anything I could have found to spark recollection had been lost or destroyed. Only the shell of a home had survived against the passage of time.

I heard the crunch of Keelan's boots as he followed me in. "There's nothing here." I breathed, more to myself than to him.

But I wandered in the remains, kneeling at the crumbling fireplace, running my hands over the weather smooth surface. A small part of me hoped the contact would trigger something, a memory, a vision, a chance to speak to my own parents like I had been able to with Ke's father. But there was only the stone.

In this whole place, there was only stone.

"I've seen enough." I murmured, shouldering past Keelan on shaking legs.

"I'm sorry." He said, appearing back at my side as I traveled mindlessly back down what would have been a road.

I just shook my head, wrapping my arms around myself, "I don't know what I expected. Maybe if I had come sooner—" My voice crackled, "I don't really remember them anyways. Maybe it's for the best."

"You don't have to stay." He offered, "I can find what I'm looking for and meet you back at the house."

I weighed the offer, not necessarily wanting to leave him here alone, but shaken to my core. I wasn't sure how much longer I could remain before I broke. "Will you be okay?" I asked, and I knew my face betrayed the swirling eddy of emotions.

"I'll be fine." He assured me, pulling me into a swift embrace, "Go home. I won't be long."

I just nodded, taking one more look at him as he retreated, a grim smile on his lips. I beat my wings, the gravity of the place trying to pull me back down. But I broke free, diving past the mountain's edge. The tears I had been fighting spilled over as the distance stretched between me and the city of the dead.

# 69

# Astriel

Of course, going home would not be so simple.

As I landed on the street in front of the garden gate, the iridescent fluttering of wings caught my eye. I groaned internally, praying that the tears that had dried on my skin were not visible. I schooled my features into a mask of indifference and pushed open the gate.

"Clovis," I greeted her as she flitted back and forth on nervous feet, "What can I do for you?"

"The council would like to meet with you and Keelan," Her eyes never met mine, "is he around?"

"He's busy." I said, approaching her. "What is this about?"

"They do not tell me." She stared down at her feet, the beat of her wings slowed almost imperceptibly.

"Give me twenty minutes. Tell them I will be there." I gave her one last look, and nodded sharply before stepping past, leaving the Pixie fluttering on my doorstep.

* * *

The door creaked open when I finally found my way to the meeting hall. Quiet conversation halted as I strode in, foul mood no doubt evident on my face. But it wasn't my face the gathered nobility gawked at as I stood near the door. Their eyes ran down my body— my clothes, I realized.

My silence in my home had been deafening when I entered. Every casual sign of life that contrasted so harshly against the barren ruins on the mountainside unleashing another wave of pain that crashed against my rib cage. I had dressed without seeing, without thinking. I know I scrawled a note for Keelan, so he would know where I went if he returned before I did. I did not return to my body until I stood in front of the council members.

"Expecting a fight?" Morrelin's tone, laced with disgust as his eyes ran over me, cut through the fog I had let settle in my mind.

I looked down at myself. I did not wear a dress, I did not wear white. Instead, I wore tight, dark clothes. Somehow, I had strapped myself into my still dirty leathers. Without noticing, I had donned a cache of blades.

"I was preparing to take to the skies when you summoned me." I lied, schooling any emotion on my face. "What is this about?"

"Dead soldiers in the forest." Shyla offered simply, her black eyes set on mine.

"Would you happen to know anything about that?" Morrelin asked. The rise of an eyebrow and a scanning of the dark stains on my leathers were his only indication of any emotion.

I strode across the room, lowering myself into the chair I had occupied for so long. "They marched on Phaedra. Keelan and I dispatched them in the night."

"They were coming here?" Jarrah's shimmering wings flitted nervously, her green eyes wide.

"You didn't think to alert us?" Morrelin stared accusingly, mouth slightly agape.

"We've been busy, you would have been informed." My voice was dead even to my own ears.

"Why did they come?" Shyla demanded from across the table.

"A test, I believe. From Deliana." I paused as the group stared, "She is building an army that does not rest, that does not feel pain, and they do not stop until they are killed. I think she wanted to know how they fair in a real fight."

"And how do they fair?" Morrelin asked, that hateful mask slipping in favor of genuine concern.

"They are still men." I said simply, "They fall like men."

It was silent for a long moment. The ladies cut their eyes to each other, but Morrelin kept his on me, "So you can fight?"

I nodded, "I can handle a fair number of them, especially with Keelan. He is a gifted warrior." I added, absently. I leaned forward, resting my arms on the table, "That being said, if they storm Phaedra in numbers we will not be enough. Our citizens need to be alerted of the threat, so that they may prepare."

"Prepare?" Shyla scoffed, "Prepare how? Our citizens are not soldiers." She shot a hand out and Jarrah recoiled.

"They need to be aware of the threat, so they may either take up arms or leave before it's too late."

"What you are suggesting would create chaos among our people." The male's voice pitched up, but not in anger.

"When Deliana marches, *that* will create chaos among our

people."

Shyla, emboldened by the fear that laced her voice, spoke again, "We don't even know if Deliana intends to invade Phaedra."

"She does." I gritted, frustration heating my blood, "There is no more question. She plans to take control of the tree, our people will be collateral damage. They need to be aware."

"What will they do?" Morrelin straightened, "Do you expect to fight alongside the softhearted Pixies? The Nymph artisans? Do you desire to watch water fae be cut down on dry land? We will find a way to keep the fight away from Phaedra."

I stood, slamming my hands on the table as my chair tipped behind me, the loud crack of wood on wood silencing the room.

"You ask me if I want to fight beside citizens with no training? I do not. You ask me if I want to watch the people I have spent centuries protecting fall at the blade of man? I do not. But there is no keeping the fight out Phaedra. It will come."

My breath was coming fast now, the reality of what was at stake nestling between my ribs. "Deliana intends to overtake this territory. She wields a weapon that will level our home. Allowing the citizens to remain unaware is no longer an option. If we do not at least give them a chance to take up arms or leave, they will *die.*"

I took a shaking breath, eyes traveling between the stunned trio. "We do not have the right to take away their choice by shrouding them in ignorance. They deserve to know."

Silence blanketed the room. I could only hear my own ragged breathing. The ladies looked at each other, fear in each of their eyes. Morrelin kept his glare on me, fingers tapping quietly on the wood of the table. I stared them all down.

"Leave us." Morrelin spoke with calculated calm, waving off the two other ladies, but his eyes never left mine.

# 70

# Astriel

"You are in rare form today, Astriel." Morrelin clasped his hands atop the table when the door shut behind the retreating females, "What troubles you?"

I paced up and down the length of the room, his eyes following as he waited for me to speak, "I won't be able to save them." I said finally, still pacing.

"That is war."

"Protecting the people here is my job, it is the only thing I know. It is all that I am. I cannot watch them all die because of my failings."

"You seem to forget that there is another path." He said, no emotion in his voice.

"And what is that?" I scoffed. But I halted my pacing, bracing myself on the back of the Jarrah's chair, across from the male.

"Deliana does not necessarily want the messiness of an invasion. There was a reason you were taken to the castle. She tried for an alliance first. Only when you upended those plans did she build an army."

"An alliance built on coercion and mistrust is hardly an alliance at all." I shot back, pushing myself off the chair. I turned away as memories from the castle swam in my vision.

"It is not ideal, I will admit." He said, rising from his place and crossing the distance between us. I turned to him, where he stood in front of me, "But if you are to save these people, it is the only course of action."

"You don't know what she is capable of. She will burn Phaedra to the ground only because it pleases her." Desperation had seeped into my words.

"I know you do not care for me. Perhaps you do not even trust me, anymore," He spoke softly, "but our desires are the same. And it pains me to see you this way."

I retreated, his golden eyes tracking me as I leaned against the far wall, "Morrelin, allowing that witch to lay any claim here would spell destruction for not only Phaedra, but for the world at large."

"You cannot know that." He said, tipping his head as he took another step towards me.

"I do know that. Unless Deliana is dispatched, our fate is sealed."

He sighed, "I have waged many battles, Astriel. I have won wars on scales greater than you can imagine. Sometimes they are won on a battlefield, and sometimes they are won by yielding some small thing." Another step.

"The Tree is no small thing."

"No, it is not." Another step. "But conceding a place here for her, it might save us a battle our people would not walk away from."

"And bend to the will of a power hungry sorceress who wields a weapon of complete control? *That* is a concession our people may not walk away from."

"I fear that dark fae you've been fraternizing with has poisoned your mind." Another step. "You were made for more than being the bedroom companion of some shadowy demon."

"Careful Morrelin, he has proven his loyalty." I hardened my eyes at the male, but he did not react.

"He is a distraction, he makes you selfish." Another step and his hulking form cast me in shadow, "*I* molded you into what you are. *I* formed you into the force of nature you have grown to be."

"My priorities have not changed. It is Phaedra above all else."

But he was not done. His hands landed on either side of my head, his arms caging me between them. I tucked my wings, shrinking away from him. "I turned you from a scared fledgling into a beloved queen among her people. We will do incredible things, Astriel. We can avoid all of this. One small concession, and you and I will be revered. No more council, no more fighting. When you are the queen at my side, you can finally be at peace."

I paled, mouth suddenly dry, realizing what he was suggesting, "I— I don't want that." I choked out, heart thundering inside my chest.

"Since when has that mattered?" He loosed a wry laugh, "You never wanted to become a member of the council. You did not want to become the Angel of Death, but you did. Like I said, small concessions. This is just one more. I made you into a God here, think of what we could accomplish together."

"No." I heard myself saying. His eyes widened as I ducked

beneath his arm, crossing the room before he could reach for me. "I will not turn my back on my people, but I will not indulge this fantasy of yours."

I turned the knob, slipping through the door as I heard him call from where he still stood across the room, "It would be in your best interest to reconsider."

I slammed the door, blindly pushing past a small fae on the sidewalk, the threat settling in my gut like a stone.

# 71

# Keelan

The front door shut with such force that the windows rattled as Astriel stormed into the house. I emerged from the kitchen, just in time to see the flash of white wings disappear into the bedroom. I followed, halting in the doorway, watching as she tore through the space. She did not look at me.

"What's wrong?" I asked. Her note had indicated that she would be at a council meeting, but she wore her leathers and blades. The manner of dress was out of character, but as was her blind rampage as she rummaged through the bedroom.

"Nothing." She spit, still not looking at me, she was opening and slamming drawers now, digging through their contents, "Gear up. I want to train."

I eyed her as she continued the assault on the dresser, but I obeyed. "What are you looking for?" I asked carefully, grabbing my breastplate from the pile on the floor, trying to sound casual.

"Nothing." She said again, but when she flung open the drawer of discarded daggers I heard her suck breath.

"Maybe I can—" But I did not finish.

She was inspecting the fine blade she held. Past the fall of her hair I could see her lip quiver, tears welling in her waterline. Her fingers trembled at what she beheld that I could not see. I watched her face turn to the ceiling, swallowing and blinking hard.

I opened my mouth to speak again but my voice caught. She twisted, a flash of white wings and silver blade. The solid sound of the dagger embedding in the wall next to the door was drowned out Astriel released a strangled scream that was almost a cry. She stared at it, arm outstretched, for just a moment.

"Meet me on the cliff when you're dressed." Her voice strangled as she strode out of the room.

The front door slammed once more as I continued buckling and strapping on my leathers. I worked quickly, the need to follow her overwhelming my senses. I was already walking as I locked the scabbard over my hips, once I slipped into my boots I would be after her. The glint of the blade in the wall caught my attention as I passed the threshold.

I paused, just long enough to read the inscription on the ornately carved blade.

*For my queen of angels*
*-M*

\* \* \*

By the time I had made it to the cliff side, Astriel's dagger sheaths were empty. She braced herself against the base of a thick tree, prying them from the trunk. They stuck out of the wood in a tight circle, all at the height of the average male. All of them were buried to the hilt.

She did not react when I approached, just continued dislodging the weapons from the tree with unprecedented ease. Whatever emotion she had displayed at the house was long gone. Her face was an impenetrable mask of calculating calm. The prickle of unease at the back of my neck hinted that it was no facade.

So I watched her, and when the last blade eased free of the battered oak, she leveled her gaze on me. White fire burned behind those quartz eyes. She stalked over, sheathing the final blade. My wings flared, unsure of her next move. Though all she had been through, I had never seen this in her.

"What happened?" I found myself asking, "Who is 'M'?"

She sneered at the initial, "I want to spar." She dropped into a fighting position.

I considered her for a moment, "Hand to hand or weapons, lady's choice."

"Weapons." She responded simply, and lunged.

I dodged her first swipe with the dagger, unsheathing my sword and yielding a step. She lunged again, that pale blaze in her eyes flickering in the dying light. I blocked her with the hilt, knocking her backwards and swiping for her legs. She jumped over the blade and swung again. I caught her wrist.

"What happened?" I asked again, staring her down.

"Council meeting." She responded, ripping from my grip

and slashing past my guard.

Her blade connected with the leather, leaving a soft scratch over my breastplate. Either she had dulled her blades or the tree had. Neither were comforting thoughts. "Must have been quite the meeting if you are this wound up." I swung again, the broad side of my blade connecting with her thigh guard with enough force that she stumbled sideways.

She gritted her teeth, ducking my defense and tapping the hilt of her dagger on the inside of both my thighs before emerging behind me. "You must be out of practice if your sparring is this sloppy."

I spun on her, using a wing to dislodge the blade from her hand. "If you will not tell me what the hell happened in there then perhaps I will ask them myself." I countered.

Her eyes darkened, "You will do no such thing." Without retrieving another blade she pounced, striking and blocking barehanded as I yielded step after step.

"I may just," I countered, a lie. As her emotions raged, her technique grew sloppier, leaving herself open, "I will go to their very homes and demand to know exactly what occurred."

"You will stay far away from them." She grunted, landing a hit on my ribs, "You will never attend another meeting. You will not answer any of their summons." I knocked the hilt of my sword into her stomach, sending her sprawling across the rock.

"Why?" I demanded, arms outstretched. But when she looked up at me, the fire was gone from her eyes.

"Morrelin. The blade was from Morrelin." She finally confessed, barely above a whisper. "He cannot be trusted."

So I asked for the final time that day, "El, what happened?"

And she told me.

# 72

# Keelan

Her admission of what had gone on in the meeting hall made my blood boil. The instinctive protectiveness of my mate threatened to overtake my sensibilities. The liberties he had taken, tried to take with her. I knew Morrelin to be a snake, but not to this degree.

"We have to get out of here." I growled as she finished, "We have to get *you* out of here."

"And go where, Keelan? This is my home. I cannot leave my people."

"You people who are willing to sell you out? Betray you?" Panic gripped my throat.

"Morrelin does not speak for my people." She steeled herself, but her eyes betrayed the fear, the hopelessness within.

"El," I gripped her hands, pleading, "There is no other option."

"I cannot abandon them."

"You will not be able to save them." My heart ached for her, for what this must be doing to her.

"I—" Her voice broke, "There must be something I can do. There *is* something I can do."

"You would marry him?" Bile rose in my throat as the words left my lips.

She pulled out of my grip, turning away. "Two hundred years Keelan. Phaedra has been my lifeblood for *two hundred years*. I cannot turn my back on them."

"Then we will fight." I strode up behind her, reaching out, but not quite touching her shoulder.

"You could leave." The words were barely more than a whisper, a ragged breath, "You should leave. Take a ship, sail to Allesyna, be free of this."

"I won't leave you. I can't." And it was true, my very bones called to her. My soul demanded her nearness.

She stepped away from me, closer to the cliff's edge, until the toes of her boots hung over the edge. I stopped next to her, staring out at her home, at the massive tree that loomed over it. Wind whipped the hair that had fallen from her braid across her face. She wrapped her arms around herself, but would not look at me.

"We all must pay the price of salvation." She muttered, almost inaudible. "That is what the dead king said. This is my price."

I shook my head, the tightness in my throat strangling the words, "You are wrong. He was wrong. This can't be—"

She looked at me then, tears streaked down her bruised cheek. The dampness on her face stole my breath. I could not find the words, I could not think of anything to say that would convince her that this was wrong. It filled me with a rage and despair that cratered my chest. I just stared at her.

She spoke, her voice trembling, "Phaedra is all I am.

Whatever it takes, I have to save them."

She finally looked back at me, the silver of her eyes guttering to an empty gray. "I love you, Keelan. Maybe in another life, we could have been happy."

Something in me shattered completely. I reached out to her again, ready to fall to my knees, to beg and plead for her. *Please, don't go.* But I didn't say it, I couldn't force the words from my lips.

She just gave me one last sad smile, and fell forward off the rock. I watched her take flight, her silhouette shrinking in the distance. Suddenly, the insignificant weight in my breast pocket felt so unbearably heavy.

# 73

# Astriel

I had told him everything. Everything up to the veiled threat Morrelin had issued upon my escape from him. Tears ran unbidden down my face as I crossed the city that shimmered the dying light. Behind me I knew that he still watched, still stood frozen on that cliff face where I had left him. The sorrow that racked my body made me unsteady in the sky, but I couldn't bring myself to care.

He should hate me. A small part of me hoped he would. Even as something in my chest cracked open. I replayed the words Morrelin had spit when I rebuked him. It was not a threat against me, I had known even then, but a threat against *him*. This was a sacrifice for Phaedra, yes. But also for Keelan, so that he may be spared from the dangers he did not know swirled around him.

*Even I do not rule the hands of fate, we all must bow to it.* The Mother had said. The dead king had spoken of the price of salvation. Their words collided in my mind, a dizzying maelstrom of prophecy and guidance. This was my price, to play the pawn. It was my fate, one I had tried and failed to outrun.

There was no more running. Not for the first time, I felt the walls closing in, a narrow path with no illumination stretched out in front of me. I had known for the entirety of my life that my fate was decided, that I would never have the luxury of choice. I had never flinched from it. I had never imagined that my path of fate would be this painful.

\* \* \*

I hadn't planned to, but when my boots connected with cobblestone, I was standing in front of the domed library. The sun had set, and street lamps illuminated patches of the otherwise abandoned street. A flash of color down an alley lit in my periphery, but my eyes wouldn't focus on it. Dreamlike, I pushed through the heavy wooden door, near stumbling into the empty room.

Absently, I scanned the library. There was a very good chance Moira wouldn't be here, I wasn't even sure why I sought her out. But I did, and unthinkingly, I crossed the open space. No one else was here, as far as I could tell, and the shadows cast at the ends of long rows of shelves imposed menacingly. The only sound in the space was the soft scuffing of my own boots on the hardwood.

I yanked open the ancient door to the subterranean room, leaning against the wall as I descended. When I reached the bottom, Moira sat at the large table, still pushed against the wall, buried in a scattering of ancient tomes. She lifted her head as I crossed the room.

"What are you reading?" I found myself asking, falling into the chair across from her.

"Astriel," She seemed startled to see me, "I wasn't expecting you. Were you wanting to do more pendulum work?"

I smiled weakly, glancing at the pile of bedding that still covered a large section of floor, "I just wanted to see you."

She reached across the table to take my hands, concern lacing her features. I pulled away. I saw the hurt flash across her face. "What's wrong?"

"I'm just tired." I responded, and then repeated, "What are you reading?"

Though I knew she didn't believe me she just said, "More history on the Seraphim. I found a book on prophecies. I don't want to trouble you."

"Please," I leaned back, "Trouble me all you'd like. What did you find?"

Whatever her books foretold could not be worse than the realities I faced. There was nothing the ancient fae could have written or seen that could compare to the inevitable reality. I watched her as she considered, chewing on her lip. I just raised a weary eyebrow, silently encouraging her to continue.

Finally, she relented, "There is a story here, more of a poem, that tells of the attack on the Seraphim, the one that took your parents."

I just stared at her, "And?"

"And it doesn't end with the slaughter that occurred during that battle."

"What does that mean?"

She pushed the book over to me, pointing to a passage at the bottom of the page, "It is... vague, to say the least. But

I thought, maybe, with everything you've been doing, the things you face, you might be able to make some sense of it."

I gave her a doubtful look, but pulled the book closer anyway. The majority of the poem was, at this point, just an artistic retelling of history. But as my eyes flitted lower, I saw what she meant. The last stanza was short, and ominous.

*False redemption is crowned in fire*
*Blood of stars the Gods require*
*New worlds open unveil the past*
*The stones of fate have long been cast*
*Darkness spills across the land*
*It falls with light in dying hand*

"It is nonsense." I pushed the book back across the table, shutting out the terrible foreboding that had been scrawled across the page.

"You don't think—"

"It's nothing at all, Moira." I snapped at her, more sharply than I had intended, "I'm sorry, I just mean, that could mean anything, it may have even already happened. Besides, it's just a poem."

"The rest was correct, about what happened to the Seraphim." She said quietly, turning the book to face her again, scouring the page.

"I'm tired, I'm sorry for interrupting your study." *Coming here was a mistake.*

"Let me walk you out." She jumped up and followed silently as we climbed the stairs.

She walked next to me, saying nothing else as I led us through the main floor. When my hand rested on the knob to the front door, I turned back to her, "Thank you, Moira. For everything. You've been a good friend to me, I don't know if I ever told you that."

I pulled the door open, halfway into the street when I felt her hand on mine, "I will always be your friend."

I nodded to her, and pulled the door shut behind me as I stepped onto the street.

# 74

# Astriel

The moon was high in the sky when I knocked on his door. The same door I had passed through countless times in my youth, without even the inkling of what its resident was capable of. I shuddered at the thought. I steeled myself, knocking again. I fisted the charms around my neck, listening as my circlet thrummed a soft song at my temples. A song that would never cease, I imagined.

The door opened, and I met the golden eyes that appraised me, "Astriel, I was hoping you would visit me tonight. Please, come in."

Morrelin stepped aside, still wearing his daytime finery despite the late hour. I stepped past him, into the large home. When I entered the foyer, taking in the familiar interior, a tightness squeezed at my chest. It was the same as it had always been, green and gold and opulent. Twin marble staircases climbed the walls, leading to an upstairs I realized I had never seen. All the times I had been here it had been downstairs, or in the gardens, learning and training with the Lord of Warfare.

He drifted past me, towards the sitting room, "Come, join me for a drink."

I followed him, observing the quiet emptiness of the house, "Where is everyone?"

He threw me a look over his shoulder as he retrieved two short glasses from a beverage cart, "The help? I have dismissed them for tonight. The fewer ears listening in on this conversation, the better. We are alone."

I glanced around again, the house was almost eerie without the bustling of the many servants he retained. He returned to his task, pouring a generous amount of dark liquor into each glass. He held out one, taking a sip from his own. I took it, watching as he lowered himself into a heavily embroidered chaise, adorned with stitching that depicted leaves and vines tangled into each other. I mirrored his movement, setting myself on the edge of a matching chair across the sprawling rug.

"I've considered your proposition," I started, feigning a sip from the glass. The liquid pressed against my tight lips but did not flow into my mouth. "Is it true that our union would prevent attack on the city?"

"It is," He said coolly, resting his nearly drained glass on his knee, "I have been in communication with Deliana. As long as she is met with safe passage in our lands, there will be no war."

"You've been in communication with the witch? To what end?" My circlet thrummed quietly as I stared wide-eyed at the lord.

"We have... complementary goals. She desires access to the tree, and I desire to once again reign as a king. We can help each other to accomplish those things." He threw an arm over the back of the chaise, the very picture of ease.

"And what of me, then?" I found myself asking, "What is my place in this trade off?"

"I want you. And she needs something from you. It is as simple as that." He shrugged, like it was obvious.

I scoffed, setting down my glass and rising from the chair. I felt his eyes on me as I stalked across the space, pouring a taller glass of water from the carafe. I sipped from it, desperate to moisten my anxiety parched throat. I leaned against a gold pillar near the entryway, feigning deep thought. It would be necessary to appear completely detached in front of this male, to control the conversation.

I took a long drink, "What could she possibly want from me?"

"It is such a small thing, we can worry about that later, after you agree."

"Why would I? Why should I bow to her demands?"

"Don't think of it like that. You bow to no one, we are simply uniting kingdoms." When I gave him a skeptical look, he sighed, and then continued, "She also believes that if you are not tightly leashed you will continue to derail her."

"You would be the tight leash, I presume?" I couldn't help the downturn of my lips.

"In a manner of speaking," He smiled, a mischievous glint in his eyes, "Though my queen of angels could never truly be leashed." He finished his drink, setting it on the side table and standing.

I suppressed a grimace at the title, raising my glass for another sip and finding it empty. I set it back on the beverage cart. "You have to understand that this is all very unexpected, Morrelin. Here I thought you had grown to hate me."

He stood, crossing the space between us, once again casting me in the shadow of his body, "Hate you? I could never." He lowered his voice, dropping his head until it hovered next to my ear, "Your power is intoxicating. When you would challenge me, flair those wings of yours in a rage, in the late hours of the night I remember those moments. I crave you, your fierceness, your noble ruthlessness."

His proximity made my head spin, threatening to knock me off balance, "You— you never gave any indication." I tripped over my words.

He raised his head, his eyes gazing over my shoulder, "You weren't ready. Everything had to be just perfect." In my periphery I watched him reach past me, and felt his fingertips grazing the arch of my wing.

I shivered at the touch, and stepped back, stumbling. I reached for a dagger with shaking fingers. He just looked at me, amusement evident in his features. I tried in vain to shake away the dizziness that muddled my thoughts. My breaths were coming in shallow pants. *Something is wrong.*

He laughed a little, "You are so predictable, Astriel. That is my great failure in our many years of training."

I stared at him as he approached once more, our faces so close I could feel his breath. "I don't—"

My legs were failing, my knees giving way. I felt his firm grip on my waist, pressing my body to his chest. I could not even raise my arms to push him off, "Perhaps you came here in good faith. But you have always been a jumpy, defensive little thing. I had to protect myself, you understand that."

I blinked, my mind moving too slowly to understand. But the weight in my limbs intensified, the sensations of his body against me fading away. My eyes widened, "The liquor." I choked out, my throat closing. *But I didn't drink it.*

"Close," He said. "It was in the water too. I expected that you would be suspicious of a drink I prepared for you. So I dosed the water and the whiskey glass. You would never be wary of a drink you prepared for yourself. Like I said, predictable."

"Leru." I managed to choke out, no more than a garbled sound. The room tipped, and I knew Morrelin had scooped me into his strong arms. My circlet fell from my hair, clinking softly against the polished floor. I watched the room, upside down as he carried my frozen and useless body up the stairs.

"Very astute, Astriel. It's an odd little plant isn't it? It paralyzes and removes sensation from the body entirely, but does not interfere with consciousness, or one's ability to think. I often wonder if one can sleep while in the throes, or if they are committed to lay awake, trapped in their own mind. Perhaps you'll be able to tell me in the morning, my divinity."

We reached the landing and he carried me down a long hall. I could not focus on any of it, the blood was rushing to my head which was already spinning. I wanted to scream, to fight. I wanted to stab him in the chest with one of the daggers my limp hand rested on. I had recovered so swiftly last time, maybe I would be able to this time as well.

As if he could hear my thoughts, "I know you have been struck down with Leru before, from the dagger I had given that useless Elf. The male you've been associating with shared that you recovered exceptionally fast." He had given the dagger to Farryn. The realization set off a throbbing between my temples. *He isn't just in communication with*

*Deliana, he is working with her.*

"You'll have to forgive me," He continued, "The dosage in the water had to be increased substantially, I don't know how long you will be like this. I hope it is not terribly unpleasant. I'll ensure that your needs are met until you are well."

I heard him softly kick open a door. The scenery changed, this room was opulent, yes, but nearly completely devoid of decoration. A four poster bed stood in the center of the room, with a dresser and wardrobe across from it. But there was nothing hung against the expensive wallpaper, nothing atop the dresser. Even the attached bathroom had been stripped to bare bones.

I realized with no small sense of horror, that this room had already been prepared for me. There would be nothing I could use to defend myself, no candlesticks or fire pokers to fend him off. He had made me a prison cell with the elegance of a royal suite. He had been planning this for a long time. He had been planning for me to refuse him, and for him to still be able to keep me here.

He set me gently on the bed, looking me over as he did, "Let's make you more comfortable shall we? I'll remove your leathers." His hungry eyes ran over my body, "We will be leaving in the morning. I will have a female servant tend to your needs before we depart. Is that alright?"

He stared down at me with a wide smile across his face, knowing I couldn't respond. I couldn't move enough to even sneer at him. So he got to work, unbuckling straps and manipulating my limbs. I could hear my daggers and sheaths being removed.

One by one the pieces came off. He glowered at them as he tossed them into the hallway, no doubt to be gathered up and discarded. Because they were a gift from Keelan, because they bore the mark and scent of another male.

When the final bracer fell away, he just stared, as if perplexed by what he beheld. The *Serch Bythol* I realized. The binding, I felt a swell of hope that it would ruin me in his eyes, that I had already been claimed. *A claim I just severed.* I tried not to think about it.

But he just tutted, "Well, we will have that removed, of course." And then, without even a farewell, he left.

I listened as the door shut and locked behind him, blanketing the room in darkness. I listened to the scraping of leather and fading footsteps. When there was no more sound, I stared at the ceiling shrouded in darkness because it's all I could do. *This is my price.* I reminded myself even as I hoped that the Leru would freeze my lungs and heart and let me suffocate peacefully.

But my lungs filled, and my heart beat, and distantly, as if I had imagined it, I felt a single tear slide down my cheek.

# 75

# Keelan

*The entire night.* I sat on that barren cliff for the entire night. Unmoving, adrift, listless, completely and utterly lost. She left me. Not because she didn't love me, but because her duty to Phaedra drove her to it. For a moment, as I glared out at the city below, cast in the glow of the rising sun, I hated it.

I hated Phaedra. I hated its people. I hated the tree. I hated the Mother.

But I did not hate Astriel. Her fierce protectiveness of this place was so entwined with who she is. I loved her so fiercely for it, even when it was the very thing that ripped her from me. I should not have let her leave so easily, I should have come up with a solution better than this.

*Morrelin.* His name set flames ablaze in my mind. He had done this, he had taken her away from me. He had used her as a pawn, a chess piece in the game of war. He had promised peace in exchange for her loyalty. Did he know what she was capable of? Did he have any idea the force of nature he intended to contain? Before long he would.

As the sun crested over the city, I resolved myself to fix this.

She spoke so flippantly of her price for salvation. I would not let her pay it. Fates be damned, I would not allow her to suffer at the hands of cruel destiny. I dove off the cliff.

* * *

My feet had barely hit pavement when the small, mousy haired female barreled towards me from Astriel's front door. She was disheveled, her hair falling out of the clip that contained it, her simple linen dress crumpled in places. I grunted as her small fists pummeled my chest plate, tears streaming down her face. I gripped her wrists, holding her away from me as she thrashed and screamed. With wide eyes I watched the previously meek librarian swear and curse me.

"Moira, what are you doing here?" I asked, incredulous. As she pulled away from me, I released my grip on her.

"Where the hell have you been?" Her fists were still balled at her sides. "I have been waiting here for hours. Have you seen Astriel?"

"Yesterday." I responded, my chest tightening painfully. "Why?"

"She came to see me last night at the library. There was something off about her." She squinted her eyes at me.

"Don't bother playing coy, seer. Why are you here?" I crossed my arms.

She bristled at my tone but continued, "I saw what happened between you two and oh, she is such a… but you just let her and… anyways there was this book…" She was practically shaking.

I grabbed her by the shoulders, stooping until we were eye to eye, "Moira, what is it?"

She took a shaking breath, "When I touched her I didn't just see her memories, Keelan. I saw her future, or at least I think I did."

"You can do that?" I asked.

"I didn't know I could. Or I guess I still don't. It may not even be a true vision, I may have only seen what she *thought* her future would be." Her eyes flitted back and forth, as if seeing two different realities, "But either way Keelan, it's bad. You shouldn't have let her do it."

I gritted my teeth against the final statement, knowing it was true, "Moira, what did you see?"

When she told me, the thing in my chest that had been tortuously aching, broke completely.

# 76

# Keelan


I did not wait for Moira to finish before I wrapped her in my arms and took off, back into the sky. What she had said, what she had seen, the details didn't really matter. Moira didn't know if it was a true prophecy or just El's anxieties. I didn't care, I would protect her regardless, once I found her. But first I had to find that bastard of a fae.

I would kill him.


* * *


I knew only what side of the city Morrelin's house was on, but not which was his exactly. I could get us close, but I needed Moira to come. If Moira had seen it when she touched Astriel, then she could help me identify it. I didn't know what it looked like, and tugging the bond, trying to follow El with that sixth sense wasn't working. She was blocking me out.

The librarian screamed as we took flight, her arms

wrapped around my neck and her fingers gripping my shoulders so hard I could be confident it would leave bruises. "You have to open your eyes, Moira. I need you to look."

She shook her head feverishly, squeezing her eyes tighter, "If I look down I'm going to be sick."

I clenched my teeth, resisting the urge to snap at her, "This isn't a casual flight Moira, we have to find her."

She peeked one eye open, glancing over her tense shoulder, and her nails dug into my back harder, "I can't do it! I think— I think it has a green door, edged in gold, do you see that?

My teeth clenched harder, "No. What color was the roof?"

She considered for a moment, "Light brown, almost beige. It's a tiled roof."

That was something I could work with. I banked to the left, the fae in my arms squealing with the movement. The urge to drop her was not insignificant. I could certainly have flown faster without her. And the maelstrom of emotions was interfering with my sense of protection for anyone other than my mate. But I steeled myself, even if she drew blood, which she was growing dangerously close to doing, I would not drop her.

It was only a few more agonizing minutes before we found the house with the beige tiled roof and green door. Looking at it, I realized that I could have identified it without her. Nearly a mansion, the Tudor style estate towered over the neighboring townhouses. Surrounded by a sprawling yard, it offered ample privacy from prying eyes. The thought filled my vision with red.

I dropped Moira, looking sick, none too gently just inside the towering wrought iron gate and tore down the pathway to the door, banging my fist against the solid wooden panel. Verdant paint flaked off beneath my fist, the sturdy barrier straining on its hinges. I'd turn the thing to splinters if I needed to.

I whirled on a light touch tapping my shoulder. Moira recoiled when I snarled, and then pointed further down, past a curve in the wall. "Keelan, the servants' entrance is open."

I schooled my emotions only enough to offer an apologetic look to Moira. I suspected she never truly cared for me, and stomping around like a raging brute certainly wasn't helping. I hurried in the direction Moira had pointed. Footfalls close to silent, she kept directly behind.

"What exactly is your plan?" The librarian whispered over my shoulder.

"I'm going to confront that piece of shit and demand to know where El is. And then, whether he tells me or not, I'm going to kill him." I could almost feel her shudder behind me, but she said nothing.

The smaller weather-worn door creaked open and I peeked in. It led into a kitchen, an empty kitchen. We crept across it, heading for the double doors that I was sure would lead to the common areas. We emerged into an opulent receiving room. The space was empty. I stalked around the wide space, she had to be here. She had to be. I called out, the sound echoing through the space. The only reply was a resounding silence.

I climbed a set of stairs, leaving Moira to search on her own. We split up and cleared room after room. Not a soul resided in these walls, not even staff. Any sign of life had been swept away. But every so often, I could have sworn I could scent her. Faint and distant, not enough to follow.

I slammed the door to an un-decorated bedroom, anger and frustration turning molten in my veins. I had to find her. The thought of what the Nymph wanted with her, what he could be doing to her— I couldn't bear it. I would kill him slowly, I decided then. I would tear him to pieces until he experienced the agony of having a part of you stolen away. I would make him feel the way I felt now.

Lost in my anguish, I grabbed a narrow table and sent it flying backwards down the hall. A vase of flowers shattered, the tiny ceramic figurines that decorated the top scattered across the carpet runner. I heard a startled gasp from behind me. I panted, staring at the ruined rug beneath me.

"She's not here." I grated out, the words laced with venom. "Your vision was wrong."

"She was here." Moira murmured.

I turned to her, a sense of hope I hadn't dared to feel creeping into my heart. She stood at the entrance of the hall, head hung low. She carried something in each hand. In one, a leather bracer, a piece of her armor. Geometric constellations tooled into it. The set that I had given her.

In the other, dangling weakly in her tiny fingers, was a ring of metal. A silver circlet, intricately braided into the visage of glistening vines. In the center, where it crested into a peak, the mark of my mate. The enchanted moonstone glinted in the dim light.

My shadows stirred, reacting to the items. *We're too late.* I felt my fist connect with the wall at the same time they erupted. Darkness exploded around me. I became it, allowing the grief and anger to consume me. I allowed that kernel of vengeance and all consuming rage plant itself in the gap of my heart.

When my vision cleared, I dared look around. Moira has retreated further, her eyes wide with horror. There was a hole in the wall, where I had hit it, plaster dust still hanging in the air. Panting, my eyes traveled back to where the shadows still retreated to their normal place, the sight was unfathomable.

The wall, the entire end of the hallway, previously decorated with expensive wallpaper and paintings, was completely blackened. Not in the way of smoke or fire, I realized, but like the color of it had just been... removed. Even the light from the window seemed to avoid the absence that had been created. I ran a finger over it, there was no residue, and the structure did not crumble. But it was different, cold and hard. No longer wood and plaster, but something like stone.

I looked over my shoulder, at my own back. The shadows still swirled restlessly, almost angrily. Beyond them, I noted, my wings were darker. A black that absorbed light. The feathers were indistinguishable, it was only the shape that remained. A pair of black holes connected to my body.

# 77

# Keelan

A dove, pecking at the grass, something so normal, so pleasant, when nothing else was. I watched it, its white wings tucked tightly to its sides. Another wave of grief crested in my chest, crashing against my rib cage. I buried my face in my hands, pushing out the thought, the inescapable image of Astriel. They way she soared, how her own wings flared when she was angry or excited, how they could extinguish candles when we—

I banished the thought, it would do me no good. My wings had gone back to what they always were, the void of them gone and returned to their raven hue. The shadows had calmed considerably as well, though they still whirled in an agitated sort of way. Moira and I had not spoken of it, the damage that I had done, unbidden.

Now, she slept, curled into herself on Astriel's reading chair. She hadn't rested the night before, waiting for me on the house's stoop. I was too late. We hadn't found Astriel. I failed.

I was at a loss for what else to do, so we came here. *If I hadn't spent the night brooding on that mountain, we could have saved her.* I knew I needed to sleep, but I couldn't bring myself to, not when my mate was in the wind with a psychopath who could have taken her anywhere.

So I looked out the window again, glaring at the dove, resenting it for being what it could not help but to be. As it hopped across the yard, tipping its head this way and that in search of seed, I noticed it. The creature had something stuck to its leg. Not stuck, attached.

I shot off the couch, quietly as I could, so as not to wake Moira. I flung myself at the door, yanking it open with so much force the hinges creaked. The poor bird startled as I barreled out into the yard, fluttering a few steps away. I slowed my movements the best I could.

I could not afford to scare it off, not if it carried a message. I approached the dove, my footsteps light. It pecked at the ground, seeming to relax now that my movements had steadied. I studied it as I approached. Yes, there was something attached to the bird's leg. It stepped clumsily around the offending item as it pecked around in the grass.

I scooped the bird off the ground, tipping it over to get a better look at what it carried. Its only objection was a small coo as I palmed the creature. A small roll of paper had been tied to its leg. I gently removed it, careful not to damage the bird's all too delicate limbs.

I set the dove down, content to continue its hunt for seed in the grass. Straightening, I unfurled the small letter. I recognized the handwriting, though it was not written in code, I knew it came from Edward. A short message, one written and sent hastily. Only three words scrawled across the parchment.

*She is coming.*

# 78

# Astriel

Three days. Three days lost in a haze, stuck in a body that did not belong to me. I knew the answer to Morrelin's musing now, I did not sleep. No matter how heavy my eyelids became, or how desperately I pleaded with the Mother or the angels or any dark God who may hear me, I did not sleep. I watched with hooded eyes as a young servant girl periodically entered the cramped carriage I had been laid in. Human or fae, I did not know. I just stared when she poured minuscule amounts of water down my throat.

I tracked the time by the sun whenever she entered and departed. Five times a day, it seemed, she would enter and force water into my uncooperative mouth. If it had been laced with anything, I couldn't tell. I could taste nothing.

Before we departed, she had dressed me in a long crisply white gown with a far too low neckline and sweeping layers of sprawling skirts. *Like a corpse.* Perhaps that is what I was, perhaps the Leru had killed me, and this was my afterlife. Perhaps this was purgatory, and I would be trapped in the body of a corpse until the end of time. The thought was almost comforting, though I knew it wasn't true.

I also could not tell if the carriage moved. It must have, I figured, but I could not discern how frequently or how far. I could not feel it, and there was nothing in the mobile coffin that would shift or sway that would indicate it. I stared at a wooden ceiling, simple and utilitarian. Human construction.

By the end of the third day I had counted the number of nails in the ceiling over a hundred times. Each time coming up with a different number, the lack of sleep and food affecting my mind. I did not care. *This is my price.* But as the servant girl left for the last time on the third day, the moon in the sky behind her, I felt my fingers twitch.

I felt the rough wood I laid on, I felt the mugginess of the still air. But only in my fingertips. Nowhere else. Maybe I would have cried if I could have, but the inability to move had turned my well of emotions into a shallow pool. Resignation, that is what I felt.

It was all I felt.

\* \* \*

The morning of the fourth day, instead of the servant girl, Morrelin entered the carriage. He sat beside me, an arm resting on a propped up knee. I could move up to my wrist now. I clenched my hands into fists as he approached, my only show of defiance against him.

"Betina says the effects of the Leru are starting to wane, that is exciting." He smiled down at me, "I have waited so long for this, my divinity."

So the servant's name was Betina, not that it mattered. I turned my eyes away from him, instead training them on the opposite wall. How many times had I counted the nails there? I did not know.

"So ungrateful." He sneered, a viciousness edging his tone, "Most females would rejoice to have a male such as myself so devoted."

He grabbed my chin, turning my head to face him until he was all I could see. He wore his finery, a dark green tunic with gold edging, brown breaches. His yellow hair was slicked back, a single tendril escaping and falling into his eyes. It occurred to me that I had never seen his hair out of place.

His face softened, "The moment I met you I knew you would be mine," He mused, his gaze turning faraway, he still held my chin, "Your parents were so desperate for answers, for why you were like this."

He released me, reaching past my face, bringing a piece of white hair into my vision, rolling it between his fingers, "You were angel blessed, that much was obvious. But why? In my entire life I had never beheld a Seraphim like yourself. They were all... over sized birds." His face contorted into disgust, before his eyes softened on me again, "But you, you were a fresh faced goddess in the flesh. Or, at least, you would be.

"I knew I could mold you. If given the chance I could foster all of that endless potential. Your parents, however, were distrusting of me. They wanted you to grow with the Seraphim, to become one of them." That scowl returned, "How could they be so short-sighted? My divinity, living with and learning from the rabble. I couldn't bear it.

"I urged them to send you to the capital school. I demanded

they let me train you in the ways of war and conquest, of nobility. They were fools, they refused and rebuked me again and again. They conceded, only a little, to send you to the school instead of the southern continent, but it was not enough. I waited as long as I could, Astriel. But they would not see the light, your light."

He dropped the hair he had been holding aloft, seeming lost in contemplation. I should have been afraid. I should have been scared of him. I should have been enraged and eager to kill over the way he spoke about my parents and my people, my true people. But I wasn't, I could not bring myself to care what he confessed. It did not matter.

He took a deep breath, and spoke again, "I didn't want to do it Astriel, you have to believe that I didn't. They gave me no other choice." He leaned in close, something like pleading in his golden eyes, "When I brokered that deal with King Byron, when I informed him how most effectively to attack, I did not know. I did not think it would destroy you as it did. It broke my heart to do that to you, my divinity. You were so grief stricken over them leaving you, for so long you mourned them.

"I couldn't tell you the truth of course, not when you were already in such a state. But despite it, with my help, you bloomed. Through it all you flourished. Look at you now, even as you lay here, you are divine. I made the right choice. I know I did. I rid the world of a nuisance, and was able to give you the life you so desperately deserved."

He stood then, eyes raking over my body, stooping in the small space, "I beg your forgiveness, divinity, I did what needed to be done." I watched him as his expression changed, as if he heard something just outside that I couldn't, "It is nearly time, my queen. Soon this dreadful task will be over, and we will be happy."

He grinned before he hopped out of the carriage, shutting and locking the door. His admissions should have crushed me, would have broken me, if there was anything inside of me to be broken. But I just turned my face back to the ceiling.

There were sixty-eight nails.

# 79

# Keelan

I flew for hours, wearing my leathers and my family sword. I had left Moira to sleep off her exhaustion in the chair, wound in a tight ball. *El's chair.* Edward's message offered no detail, nothing beyond those three words. So I flew, over the city, over the forest. I searched for signs of an army, I searched for signs of Astriel. But there was nothing. The residents of the city proceeded with their lives in peaceful ignorance.

I pulled and pushed on the bond between us, begging to hear anything from my mate, but I felt nothing in return. She hadn't broken it. I was confident I would know if she did. And she was still alive, I knew that to be true. I could feel the bond, like a golden thread, I just couldn't get to her through it.

I wondered if she could hear me, if she knew how feverishly I hunted for her. She must, she must know that I wouldn't have given up. But our parting had been so final, at least for her. *Another life* she had said. That perhaps in another life we could have been happy.

But there was no other life, not for me. She was the very

blood in my veins, the fire that burned unrelenting in my chest. We would be happy in this life. I would make sure of that.

\* \* \*

I returned to the house as dawn began to break. I had flown through the night, I realized, so lost in my own empty turmoil that I hadn't noticed the time slipping away. I flexed my wings as I stood on the stoop, the tightness indicating just how far I had pushed myself. How long has it been since I slept? A day? Two? Probably too long, but I couldn't find rest, I couldn't just let the time slip away like that.

When I pushed into the house, I noticed the chair was empty. Straining my ears, I realized the entire house was empty. It was suffocating. I didn't realize how much of a comfort Moira's presence had been, even as she slept. Her closeness to Astriel had the effect of easing, just a little, my mate's stark absence.

As I stalked across the empty room, I noticed the slip of paper that had been left on the coffee table. Unbuckling my leathers and letting them fall to the ground, I picked it up. Moira had left it, written in her perfect, flowing script. She had gone back to the library in search of more answers.

I scoffed as I balled the piece of paper in my fist and dropped it on the rug. It would be a fruitless endeavor, a waste of time. But, I suppose when a librarian is trying to find solutions, the library is the only place they could think to go. If it made her feel better, that's fine, it's not like we were making any substantial progress here.

I dropped into the couch, exhaustion pulling at my very bones. I tried again, to shoot a message down the bond and was met, once again, with nothing. Groaning, I leaned back, that all too familiar hopelessness strangling my heart once again. I stared at the ceiling, wracking my brain for answers.

Perhaps I would send a letter to Edward, though surely he would have alerted me if he had spotted Astriel at the castle. *If he is even still alive.* The thought rang out before I could silence it. He was alive, he is. But the last message he had sent, so short and hurried, was concerning. Yes, I decided, today, I will fly to the castle. And if anyone got in my way, I would cut them down. I just needed to rest my eyes for a minute.

\* \* \*

A pounding on the door had me lunging to my feet. I cursed as the room came into focus. Through the windows, I could see the sun had set, I had lost the whole day. I rolled my neck, grimacing at the twinge of pain from sleeping on the couch.

The loud knocking sounded again, and I strode to the door, flinging it open. "What are you doing here?" I growled at the small female on the stoop.

"We need to talk about Astriel." Jarrah spoke with more confidence and ease than I have ever witnessed.

"Why should I speak of her with you?" I asked, looking the Pixie up and down.

"Because we both want to save her from the fate she has chosen for herself." She shifted, revealing the nervous fae that she always kept close, "Clovis has been following her, she has seen things that perhaps you would like to be aware of."

Begrudgingly, I opened the door wider, still glowering as I stepped aside and let the Pixies pass. "Why, exactly, have you had Clovis tailing Astriel?"

Jarrah did not falter, "I have had my suspicions about Morrelin's intentions for a long while now. He always seemed to take an… inappropriate interest in our lady of the skies. But recently, he has become more bold. Astriel has been our ward for so long, Keelan, she is like a child to us. To us ladies at least."

"You suspected he had ill intent and did nothing? For two centuries?" I saw Clovis flinch at my rising voice.

"We hoped for the best of him, Keelan. Though I admit, I wish we would have acted sooner." She wrung her hands, looking down.

I schooled the irritation on my face but I couldn't truly release it, "How do you even follow her without being noticed, Clovis. You're not exactly inconspicuous."

It was true, she was short, even by Pixie standards, but not invisible. Her stormy skin and shiny black hair was distinctive, unlike any other fae I had seen. And those wings, even when she wasn't flitting about nervously they gleamed with an iridescent rainbow. She was quite a beauty, I couldn't imagine her fading into any background.

Those nervous wings fluttered as she responded, "I think that I have been in the background of their meetings for so long they don't even notice me, if I'm being honest. Even you have overlooked me when I do not directly request your attention."

A feeling of shame washed over me as she spoke. It was true, she was in the periphery of so much and so infrequently directly involved that her presence slips focus. "I'm sorry, Clovis, if I ever made you feel—"

"I like it that way," She interrupted me, "that is how I have this information for you."

I shook my head, banishing my own self loathing, "Of course, what have you learned?"

As it turns out, she had learned quite a lot. She had stayed after the meeting to listen to what Morrelin had to say to Astriel privately. She had been there when Astriel went to Moira at the library. She had camped out at Morrelin's when Astriel visited him.

I felt my rage boiling with every sordid detail. He had threatened her. No, he had threatened *me*. And it had made things more clear, her departure from me, her urging me to leave, it wasn't just for Phaedra. She gave herself over to that maniac in an attempt to keep me out of the cross hairs. My skin prickled at the thought.

What was more, she had seen an unmoving Astriel being loaded into a human made carriage. By her accounts, she had tried to follow their procession, but lost them somewhere in the north of the city. I had spotted no mortal made carriages on my patrols and I cursed under my breath. I hadn't been looking for them, I should have been.

"If they went north that means they were not headed to the human castle." I contemplated, "Why would they be going north?"

"There is the port city to the north of the forest." Jarrah offered, sadness in her eyes.

If they had taken her to the port, if they had crossed an ocean with her then there was truly no way to find her. I refused to accept that. Not that it made sense, I couldn't think of any reason they would remove her from the continent. But still, it was a possibility, albeit a far fetched one.

"And we haven't seen any sign of the Nymph either?" I asked both the females.

"No," Clovis said sadly, "He disappeared when she did. I am confident he is staying close to her. I will keep an eye and ear out."

I cursed "Tomorrow I will travel to the north. I will search for her there."

"I would not advise that, Keelan." Jarrah spoke carefully, "The information Clovis has gleaned is not all."

I leaned back in the chair, already grimacing, "What else?"

She and Clovis locked eyes before they turned back to me, "We have sources that claim an army is being formed at the edge of the human kingdom."

"We already knew she was building an army."

"They are gathering at the edge of the forest." Jarrah spoke slowly, "They appear to be readying to march."

My eyes widened, "How many?"

"North of ten thousand." Clovis whispered, her voice trembling.

"We cannot fend off an entire army, even if Astriel was here. We will be forced to surrender."

Jarrah stared for a long moment before she spoke again, "I have taken the liberty of informing the residents of my territory of the threat, so has Shyla." I gawked at her, "Some, mostly families have decided to evacuate. But, a great many have agreed to fight."

"They are untried, they have never seen war. Jarrah, it will be a slaughter." I shook my head in disbelief.

"This is Deliana's army," She reminded me, "Even if we were to surrender it would be a bloodbath. At least this way our people have a chance to defend themselves, their home."

I knew she was right. I also knew that I had to find Astriel. *Soon*.

# 80

# Astriel

By sunset on the fourth day, sensation, though not control, had returned to my legs. It was enough, Morrelin had told me, gesturing for two guards to remove me from the carriage. Human guards, I noted passively, wearing the royal colors. They held me between them, grasping my arms as they half carried, half dragged me across the uneven terrain. The hem of the dress I wore tangled around my bare feet and scraped across the dirt.

I tried to move in step with them, but even if the poison was waning, I was weak from not eating. My legs trembled terribly beneath me, giving out when I tried to carry my own weight. I could almost feel the mens' hands on me, the pressure of their grip on my arms. I knew my wings were dragging through the dirt, I couldn't, or wouldn't lift them. I didn't know the difference anymore.

Blindly, I followed their guidance, allowing them to direct me across the windswept plain. My voice had not yet found me. I couldn't ask them where we were, where we were going. I kept my eyes unfocused, my attention instead entirely centered on the pained beating of my heart. It still beat, for better or for worse, I was alive.

They dragged me, stumbling and tripping, to a large post in the center of a wide space. It was newly erected, the wood still wet and the air smelling like freshly turned soil. My eyelids were so heavy, I just wanted to sleep, I needed to rest. The men halted, and I felt rough fingers on my forearms.

When my eyes opened, Morrelin was in front of me. I heard the clinking metal before I saw the shining metallic cuffs. *No. No more shackles.* I willed myself to fight off the guards' grip, but only succeeded in weakly kicking out. My foot barely left the ground, but effectively compromised my already precarious balance. I felt myself falling before the guards grunted and pulled me back upright.

Morrelin tutted, "It is not iron, my divinity. It is silver, it will not hurt you. They are just a precaution, we need you to be able to access all of your power for this task."

The sight of the restraints had awoken something, a deep terror I had not realized I still carried. I opened my mouth to ask, or accuse, or scream at him, but my voice was still locked in a vice. Only a squeaking cry escaped my cracked lips. My eyes darted from him to the cuffs and back again. Silently pleading against them, wordlessly begging.

He ignored me, looking away and locking them onto my wrists. I shut my eyes against the sensation of the cold metal containing me. I knew they did not hurt, but I could feel it, the phantom burning. The agony that sometimes still crackled across the scars on my wrists. I don't know if I moved, but when I opened my eyes, I was on my knees.

I panted hard, shutting out the memories of my last

entrapment that felt so near. The men who had been supporting my weight retreated, I heard the scuffing of their boots as they backed away. The rattling of the chains echoed in my head. My shaking hands clenched the fabric of my skirts, nails tearing through the soft weave.

"Get her up!" I heard Morrelin command.

"Sir, she—"

"I don't care! Get her to the post!" His voice was menacing, but laced with trepidation he tried to conceal.

I don't know what I did to scare the men. I couldn't see anything past the horrible, glittering silver. But I felt them haul up this body again. Harder this time, more roughly. The thing in my chest beat an uneven rhythm. White hair fell in the face I hadn't realized was wet with tears. As they fully dragged the collapsed body that held me to the post. I did not struggle against them, my eyes never left the cuffs.

Until they were wrenched above my head, out of my vision. I heard the clattering of metal on metal and then the men withdrew once again. I found the strength to look up. The chain linking the silver bonds had been tossed over the curve of a heavy metal hook buried deep in the post. It suspended my weight, high enough that the heels of my bare feet were lifted off the ground.

Sensation was returning in earnest now. I could feel the rough hewn wood scraping against the sore bases of my wings. My shoulders ached against the weight of being hung by my wrists. I forced myself to focus, bringing my tattered mind back to this weary body.

Morrelin stood in front of me, his chest heaving. I glanced around. At the caravan of wagons, the bustling battalion of mortal guards in royal colors. Through the strands of limp hair that stuck to my damp face, I took in my surroundings. With horror, realization dawned on where we were. High in the mountains, a cliff falling away to overlook the city bathed in fading light below, surrounded by the crumbling ruins of a civilization.

My throat was tight, but I forced the pained words, "Why did you bring me here?" It was a fractured sound, and Morrelin started when he heard it.

"Divinity, you have found your voice. Thank the Mother for that, you will need it."

"Why am I here?" I cried out again, clearer but strained. I pulled against the cuffs that suspended me, they did not budge.

A cruel laugh broke from my periphery, "There is no better view of your city than from here." The voice was a claw dragging down the back of my neck.

I whipped my head towards the sound, the pain that erupted from the movement set black spots dancing in my vision. I tried to blink them away, but I could still see her through them. She strode across the open space, a dark cloak concealing her face and form entirely.

She stopped in front of me, pulling back her hood. "It's a bit poetic isn't it, the last of the Seraphim returning to the place her own kind were slain like dogs. I thought you would appreciate my thoughtfulness."

Those ember eyes, filled with contempt, and something frenzied and wild, leveled themselves on me. I stared at her, unable to find anything to say. Deliana closed the distance between us, close enough that her smoky scent filled my nostrils. But my attention was pulled higher. I could see it then, in all of its cursed glory, the crown she wore atop her unevenly woven charcoal braids. *The World-Breaker.*

It was not encrusted in jewels as I had expected, just fine blackened metal, not even engraved. Though that did not take away from its otherworldly beauty. The shape was so expertly formed it looked as if someone had trapped a living flame inside of it. When she moved I could almost see the fire licking at the air around her head.

"Astriel, I have been looking forward to this day for a very long time." A cruel grin spread across her sharp face.

# 81

# Astriel

The sorceress did not waver as I gawked at her. "Don't act so surprised, girl. You knew how this would end." She examined her fingernails with casual disinterest.

"Morrelin," I choked on the words, turning to the fae behind her, "you cannot trust her. She will betray you."

She laughed again, "Do not listen to her, she does not know how far our agreement extends."

I fought through the maze of fear in my mind, trying to find something, anything that would at least delay whatever she had planned. I only came up with one thing. "Morrelin, you have been striking deals to win my hand for centuries. But when I was at the castle she tried to pair me off with the ancient king." I watched him for any reaction, confusion lined his face.

I panicked, the chains clanging, "She never would have let me come back to you," I forced a sad sound from my throat as the words tumbled out, but my tears of desperation were no facade, "When she realized I would not be with the king, she marked me, she used some magic to make me think I loved Keelan."

Morrelin stared at the dark queen, "You vowed that she would be returned to me. And yet you promised her to the human king, and then it was you who bound her to that crow?"

"Contingencies, Morrelin." Deliana regarded the male, "She always would have been returned to you, our deal was still in progress. I am here to break the binding for you, aren't I?"

My heart lurched, but speech was coming more smoothly now, the poison grip fading. "My love," I looked again at Morrelin, the words a burning acid in my throat, "I escaped for you. I did not see it then, but I see it now. I knew she would never let me come back to you. Please, take me home before she hurts me again."

Morrelin took a step towards me, rage and sadness warring in his golden eyes. Relief flooded my lungs, a short lived respite. Deliana sneered, putting herself between me and the male. A flick of a hand and he was trapped in a ring of fire.

"That is quite enough. Your weak deception will not derail today's events." She turned to Morrelin, "And you will not be taking her anywhere until I am done. And then you may have her."

My heart dropped, even if I could convince the lord to take me from this place, he wouldn't be able to. It was too late. I saw his face through the climbing blaze. He glared at her but nodded silently. And the fire was gone, the ground not even scorched where it had burned.

"We will be home soon, my divinity." He sounded almost remorseful. He did not meet my gaze.

Deliana grinned, content with his acceptance. A deviousness glinted in her smoldering eyes. "I will begin the preparations." Was all she said before stalking off into the encroaching darkness.

Morrelin stood in my vision, alone now. "Please," I begged him quietly when I was confident the witch was out of earshot, "She is manipulating you. She will kill us both."

"No, she won't. I have her word." Morrelin looked at me again, "You will do what needs to be done and we will leave."

"What is it exactly that she wants me to do?" I asked, dread pooling in my stomach.

Morrelin grinned, seeming pleased. "We will free you from the binding mark, and then you will perform The Opening."

"The Opening?"

His smile widened, "The tree is a gateway. When you tap into its power, you will be able to open that gateway, permitting passage through it."

"For what?" None of it made sense, my part in this made no sense.

"Whatever manner of being deigns to walk through it, I suppose." He said, rubbing a hand over his stubbly jaw.

"Morrelin, you told me that we would avoid an invasion of Phaedra if I united with you. You are asking me to open a door in the middle of it. I won't do it, I don't even think I can." I shook my head, yanking at the chains fruitlessly once again.

He approached with wide, excited eyes, running his hands down my waist. "You can and you will though, my divinity. It is not an invasion. They will be subjects of Phaedra, and Deliana's kingdom. We will be an unstoppable alliance, we will rule them all."

I suppressed the urge to kick out, to recoil from the Nymph's touch. His words were sinking in, weaving together an unimaginable truth that froze the blood in my veins. He had laid the perfect trap, whether he realized it or not. Coming to him never would have resulted in peace for Phaedra. The understanding rocked me as if I had been struck.

Suddenly, a rhythmic drumming started in the distance. The sound had just reached me when Morrelin released my waist and turned. In the dying sunlight, thousands of tiny lights had ignited in the forest. The sound grew louder. I watched Morrelin pale at the sight. I could only look on in horror as they emerged, a sea of emerald and glinting metal pouring out of the treeline. Soldiers, Deliana's soldiers, were invading.

I screamed, thrashing violently against the post. I felt the metal cut into my wrists, and fractured splinters broke from the post beneath the mindless battering of my wings. I could not free myself, tears stung my eyes. I cried out in a warning that I knew was lost in the vast space between me and the city. I had offered myself to Deliana on a silver platter, and now my people were going to die for it.

# 82

# Keelan

I couldn't find her. Days had passed. I searched in the sky, I questioned anyone with ties to Morrelin. No one knew anything. It was as if they had just disappeared in the wind. I tugged on the bond constantly, begging for her to respond. Pleading with the silver lines to tell me anything.

I was only met with silence. Moira stopped by a few times a day, dropping off food, reminding me to eat and sleep. A few times, not too gently, she encouraged me to bathe. None of it was important to me though. Nothing mattered outside of getting my mate back.

How could I live? How do I survive like this? There was no life without her, I had been cleaved in half. I was an open wound that leaked and oozed. The worst of it was that there was no one else to blame, not truly. I had let her sacrifice herself for some fraught cause.

The house had become a war zone for my turmoil. I had torn the curtains down, shattered a mirror, and broken the coffee table. There was no outlet for this anguish, it was all I could do to not start terrorizing the city's inhabitants in search of answers. Moira did some cleaning when she came, but the scars of my self hatred remained.

The worst of it occurred in the bedroom. Sleeping alone, in her bed, without her warmth felt like sacrilege. And every time I entered or exited the flicker of the silver blade that still dug into the wall mocked me. I briefly considered yanking it out and discarding it. But it was a focuser, a conduit to channel all of this torment.

* * *

The passage of time had lost all meaning when Clovis burst into the house, no longer bothering to knock. I stared at her, the torn pieces of a shirt still in my hands. She didn't seem to notice, she just crossed the room to me on nervously fluttering wings. She hopped over the scattered remains of my last outburst.

"What do you want?" I growled, throwing the shredded cloth into the couch.

"We are out of time." She panted, face flushed.

"What are you talking about?" The words threatened to send me over the precipice again.

"The human army marches, They are invading Phaedra. Now."

# 83

# Astriel

Deliana returned a long while later. She waited until my arms had turned to jelly above me, my throat hoarse from screaming. My wrists were raw and bleeding, my wings bruised and feathers snapped from the struggle. I set my jaw in a hard line as she stalked past the interspersed fires her men had set. This time she did not smile, she regarded me with the casual disgust of an insect beneath her boot.

"Summon him." The witch spoke with lethal calm.

"No." I spit at her feet.

"Do not test my patience, child. Summon the male."

I did not speak again. I just stared directly into those hellfire eyes. She smiled. Not the calculating smile she often bore, but one that showed too many, too sharp teeth, one that was less controlled. She looked over her shoulder, to the seemingly endless force that still flooded the plain that led to the city proper.

"Can you feel him, Astriel? The way he fights for your city? Can you see him being overwhelmed by my forces?" I could. Even at this distance, flashes of black emerged within the mass of soldiers. The fire that threatened to consume the lowlands casting the long shadows of his wings across the plain. "He will be cut down soon if you do not summon him. It will be your fault when he dies."

She did not seem to understand that if he fell then I would too. *If you die, we die together.* Our marks called to each other. If we fall, I accept it. I would not subject him to Deliana's wrath. Not again.

"Summon him." As if I could even do that, as if I knew how. I had, in times of need, been able to send a message through the rune, but it was no summoning. She didn't seem to understand that either. But still I kept the bond locked away, somewhere deep inside of me, hidden, and silenced.

"No." I said again, the strength in my voice was all I had. Below the surface was a ruinous wind of fear and despair. I had done this, I had condemned my people.

Her face contorted into an ugly mask, "Then I will."

She had a bony hand wrapped around my forearm before I could think. The movement opened another wound against the silver that suspended me. Blood trickled beneath the shackles. I opened my mouth to cry out but it was too late. An iron dagger flashed across my vision, and was brought down with lethal swiftness.

I screamed, the sound of it echoing in my skull. Pain like white fire wrenched me off the balls of my feet. I dangled from the bindings, black filling my vision. I heard a male shout. In my periphery, I could see Morrelin lunge forward before he was once again enveloped in a blazing cage. The darkness swelled and receded, nausea roiled in my gut.

"You said you wouldn't hurt her!" The Nymph screamed from within the wall of flame.

I forced my head up, to see what she had done. Directly though the Serch Bythol, which now flickered with internal light, was a deep and wide gash. Nausea crested as I beheld the wound that cut nearly to the bone, a gaping window of raw flesh. The edges smoked and sizzled. A river of crimson poured down my arm, staining my white dress, pooling beneath my feet.

"You have killed her!" Morrelin shouted again, unadulterated rage filling the words.

The witch glared at him through the flame, "He will sense her pain. It won't be long now." In my last moment of consciousness, I prayed to the Mother that she was wrong.

# 84

# Keelan

The hoard was an onslaught with no end. Under the cover of darkness they marched out of the treeline to the thundering boom of war drums that seemed to shake the city itself.

I had spotted Jarrah at the edge of the farmlands, surrounded by her people. They armed themselves with farming and gardening tools, some only wielded kitchen knives, too few of them carried swords. Her eyes were filled with fear, for herself and her people. But the invasion was here now, whether we were ready for it or not.

\* \* \*

Without great fanfare, Clovis and I had split ways. She went off to find her lady and assist her militia. I flew directly into the front lines. I armed myself with everything I could find a place for. Including the treasure I had found at my parents' home. It would not help me in the battle, but I kept it close, as talisman of hope. A silent prayer that we would walk away from this.

As I dove into the fray, it was with no small horror that the nature of these warriors dawned. They were like the sentries in the forest, the dozen that took Astriel and I both to dispatch. It was evident in their fighting that many of them were not trained in combat. They were sloppy, and easily distracted by the chaos that had taken hold around them.

They fought like wild animals, tripping over each other and swinging their blades with reckless abandon. I only saw the full extent of it when a youth, no older than thirteen, jumped on top of me. He knocked me off balance, pinning my wings beneath his boots. Somewhere, he had lost his sword, if he ever wielded one. Instead he fought with fists and nails and snapping teeth.

Our faces were mere inches apart when I finally ran a dagger across his throat. But even as his blood rained down on me, it was his eyes, glassy and shadowed, that shook me. These humans fought without sight, not true sight. And watching them attack without retreat, without any sense of self preservation elicited a shudder, even in the midst of battle.

Some small part of me wondered while I tore through the horde, flying above them when the bodies became too thick, if a human still resided in those bodies. When cut, they bleed, but if they felt it they did not react. They did not speak, they did not cry out, they only snarled and growled when they attacked. An army of the undead. Their bodies lived, their blood lust remained, but the mind had been vacated of all else.

On some level, it appeared that they could think. Or, at least they could think enough to follow orders. A small group had breached the line that the fae farmers had been holding, barreling towards the small village in the midst of fields. As they ran, they dragged torches across the grasses, leaving a trail of flame in their wake.

I tore after them, leaving the center of the fight in pursuit. As I flew low above the mass of bodies, I cut down as many soldiers as I could before they could engage the militia. It was an insignificant contribution. Alone, I was not enough.

I tried not to notice how many fae bodies were littered among st the soldiers. Green uniforms served as the backdrop for the barrage of colors the un-uniformed fae wore. I soared over crumpled iridescent or leathery wings, and rainbows of bloodstained cloth. Their eyes clouded and glazed as life was struck from them. Too many were falling, too fast.

I landed in the center of the group. Six mortals with death in their eyes. One threw her torch down and unsheathed a chipped and dented sword. In two steps she was cut down, and the rest of her group lunged. I rolled between them, slicing for their middles before plunging the sword into their backs. The final man struck quicker, running a slice across my shoulder before I launched a dagger between his eyes.

The last of the group fell, but the fires that they had set were growing, merging together and spreading in a hellish blaze. I looked on helplessly, watching thatched cottages and barns were consumed by the ravenous flames. I forced myself to look away, to focus again on the battle at hand.

The desperate sounds of cattle and sheep and donkeys filled the air here. Over the resounding clashing of metal and screaming their cries crescendoed in anguish.

A young, dappled stallion broke through the wall of a barn on the precipice of collapse, wood splintering against his shoulders. His steps unsteady, eyes wide and white with fear. His nostrils flared open as he ran and spun and stumbled over bodies. With nowhere to go, blinded by the atrocities unfolding around him, he leapt directly into the wall of flame.

I could smell the burning hair and hear his final cries before I broke away. I turned back to the onslaught, shaking out my already fatigued muscles, preparing to launch back into the center. The thought of Astriel entered my mind unbidden. I allowed myself to linger on it for just a moment. To picture her eyes, her hair, to imagine her scent and how it mingled with mine.

I tucked the image away, saving it as a reminder of why I would fight so hard. We would win out against the invasion, and then I could return to her. The stoney resolve settled in as I tightened the grip on my sword, the eye of the dragon gleaming in the firelight. In a single wing beat I was back in the sky, eyes scanning where I would be needed most.

\* \* \*

The farmers turned fighters were surrounded. Their numbers dwindled with every second. Behind them, I could see an approaching force from the east. A muted tangling of forms that slithered towards the battlefield. Selkies and Water Sprites, Undines tearing across the land on the backs of ferocious Kelpies.

I did not get the chance to feel the relief that Shyla had rallied forces of her own. My body stiffened in the sky, the beat of my wings turning uneven. A shock jolted through my mind. An internal screech rang in my ears, drowning out all other sound. I fell back to the ground, stumbling and panting.

And then I felt the searing pain that cut straight down to my center. I groaned, steps faltering. My sword nearly escaped the grip of my now clammy hand. *What is happening?* My shadows whirled in wild tendrils, reaching down my arm. I blinked away the swimming in my vision, looking down.

The mark that had been so silent these last days hummed beneath my skin. I stared, the fraught battle and encroaching fires momentarily forgotten. The silver knot flickered an irregular pattern, alternating between near blinding and dull. *Home.* It screamed into my bloodstream.

There was no conscious thought. A force I did not understand sent me skyward again. The battle was white noise against the screaming between my temples. I did not even look back as my wings carried me north, away from the chaos and destruction. Home. Astriel called for me. There was nothing other than that.

I raced for the mountains. The call of my mate vibrating in the core of my very being.

# 85

# Keelan

As I neared the place that called to me, the soft glow of campfires came into view. They brought her to the fallen city of the Seraphim. I cursed myself, they brought her north, and yet I did not check the mountains. I had flown by them, over them, and yet I never saw the caravan that was so clearly in view now. I failed her then, I would not fail her now.

I could not see her, but I could feel her, faint as it may be. The mark's frequency increased as we approached, but her call had once again gone silent. Still, I knew where to go. The tug I had been praying for these past days finally pulling me towards her. I don't think I could have strayed from the path if I tried.

\* \* \*

My boots skidded against the loose ground as I landed hard on the cliff side. The hairs on the back of my neck prickled as I scanned the ruins. Fires lay abandoned, there was not so much as the shuffling of feet or distant exhalation of breath. But I knew I was not alone.

The hidden threats were forgotten when I laid eyes on her. She hung limply from a tall post, her head drooped between her arms. Her silver hair was stained dark in a curtain, concealing her face. I raced towards her. She was covered in dark. thick blood, so much blood. When I reached her, I held her face. Her comforting warmth was gone, her skin was ashen and cold beneath my fingers. The light of her had dimmed, had been drained from her.

"Astriel! Mother above what have they done to you?" I cried and begged as I shook her shoulders, "Astriel it's me, it's Ke. I found you, I came for you."

But she did not stir. I reached up, grabbing for the chains. "I'm going to get you out of here, El. I'm going to take you somewhere safe, but you need to wake up. I need you to wake up."

"How sweet is that? Coming when you're called. She has you better trained than I could have hoped." A voice crooned from somewhere behind me.

I turned, unsheathing my sword and thrusting the other hand behind me, placing it protectively on Astriel's waist. The still warm blood flowing down her body slicked my fingers and emboldened my rage. Keeping contact with her, keeping her protected, was my only thought. Nothing else mattered.

"I'm taking her." I growled at Deliana, stalking out of the shadows, "I will cut you down if you try to stop me."

She laughed. Her eyes were unfocused, her hair beneath that crown was frizzy and streaked with gray that hadn't been there before. "I can't allow that Keelan, darling. I still need her to do one more thing for me, and I need you out of my way." She snapped her fingers.

Vines slithered out of the darkness with preternatural speed. I sliced and cut at them as they closed in, raising up their ends like the heads of snakes. My body was weakened from hours of fighting. My muscles screamed against the exertion. Astriel's fragile state was compromising my own.

A vine struck out, wrapping around my sword arm, wrenching the blade out of my hand. I yanked against it, trying to break it off. My other hand still on Astriel's waist. But another wrapped around my ankle, dragging my feet out from beneath me. I hit the ground with enough force to knock the wind from my lungs.

They pulled me along, breaking contact with my mate. Scrambling, I fisted daggers in both hands, slicing and sawing at the vines. The more I cut, the more there were, and it didn't take long before they completed their assault, pinning me to the ground.

I gritted my teeth against the vines that wound around my neck as Deliana approached. Morrelin, hands contorted to control the vines, stalked up just behind her. I glared at them, not daring to look back at the rapidly fading female on the post. I would not let them see the fear that gripped my chest tighter than the vines.

"Let us leave and take Phaedra. You've won." I choked out, addressing the grinning witch.

She tutted, "That is not an option. Taking Phaedra is secondary to what I need." She looked me over with a predator's glint in her eyes, "You though, are problematic. She can't do what I need her to do with your darkness muddying the waters."

"She will finally be free of your malevolent influence." The Nymph spoke now, "My divinity should never have been binded to a hell spawn such as yourself."

I was not given the chance to reply. I watched as he cut Deliana a harsh look that she ignored and then turned his attention back on me. With a flick of his wrist one my arms was shifted away from my body, palm up. The vines retreated from the junction of my elbow, revealing the Serch Bythol.

Deliana stepped around me. She knelt, laying a bony hand on the mark. I struggled against her touch, but the vines only tightened. I watched in horror as she mumbled words in a language I didn't understand. Her eyes closed, she recited the inverse to the chant she had used the night of the binding.

Lightning coursed beneath my skin. It struck and shuddered at my organs, in my mind, in my heart. I knew I was screaming. It was inescapable, all consuming agony. I was being flayed open, skinned alive, pulled apart at the seams. Something had snapped and shattered in my core, lodging shards into the underside of my ribs. She completed the incantation and removed her hand.

She had carved something out of me. I tried to crane my head, to see what she had done. Where the mark had been was now just clean skin. Not even a shadow of the knot remained. I laid my head back, breathing heavily against the torrent of pain, unable to otherwise move, when I heard her scream.

"Ahh, she's awake. Good." Deliana spoke, looking past me. "They are unbinded, do what you will." And then she stepped out of view.

*Unbinded.* The word echoed in my head as a grinning

Morrelin stepped over me, a foot on either side of my chest. Distantly, I could hear Astriel screaming, crying, begging for something. I wondered if she felt what I felt, I wondered if it hurt.

But the shadows were closing in, unconsciousness looming. Even the Nymph who glowered down at me turned fuzzy at the edges. Something glimmered in his hand. The vines tightened, strangling my breath.

Then I felt the dagger plunge into my chest.

# 86

# Astriel

I always thought that death would be a gentle embrace. The sensation I felt when too much blood ran unbidden from my arm. The soft coaxing into that liminal space that was not sleep. But when I woke to the unrelenting assault on my senses as something unnamed was being torn from my very soul. I knew that was death calling me home.

My eyes opened in darkness. The memory of where I was and what had been done to me pulsing like a dying sun between my ears. I looked outwards, over the expanse of my home. Everything was burning. I knew that if I could feel anything outside of the shredding of my insides that I would mourn it. But I could only see it, only abstractedly acknowledge that it was a great tragedy.

But then I heard the screaming. Head pounding, I turned to the sound. On the ground was darkness smothered in a warped visage of nature. A male, Morrelin, I remembered, stood near the teeming mass of plant life. A woman, Deliana, crouched next to it, concentration lining her face. Another wave of tearing ricocheted around my body, pulling a scream from my throat.

I blinked, trying desperately to shove down the pain so I could *focus*. Suddenly, the entire image came into agonizing clarity. It was my mate beneath the witch's hand, his face contorted in anguish. I screamed his name, I pulled against the unseen pressure that kept me in place. Warmth ran down my arm.

She looked at me, rising from her place next to a now panting and ashen Keelan. I screamed at her, I begged her to save him. I promised anything, I would rake myself across hot coals for her just so long as she let him live. But she only smiled.

My ears were ringing, my own voice not reaching them. Out of the corner of my eye, I spotted the gash that was once again a torrent of crimson. I knew she had cut through the binding mark, but when I looked, it cut through only pale flesh. I still had scars, I still had open wounds, I could see them. There was no mark.

Deliana was upon me now, speaking, but I couldn't hear her. A wicked grin split her face, her burning eyes were hungry. She lifted her arms but I did not watch them. I stared at my arm, at the utter absence of the binding.

*She unbinded us.* I looked back over her shoulder. Her body obscured Keelan, but I could see Morrelin. He stood, anger in his eyes, a dagger held high above his head. A scream choked in my throat. The dagger surged downwards. I could feel the blade hit home in my own chest.

Burning cold metal connected with my temples. The world disappeared, I fought it, but the presence of something intangible and yet oppressive overtook my mind. I was slipping, I knew that, but my resolve to fight it was weakening. I only heard one thing as my mind emptied, a breath of air, an exhale from nowhere and everywhere.

*Finally, we are united.*

\* \* \*

A realm of all consuming flame, it licked at my feet but it did not ignite the fabric of the dress that pooled within it. Instead, the dancing blazes softly caressed my feet, my ankles, a lover's touch. Gentle and explorative, a consciousness all to themselves. I could almost hear the tufts of heat whispering to each other, quiet questions and statements.

Their murmurs were drowned out by a screeching in the distance. I started at the sound, the fire pulled at my skirts like a shy child. They grew closer, their warmth grazing my senses. When I turned, smoke darkened scales and leathery wings flooded my vision.

I stumbled backwards. The force of wind blown forth by the incomparably sized reptile landing with a heavy sound knocked me backwards. Talons as long as my forearm scraped against the brimstone as it stalked across the barren space. It bore a mouth that hung slightly ajar, overfilled with razor sharp fangs like spearheads.

As it neared, towering over me, it released a hot sulfurous breath through wide nostrils. The glare from its yellow slitted eye cut through to the center of me. I watched muscles ripple beneath the dinner plate scales too thick to be pierced by any weapon.

I should have been terrified. I should have recoiled from

the beast as it lumbered ever closer. Dark rocks shattered beneath its massive feet. The fire that burned like hellish grasses leaned away. But even alone with a beast of legends on an unforgiving plain, I was not afraid.

*You who wields the World-Breaker, have you come to release us from this place?* The beast sniffed, his yellow eyes traveling across my body which was so insubstantial compared to his.

I raised a hand, absently feeling the place above my head. My fingers grazed metal cold as ice. Had I placed it upon myself? I couldn't remember. I remembered darkness, and pain. I did not remember where I would have found a crown.

"I don't know." I addressed the dragon, dropping the hand to my side, "I don't know why I'm here."

*What are you called in this life, child?*

I opened my mouth to respond, but could think of nothing to say. Did I have a name? Was there anyone who addressed me that would warrant one? "I can't remember."

His head tipped to the side. *You wear the crown. You are The Fallen Star of prophecy. You are the foretold. Astraea.*

"Astraea," I rolled the name around on my tongue, tasting the sound of it. It was familiar, and yet not, like it fit, but chafed. "What is this place?"

*Perdition.* The creature growled. *The ancient kinds have been entombed in this underworld for millennias. You are our savior, our liberator. It is written that you will open the gates.*

"What gates? I don't know how to open them." Something was missing, something fundamental. The beast with ancient eyes simply craned his head, huffing a breath as he looked past me.

When I turned once again, the flames that licked at my heels grew excited, staining the hem of the dress black with soot. I walked forwards, the surrounding fire splitting, creating a path. I hadn't seen it before, the looming doors of iron embedded in the towering stone walls. I heard the thundering steps of the dragon approaching. His massive head hovered above my shoulder.

*We were tricked into this imprisonment by the old Gods. The gates tell the story, as well as how we will be released.* His head tipped up and I followed his gaze.

Carved into the metal were images. Formless beings casting down lighting and fire onto masses of oddly shaped bodies. A lock being forged. A night sky filled with bodies. A meteor colliding with the planet.

I followed the story I felt I had already known. A woman's figure surrounded by stars. A raging fire. A lock, shattered. Those oddly shaped bodies surrounding a tree. An army of angels. A city in ruin.

"I don't understand the ending." I said to the dragon.

*You will not until the prophecy is complete.* He responded.

I reached out, grasping onto his rough hide as a wave of dizziness knocked me off balance. The dragon's scales cut into my palms, red smeared across his dull coloring. He leaned into the touch, pushing me back to my feet. His citrine eyes studied me as I blinked it away.

I steadied myself, releasing the grip on him, wiping my hands on the bodice of my dress, "How do I open it?"

*Place your hands on the gate, and will it to open.* The creature sucked in a large breath, as if in preparation.

I looked down. I was covered in scars and leaking wounds that should have hurt, but I couldn't feel them. The dress I wore was covered in blood, was it mine? I appeared to be freshly injured, and yet I did not hurt.

My red smeared palms bore scars, burns. Had they always been there? I searched for some recollection, but found none. There was only the smudged and bisected image of a lock on one, and on the other, a key. Complementary to each other, one gracing each hand.

"When I open it, will I see you again?" I asked, not entirely sure why. He was a beast of legend, capable of ending my life with no more than half a thought, and yet I trusted him, a small comfort in this foreign place.

*I will be forever indebted to you, Astraea. When you call, I will answer.* He tilted his head down ever so slightly. A dragon's version of a bow, I realized.

I walked towards the gate, hands outstretched, "I don't even know your name." I said. The metal began to glow red as I approached.

*Zephyrus.*

The name was the last thing I heard before my world erupted. The flames that touched me so gently before now wrapped around my body in a whirling spout of heat. I wanted to recoil, to remove my hands and escape the blinding agony, but I couldn't. An unbreakable force held me to the door.

I had felt pain like this before, I realized. There was someone I cared about that had been taken from me. The wisp of a memory steadied my breath even as it came in painful pants that tore at my throat. There was someone I needed to find, someone I needed to save.

I couldn't save them until I opened this door. So I willed it. I poured every ounce of desire into opening the door. I channeled the surging fire into a mighty weapon. My vision narrowed into a pinprick, the ground I stood on grew unsteady. The whole world shook as I clung to that burning gate.

And then the crack of something giving way, the creak of metal. I pushed and pushed as the barrier before me started to move. One step in front of the other on legs that were swiftly failing.

I screamed at my own hands. I commanded the resisting barrier to yield to my touch. And then, through the door, light. The pain released me.

The gates to Perdition yawned open.

# 87

# Astriel

I opened my eyes, a new kind of pain erupted all over my body, striking to my core. My body, I was in my body. Astriel, My name is Astriel. I am in the ruins of the Seraphim township. I am trapped, no, I am not. I looked down at my bleeding hands, my bleeding arm. But there were no shackles.

I was kneeling, pebbles digging into my knees. I looked up, they still hung on the hook, empty, still locked and closed. When my eyes once again fell downwards, I felt it, the weight upon my head. I jolted, hand coming up and tearing the burning metal away. The crown seemed to hiss and whisper, begging me to take it back, to wear it once again.

*I opened the gates.* I suddenly remembered the strange vision, the strange place. But it was no vision, I was there, I pushed the gates open with my own two hands. I shot to my feet, unsteady as I stumbled forward. I surveyed the area around me, memory returning in fragments.

"I've done it!" Deliana cried out, her face contorted in wild ecstasy, "Come to me my dark subjects. Behold your savior."

Down below, the burning city erupted into screaming chaos. From the flame licked plains around the tree, creatures emerged from nothing. Figures that flew and slithered and ran at unnatural speed flooded Phaedra. I had done it. I opened the gates, I was the one that unleashed Perdition upon my people.

Deliana kept calling to the horde that tore through her own men. She looked at me, at the crown on the ground. She was frenzied, and hissed as she lunged like a crazed animal to the discarded ring of metal. In the distance, a vast shadow took to the skies. She squealed with the glee of a child, donning the crown again as the massive silhouette directed itself towards the mountain.

My gaze fell past her, to the crumpled heap that lay motionless atop a pile of dead vines. "Keelan!" I screamed as I ran for him, rocks and sticks cutting into the bottom of my feet.

I slid up to him, dress tearing against the rough ground. The hilt of a dagger stuck out of his rattling chest. I ran shaking hands over him, across his chest, up his throat. I cupped his colorless face in my hands.

His eyes opened just slightly, eyelashes fluttering as they did, "You're going to be okay, Keelan." I ran a hand down his hair.

"I'm sorry, Ke." I mumbled into his neck as my other hand wrapped around the hilt of that dagger, "This is going to hurt, I'm sorry."

As smoothly as I could, I wrenched the blade out of his chest. His eyes shot open, a sputtering cough erupting from him. Blood colored his lips, so stark against the paleness of the rest of his face. As swiftly and gently as I could manage I unbuckled his chest plate, casting it aside.

I could stanch the bleeding. I didn't know how to heal but maybe I could slow the flow, I could keep him alive until help came. Moisture struck the back of my hands where they stacked on top of the wound. Tears, I was crying. I wiped my face on the shoulder of my dress, trying to clear my vision.

"You're going to be okay, my love. We are going to get you out of here." I tried to smile, "I'll make sure Elia makes you that good brew, you won't even be able to tell this happened." His shadows covered his chest, they covered my hands, like they were trying to help.

His arm moved, slowly and weakly up his torso. A rattling breath sent him into another coughing fit. I did not move. His trembling fingers dug into his breast pocket, gripping something there. I watched his face. His other arm slid across his chest, his fingers wrapping around my left wrist, tugging.

"I can't release the pressure, Keelan. I have to keep the pressure on." He tugged again, his eyes pleading.

I relented, pressing harder against the wound with my right. Our blood mingled in the dirt beneath us. His eyes stayed on me as he placed something on my finger. Confusion colored my face as I lifted the hand out of his shadows. Even in the moonlight I could make out what it was.

On the third finger on my left hand sat a silver ring. Atop the delicate hoop was an intricately cut sapphire. It shifted in blues as dark as night itself. The band was engraved in such small lettering I couldn't make it out. Ke's eyes silver rimmed with the question.

"No, no Keelan. Don't do this now, not until you're better.

We have time—" But a pressure around my legs cut me off.

I kicked at the intrusion, screaming against it as it pulled me away. My hands slid from Keelan's chest. I thrashed as the blood once again ran in earnest. His eyes followed me as I clawed at the ground, trying to break free, struggling to return to him.

"That is quite enough of that." A male voice boomed from behind me.

I twisted on the ground, feathers snapping. Vines wrapped around my legs and snaked up past my hips, "Let me go!" I screamed at Morrelin, "You can't let him die!" I tugged and ripped at the plants but they kept growing, they kept dragging me away,

"We are leaving." He scowled down at me, "Now."


A thunderous collision rocked the mountain as the words left his mouth. And I saw his face pale as his eyes fell behind me. I twisted again, needing to know what captured his attention. At the cliff's edge, dwarfing even the evergreens, was a dragon. With yellow slitted eyes, it regarded the human and fae littered across the rock.

Deliana stormed up to it, waving her hands in the air, "Great beast, it was I that freed you. I am your queen. I wear the crown."

She once again donned the metal crown of flame, but she had also created one of her own. True orange fire that danced in the wind. Enchanted to not burn her, it encircled the metal flames, real and rendered danced together to a horrible song. She stepped closer, but the dragon did not yield.

"Zephyrus!" I screamed desperately, and those yellow eyes turned to me, the slitted pupil widening as his attention locked on me, and then the male behind me.

Deliana whirled, pointing an accusing finger, "It will do you well to hush, girl. You have no idea the creature that you—" But she was cut off, her body wedged against the dirt, the crown of flames extinguished.

In a lazy swipe, the dragon had used one viciously taloned foot to pin her to the ground. In the same deep voice that I had heard in Perdition, gravelly and without a true source, the dragon spoke. The message booming across the plateau. *Careful how you speak to her witch. I serve Astraea alone.*

Deliana breathed a garbled sound, her eyes wide. She tried to raise an arm, to reach towards me as more wet noises escaped her. But whatever she had meant to say, would be her secret to keep. Before I could blink, Zephyrus stepped forward again, and the witch was crushed beneath his weight. I couldn't help but look as the crown rolled away, once again calling for a master.

Nausea roiled as the dragon continued his advance, red footprints coloring the dust behind him. I felt the pressure of the vines lessen as I heard Morrelin stumble backwards. *You will not walk away from this rock, fae.* Zephyrus rumbled as he stepped past me.

I turned my head away, shielding it with my arm. Morrelin babbled some crying plea for forgiveness. He did not get to finish before the sound of snapping jaws and crunching bones filled the air. The vines that held me withered to dust. I did not dare look back as I tore off across the space, back towards Keelan.

I did not falter when I heard human screams or metal clattering against the ground. I blocked out the noise of wood splintering and bones shattering. I knew what was happening. The mortal soldiers on the mountain with us were either retreating from the imposing reptile or being consumed by him.

It was all forgotten when I fell to my knees next to my mate. This time, when my hands landed on his chest it rose and fell in shallow gasps. A wet rattling and sucking every time he breathed. I touched his neck, a cold sheen of sweat slicking my hands.

"Keelan it's okay, Deliana and Morrelin are dead. We are safe." A sob broke from my lips.

But Keelan's eyes did not open, his eyelashes did not even flutter. The blood from the wound on his chest had slowed, but I knew it was because there was nothing left for him to bleed. I fell into him, wrapping my arms around his neck as I called his name, as I brushed the hair back from his face. I listened for the heartbeat that had grown so faint.

"Keelan, please," I begged, fisting his shirt in my hands, the ring he had given me digging into my tear streaked cheek, "Come back to me, Ke. Come back to me, and we will get married. Come back to me and we can be happy in *this life*." I felt his chest fall, and it did not rise. I heard one final, weak flutter of his heart, and then silence.

The mating bond unraveled, unable to carry the weight as Keelan left. And then it snapped. And it did not hurt. It was not the all-consuming agony that the breaking of the binding had been. This was worse.

I had been hollowed out. There was only a void where my heart used to beat and my soul used to dance. There was absolutely nothing at all. Tears fell, my breath wracked against my ribs, but I couldn't feel it. Without that connection, I felt nothing.

And that nothing swelled, and crescendoed until I could see nothing, hear nothing, smell and feel *nothing*. And then it swelled again, and I decided that if I could feel nothing, then I would become nothing. But then it swelled one final time, if there was no Keelan, there was nothing.

I knew distantly that a light was growing, I did not care. I let the light consume us.

# 88

# Astriel

I lifted my head, squinting into the all consuming brightness that I knew I had created. I imagined that the entire world was blinded by my grief. It would be fitting, to plunge everyone and everything into a bright void like the one that gaped in my chest. Maybe I could burn myself out, maybe this grief would kill me. Another sob rocked my body and the light hurled itself further still.

I gripped Keelan's cold hand, bringing it up to my lips, whispering into his palm. All the things I should have said, everything I needed to apologize for. I told him about the first time I knew I loved him, I cried as I recounted those first fraught days where I thought he was a monster. I apologized for being the reason he was dead.

With every word his shadows seemed to stretch out across the blood stained ground. Dense and thin, they moved like a dark liquid. I wondered if they too were dying. I wondered if shadows *could* die, where they would go. I wondered if they would stay with me if I asked.

But I did not ask, I just watched them spread across the

ground. They puddled around us, absorbing the light that I couldn't stop now. They created a shallow pool so devoid of light that I hoped we would fall through it, be absorbed by it. But then tendrils of shadow began to climb.

They swirled upwards, creating spindly bars that cut through the oppressive white. They rose until they met above my head. And then, like a wall of water, they dripped downwards, containing my light. They created a cocoon, an impenetrable barrier that blocked out the world.

"What are you doing?" I heard myself cry, Keelan's hand still in mine.

And then it shattered, with a boom that echoed in my bones. Casting my light out once again. But it was different now, my light fractured. Instead of light that consumed, it only illuminated.

A gathering of forms surrounded us.

I stared up at them, not releasing the grip on my mate. *Still my mate, no matter what.* Surrounding us were hundreds of winged fae, emitting their own light. Many of them wore fighting leathers and weapons, a few held children. Some were simply wearing the plain dresses and tunics of everyday life. They looked on stoically, if not sadly.

A female stepped in front of the others, her blue eyes the clearest part of her spectral form. But on her back, I could see the less than solid sage green of her wings, "My daughter, we came when you called." She said softly, hands outstretched.

"Mom?" My voice cracked.

She nodded, crossing the space between us, her Rosie linen dress flowing as she walked. She knelt at Keelan's side, across from me. "We have come to fight for you, Astriel. You only need to tell us what to do."

"Save him." The words tumbled out before I could stop them, "Save Keelan. Save my mate."

"My star," She reached across him, cupping my cheek in her soft hand. I leaned into it. "that is no simple task."

"You are a healer." My eyes bore into hers, the soft azure full of sorrow, "You can save him. *Please*." The last word was no more than a lost breath.

"You cannot take him back without giving something in exchange," Her words were soft but firm, "The cosmos demand balance. You would have to sacrifice something."

"Anything," I cried, "I will give anything to have him back."

My mother nodded, her warm touch falling from my face. She rested both hands on Keelan's chest. A male broke from the group, approaching and resting a hand on my mother's shoulder. His moss green eyes met mine, chestnut wings tucked in behind him.

"Hello, angel." His smile was so warm and familiar.

"Dad." My throat tightened with tears.

And then three females emerged from the crowd, their yellow feathers fluttering on the wind. They smiled, but said nothing, just each placed a hand on my mother's other shoulder. And then the rest of the Seraphim followed suit. They created a chain of bodies, an unbreakable link of power.

My gaze fell back to my mother, whose face was creased in concentration as she leaned over Keelan. "No more Seraphim blood will spill on this mountain." She said quietly.

And then there was a different light, one that drowned out my own. A swirling warmth that reflected the many colors of Seraphim wings that occupied the mountainside. I squinted my eyes against it, but did not release Keelan's hand. The color slowly returned to his skin and lips. Heat reentered the unnatural cold in his body.

My mother released him, and the light that warmed the mountain faded, "It is done." Her voice was softer, almost weak. Her edges flickered.

I looked away from Ke's once again tanned face, and turned my eyes to her. "Thank you." I breathed, the hole in my chest slowly refilling.

"Now we fight for your people." My father grinned down at me, unsheathing his glowing sword.

My mother stood, running a hand over my hair before straightening. She and my father shared a lover's look. My sisters held each other. Their eyes, in varying shades of green tinged brown, glittered in the blanketing indigo of impending dawn as they smiled at me.

"You have made us so proud, daughter." My mother whispered, her eyes rimmed with tears.

And then, in one sweeping movement, the Seraphim took flight, and they dove down to the city that burned and bled below.

# 89

# Astriel

My attention was pulled back down at the sound of a long groan, "Keelan?" I choked. It seemed so precarious, so fragile that I was afraid to breathe.

His eyes opened, pupils dilating when his gaze met mine. He groaned again, trying to pull himself up. I used one hand to help his rise, and rested the other on his chest that was no longer bleeding, no longer an open wound. Only a pink scar remained.

My heart leapt when I saw it, the wound that took him away from me, now healed. I wrapped my arms around him, crushing my mate into me. He exhaled a sound of pain, but when I tried to pull away, his arm snaked around my waist, holding me to him.

He inhaled deeply, breathing me in, "You're okay." He murmured into my hair.

I choked on a laugh mixed with a cry, "You came back to me."

He pulled away, dark eyes meeting mine, and then fell downwards, scanning over my bruised and bloody body, he cursed. "El, you're covered in blood, are you—"

"I'm okay." I cut him off, and it was true, he was alive in front of me. I was okay.

A thundering approach caught our focus, and Keelen cursed again, scrambling to his feet. He pushed me behind him even as he grimaced, reaching for the sword that wasn't at his back.

I pushed around him, running up to the dragon that lumbered across the ruins. I threw my arms against his enormous, blood speckled neck, "Thank you, Zephyrus."

The beast rumbled, deep in his throat. *The humans are gone from here. Shall we join the fray?*

I looked back at Keelan, whose eyes were cutting between the massive reptile and his sword that lay discarded in the dirt a few feet away.

"He is with me," I addressed my mate, "Zephyrus killed Deliana and Morrelin, he saved me."

Ke eyed the dragon suspiciously, but relaxed ever so slightly. "We need to return to the battle, if you are able."

I looked out over the city below. Fire burned in every direction, flashes of spectral winged warriors cutting through the still fighting horde of green clad humans. Those beings of odd shapes were interspersed among them, though I couldn't tell who was the victim of their slaughter.

*The others of Perdition are only loyal in this battle. They fight the humans as well, but when the fighting ceases they will leave. The debt will be paid.* Zephyrus answered for me, his citron eyes watching the chaos unfold. *Your wings are damaged, I will take you down.*

"Absolutely not." Keelan objected, stooping to retrieve his sword and discarded chest plate.

He opened his bloody maw in a snarl of frustration. *Yours are as well Dark One, you will fall before you fly.* His nostril's flared as he scented Keelan, Giant pupil dilating as he saw something I couldn't identify.

I rested a hand against the side of his head, "If you will take us, we accept." I assured him, turning my pleading eyes to Keelan.

He sighed and nodded, shadows once again stirring around his shoulders. The dragon lowered himself to the ground, slitted eyes widening. I clambered atop him, ignoring the smarting pain of my injuries. And gestured for Keelan to follow as I settled just ahead of the massive wings tucked into his side.

He shook his head but followed, sheathing his family sword and taking my hand to help him up. He sat behind me, not even fully seated when Zephyrus released a sound of amusement before rising. He ran for the edge of the outcropping, spreading those huge membranous wings and taking flight.

\* \* \*

The landing was an ungraceful jolt, throwing me against Zephyrus's rough shoulders and Keelan into my back. I looked out over the blood soaked battlefield, at so many fallen. To the north, fae of every kind slumped against the ground, or still fought against the onslaught. To the south, lines of human soldiers had been split by horned creatures, wolves of unnatural size, flame wrapped winged humanoid

449

beings. Alongside them were the apparitions of Seraphim warriors.

The sight was one of dreams and nightmares, and yet they all fought for us, they fought for Phaedra. A debt to be paid by some, a call home for others. The human forces did not show fear against the extraordinary resistance, but their forces were dwindling. At the treeline, there were no more men flooding out of the forest.

Keelan slid off the mount, landing with a grunt of pain on the scorched grass. He held out a hand for me to take, to come with him, "I have no weapons." I called down to him, realizing that I was not dressed or armed for a battle like this.

He reached for the daggers in his belt, but Zephyrus spoke. *Astraea stays with me. We will fight from the skies.*

"You are not taking her." Keelan growled at the beast.

*You will have her fight injured and nearly unclothed?* And then his massive head turned to me. *This is the male you gave so much for?*

I suppressed a grin at the opposing protective forces, "I will fly with Zephyrus, it will be safer." The human forces that had been split by the dragon's landing were once again closing in.

Keelan made to object but Zephyrus was already spreading his wings in preparation for the takeoff. I called down to my glowering mate, "We will find you when it is over."

And then we were airborne, gliding low above the mass of bodies. I gripped desperately against a horned protrusion at the base of Zephyrus's neck. It was all I had to keep steady as his body flexed and contracted. I watched as his lengthy tail swept through masses of green clad men. The sound of their bodies cracking and crumpling against each other a sickening song amidst the chaos.

*Where do we fight?* The dragon asked from beneath me, even as his extended claws tore through a group of men pinning a small force of fae against the side of a burning barn.

I looked out across the battlefield, at which factions would benefit most from the unstoppable power of a colossal animal, "Into the city." I finally yelled over the wind. Men had broken off from the main battle in favor of burning houses and slaughtering civilians.

He banked hard, headed northeast. As we rose over a sprinting mass of unchallenged soldiers, Zephyrus loosed a roar. Not only a roar, I realized, but a wall of flame that incinerated the men mid step. I looked back, all that was left were piles of ash and warped metal.

When we landed in the city square, the screaming of the families escaping human soldiers filled the air. Mothers holding children crouched against the cobblestones, shielding their children from the beast that carried me. But more men were approaching, tearing down the road to the city proper. These people needed to move, now.

"The dragon fights with Phaedra." I shouted to the terrified fae, "Get somewhere safe, arm yourselves."

Terrified females looked up, distrusting. But then they saw me, spreading my wings as far I could against the pain in my shoulders. They needed the Protector of Phaedra. I would give it to them. The few stragglers only just ran out of the way as Zephyrus galloped towards the opposing forces, his talons shrieking against the stone.

It only took a breath for the men to fall. He slashed and

swung that flexible tail, knocking men into stone walls. His teeth tore through armor and flesh with practiced ease. But he dared not use his flaming breath, not this close to so many buildings. Not when so much was already ablaze. He took only a moment after the last of them fell, to huff deep breaths and lick the gore off his maw. Then, lurching forward, we were back in the air, returning to the battle.

# 90

# Astriel

The sun blazed high above us as the last of the humans fell. Their bodies piled high across the scorched plains and within the dirt streets of the small villages they had wrecked. Interspersed were the bodies of fallen fae. The living stepped over and searched through them with devout reverence.

Zephyr hadn't yet truly landed when I leapt off his back, running barefoot across the plain into the weary arms of my mate. He had survived the battle with only minor wounds, the majority from tripping over fallen blades as he ambled through the corpses of friend and foe. His embrace was fierce, too tight to truly be comfortable for either of us in our damaged states.

I pulled away, and we watched the ghostly Seraphim disappear, dissolving into mist as their fights concluded, none of them came to offer farewells. The monsters we fought alongside took to the skies, or stalked off into the forest, their life debts paid. Only Zephyrus remained, watching with those slitted golden eyes. Even the fae who battled alongside the other hell beasts gave him a wide berth.

But still, so much fire burned, everywhere. The plain and fields had long been turned to ash, but the edge of the forest and the thatched cottages that had become the center of the fight remained ablaze, if not smoldering cinders. Kelpies and their riders did their best to stanch the damage, but much of it was already done. Families who had fought so valiantly wept at all they had lost.

It wasn't until screams rang among the gathered that my mood fell from our victory. A Pixie pointed across the field, toward the spiritual center. My eyes widened in horror as I beheld the sight. Fire unchecked had spread across the place of so many solstices and equinoxes. And the towering tree that stood in the center glowed with heat. The fire hadn't licked up the sides and feasted on the foliage, no, it had corrupted the very core of the tree.

I screamed, taking only a few steps towards it before Keelan grabbed me by the waist. He held me to him, whispering empty reassurances as I struggled against him. I needed to go to it, I needed to save it. But I knew, in a way that I couldn't accept, that it was too late.

I cried as a thundering crack sounded across the land, and I fell to my knees. Keelen still held me as I gripped at the ground, at the grass that was no longer grass. A deep breaking rang out as my people gasped and sobbed. I couldn't tear my eyes away from the tree that was overwhelmed with internal fire. I couldn't breathe as that ancient monolith listed dangerously to one side.

And with a crash that shook the world, the tree of life fell.

Printed in the USA
CPSIA information can be obtained
at www.ICGtesting.com
CBHW051728271024
16400CB00040B/969

9 798991 667906